THE

WORDS

FOR

HER

Lawrence & Gibson Publishing Collective
www.lawrenceandgibson.co.nz

The Words for Her, by Thomasin Sleigh
First edition published in Aotearoa New Zealand by Lawrence &
Gibson, 2023

Printed and bound at Rebel Press, Trades Hall, Te Aro,
Te Whanganui-a-Tara Wellington.

A catalogue record for this book is available from the National
Library of New Zealand, Te Puna Mātauranga o Aotearoa.

ISBN 9781738590315

Cover design: Judith Carnaby
Copy editor: Brydan Smith
Page design: Murdoch Stephens

THE
WORDS
FOR
HER

Thomasin Sleigh

Lawrence & Gibson

1.

I'll start with Jade because she's the reason I'm writing this.

One day, when she was a toddler, small and stubborn, we were down at the end of the beach. I'll describe it, because that's what I do, what I've always done. And it's a relief to remember and write it down here, to let these words finally come out.

The sea was calm and flat, and the beach was empty, but out above the waves a hungry crowd of gulls swooped and circled close to the surface of the water, hunting fish. I was half watching them and half watching Jade. She ran into the sea, let it touch her toes, and ran out again, giggling. She was having fun, but things could quickly change. She might fall and soak herself, and she really didn't like any part of her clothes to get wet, or she might stand on a sharp rock. Tears were never far away.

We spent a lot of time at the beach then, but I remember that afternoon because Jade spotted a starfish on the sand. It was tiny and pink and covered in lumps. She crouched down and pointed at it. 'Star!' she said, looking up at me and grinning. This was a new word. I hadn't heard her say it before. 'Star!' she said again and pointed at the sky. 'Star!' She stood up and pointed at my throat.

I reached up and felt my gold star necklace. She had never said 'star' before and now they were everywhere around her, so different from each other but still the same, a new thing with a new name.

She was making connections all the time, new words, like a series of mini explosions, fireworks in her brain. And I was with her every day, so I saw all these moments when a pattern appeared for her, or she found a word to describe what she saw. Making the world make sense.

A wave came in and covered the starfish and went out again. Jade didn't run away but crouched to peer at it as the wave retreated. I thought she might pick it up and chuck it into the sea, but she only stared at it.

I remember that moment, or I remember that photo, because Jade was so still around the starfish, the way she stared at it, her hands pressed down into the wet sand to steady herself. Over the noise of the sea I heard her repeat to herself, 'Star, star, star.' Amazed at the thing and the word and the link between the two.

I backed away and took my phone out of my back pocket. 'Jade!' I called, to make her look up. She did, and I took the photo. The sea and the sky in the background, Jade in her purple T-shirt and baggy leggings, her face in the silly scrunched-up smile she only made for photos.

After I took the photo, she jumped up, all crazy energy again, and ran to look over my shoulder. Even then, when she was so young, she knew she would find herself there, a small version of Jade, and that she would see the starfish again and it would be clearer and better and brighter in the image.

2.

I was watching the news on TV when I first saw it happen in real time. Jade lay on the carpet in front of me playing with her family of toy horses. She had them arranged in a circle, with her favourite black horse in the middle. A horse meeting was going on, sometimes I'd heard her call it 'a meeting of hooves'. I heard her whisper, to herself, to the horses, 'Don't get lost, Black Star, follow us out to the plains.'

Fish fingers were in the oven. A pot of water waited on the stove to boil the peas and corn. The lounge window was open and we could hear the chatter of kids playing on the school field behind our house.

Maybe it didn't happen exactly this way. But there were things that repeated in our lives at that time. Fish fingers, the sound of kids playing in the school, Jade's toy horses.

On that night, it would've been some combination of these things. I remember Jade on the floor, the way she lay with her head on its side, resting on the inside of her outstretched arm, the other hand galloping a horse across a field of grass, or towards the edge of a cliff, or a beach at sunset, whatever place Jade had imagined for her horses to roam.

There are facts, real things that I write down. I want to get this first part down quickly. I want this to be known, for Jade, for Mum, for Miri, even for Guy. And for me, it's already a relief to write. It's a way to lay it out and remember the order of things. I need to get these words out of my head and onto the screen.

This is for Dad too. This is the thing he always wanted, for me to tell him what was happening and what things looked like. Maybe I'll be able to read this to him and show him what he couldn't see, or somehow I'll get this to him so he'll know that Jade and I are safe.

Jade, for sure, will have questions about how it happened when she gets older. And it's true, I can't remember it all, but I can write it down as best I can, not hiding anything, not making anything up, just writing it down so that Jade will have it and she'll know why I did what I did and why it was the best thing for us.

Because we've gone out and I don't want to pretend that it hasn't happened, or to write this without being honest. I'm tired of pretending, of keeping quiet. I want to be totally open now.

So, let me start this again. We were at home. Jade was playing horses in the lounge. I was scrolling through something on my phone and then I looked up and the TV was broken.

I remember thinking, Not the TV too, for fuck's sake. Because the washing machine had broken the week before, and that always happens, doesn't it? All the appliances break at the same time, and then you have to get a WOF and the car needs four new tyres, and before you know it you're down two thousand bucks, just when you were starting to save a little bit.

But it wasn't the TV that was broken, it was the image. Or, actually, just a small part of the image.

I muted it because Jade hadn't noticed yet and I didn't want her to, not until I could figure out what was going on. The two presenters, a man and a woman, sat next to each other. The man had a bland, tanned face and short hair. He looked tidy, symmetrical. The woman was in a red blazer that was so thick and firmly ironed that it didn't respond to the slight movements of her body, as if it was a shield against the camera.

But it didn't help her, this red shield, because she was going out.

Small sections of her were fading. It was as if she had been punctured by tiny needles and the glossy blue background that was behind the news desk was bleeding through, into her body. Her hair disappeared. And then it rallied and came back again for a few moments, before disappearing again. It was the other presenter's turn to speak, and as he said his part, his mouth moving silently because the TV was still muted, she faded. Her eyes went, then her head, so that she was only a torso in an ugly red blazer.

The man had no idea what was going on and he kept speaking. The woman didn't know either and I saw her hands, lonely now, cut off at the cuffs, the only part of her on the screen, moving across the shiny surface of their desk, reaching to lightly touch the tablet that lay in front of her.

The camera began to move then. Shifting to the left, to focus on the man and cut out the space where the woman used to be. Her negative space was a big problem. The camera slowly zoomed in until the man filled the frame, his lips still moving as he finished his script. Then it cut away from the presenters and to the news report they had introduced, a shot of a canal somewhere, then Rangitoto, then something else. I don't know what it was about.

I wanted to look away, but I also really wanted to see. It was fast, without any warning. Her image kind of broke up and fell apart. I wrote 'disappeared' before, but it wasn't really like that. That's not what it looked like. It was more like she was punctured, sort of pierced by light, and it meant she couldn't hold together very well, as if she had lost her ability to *be*. Be a person. Or an image of a person. Later, I kept thinking of her sad, lost hands moving across the desk and gripping the little tablet in front of her. That stuck with me. Why did that seem so sad? I don't know, but it did. Like she was clinging on to it to stop herself from going.

What had happened in the newsroom as she was going out? There wouldn't have been much time to react. But they would have seen, on their monitors, just what we saw, the woman fading, and they would have known that there was nothing they could do to stop it. They had to let her slip away and refocus the camera on something else.

I reached for the remote and turned the TV off because I didn't want Jade to see. But when I looked down, I saw that she had been watching the whole time. 'She went out, didn't she?' Jade asked.

I didn't know what to say. I didn't want her to be afraid, but it seemed dumb to lie.

'Yes,' I said eventually, 'I think so. I think that's what it looks like, when it happens.'

Jade said nothing. She was still lying on her side on the carpet.

'She's okay though, you know that, right?' I said, prodding her with my big toe. 'She just went out.'

Jade rolled onto her back and looked up at me. Here she is. I want to stop and look at her in these words. Her hair fans out around her head and her knees are smudged green with grass. She is six.

'We don't know if she's okay,' she said.

I couldn't tell if she was scared. Or worried. Or what.

3.

It was a little while later, maybe a couple of weeks. Jade was asleep. I went in and checked on her and her cheeks were pink because she had burrowed down under her blanket even though all she really needed was a sheet. I uncovered her and shifted her head up onto the pillow. She slept so deeply at this early part of the night. Totally spent after a day hooning around with the other kids at school.

I went into the kitchen. I was probably tired. I'd worked all day. Jade went to school and then to our friends, the Rewetis, who lived down the end of the road, until I finished work and came to pick her up at 5:15. Ben Reweti worked at the mill too, but he started early and his shift finished at two, so he could meet all the kids when school finished. I kept trying to pay him and Ange for looking after Jade, but they wouldn't let me. They'd just shake their heads and say, 'Nah, she just watches TV with the kids, it's no trouble.' But I knew they were doing me a massive favour, so I tried to be on time to pick Jade up. Or even be early, if I could. But I had to work until five, so there was only so much I could do.

Jade and I would come home and quickly get some dinner together and Jade would show me what she'd been working on at school, and we'd watch some TV, and then we'd be into the whole going to bed routine, and she'd have a bath and brush her teeth and all that.

After she was in bed, I'd tidy up the bathroom and the kitchen and make us sandwiches for the next day. We never had time to make lunch in the morning.

Okay, actually, sometimes, especially in the summer, I wouldn't be quite so organised, and after Jade was asleep I'd sit on the backdoor step and have a ciggy instead. I wasn't supposed to be smoking. I definitely couldn't afford to. I'd have all those thoughts that you have when you're trying to stop something. I had a kid, and all that. But then I'd be like, you've been working all day and looking after Jade, and it's just one smoke. And in summer it was nice to be outside while it was still light and listen to the cicadas and the lawn mowers and the cars going by.

That evening, I was in the kitchen doing something when I heard a thud from out in the backyard.

It must've been about 8:30, because I looked out the window and it was nearly dark.

In those days, I tried hard not to be afraid. It was like a game that I played with myself. We didn't really know what was happening with the gaps, and there was a lot of dodgy information about, but, at home, I tried to keep things normal, and not be freaked out or show Jade that I was worried. Keeping her safe and looked after, that was my main goal.

Often though, even then, before it all began, in the evenings when Jade was asleep, I felt like our little house was too delicate and insecure. It used to be a state house, a flaky weatherboard cube with a small set of concrete steps leading up to the front door. It was too easy to get in. Too easy to get at us, with the windows wide open in the summer. I'd go in and check on Jade, six, maybe seven times. Just making sure that she was still there and she was okay. I'd check the locks on the doors and make myself all stressed out.

But some evenings, things would be easy, and I'd be chill and not worried and just enjoying the summer night. The backyard was a safe place and Whakatāne felt a long way from the chaos of the world.

The night I heard the thud, I was in the kitchen, and I stopped and listened. Outside, it was still. Had it been something falling? The shed door banging closed? I was sure I hadn't left it open.

The kitchen window looked out over our small backyard. There was harakeke down the back, by the fence, and a little shed.

I wiped my hands on a tea towel and went out the back door and into the garden. I walked down the fence, round the lemon tree, pulled open the shed door and turned on the light.

Nothing. Just the messy shed, the old lawn mower leaning against the wall. I hated that lawn mower. I reckoned the landlord should sort the lawns for us, but he was lazy as and had to be hounded for weeks to even fix a leaky tap.

I left the shed and stood up on the edge of the garden bed so that I could look over the fence at the school field that was behind our house. Empty. All the kids at home and tucked up in bed. The painted white lines of the cricket field looked strangely bright in the dimming light.

I went back inside, finished the dishes, watched some TV, and went to bed.

In the morning I went to wake Jade. She'd pushed off her sheet and just lay, all sleepy and floppy, at the very edge of her mattress.

We went to the kitchen where I made a cup of coffee and Jade crunched Rice Bubbles at our small table. We went around the house, getting ready. I made her sandwiches and packed her bag. I remember that we didn't talk much and we had the radio on.

Jade waited for me in the lounge while I straightened my hair in the cloudy bathroom mirror.

When I sat down on the couch to put on my shoes, Jade moved over from where she was sitting at the opposite end. 'Do you think,' she said, coming in close, putting her arms around my neck, her breath full of toothpaste, 'that someone has been in here?'

I paused and took a moment before squeezing my foot into its shoe, because I'd spent the morning hoping that she wouldn't notice. I said, 'No, I don't think so. You mean in the house? Nope.'

Jade let go of my neck, shuffled back to the other side of the couch, and frowned at me.

But she was right, I think. It felt as if someone had been in our house the night before. Had they been here and walked around and looked at our stuff?

Jade was annoyed at me for pretending, but what was I supposed to do? I needed to protect her and I needed our house to be safe for her. She was too young to be aware of these things. But she just kind of *knew* stuff, and I couldn't hide things from her. It was as if she could feel the shaking inside me as I pulled on my shoes, trying to look chill.

In the car, the radio was probably playing Fleetwood Mac or something, and I would've hummed along while Jade eyed me in the rear-view mirror. I dropped her at school and she slammed the car door.

Thinking about Jade's face in the rear-view mirror reminds me that part of the point of all this is to describe Jade when she was six, now that I can't see her at that age anymore. I feel like I've lost something, lost a part of her. But I don't regret my decision. Things are better the way they are now, I think.

Jade had an exaggerated way of frowning at me that looked so funny that it was hard not to laugh. She was angry, but if you didn't know her, you'd think she was acting.

Here she is, looking at me in the mirror. Jade is small but tall for her age, with long legs. When she walks sometimes she does these little skips, as if she can't contain her energy, it just bubbles up out of her. She has brown, straight hair like mine, but I cut hers into a bob that I hope looks cute, but mostly looks messy.

What else? She is easy to dress, clothes slip onto her, as if her arms and legs are smoother than other people's. She wears leggings and T-shirts with faded pictures of dolphins on the front and socks with holes and she has a purple backpack for school.

Okay, I'll write some more later. That was just a start. Maybe I'll learn how to describe her better as I get more of this down. In a way, this is a practice, and I'm testing out these words for her.

When Jade and I got home in the evening, the feeling of the morning had disappeared, and Jade was in a good mood. She'd been using a Spirograph at school and had a pile of patterns that she showed me, spreading them out over the kitchen table and telling me why each was important. 'This one is a green jewel that the princess has collected,' she said. 'Cara said this one is a symbol of peace.'

We ate pasta in front of the TV and didn't talk about the morning. I told myself that we'd made up the presence that had been in the house the night before. Back then, it was easier to shut that thought out.

When Jade was in bed, I sat on the floor beside her and told her the next chapter of our story about taniwha and mermaids. She was sleepy but she watched my face closely, taking in the words, sometimes repeating things quietly to herself, details that she wanted to remember. She said as I was leaving the room, 'Night, Mum. I hope it's just us tonight.'

I was on my phone that night when I first came across the Seeing Camps. Gaps who had a particularly strong bond with their images, vloggers or Instagram influencers, people who had left thousands of holes across the internet when they had gone out, a group of them had started the Seeing Camps. It looked like the first ones had been set up in Utah, or somewhere else deserty and middle-of-nowhere-looking in the States.

For those who have gone out and need a sanctuary, the website read. *Join us at Brighthome Seeing Camp for a total immersion healing experience. Learn how to tap into your new wholeness and leave your image behind. Embrace your 'now' energy and release the inner vibrancy that going out affords.*

A couple of pages further into the site there were parts that seemed to promise to reverse the effects of going out, but they seemed to be pretty dodgy. The words made it hard to understand what they were really saying.

Participants in Brighthome Seeing Camp's group meditation and imaging therapy sessions have seen a near return to presentness. In addition to these, we have developed an innovative and scientifically proven module in image location and acknowledgement that shows a 90% response rate. This module involves, but is not limited to, image-affirmation therapy, image-replacement solutions, and image reconstruction. Contact us today to see how Brighthome Seeing Camp can reduce the immediate effects of going out and ensure you are fully seen again.

Could they really bring someone back?

I scrolled through the site, which was covered in images. The cabins had been built in a flat, empty field. Even though the environment looked really boring the photographer had gone for it and documented every detail, zooming in on the heads of grass, fence posts, and the gravel driveway, in what seemed to be an over-the-top level of detail.

All the symbols of luxury accommodation were also recorded. There were rolled white towels, bedside tables with fancy orchids in vases, beds with too many pillows. I tapped on their Instagram and there was more, fruity muesli, cows leaning over a fence, papers laid out on a reception table. Everything was pristine, high quality, and empty of people. Or, I reminded myself, looking closer at the photos, maybe there were heaps of people there already, maybe it was packed, like a music festival, filled with bodies, elbowing each other out of the way, meditating, eating muesli.

I looked at a post about the swimming pool and the surface of the water was smooth, but there were choppy areas too, where gaps had once stood and disturbed the water around them.

4.

Mum and Dad often looked after Jade on Sunday mornings if I had stuff to do. They lived where they've always lived, on the edge of Whakatāne, in the house where Guy and I grew up. I have words for every tiny part of that house. An old villa on a biggish property, seriously in need of a paint job, hidden away from the road by a thick macrocarpa hedge that I used to hide in when I was a kid. There were small pockets in between the branches that I'd squeeze into because it was the best place for hide and seek. If Guy and I were both hiding, we'd sprint to the hedge, and then we'd wait, quiet, grinning at each other, as the other kid went round and round the house, getting tired and pissed off because they couldn't find us.

Jade liked running around in Mum and Dad's garden. It was big, but it was a bit of a mess, really. There was an old car, falling apart and overgrown with grass and weeds, rusted tin drums, out-of-control rhubarb, a row of beer cans that Guy used to shoot with his air rifle, and a sludgy pond with a goldfish. Things hadn't changed much since I was a kid. Mum was busy and didn't have much time or energy to tidy up and Dad couldn't mow the lawns.

Jade and I didn't talk about the person we'd felt in our house when we went round the following Sunday. I didn't want to get into it all with them, didn't want to think about it. I pretended that nothing had happened. And I had no proof, only a feeling, a feeling that Jade and I made between us.

Jade didn't say anything, either. She was good at keeping secrets. I think she liked having stuff that only we knew about because it made our little team more special.

Mum was getting something out of the letterbox and she waved at us as we turned into the driveway.

Jade jumped out of the car and ran up to her and Mum bent down to give her a hug.

'Look at this, Nan,' Jade said, holding out one of the patterns she'd drawn.

'Let me see,' said Mum, putting on her glasses. 'Nice one. I like this green.'

'It's a gem. You can have it. I'm gonna check the fish.' Jade sprinted off across the garden.

'You used to play with a Spirograph when you were little too,' said Mum.

What would we have talked about then? Probably Dad. I would've asked, 'How's Dad doing today?'

And Mum would've replied, 'Oh, you know, he's getting along. So-so.' Something vague like that.

Dad had already been blind for twenty years by then. It had happened at the mill. Like a lot of boys in Whakatāne, he had left school and started working at the mill when he was fifteen. Started at the bottom and worked his way up to foreman. The mill grinds up radiata pine and turns it into cardboard packaging, boxes and cartons and other kinds of containers. Well, it used to anyway.

Dad was checking a rookie's work, monitoring one of the boilers, but the pressure was all wrong and the valves hadn't been closed off properly. Dad got burning hot water in his face at high pressure. He was badly burnt and he went blind.

I don't really like to write this down because I've always tried not to think about what that moment would have felt like for him. There's too much pain. He probably didn't have time to think, to really be aware of what was happening to him.

To the mill's credit, they had emergency practices in place and they moved quickly. It could've been worse. I remember waiting nervously the day he came home from the hospital. I was with Guy and Aunty Jill, and Mum and Dad came up the driveway, then Dad got out of the car and Mum guided him through the front door. She was so gentle with him. Dad felt for the doorframe, feeling for the arms of a chair to sit down in. I was afraid of him and afraid of what our lives would be like now.

After bustling around for a bit, Aunty Jill left and we were all alone, together in our quiet lounge. I thought about turning on the TV but I realised what that would be like and I felt weird. I wanted to scrunch myself up. Mum got up to make a cup of tea and she asked if anyone else would like one, but we just sat there without saying anything. I remember that moment, feeling as if our home was different with this new Dad in it. His blindness made us less present, less *there*, but the interactions between Mum, Guy, and me felt bigger, like we were acting, with Dad's hopeful eyes turned towards us, trying to make out what was going on.

Things changed though, of course. Pretty soon Dad had all his systems set up so that he could get around and do some of the things that he used to like to do. When I found him that Sunday, he was sitting at the little table in the kitchen polishing some old silver cups and listening to his screen reader tell him the news from his phone.

He turned his head towards the door when I came in and told his phone to stop. I sat down and watched him carefully dip his cloth in the cleaner, judge how much to soak it, and rub it onto the small cup he was holding. It was one of Guy's rugby trophies. He had played a lot when he was at high school, he'd been in the first fifteen, on the wing.

'How're they looking, J?' Dad asked.

I sighed. He wanted me to colour for him.

'I can't today, Dad, I'm going to the gym.'

I leaned against the doorframe. The swirls of Dad's cloth cut swathes through the grey grime on the cup, uncovering the shine. There you go, Dad, that's what you wanted me to tell you, how they were looking. I'm writing it now.

But I wouldn't say it, not that day. I was in a rush. I also knew that if I hung around long enough he'd know that I was worried about something, about the person who'd been in our house. He had a way of figuring these things out. And I didn't want to talk to him about it, I didn't want him to worry. I wanted to handle it by myself.

'Why don't you stay a bit?' Dad nodded to the seat next to him.

'No, I'm going to a class today, starts at 9:30,' I said.

'Can you get me some water and another rag, then?' he asked.

I went to the kitchen and found an ice cream container. While I waited with my hand under the tap for the water to heat up, I watched Jade and Mum through the kitchen window. Jade was plucking daisies out of the lawn and putting them on the rocks that surrounded the pond. She was going to make a daisy chain.

Here's another way that Jade looked when she was six, a disintegrating daisy chain hanging around her neck, or tangled up in her hair, coming apart and sharp smelling. Don't let me forget this. I write it down here. I write Jade down here, on the screen, so I can see her.

'You okay?' asked Dad.

I took the container of water and a new cloth and put it down next to Dad on the table. I showed his hands where they were. 'Careful,' I said, 'it's hot.'

The backdoor opened and Guy came into the kitchen.

'Dad, that water is hot,' he said. The dutiful son.

'He knows. I told him already,' I replied.

'Giving your old trophies a clean,' said Dad. 'Mum said they were getting a bit grimy.'

'Uh huh.' Guy went to the fridge, looked inside, closed it again, and leaned against it, looking at me. 'How's it going, sis?' His phone buzzed in the pocket of his hoodie and he took it out and tapped out a message.

Jade burst into the kitchen and said, 'Mum, we're going to make cheese scones!'

'Sounds good,' I said.

Guy sat down at the table. 'Sounds like something I should stick around for,' he said, still looking at his phone.

He wanted something from Mum and Dad, to borrow their car, borrow some money, for them to cover for him in some other way. That was the only reason he ever came round to see them. But he wouldn't ask while I was there. This was a game that we played. I looked at my phone too, tempted just to hang around to stop him from asking. 'Maybe I should just stay for scones too,' I said.

Guy focussed on his phone and pretended that he hadn't heard me.

'We can save you one,' said Jade. 'Do you want some help, Pop?' she asked. Dad had moved on to wiping the Silvo off with the cloth. 'You're good at rugby, Guy,' she said. 'You've got a lot of trophies.'

Guy scratched the stubble on his chin and grinned.

'He was bloody great,' said Dad. 'Used to fly up the wing. Crowd cheering. Best player on the team.'

'Why don't you play now?' Jade asked.

'Got other things to do, don't I?' said Guy.

'That one's probably done, Dad,' I said. The trophy Dad was holding gleamed in his hand. 'It looks good.'

Dad set it down on the table and, though there were a few little patches that had been missed, it did look good.

'I gotta go,' I said. 'Be back in a few hours.'

I went out to the car, gritting my teeth. I left Guy to sponge whatever he needed off Mum and Dad. I couldn't be bothered with him that morning. Left Mum and Dad to say yes. Because they always said yes. That was just how things worked in our family.

5.

I didn't have a lot in common with Bex, but her daughter Cara was one of Jade's good mates, so we'd spent a bit of time together since the kids had started school. She worked at the council, I think, and she had another daughter who was a bit older. We had chatted at school things and Cara had come round to play at our house a few times, but we didn't really know each other, so I was surprised to see her on my doorstep at eight o'clock at night.

I let her into the lounge and turned off the TV. I'd been watching some crap cooking show.

'Sorry to interrupt,' Bex said, 'but I was just at a work thing and I was driving back home this way and I saw your place and I thought I'd pop in.'

It was fucking weird, is what it was. But I smiled and said it was fine, that it was nice to see her, or something like that. 'Do you want a cup of tea? Glass of wine?' I remembered that I had a half-open bottle of sav in the back of the fridge. It'd probably still be okay.

'I wouldn't say no to a glass of wine,' she said.

I didn't really want her to pick the wine because that made it seem like we were better friends than we actually were. I couldn't even remember what it was she did at the council. Events or something?

I poured the wine and we went back to sit in the lounge. It seemed weirdly quiet with the TV off. I wished I had put on the radio in the kitchen just for some background noise.

Bex started talking about Cara and something she'd done at school. At least we had the kids to talk about. I could pretty much talk about Jade forever, things that she had said and done and the ways that she was changing. And Cara was a cool kid. She and Jade played really well together.

Then Bex asked me, 'Are you ever freaked out, with you and Jade here, I mean just the two of you?'

'What do you mean?' I asked.

'With the gaps.'

'Well, there's not that much I can do about it. We just have to sit tight and see what happens.' I shrugged.

'That's what I mean, sometimes I feel like I just want to keep the kids home with me forever. I feel like it could happen to them while they're at school and I wouldn't be there and… I don't know. Do you know anybody that it's happened to?'

'No.' I didn't think twice about the lie. Was it a lie? Sort of.

'I don't think it's happened to anybody in Whakatāne.'

Bex was fidgety. She played with the buckle on her handbag and kept picking up her phone, as if she was checking the time. If she was in such a hurry to get home, why had she come here? I felt like she was building up to some big question but didn't want to ask it. It had been a couple of years, but everyone was still scared. There was still a lot that we didn't know and everybody was happy to chip in with their two cents, even if they didn't know anyone who had gone out. There was lots of bullshit out there.

I had finished my wine, but Bex was taking an age with hers.

'Did you go to school with Miri Neeson?' Bex asked.

'Miri? Yeah, I did. How come?'

'Oh, someone just said that you knew her. I know her brother.'

'Jared. Yeah.' Jared was a dick.

There was a silence that I didn't try and fill. I didn't want to talk about Miri. Bex was starting to piss me off.

'Have you seen her recently?' Bex asked.

'Miri?'

'Yeah.'

'Nah, she's in Auckland, I think. We sort of lost touch with each other. Dunno.'

Miri. Beautiful Miri. Beautiful bossy Miri. When we were kids, we'd leave little messages for each other under a brick in the shed out the back of her place. There was a route through the paddocks, along the line of pine trees, which connected her place to mine. We went to primary school and intermediate and high school together. Did gym together. Sat at the back of biology class and graffitied the desks together. Yeah, I knew Miri.

'Jared said he hadn't heard from her in a bit. I heard things got a bit crazy for her. She'd lost it, you know?'

I didn't say anything and I didn't care when Bex looked awkward. She finished her wine and left soon after that and I watched from the window as her car drove away down the road. I checked the locks on the doors and went to bed, but I couldn't sleep. I wished I hadn't drunk a glass of wine. I lay there listening to the small sounds of the house at nighttime, all its clicks and hums. I got up and went and sat on the floor next to Jade's bed. Her *Frozen* duvet had slipped off, so I straightened it out.

Jade asleep. Here she is. Look. Her eyelids quiver as if her eyes are searching, looking for something. Her eyebrows are small and soft. Her left eyebrow has a slightly different arch to the right one. Her mouth is closed, and her breath is so light that I have to lean in very close to feel it against my cheek.

I went back to bed and it felt nice and cool again. I lay there and thought about Miri and where she might be. I lay there and thought about what Bex knew and what she had wanted to ask me but wouldn't say.

6.

I need to try and keep the right order of things. The first time I saw someone go out on TV, then the first person who went in Whakatāne. Sure, there were lots of rumours before then, friends of friends, and such and such's uncle, but most of it was total crap. People just trying to feel special and saying shit that they had no idea about.

One evening, Jade had only just started school, I'd left work and was driving to pick her up when I saw a real estate billboard, one of those ones that was advertising a real estate agent, not an actual house. I clocked it because it looked wrong. There was a big gap where the smiling person should be. They always have them patting a Labrador or kissing a baby or something, trying to look like caring people. The tagline name on the billboard said, *Terri McKenzie: family comes first.*

I got Jade from the Rewetis and my phone rang as I was unlocking our front door, juggling Jade's school bag and a bag of groceries.

'Did you hear?' It was my mum.

'Hear what? Just wait a sec, I'm trying to get through the front door.'

I got everything inside, dumped it on the kitchen table, and picked up my phone again. 'Did I hear what?'

'Terri McKenzie has gone out.'

I realised what had happened with the billboards. She was gone. I waited until Jade had gone down the hall to her room because I didn't want to talk about this in front of her.

'Jodie? Are you still there?' Mum asked.

'Do you know her? I mean, did you?'

'No, but she's Pam's daughter. You know Pam McKenzie? I used to do Weight Watchers with her.'

I didn't remember Pam. I didn't know Terri. 'You've talked to Pam?'

'She called me this morning. Oh Jodes, she's so upset.'

'And how's Terri?'

'Well, Pam said that she was resting. That she was really tired.'

'When did it happen?'

'Yesterday afternoon, Pam said.'

'Did she... did Terri feel anything?' I didn't know how to ask this either. But I'd heard that it could be painful, for some people, and that the pain could go on for a while, like a muscle injury.

'Pam didn't say. She did say that Terri knew, somehow, that she'd gone. A friend called her and told her that her billboards had been vandalised. You know she's a real estate agent? Very successful too, has done well for herself. They called her and told her about the billboards, but Terri already knew, Pam said, that it had happened, but she just hadn't told anyone. She didn't know how to.'

Mum and I were quiet for a moment, thinking about that, how Terri had kept it to herself for an afternoon. What would her life be like now?

I hung up and I went down the hall and found Jade in her room. She was crouched on the floor arranging a tiny plastic tea set. I sat down because I wanted to be close to her and she poured me a tiny cup of nothing-but-air tea.

At the time, there were no patterns to the gaps, as far as anyone could see. It was random. No one knew when the first person had gone, but most people thought it must have been a couple of years ago. People had thought, at first, that it was spread via contact with someone who had gone out, that it was like a virus and could be passed along by touching hands, or coughing, or little kids smearing their grime on each other.

But it wasn't like that. They'd done tests and they couldn't get it to transmit that way, or sometimes it did and sometimes it didn't. There were lots of gaps in South Africa, around Pretoria. Thousands of people, apparently. And in Vietnam, and in the middle of the USA. But it was also random and people went out who hadn't had any contact with other gaps, and nobody could figure out why. In New Zealand, there had been about twelve gaps, at that time, scattered all around the country.

Rick, down in Mosgiel, said that he hadn't felt a thing. That his mate was trying to take a picture of him at the pub on his phone and it was then that they twigged that Rick didn't show up in the photo, even when his mate held his phone up right in front of him, he didn't appear. He was gone. I heard sound bites of an interview with him on the radio and read stuff that people posted on Facebook. Rick seemed okay. He said it wasn't sore, or uncomfortable.

Some gaps were happy to talk to the radio, but others wanted to keep to themselves. And fair enough too, because the media were like a dog with a bone. Christ, it was awkward watching them try to figure out how to interview people when they'd gone out. A gap on camera was just an empty space, so they had to interview them in person, keep the audio and then play that over top of stock footage of places the person was talking about, or shots of the journalist nodding, like they really cared.

Rick talked to the press heaps but then, after a few months, he stopped and went quiet. I kept googling to see if I could find a follow-up interview with him, to see how he was doing after the first media storm had passed, but I couldn't find anything. Maybe he'd had enough. Some people said that something else was happening that they weren't telling us about. I didn't really know who 'they' were. The government maybe, or the gaps.

Later in the evening, after Mum told me about Terri, I went on Facebook, and because it was Whakatāne, it turned out I was only one friend removed from Terri McKenzie. Her profile was private, but I could still see her profile picture. There was a man, kind of hot in a normalish way, standing on a beach with a sunset in the background. He was leaning on this weird angle because that was where Terri had been, before she had gone out and made the image all messed up and meaningless.

Broken-up images like this one became familiar. I'd be on my phone and come across a website in ruins. Someone who had been really involved in the site had gone out and now all the images were splintered and full of holes, as if some graphic designer was following a crazy idea. Or, I'd be checking a site and there'd just be the tiniest little clue that someone had gone out, a frame where someone used to be, or a person's arm stretched around an empty space, the people all fitting together wrong. Sometimes it was someone in the very far background of an image. Just the tiniest thing, but it made all the other images out of kilter, like it had a domino effect on the rest of the screen.

At that time, early on, people tried heaps of stuff to bring people back and make them show up again. They tried special lights, tried running computer programmes that dug away at the digital files to see if the person was somehow still inside. People rewrote whole operating systems and created totally new ways of capturing digital images. I remember that every couple of months during that year, there'd be a big announcement of 'a major breakthrough' that showed great 'promise', or whatever. But it'd come to nothing and the number of gaps would keep going up.

It wasn't just tech stuff either, a lot of people said that the secret was inside the person who had gone out, like, deep down in their body. They ran all kinds of tests and x-rays and examinations to see if there was something in the blood, or the brain, or the heart, something that had changed in the gaps so that they repelled any lenses. About six months or so after the first gap, one doctor claimed that she'd discovered an anomaly in the skin of all the gaps. I can't remember the details, I'd have to google it again, though it's probably impossible to find online now, but she said it was some cell or DNA or something that had twisted and changed. She said that this made the gaps respond differently to light and the way that phones and cameras *saw* them. Everybody went on about it for a while, but it ended up coming to nothing. A bunch of people went out in Malaysia and none of them had this twist. They didn't follow the same pattern, so all the scientists had to go back to square one.

Everyone was trying to figure out what the hell was going on.

The borders between countries had shut when they thought that going out could be spread by touch, or in the air, and I was worried about my job and the mill, because we had so much international business, but things seemed to keep ticking along, for a while, anyway. And when it became clear that this wasn't the way it worked, that it couldn't be controlled by keeping people away from each other, borders started opening up again.

We were told to 'keep alert' and 'stay vigilant'.

Jade asked me what 'vigilant' meant and I told her, 'To keep a lookout.'

'But what are we looking out for?' she asked.

'Anything weird, something we haven't seen before.'

Jade thought about this. 'Do you think when people have gone out we can see them more? Or less?' she asked.

'Well, we can't see them in pictures anymore,' I said.

'We can't be vigilant for them in pictures, but we can be vigilant for them in real life.'

'That's right.'

'So, if we notice anything different about a gap in real life, we should tell an adult.'

'Yep.'

'And if we see a picture where they should have been, we should tell an adult.'

'Yep.'

'We've all got to keep noticing.'

'Yep.'

'And be vigilant,' said Jade, nodding to herself, locking this away.

And we did, I guess. We looked at each other differently. Especially after Terri went out. She was the first person I knew, or the first person close to us. Even though it looked like the internet was being eaten up and more bits kept disappearing every day, it still felt like the gaps were far away, and they might figure out a cure before they got any closer. But then, with Terri gone out, they were close.

Her billboards came down. Terri didn't talk to the media, though they must have been hounding her like nothing else. They announced that she was the thirteenth person in New Zealand to go out and that the situation was being 'monitored closely'. What did that mean? We didn't know. We were just told to stay vigilant.

7.

I love that Renee comes in here and I get to write about her. It feels like a way of caring for her, in return for all the ways that she has looked out for me.

A few days after Terri went out, Renee's face popped up on my screen while I was at the kitchen table paying bills on my phone.

'Jade gone down?' was the first thing she asked.

'Yup,' I said.

She walked around her kitchen, holding her phone in one hand and tidying up with the other. She always did this when she called me, doing a million things at once. She put something in a cupboard and fumbled with the phone. I saw blurred stripes, possibly Renee's top, and then a greyish black. 'Fuck!' she said.

'Put it down somewhere,' I said.

She balanced her phone against something so that I could watch her move around the kitchen, but mostly I had a view of her kitchen bench.

'What's up?' I asked.

'Just seeing what's going on,' Renee said.

'Where's Trace?'

'Some work thing.'

'Did the kids go down okay?'

'Ari had a meltdown about getting the wrong towel after his bath, but otherwise they were pretty chill. Hugo has a cold. I can hear him snoring from here.'

I watched Renee unload the dishwasher for a bit. She lived in Sandringham, with her wife Tracey and their two boys, Ari and Hugo. They had a nice house. A nice kitchen. Tracey was a lawyer and Renee was an analyst, worked for the council.

Renee stopped tidying and looked at me. 'I heard about Terri McKenzie,' she said.

'Yeah. Did you know her?'

'Nope. She was a couple of years above us, right?'

'Yeah.'

Renee washed her hands, dried them on a tea towel, and picked up the phone again. I watched her face up close as she went outside and sat down on the stairs of their deck. I saw the yellow blobs of their lemon tree over her shoulder and a stretch of purply sky.

'Looks like nice weather,' I said.

'It was so nice today.' Renee paused. 'Have you seen my mum recently?'

'I popped in a couple of weekends ago. She made me take some of her gross grapefruit.'

Renee snorted. 'I quite like those grapefruit.'

'No, you don't.'

'I was talking to Trace about coming back. With Terri McKenzie, it feels like…' Renee trailed off. I could tell that she had 'self-view' on and was looking at herself. Her eyes darted down to the corner of her screen and she tucked her hair behind her ears.

'I'll keep an eye on her,' I said. 'Even if you're here, there's nothing you can do. It'd be hard for you guys to leave Auckland. What about your jobs?'

'It said on the news today that China are rounding up all the gaps and putting them in some facility together. They said it was a 'treatment facility',' Renee did the quotes marks with one hand, 'but who the fuck knows what they're doing with them.'

'Can they force them?'

Renee shrugged, then said, 'Have you seen Terri around? Do you think she… do you think she looks different?'

'I haven't seen her. I think she's just keeping to herself. Mum talked to her mum, they're friends. She said Terri was okay, but a bit tired. I saw a thing online, a kind of retreat, like a health spa, where gaps can go. It said it could bring that all back, the energy, and everything.'

'I reckon a lot of that stuff is bullshit,' Renee said.

'Yeah, probably. But you'd hope, right, that someone is figuring out how to help? Someone needs to do something.'

Renee didn't say anything. She was looking beyond her phone, out at her garden. She and Tracey had a big backyard. Renee had planted a row of feijoa trees along their back fence and they had a giant trampoline in the corner of the lawn that Ari and Hugo basically lived on. To be honest, I was jealous of their life. Jealous of their fancy well-paid jobs and the fact that Renee had got away from Whakatāne. Ari and Hugo were five and four, only a year apart. Renee had had Ari and then Tracey had got pregnant with Hugo soon after, they had the same sperm donor, a friend of a friend. Tracey had wanted them to be close in age, so they were. Tracey liked to plan and seemed to have a way of making everything fall into place. They'd bought a house in Auckland too! And who could afford that?

Renee shifted her focus back to her screen.

'It's nice to see your face,' I said.

She smiled. 'Yeah, who knows for how much longer.'

'Don't say that. It won't happen to us.'

'How do you know?'

I paused. 'I just know.'

'We could still just talk, on the phone, if one of us went.'

I wanted to stay on the call, but Renee turned her head, then said, 'Gotta go, I think Trace is home. I'll see you later.'

We waved at each other and hung up.

For a second, I wanted to call her back straight away and see her again. Like, I should hold on to her image just for a little bit longer, because she might go out. It was new, then, that feeling, but it became more normal, the sadness of hanging up on someone, or looking away from their picture, and not knowing if you'd see them again.

8.

I guess I should write about Johnny. I hardly think about him now, but he's important to this, and I need to go back, because there is stuff that Dad still doesn't know, and for Jade too, if I give her this to read.

I met Johnny at a party in Whakatāne when I was twenty-two. He told me he was twenty-five, but I found out later that wasn't true.

I'd just moved back to Whakatāne after two and a half years in Auckland. After high school I'd worked in hospo for a while and then, when I was twenty, I'd moved to Auckland to be a duty manager at a bar in Ponsonby, after a friend from school hooked me up with the job. I was excited to move, to get away from the bay.

I lived in a crappy house in Kingsland with five other flatmates and worked full time at the restaurant, running the evening shift. I felt lucky to have that job and I worked hard. I'm a night owl, so the hours suited me. I was young and things were a bit loose. I drank too much, and I definitely smoked too much. But I had fun and I held it together. The friend who had got me the job, Hana, ran the bar. We got on really well and ran a tight ship. We didn't put up with any bullshit and we had each other's backs when we needed to, because there are some real arseholes out there.

In my second year working there I started saving some cash. Just a bit every week, but enough so that I could pay for a couple of psychology papers at Auckland uni in the second semester. Some of my flatmates went to uni and I was interested in what they were doing. They told me how it all worked, because otherwise, I don't think I would have had enough confidence to go. No one in my family had been to uni before and, before I had moved to Auckland, it didn't really seem like it was something I could do.

I picked psychology because I was interested in people, how they thought and acted and why they did what they did, and it seemed like the subject for really getting into all of that.

Looking back on it now, it was crazy. I'd work at night and go to uni during the day. Young and lots of energy, I guess. I'd go to the restaurant on the way to class and get whoever was opening up to make me a free short black that I'd knock back and then head on to my lectures for the day.

One mid-term break I took leave from work and went back to Whakatāne for a week. I had an essay to finish and I read my course notes in the lounge while Dad sat in his big chair and listened to the rugby on the radio. Dad wanted to spend time with me, but he didn't want to interrupt my work. Mum came in every now and then and offered us cups of tea and raspberry slice that she'd made specially for my visit. They were so impressed with my uni work, like I was working on something super-secret, something they could break by talking to me the wrong way.

I don't remember where Guy was living at this point, but he turned up and came into the lounge. He sat, munching biscuits, in the chair across from Dad. 'What're you doing?' he asked.

'Just some uni work.'

'Uni, huh. What's it about?'

'Just reading a lab report.'

Guy was silent for a bit and brushed the crumbs off his top.

Then he asked, 'What are you going to do with this psychology degree, then?'

'I don't know.'

'Where do psychologists even work?'

I ignored him. Dad shifted in his seat, then got up and went into the kitchen. 'Are you okay, Dad?' I called.

'Fine,' he said, and I listened as he walked slowly down the hall.

I closed the course notes and drummed my fingers on the cover.

'Please,' Guy said, 'don't let me interrupt.'

'I'm done.'

Down the hall, a door clicked closed. 'Mum seems stressed,' I said to Guy.

34

'Mum?'

'Yes, Mum.'

'She's okay.'

'No, Guy, she's not. It's hard work taking care of Dad. And she's doing a lot of relieving at school, one of the other teachers has cancer, so she's there all the time.'

There were other things that I'd noticed too. The house was messy and the fridge stunk like there were weird old things at the back that had to be chucked out. The night before, I had heard Mum on the phone in her room and it sounded like she was crying. She might have been talking to Jill, her sister in Masterton. I'd stopped for a moment at her door and listened, but I couldn't hear what she was saying, only her muffled voice.

I had asked her, the next morning, in the kitchen, 'Are you okay, Mum?'

'What? What do you mean? Yes. Of course. I'm fine.' Dad was trying to empty the dishwasher and Mum was guiding his hands to the cupboard shelves. 'Dad just needs a little reminder sometimes. He knows what he's doing. You've got it, yep, that's it, Ray.'

Dad wanted to help and Mum wanted to let him, because it made him feel good, even if it meant he got things wrong. It'd been like this ever since Dad had had his accident. But it meant Mum had to help Dad to help, so things took twice as long and often went wrong.

I said to Guy, 'Mum needs help with Dad. How often do you even come around here? Do you ever come and help Mum out?'

'And pissing off to Auckland helps?' Guy grinned and scratched his leg. 'Don't come back and give me shit about helping Mum and Dad when you don't even live here anymore.'

This was true. I went back to Auckland but I kept thinking about Mum and Dad. I called them but I knew they didn't tell me what was really going on with them. Mum didn't tell me about how she was getting up at five in the morning to make sure she had enough time to help Dad have breakfast and get everything ready that he would need for the day, before she went to work. I only knew this because Dad let it slip one time. Or how she'd give up her lunch hour to drive home and check up on him, make him some sandwiches, or take him to a friend's place for the afternoon, or an appointment.

Mum had to work, but it was wearing her out. When I called her, she was always tired, and she always had to rush to do something else, like help Dad up, put the potatoes on to boil, or prep for her classes.

I was in an afternoon lecture when I got a message from Guy: *At the hospital with m and d. dad fell.* I quickly packed up my stuff, left the lecture theatre, and called him. 'What happened?'

It was hard to hear. It sounded like he was standing in an echoey corridor with people talking all around him. This really pissed me off. I felt like Guy had done it deliberately to annoy me, to keep me from hearing what was happening, and to keep me separated from Mum and Dad.

'What happened?' I said again, and someone who was walking past turned to stare at me, so I must have been yelling. I sat down on a bench and tried to keep calm.

'Dad tripped on something and bashed his head on the kitchen bench. Mum found him when she got home. He must've blacked out for a bit.' Guy said something else, but I couldn't hear him.

'Where is he now? Is he okay?'

'They're in with the docs. Doing some scans or something. He's better.'

'What do you mean, better?'

'I dunno, he seems better.'

'Fuck.'

'Mum said there was a lot of blood.'

'Fuck. I knew something like this would happen.'

'How?'

'Because Mum is fucking stressed, Guy, and Dad needs more help!'

The background noise flared again, all these weird rattles and beeps, a flurry of voices hurried past. 'Where the hell are you?' Then, I said, 'It doesn't matter. I'm coming home. I'll catch the bus.'

I did catch the bus and came home and Mum was all thin and worried and Dad had this great big square plaster on his forehead and Guy was lurking in the background trying to act like he was helping. Christ, what a mess. I tidied up the kitchen and mowed the lawn, which was a mission because it was ankle-deep in most places and Mum and Dad's lawn mower was a piece of shit. During the day I took Dad to the TAB so that he could listen to the horse racing and place some bets, and I made sure he took his meds at the right time. I cooked dinner so that everything was ready when Mum got home from work.

After a couple of weeks, Dad's head was looking better and they both started telling me to go back to uni. I said I was going to take the rest of the semester off and then think about what I was going to do after that, and that it was easier for me to start again at the beginning of a semester. I didn't tell them that I had found someone to take my room in our flat and that Hana had packed up most of my stuff. About a month after Dad's accident, a package arrived at our place with my psych books, but I managed to grab it from the courier before Mum and Dad saw it.

I think I told myself that I'd take a year off from uni and make sure that Mum and Dad were okay. I needed to figure out how to get someone to help Mum with Dad's care. But, looking back, maybe I was scared of Auckland and stressed out about the 200-level papers. Just before Dad had fallen, I'd got a C– on one of my assignments, the worst mark I had got so far. I had joked about it with my flatmates, 'C's get degrees!', but I was actually annoyed and confused because I'd been getting good marks until then. I went back and reread everything but I couldn't figure out what I had done wrong. Had I completely misunderstood the essay question? I doubted myself, so maybe moving back to Whakatāne was a way of getting some control back and creating a situation where I could be in charge again.

Whatever the reason, I stayed, and when a job came up on the reception at the mill, I applied and, I don't know, Dad had worked there for ages and he'd had his accident, and maybe that's why I got the job. I told myself that I'd just work there for a bit and that I should take the job because I should be paying board to Mum and Dad and contributing to all the other house stuff too, and my savings were running out.

I'd been back in Whakatāne for about a year when I went to a party at my friend Kat's place. It was summer and Kat had the barbecue going in her backyard and everyone was drinking and the sun went down and the music turned up and a few drunk people started to dance on the deck.

I had clocked Johnny soon after I'd arrived because I knew most people at the party, but I didn't know him. He had dark hair and a black T-shirt and was skinny, almost scrawny. But Johnny doesn't get to be described, except, I guess, I should say that I thought he looked good, because that's true, and that's important.

We ended up sitting next to each other on beanbags on the deck, watching the drunk dancers swaying and traipsing in and out of the open French doors. Johnny was sitting with the bright lights from the house behind him and I couldn't see his face in the shadows, so it was hard to figure out how he was reacting to what I said. I had to guess, in that, our very first conversation, what he was like from his posture, his voice, the way he laughed. And it was nice, his laugh. We started taking the piss out of some of the dancers. He told me that he worked on a kiwifruit orchard just out of town, that his family were from Gisborne. I can't remember now, but there were other things that probably impressed me. We talked about music, he liked some of the old bands that Mum listened to, The Kinks, Roy Orbison, stuff that I didn't expect him to know. Jesus, it seems so pathetic, now. I told him about high school in Whakatāne, what subjects I liked, what my friends had been doing since school.

A friend of his came and took him away. I was tired, so I went and found Miri, who was supposed to be driving. She went to pee, and I was waiting for her in the passenger seat when Johnny knocked on the window. I wound it down and he asked, 'Where are you going?'

I laughed. 'Home.'

'Some of us are going down to the beach. Come.'

That was the way it was with Johnny. No invitations. Just instructions.

But I didn't know that then, so I went with him. I got into the car with him and his mates and we built a bonfire at the beach and smoked a spliff and some people went for a swim and came back in their wet undies and dried themselves as best they could in front of the fire.

The next day, Johnny texted me, *come for a drive*, and we did. We were hungover, so we went all the way to Ōpōtiki and got fish and chips. On the way back, I was drinking a Coke and resting my feet on the dashboard and Johnny picked up his phone and put The Kinks on and I had this sudden thought that a boy had never listened to me before. Like, really listened. Listened so that he remembered and then did something based on something I had told him the night before.

It was like a drug, being listened to, being remembered, and so, that summer, I told Johnny everything. There wasn't anything special or important about me and my life, but I felt like there was, when Johnny listened to me with his look of focus and concern.

We went to the beach and the movies and drove together down to a music festival in Hawke's Bay. Johnny shared a flat with two friends from the kiwifruit orchard and I stayed there more and more, though I still helped at home, stocking up Mum and Dad's freezer with dinners and coming round on the weekend to vacuum and take Dad out to the pub.

Johnny worked from Tuesday to Saturday and had Sundays and Mondays off. I worked a normal week, so Sundays were our only day to hang out together. We'd wake up late and I'd make scrambled eggs and we'd eat them outside, on the rickety table he and his flatmates had made out of packing crates from the kiwifruit orchard. We sat in old wire outdoor chairs that had been picked up from the side of the road, or maybe even left there by the tenants who had lived in the house before. They were the kind that left the imprint of a grid on your legs, or any part of skin that pressed up against them.

Those mornings, nothing to do, smoking and wearing my pyjama shorts, my bare legs stretched out in front of me and resting on the crates, feeling sexy and knowing that Johnny's flatmates were checking me out, and also feeling like my decision to come back to Whakatāne was the right one, because here was Johnny, sitting across from me, wearing a black T-shirt even though the sun was already hot, Johnny, who looked up from his phone and said, 'We'll go for a drive to Matatā and see Josh.'

I went to Matatā and saw his druggie friend Josh who grew weed and had a freaky Alsatian called Chewbacca, even though I didn't like Josh or his gross dog. Johnny made plans and I did as I was told because I was dumb and in love and couldn't see him for what he really was.

I was at Mum and Dad's house on the day that I finally felt that something was wrong. Actually, I'd known something was wrong before then, but I'd ignored the feeling, pushed it to the back of my mind.

Dad was in the lounge listening to the radio and Johnny and I were in the kitchen. I was making Dad a cup of tea and Johnny was looking at his phone.

'*The Avengers* is on at eight tonight, so we'll go to that session,' he said.

I quickly dunked the teabag and put it in the sink.

I replied, 'I'm going round to Miri's tonight.'

Johnny looked up. 'We're going to the movies tonight.'

'Why don't you go with Adam?'

'I told you this morning.'

I poured milk into Dad's mug and when I didn't say anything, Johnny said, again, in a changed voice, 'I told you this morning.'

I turned to look at him and he hadn't moved but I could see a new tension curled inside of him. He shoved his phone into his back pocket and looked past my shoulder, out the kitchen window, and into the garden. I realised Dad had turned off the radio and I could hear the drone of someone mowing their lawn.

'I'm sorry,' I said. 'I promised Miri ages ago. I'm helping her with her CV.'

He said nothing, still not looking at me, then turned and left the kitchen. The front door banged closed, and I heard his engine rev and the gravel crunch as he turned too quickly on the driveway.

I went into the lounge and put Dad's tea on the little table beside him, taking his hand to gently show him where it was. 'Where'd Johnny go off to?' he asked.

'He remembered he had something to do,' I said.

'Shouldn't go that fast down the drive. Mum could've been turning in.'

Dad reached out with both hands and found his mug.

'I'll tell him.'

That was the first of many excuses that I made up for Johnny. I said we couldn't go to things because he wasn't feeling so good or he'd been working overtime, so was tired and needed to take it easy. The truth was that he didn't like going to things that my friends had organised, like games of touch at the domain, or drinks after work, because he wasn't in charge, or didn't know everyone there, or there was some little thing that put him off. Johnny liked to be in control. He didn't want to be the centre of attention. He was actually pretty quiet in big groups, but he watched. He watched and he remembered. He judged people. And he didn't like it when conversation turned to a topic that he didn't know much about because he hated being at a disadvantage, or that someone might think they were better than him.

I didn't realise these things all at once, but I slowly began to hear Johnny's instructions, his demands, and the way that he spoke to me, as if I would do whatever he said. Because I did. I loved him, and I loved being around him. He sent me links to songs that he thought I'd like and brought me coffee in bed, while I watched him get ready for work.

So I made up all these stupid excuses for him and backed down and went along with his plans. And I became a bit smaller, a miniature, limited version of me.

I remember Renee, who still lived in Whakatāne at the time, turning to me while I was waiting for Johnny somewhere. I was supposed to be driving him home and I was tired and wanted to go, but he was pissing around with his mates and ignoring me. Renee said, 'You know you could just go and he could get a ride with someone else?'

But it had never even occurred to me to leave, because I didn't want Johnny to be angry, for him to get tense and silent and watchful.

He never hit me, but I felt that he might, he could, and that he wanted to. And that's why I started shading myself, to protect myself from Johnny's silent threat, this threat that I followed around all day.

When I started shading, it was subconscious. I didn't know what I was doing, it was just a survival mechanism that kicked in, a feeling, a way of thinking that came naturally to me.

It's still dangerous, I guess, to write this down in detail here, but I'm trying to figure it out for myself, and for Jade, so that she can try to understand how I knew how to do it, where it came from, and why I had to. It's helping, and I'm starting to see things clearer now, as I get this onto the screen.

I started shading with Johnny so that he wouldn't focus on me so much, and it'd calm things, and calm him. It's messed up, because it was his listening to me so closely that made me such a sucker in the first place, but later, I wanted him to look away, to stop seeing me so that he wouldn't get angry.

So, here's the first time I shaded. Or maybe I had done it before, and I hadn't realised? I don't know. Anyway, Johnny was picking me up from work and I was late. A whole lot of shit had gone down just as I was about to leave, a supplier had started complaining about unpaid invoices, which, it turned out, had been paid, but I had to track back through some messy records to sort it all out.

It was taking ages, but I had to do it before I left, and I had texted Johnny, *So sorry, have to sort something, be out soon.* But it was complicated, and the more I rushed and worried about Johnny waiting, the more I made mistakes and couldn't find what I was looking for.

I was half an hour late when I finished and felt like I could leave, even though Nicola, who was in the office with me, was still sending final emails to calm people down. She waved me off and said something like, 'Go. I'll finish this up. What a shit show.'

I grabbed my bag and ran through the front doors and out onto the footpath. The road was busy, but I saw Johnny's car parked on the other side. The windows were tinted, and I couldn't see what was happening inside, but I knew Johnny would be there, simmering, scrolling through his phone. He hadn't replied to my text. He hated waiting.

I stood for a moment and thought about leaving, just going back into the mill, and texting to say that I had to work even later. But that would just make things worse. I remember thinking that I would have to face up to him sometime, so I may as well just get it over and done with.

The car's headlights turned on and Johnny revved the engine. He had seen me.

I waited for a gap in the traffic and darted across the road, opened the passenger-side door, and got in. The car was hot and smelt like McDonald's. Johnny said nothing but revved again and pulled out into the traffic, too fast.

'I'm sorry,' I said. 'I had to stay and sort that out.'

Johnny was silent. He sped up then came to a sharp stop at some lights. I jerked in my seat and had to put my hands out onto the dashboard to steady myself.

We started up again with a burst of speed, leaving the other cars at the intersection behind us. Johnny left town, heading south. I didn't know where we were going. We hadn't planned to do anything special. We were supposed to be going back to his flat.

'I don't have time to piss around waiting for you,' said Johnny. 'Nicola does the invoicing.'

'I had to help her.'

'No, you didn't. You just wanted to make me hang around like your bitch.'

Johnny turned to look at me, but I didn't want him to, I wanted him to look at the road. He took a 75 kph corner at 110 and sped up on the straight that came afterwards. I gripped the handle above the passenger-side window.

Johnny took one hand off the wheel and reached down to the compartment between the seats for a smoke, then, with the same hand, dug down into the pocket of his jeans for a lighter, raising his hips to get at it. Hurry up, Johnny, I thought, get your hand back on the wheel. He lit the cigarette and took a drag. The hand with the fag came back to rest for a second on the wheel, before it returned to his mouth.

I didn't feel angry, I remember feeling scared and wanting to get out of the car. And also, I felt bad, actually bad, that Johnny had had to wait for me, that's how deeply he'd got inside my head. I couldn't see that he was just a waster who pissed around at the kiwifruit orchard and played too much Call of Duty.

We were going too fast. The road zipped towards us and the car ate up the white lines. Johnny took a drag on his cigarette, changed gears, and let the car sway out over the middle line, just gently, deliberately, yeah, as if it didn't matter, as if he was testing me, forcing me to say something, to say that I wanted him to stop and let me out.

A truck appeared at a corner ahead and Johnny corrected just in time. I held my breath as we sped past and felt the pressure of the truck's displaced air, saw its row of rolling wheels, the wheels so big, seen up close.

Green fields skimmed past outside my window. Too many things to look at. Too many things to keep hold of. The sign for a fertiliser company, 'Richter's Agri-gro', appeared ahead of us, then was gone in a second. 'Richter's Agri-gro,' I said. A hedge of macrocarpa. A primary school. More fields, scattered with grazing sheep. As I saw them, I said these things aloud too. The sign for a railway line, then the railway line. Johnny slowed, just enough, the engine grunting and complaining at his clunky gear shifts, and I turned, as the car bumped over the tracks, to see them stretching out into the distance, the grass alongside them, dry and dirty looking. Next came hay bales wrapped in plastic. A rabbit hopping next to the road and suddenly changing direction to slip under a fence. An orchard. A garage with a black ute parked out the front. I saw these things and I said them. I saw them and said them. Saw and said. The black lines on the road in front of us where someone had pulled on the hand brake and black smoke had come out behind them. A turnoff to our right. A give way sign.

Johnny looked at me, when I spoke, but the radio was loud and I wasn't sure if he could hear me, and he turned back to the road. I saw the things and I said them. I wanted to anchor us. A field. A field. A wire fence. A house. A barn with a rusty roof. It was as if each thing, each word for the thing, was piecing together a parachute that dragged on the car, slowed it down, eased the pressure, a weight of words.

I started to look around at the inside of the car and gave each thing its name. The dust on the dashboard. The worn carpet under the driver's seat. The discoloured patch next to the radio where something had once been stuck. Each little thing in its place, with its words around it. I said them.

Johnny looked at me again and the car slowed a little. He rested his elbow on the lip of his window. The lip of his window. The lip. The windscreen wipers. The broken handle on the glove box. The... I paused to think of the right word. The right word was important. Being specific was important. Velour. The tired, black velour on the passenger seat, stitched in a grid. The shallow indents of the stitching, running parallel to each other.

The car slowed down. A stop sign. Block white letters on a red background. S. T. O. P. The car stopped. The song on the radio. 'Two white lines,' I said. 'The blue see-through strip at the top of the windscreen,' I said. Johnny looked both ways and we started moving again. He indicated, turned left, and I saw we were taking the road that would lead us back to my parents' house.

Johnny opened his window and flicked away his stub. He shifted in his seat, leant back slightly, relaxed. I spoke quietly, all the time, naming the roads as we passed, saying the numbers on the letterboxes. At an intersection, he slowed and turned to look in my direction to check the road, but he didn't see me. He looked right through me and quietly sang along to the radio.

The goat on the berm. The letterbox. The gravel driveway. The ruts in the gravel from all the cars before. We pulled up at Mum and Dad's place. Johnny left the engine running and tapped the steering wheel with his index finger. 'See ya,' he said, not looking at me.

'Thanks.' I unclipped my seat belt. 'Thanks for the ride.'

Johnny frowned slightly and scratched the back of his neck.

'I'll text you later,' I said, opening the door.

'Yeah.' He leant over and kissed me. His lips felt cold and dry and his breath was smoky.

I shut the door and Johnny drove down the driveway. I stood and watched the car ease out onto the road, moving slowly now. I stopped naming the things and their little spaces. I closed my eyes and when I opened them again I let the objects and places and their specific words drift away from me.

I turned and opened the front door. 'Hi?' I called.

'I'm here,' Dad said, from the lounge.

I went in and sat down on the couch across from Dad's old chair. I bent my legs up underneath me and tucked my shaking hands in between my thighs.

Dad had the radio on and a cup of warm tea on his table.

'Where's Mum?' I asked.

'Out the back. Getting the washing. Johnny dropped you off?'

'Yeah. He got me from work.'

Dad nodded and reached for his tea, his hand pausing to feel its heat from the side of the cup before he picked it up. We sat in silence.

'What's it like out there at the moment?' he asked. He had a way of asking this, quietly, gently, as if he didn't want it to seem like he'd been thinking about it all day, as if it wasn't that important, when I knew that it was.

I closed my eyes. 'Bright,' I said. 'Blue sky. Summer. People driving home from work and school.'

'Yeah?' Dad put his tea down and leaned in, eager now, and forgetting to pretend it wasn't important.

'You need to wear sunglasses outside. All the lines of the roofs are hard against the sky. You know, like, sharp, like they've been drawn with a ruler. Everyone's roof is grey. All the new houses have dark-grey roofs and dusty-blue wooden walls. Sometimes they have different coloured doors, like fire engine red, or tangerine orange.'

I lay down on the couch, my eyes still closed. Then it came on all of a sudden, an extreme tiredness, so that I couldn't even sit up and had to sink down into the cushions.

I kept talking for Dad because this was what we did. He asked and I described things for him, described the world he couldn't see. I could go on for hours, just talking about the tiniest things. Some days he wanted to know what outside looked like, and sometimes he just wanted me to talk about a room at the mill that he could remember, like the staff room, or the dirty area at the back of the car park, where they stacked old pallets, and the smokers gathered. I could talk about these places for ages, just talking about the carpet and the smells and the windows and the lights, drawing it all up for him, describing it so that he could see it again.

They were the same, in a way, the colouring for Dad, and the shading from Johnny. I can see that now, from a distance. But with Johnny, it was so that he didn't see me anymore, and so he forgot I was there and forgot what he was angry about. I shaded myself and brought up the colours of everything else around me so that I disappeared.

I hadn't thought about it clearly, in the car, with the fields speeding past outside, and Johnny smoking. I had started doing it because I felt like it was a way to calm things down, and to calm him down. I knew I could do it because I'd done it for Dad for years. I had created spaces for him, made things clearer, put images into words that became images again, in Dad's head.

I can't remember now, how I felt about the shading, as I lay on the couch across from Dad. Did I think that it could save me? Did I think that it'd change Johnny?

I remember being tired, so tired that I couldn't move any part of my body, except my lips, so I kept telling Dad about the colour of clouds and the cars in the supermarket car park and the names of cereals and the patterns on their boxes and thickness of the grass on the back lawn, the seed heads of the grass growing higher, my eyes closed, sort of aware of Mum coming in through the back door and standing in the doorway, listening and looking at us.

9.

I felt relieved after I shaded myself from Johnny, because the longer we were together, the angrier he got, and I was running out of options.

Sometimes Johnny's was a bottled-up anger, a small anger caused by small things. Some drunk person would blurt out an opinion at a party that he didn't agree with, or felt was meant to make him look stupid, and Johnny would be pissed off. He'd grind his teeth and roll his cigarettes tightly into mean, pinched tubes, not smoking them, but putting them back into his bag of tobacco, storing them up for some time in the future.

'Who the fuck does he think he is?' Johnny would say, in the car, late, after a party out in the wops somewhere. 'Dissing The Clash. The Clash! Fuck.' He would hammer the wheel with the heel of his hand and gun the engine. 'Let's get out of here.'

'Are you drunk?' I'd ask from the passenger seat, as he backed down the driveway and out onto an empty country road, a pitch-black night. But no, Johnny didn't really drink much. He was angry at the world, but sober, and clear-eyed.

A sober anger, yes, but sometimes, Johnny's was a big anger. A shouting and spitting anger. A pressing-me-up-against-the-wall anger. A 'What the fuck did you say to me?' anger.

Johnny took me to meet his mum, Pat, once. His parents had split up when he was a kid and she lived by herself in New Plymouth. He didn't talk to his dad, who was in Gisborne, and he didn't seem to have any contact with his sister in Auckland. She worked for an insurance company, or something, and he never told me anything about her. Was she older or younger?

We went down to New Plymouth because he 'wanted me to meet

his mum', but I think he just wanted to go for a long drive because he'd got a new car and wanted to test it out. He was calm and jokey and enjoying himself on the way down. He had The Strokes turned up loud and hassled me for looking nervous. 'She's going to love you, babe,' he said, and stroked my leg.

We stopped at a small house in a suburb on a hill. It was a grey afternoon. Johnny knocked on the door and grinned at me, gave me a little kiss. We saw shifting colours through the patterned glass in the front door before it was opened by a small woman. I remember her being so little, with this little voice, and this little way of moving around.

She was surprised to see us. 'Johnny, what are you doing here?' Her hand went to a gold cross hanging on a chain around her neck.

'I texted you, Mum, I told you I was coming down, to visit.'

'Did you?'

'Yes! Last week.'

'Oh dear, did you? I don't remember.' She looked at me.

'This is my girlfriend, Jodie,' Johnny said.

'It's nice to meet you,' I said. I leant in to hug her and felt her body stiffen in my arms.

Pulling away, she said, 'Yes, well. Come in, I suppose. I'm going to have to go to the supermarket. I've got nothing at all in the cupboards.'

We followed her down the hall and sat at the little table in her kitchen. The kitchen was tidy and smelt like cleaning spray.

Pat put the kettle on, and Johnny chatted away about the drive down, about his new car. He was acting weird, like, all out there and talkative and relaxed. He was never normally like that. He was usually sullen or sulky or watchful.

Pat nodded and carefully poured milk into the mugs she had put out. She didn't talk much and she didn't ask me any questions, so I found myself just volunteering random information to her, like where I worked in Whakatāne and how Johnny and I had met.

After a while Johnny went out into the back garden and mowed the lawn. Pat didn't help him find the mower, or tell him about the sticky starting mechanism that we heard him struggling with for several minutes. The kitchen window had a good view of the back lawn, but I remember Pat never looked out, to check on Johnny, to make sure he was doing it right. It was as if when he left the room he had just disappeared.

I sat in the kitchen with her and tried to make conversation. She'd often say 'Oh, but I don't know much about that', and that was the end of a topic.

That night we had fish and chips for dinner and watched something on TV. Pat showed me where the sheets were and I made up the bed in the spare room. Johnny and I sank into each other on its spongy mattress.

Pat worked at the New World and she had a shift the next day, so we said goodbye in the morning. Johnny kept offering, 'Is there anything I can do for you before I go, Mum?'

'Oh no,' Pat said, 'don't worry. The house is holding up.'

'I'll see you again at Christmas, okay?'

'Yes, yes, okay.'

Pat didn't seem to be listening, she was sorting out her cup of morning coffee. The small radio sitting on top of the fridge burbled away. Pat hadn't had any breakfast herself, and hadn't put anything out for us, so I looked in the cupboard and found a box of Weet-Bix.

'Oh yes, there you go, there should be enough for you two,' said Pat, when she saw what I had found. 'I was planning on bringing some things home after work today.'

I gave Pat an awkward hug before she left and Johnny went outside with her. I watched them from the lounge. He was standing in the driveway and talking and talking, then he pointed to the car's bonnet before opening it and checking something inside. He waved her over and indicated something. She hitched her handbag up on her shoulder and shook her head.

He desperately wanted to help her, to do something useful for her, but mostly I think he wanted her to notice him, and to care. She seemed confused by his enthusiasm and his chatter. She didn't know where to look, or how to respond. The very fact of him, his being on her doorstep, or in her kitchen, surprised her. No, not surprised even, she seemed uninterested.

In the car on the way back to Whakatāne, Johnny said, 'Mum really liked you.'

'She did?' I asked.

'Yeah, she told me.'

Johnny was probably lying. I couldn't imagine Pat expressing a strong opinion about another person. But Johnny wanted his mum to like me. He wanted her to have said, when they were unwrapping the fish and chips together in the kitchen, or when I was brushing my teeth, that she thought I was lovely, a really lovely girl. Maybe he even convinced himself that this had happened, and that she was the type of person who said stuff like that.

I write about this visit here, because sometimes I see the way Jade looks at me, craving my attention, and needing my entire focus to be on her, and I wonder if Pat ever completely looked at Johnny, or when it was that her attention drifted away from him. When she divorced? When Johnny became a teenager? And I wonder if Johnny's anger grew out of this disinterest, because kids need parents to be interested in them. Even if it's half-pretend, they need someone to nod and smile and ask questions. And I imagine Johnny fighting for that attention, and the fight staying in him, somehow.

Johnny was happy for a bit, after we'd been to see his mum, it settled him. That's probably why I thought it would be okay to go out with friends from the mill after work and have a few drinks, without Johnny, who was working a late shift at the orchard. We went to the pub and then, because it was summer and sunny, took takeaways down to the beach. As the sun went down, a few people dragged driftwood into a pile and lit a fire.

Miri was there, by herself, which was weird because I didn't see her much in those days. She lived in Whakatāne but she'd started going out with a new guy and she was always round at his place. She could be obsessive like that, Miri, single minded. When we were kids she'd pick up on some new thing, a new band, and she'd obsess over it for months. She'd make me sit next to her while she downloaded every single song she could find on the internet. This was in the days of those early download sites, and I'd get bored of watching the download bar inch across the screen. But she'd freak out if I tried to leave and say, 'Just one more. The next one will be faster.' Then we'd lie on the floor of her big sister's room and listen to the whole lot, played through her computer's crappy speakers, Miri writing down the lyrics and repeating sections over and over so that she got them exactly right.

Once, I looked through one of her notebooks, where she wrote these lyrics. It was packed with words, all written in Miri's tight, tidy handwriting, every page filled and neatly divided with ruled lines. There were hundreds of songs in there, but also stories. I'm not sure if Miri had written them or if they were copied from somewhere. I started to read one, but I heard Miri coming back to her room and I knew she kept these books secret, so I stashed it back under her pillow.

At the beach that night, when the sun went down, the sky grew big and dark and so did the sea, a black plain stretching away from the shore. People sat next to the fire and picked at the left-over hot chips, cold and fatty in their nest of newspaper. Miri had brought me some more beers and it was so nice to be next to her, just her, with the heat of the fire on our faces.

Johnny turned up just after someone had dragged over another stack of driftwood from further down the beach and thrown it on the fire. The flames rose towards the night sky, sparks leaping and wood snapping. I knew that he would come. He always came to wherever I was. But my heart still began to thud when I saw him on the other side of the fire. He looked over at me and I could see the warmth of the last couple of weeks had left him and the tension was back.

I was standing next to Miri, and I saw that she'd seen him too. Miri hadn't said anything to me about Johnny, but I knew she didn't like him because she was my best friend and I didn't need her to say it out loud.

Johnny began to walk around the fire towards us and this time, again, the shading started even before I was aware of it. It was an instinct, like a small animal darting into the bush.

'Fire,' I said, the word rising out of me. 'A big fire, the sparks leaping and wood snapping. The sky is big and dark and so is the sea, a black plain stretching away from the shore.'

Miri sipped her beer and we both watched Johnny walk towards us.

'The newspaper is a nest,' I said. 'The sand is cool and smooth. A bottle of beer. A pile of wet clothes. The Southern Cross. The end of a burnt log.' I was picking up speed, but I spoke quietly, keeping under control, finding a rhythm. 'The chips are cold and fatty. The bit in the middle of the fire is very hot, very red, a red that you can't look at. Four bottles of beer, lying on their sides. One of them has a tiny bit of liquid at the bottom.'

Johnny was near us, but I could sense his attention had drifted. He looked past my shoulder, at the group standing behind us. He looked down and put his hand in his jacket pocket, as if to get something, his phone maybe, but when he took it out there was nothing there.

I continued, 'Miri is wearing a black hoodie and blue jeans. She has rose gold nail polish on. She has black eyeliner on her top eyelids, one side swoops out slightly longer than the other. She has a nose piercing, a tiny gold stud, like the top of a pin.'

Johnny stood next to us, unsure, half of his face in darkness. 'The newspaper is a nest,' I said. 'The sky is big and dark and so is the sea, a black plain stretching away from the shore.'

Johnny moved on and stood with the group behind us. I watched him roll a smoke.

Miri and I drank our beer. I knew she'd heard me. But if there was anyone my secrets were safe with, I knew they were safe with Miri.

Someone next to us laughed and we heard Johnny laugh too, trying to keep up, and his laugh turned into a cough, and he tried to say something but the words were choked.

The fire sunk in on itself and as it got darker we huddled closer to its warmth and light. It was dark that night, like all the nights. The sky was big and dark and so was the sea, a black plain stretching away from the shore.

10.

There was a school fair, I remember, when Jade was Year Two. It was a sunny day and the stalls were arranged around the netball courts. Someone had laid out a stack of sports equipment so the kids could play, and Jade and her friends had grabbed a long skipping rope.

I took a video. Jade waited, watching the rope loop round and round, controlled by two girls at either end, before running in, her arms raised and jumping, jumping, jumping.

She jumped a couple of times before she jumped too low and the rope looped around her ankles. She untangled herself, smiling and proud. It was the longest she'd ever jumped with the big rope, and she joined the line again, wanting another go. She looked over at me, across the courts, and saw me filming. I stopped the video and waved.

I still have the video and I stopped writing to look at it on my phone now. Jade isn't there and the rope tangles around an empty space and then rights itself into a long line again, pulled taut by the two girls at either end, who stare at the gap between them.

It feels powerful to write Jade back into this scene. I remember her scanning the courts and looking for me, wanting me to have seen her and wanting my phone to have recorded her jumps, to confirm that it had actually happened and we could watch it later.

I wandered over to a bakery stall. 'Fancy an elderflower cordial?' the woman behind the table asked.

'Sure,' I said.

I gave her the money and she filled a cup with cordial and bubbly water and handed it to me. 'I gather the elderflower myself,' she said.

'Did your kids go to this school?' I asked.

'Yes, back in the day.' She laughed. 'All ancient history now.'

There was a little stage on the opposite side of the courts where a man was fiddling with a mic, trying to get it going while the PA fizzed and crackled. He beckoned to the principal who climbed onto the stage and welcomed everyone, 'Nau mai, haere mai. Now it's the moment we've all been waiting for, the raffle!' she announced. 'We've got a seriously good prize this year. A grocery hamper from New World, two movie vouchers,' she read from a list on her phone, 'even a free car service.'

She held out a cardboard box and the man who had fixed the mic reached in and drew out a ticket stub.

'Number thirty-five! Jodie Pascoe!' the principal announced.

'Shit, that's me!' I said, startled to hear my name through the speakers.

I put down my cup and I flicked through my wallet, then looked in the side sleeve of my phone case, before I finally found the ticket folded over in the back pocket of my shorts.

'Jodie Pascoe? Are you still here?' the principal said.

'Do you want me to take a photo, love? On the stage?'

The woman stood up.

I heard Jade calling out my name and saw her running towards me through the crowd.

'It's okay—' I started to say.

'Please let me,' the woman said, lunging towards me, her voice suddenly desperate, 'because I've gone out, you see, I've gone, so it's the least I can do, I want to, I really want to.'

I stepped back into the wire fence that wrapped around the courts, scratching my heel on a loose wire.

But the woman reached out and took the phone out of my hand, just as Jade appeared next to me. 'You won!' Jade shouted, smiling. 'They said your name. Can you take some pictures, please?' she asked the woman, who nodded and held my phone up.

Jade led me through the crowd and up onto the stage. I took the hamper from the principal and people clapped. 'You've won some really great stuff in there, congratulations!' the principal said. Jade stood on stage next to me and waved at her friends. I looked around, dazed, and saw the faces of the crowd looking up at me, the old woman at the back, holding up my phone and taking heaps of photos, happily documenting. Jade noticed her too and, grabbing my free hand, struck a pose, leaning out a little, away from me, and putting her other hand on her hip.

Music started playing and the crowd shifted and dispersed, moving out to the stalls and small carnival rides that had been set up at the back of the field. Jade jumped down off the stage and wove through the crowd until she reached the woman. She gave Jade my phone and smiled at her and said something. By the time I had caught up with Jade, carrying the heavy hamper, the woman had returned to her stall and Jade was scrolling through the photos until she found the video of herself jumping rope, which she stood and watched, repeating her triumph of only minutes before.

I didn't follow the woman and I didn't thank her. I didn't want to touch her. I was shaking, and I grabbed the phone from Jade because I didn't want her to touch it. Jade looked at me, confused, then ran off to join her friends.

I'd never been near someone who had gone out. This woman, with her desperate hands, her kindness, was suddenly so real, so *there*. She had gone. There'd been nothing in the news about her, or had I missed it?

I looked around at the crowds of people. The sunny day and the stalls felt threatening. I watched her from the other side of the courts, selling cakes and biscuits. Did other people know? I felt weird about dobbing her in, being the police.

I picked up my hamper and found Jade, dragged her away from her friends and bundled her into the car. She whined all the way home because she hadn't been on any of the rides. And she was right to be angry. The fair had just been getting started and I was vague about why we had to leave all of a sudden.

When we got home I checked the online advice about what to do if you found someone who had gone out. I called an 0800 number and told them what had happened, but I felt like a dick because I didn't know her name, or where she lived, or the answers to any of the questions they asked me. All I knew was that she had been looking after a stall at the fair, she was wearing an apron, and that she had wanted to take some photos of me and my daughter.

The woman on the other end of the phone sighed. 'Yes,' she said, 'they always want to do that.'

'What do you mean?' I asked.

'They always want to take photos of other people. It gives them…' She paused. 'purpose.'

'Purpose?'

'Something to do.'

'How many people have gone out in New Zealand? Did you know about her already?'

The woman didn't answer my questions but switched back to her officious tone, saying she would be in touch if there were any further questions. 'It's good that we have your details on file now,' she said. 'We may need to contact you.'

Why did the government need to know about gaps? I didn't ask these questions then. I just followed the instructions that I was given. I was freaked out, after the fair, and I felt as if I should do something. It felt too important a thing to leave unacknowledged. I felt that I had to tell someone, and something, I don't know what, needed to be done.

What was being done with this growing set of information wasn't clear, but in the weeks following it became obvious that there were more and more gaps. Lots of people had gone out but hadn't told anyone. People around the country came forward and said they had talked to cousins and neighbours and friends of friends who had gone. People swiped through their phones and found that people who had been there before had disappeared.

It was rare to watch TV without a glitch where someone used to be. These were still small, at the time, but the absences were growing. Clips on YouTube where a member of a sports team had gone out were hard to get used to. A netball would be thrown to an empty space on the court, and an invisible pair of hands would grab it and hold it for a moment, before slinging it along to the next player. Images were full of this empty energy, and gaps, but gaps that still made things happen, made balls bounce, opened curtains, and crushed grass under their feet.

There were new campaigns to get people to report themselves if they had gone out, or if they knew anyone who had gone. It was for our own good that these things were recorded, so that people could be kept safe. There were more ads everywhere, on TV, online, telling us to help keep track of this 'pressing issue'. They said that various cures were being worked on and technologists and doctors and psychologists were making progress in identifying the root cause of the problem. Was it in the mind? In the body? In the hardware?

But there were still no patterns, no connections between gaps, and the randomness of it all made it hard for anyone to know who might go out next. Governments across the world were running to catch up at the same time as reassuring everyone that they had everything under control.

I began to see more people around Whakatāne who had gone out. I saw Terri McKenzie at the supermarket. She was walking with a man, and I had this feeling that he had gone too. They seemed close, gentle with each other, as if they both understood what the other was going through. I watched from the end of an aisle as they put stuff in their trolley together. They stopped in front of the dairy section and he put his hand on her shoulder. I wanted to hold my phone up and see if they were there, to see my suspicions confirmed, but I also felt embarrassed. They had a right to their privacy, they had so much of it now, much more than the rest of us.

The official I spoke to on the phone was right too, because gaps loved to take photos. They desperately wanted to be useful in making images and recording events. Gaps were often the photographers at weddings, or the parent filming the school play. It was as if making more images was a substitute for their own presence in them. I remember the expression of the woman at the fair, reaching out for my phone. They wanted to participate in the life of making and sharing images, even if they themselves couldn't be photographed. It was a compulsion, an addiction, almost, to be near and to create pictures.

Even as I met more and more gaps in person, I didn't know how to talk to them, or what to say. I remember, around this time, talking to the office lady at Jade's school and then realising that she had gone. Gaps had a way of looking at the edge of your face, or past your shoulder, never looking you in the eye. They seemed less *there*, as if, because they couldn't be seen in images, they didn't want to be seen in real life either. But they also had a way of moving their bodies. How can I describe it? This needs the right words. They moved more freely, more openly, more… smoothly, maybe. I saw it in the way the receptionist got up from her seat and crossed the office to get something from her filing cabinet. So ordinary. But she did it in a way that was kind of unburdened. As if she could do whatever the hell she wanted. There was no one watching, no one keeping tabs on her.

I was jealous, for a second, I think, that she could move this way. I wanted that too, to be free in that way. I wanted to walk to the filing cabinet with nobody watching.

11.

Bex didn't mention Miri again after the evening that she came round and asked me questions. She actually looked like she felt a bit stink when I saw her next, couldn't look me in the eye. She dropped Cara off on a Sunday afternoon so I could take the girls down to the beach. She walked Cara up to the front door but didn't stay long, said she was going to go and do some shopping and would be back in a couple of hours.

I helped Jade and Cara get into their togs and hop in the car. On the way, we stopped at the dairy for ice blocks and chips and a Coke for me and when we got to the beach we laid out our towels and had a picnic, the ice blocks were already slushy and the girls got sticky fingers and pink smeary lips from eating them too quickly.

I took a photo of them together, sitting on their towels, pink togs, ice block sticks poking out of their mouths. Jade had made a stupid joke and Cara had turned to look at her and laughed. Except now, of course, in the photo, Jade isn't there and Cara is laughing at nothing, an empty space on the towel next to her.

I want to remember Jade in that moment. What length was her hair, exactly? Was she facing Cara too? I think she was squinting at the sun.

Cara asked me to take another photo and leapt up to strike a pose. She asked, 'Can you take one more of me, running down the beach?'

'Sure,' I said and took photos as she ran away from me and back again, deliberately scuffing up sand with her big toes.

I crouched down and Cara leaned in to look at the photos. I didn't really want her sticky fingers smearing the screen, but I let her crop the images and layer on a filter. 'This looks good,' she said, pointing at one, 'with the sea in the background.'

Jade looked too and nodded.

'Can you send them to my mum?' Cara asked. 'She'll want to see. I think...' She trailed off, sat back down on her towel and started playing with the tassels.

'What's wrong?' Jade asked, sitting down beside her.

'Mum told me I wasn't supposed to say. She's so grumpy about it.'

'What happened?'

'My uncle's gone, he's gone out.'

Jade immediately leant over and hugged Cara.

Cara looked over at me and then looked away, back down at the towel. 'Mum doesn't think I know, but I heard her talking to Nan on the phone.'

'It's okay, Cara,' I said. 'He'll be okay.'

We were all quiet for a moment, then Jade said, almost in a whisper, 'Did it hurt him?'

Cara shrugged. 'He's in Singapore,' she said, as if this might explain things. 'I think Nan talked to him on the phone. I wanted you to take photos, because I could go soon, couldn't I? Mum said it was something in our family.'

Cara jumped up. 'Come on!' she shouted, and Jade ran with her down to the sea where they slapped their feet on the sand and the waves surged up to their knees. Cara was happy again, laughing.

I sat on my towel and kept an eye on them. They knew something was up, something was wrong in their close, little-kid world and in the bigger, less-defined world of words they heard on the radio, and saw on the TV, and picked up from their parents' phones, and from the conversations of the adults around them. I knew that Jade was worried, and that she listened closely when I talked to Mum and Dad and tried to pick up any information that she could about gaps.

Even if I wanted to, I couldn't give her proper answers to her questions, because nobody had them. This idea that people in the same family shared a gene that meant they'd all go out was a classic example of the ideas that people believed because we were all just trying to hold on to something, anything, to explain what was going on.

International travel was a mess, and getting worse, as gaps had no photos in their passports. At first, gaps had been banned from travelling but then, when it became clear that going out wasn't transmissible in the normal way, temporary measures were set up so that gaps could move around again. Apparently the authorities were able to align people with their data profile to identify them at borders.

People quickly exploited the new systems, though. It turns out it's very easy to adopt the identity of someone who can't be seen by cameras. Gaps sold their identities and documents to people who were into all sorts of dodgy business. People became impossible to track, and countries with land borders had a hard time keeping tabs on who was coming in and out.

Going out was a hustler's dream. Not only were you invisible to cameras, but lots of your online life disappeared, or became, at least, patchy and hard to follow, hard to tell what was real and what wasn't. It was so much easier to slip under the radar. In places that were covered by CCTV, like London, gaps were apparently being actively recruited by drug dealers. They wanted people who could move through supermarkets and train stations and public parks, unseen and unmonitored, and this was only the beginning of how they could be useful.

Justice systems were scrambling as more and more people went out. Court documents, mug shots, video and photo evidence, all of this was vulnerable. Things that held the world together were falling apart.

I think it was in the States where there was the first trial of someone who had been in prison, before there were any gaps, because of photographic evidence. After they had gone out, they requested a retrial because the photo that confirmed their guilt no longer did so. They were acquitted, set free. It was mental! But there was no evidence anymore and the prosecution didn't have anything else to show that the person had committed the crime. I guess maybe they thought, then, that not many people would go out, or that we would figure out how to stop it or undo it. That it would just be a small thing, a thing that would go away.

That day, with Jade and Cara down at the beach, the sun had gone behind a cloud and the girls ran across the sand and back up to me and wrapped themselves in their towels. What did they look like? What can I write? Sandy toes. Their sandy toes poked out between the tassels. Cara reached deep into the bag of chips and fished out a few tiny scraps. She seemed to have forgotten about her uncle and the people disappearing from their images.

I didn't blame her, because it was still easy to forget, then, that anything was happening, when we were happy at the beach and we could see each other and take pictures of each other and everything felt normal and right.

I took another photo of the two of them, Cara and Jade, because the sun was going down and the light was all golden and they looked so beautiful and young and happy and I wanted to remember being there with them. And, as I write this, I remember how it felt, that sense that if I didn't take a photo, we might have never really been at that beach at all.

But we ended up spending ages there, that afternoon. The girls dug a massive hole and ran back and forth from the sea, filling it up with buckets. I had enough snacks to keep them going for a bit and it was eight o'clock or something by the time we left and starting to get dark.

I packed up our stuff and got the girls into the car, tucking their damp towels around them when they said they were cold.

'Can we get fish and chips, Mum? Please?' Jade begged.

'Yeah, okay,' I said.

I drove us back to town, parked outside our favourite fish and chip shop, and we got out of the car.

'Mum,' Jade tugged at my hand as we crossed the road, 'what're they doing?'

She pointed, and then I saw them too, a crowd of people, maybe sixty, standing on the corner, a block down from the fish and chip shop.

Lots of them had their phones up and were scanning the crowd and the streets around them. A man at the front of the group shouted something and shook his fist and the people around him nodded in agreement.

I held the girls' hands tightly and pulled them into the fish and chip shop. A couple of teenagers were sitting on chairs in the corner. The woman behind the counter gave us a small smile. 'Kia ora,' she said.

'What's going on down the road?' I asked.

'They're checking who's gone,' the woman said, 'they're a patrol, or something.'

'Checking?'

I could feel Jade at my side, all ears.

'Yeah, they were here a couple of nights ago too. They come in with their phones.'

'And what do they do, if someone has gone?'

The woman shrugged. 'Guess they just want to know. Keeping a record of it somewhere.'

She picked up her phone and held it up to look at me and Jade and Cara. I panicked at being so casually and quickly assessed, at being so closely looked at. I don't think she even took a photo. What if we'd gone, while we were at the beach? What would the crowd outside do, if this woman's phone couldn't see us?

Inside the panic, there was also the not-quite-there feeling that I knew what to do, and that there were words around me that I could use if I needed to. They were in my mind but also in my throat, a kind of resource, a wealth. I knew the right words for Jade, even without looking down at her. I almost want to start describing her, here. I feel her hovering in between the space of my fingers and the keyboard. I will always know the right words for her.

If we had gone, there in the fish and chip shop, would I have been able to bring her back? Would I have been able to do it, even back then?

But the woman put her phone down and turned to look out the window. We were still present.

The group of people walked past, and as they did, a couple of them stepped into the shop and held up their phones, sweeping the room, searching for gaps.

The two boys in the corner picked up their phones and held them up too, like shields against the angry crowd and all its hungry lenses, its angry looking. 'Fuck off,' one boy said, quiet but staunch.

A man took another step into the shop, aiming his phone directly at the boys. 'Watch it,' he said. I heard the vicious snapping of his phone taking photos. It was that sound of the fake shutter, opening and closing around whatever was in front of it.

'You don't need to go around checking everyone, bro,' said the boy.

'Gotta look out for the community,' said the woman, from behind the counter.

'But they aren't doing anything,' said the other boy, 'the gaps.'

'Not yet,' said the man, shifting nervously on his feet. The rest of the crowd had moved off. 'But you can betcha they're gonna. Not really here, are they? Not really part of this place. Think they can do whatever they want. Don't care about the rest of the community.'

Jade and Cara clung to my legs.

'You can't even see them properly, in real life, when they're gone,' said the woman behind the counter. 'Like, they can't keep going, without their images. They just sort of start to pass out a bit, I've seen it.'

This was the shit that people were saying.

The man nodded, stoked that he'd found a supporter, and then left the shop to catch up with the rest of the crowd down the road.

The boys shook their heads, muttered to each other, and looked down at their phones again.

'It's okay,' I said, putting my arms around the girls. I wanted to get them out of there. 'Shall we go and get McDonald's instead?'

I got them into the car and we drove round the corner to the drive-through. We parked in the queue and played I Spy while we waited.

It was Jade's turn, when she yelled, 'Look, Mum! It's Guy! I spy Guy!'

And it was Guy, standing on the other side of the road, his back to us.

Jade banged on her window.

'He won't be able to hear,' I said. The car ahead of us moved and I nudged us forward so that I could see Guy better.

He was talking to a man that I didn't know. The man was mid-dle-aged and wore a white shirt. He looked like he worked in an office. He was frowning at whatever Guy was saying, and he looked too nice, I thought, too nice and tidy to be hanging out with Guy.

Guy turned, and I looked too, and saw the patrol group with their phones up moving back down the road. The man pointed in the other direction, and he and Guy quickly walked round the corner and out of sight.

I had only seen the man for a minute, maybe, at the most, across the road and through the car's dirty window. But I knew him straight away when I saw him again, later.

The queue for the drive-through moved and I ordered two Happy Meals and then drove us home. The girls seemed to forget what had happened, but later, after Cara had gone home and Jade was in bed, she asked, 'Will those people really go into other people's houses?'

I was lying on the floor next to her bed.

'What people?' I asked.

'Those angry people we saw in town. I think they'll go and look in other people's houses to find the gaps. I wonder if they'll go into Cara's uncle's house.' Jade pulled her sheet up tight under her chin and stared at me with her grey eyes. 'They want to not see people,' she said. 'They want there to be gaps because it makes them feel better.'

'What do you mean?'

'They just like it. They seem angry, but they actually like it.' She paused. 'Maybe the person who came into our house was checking if we'd gone.'

We hadn't talked about the person who we'd felt in our house for ages. I thought about it all the time though, reliving the sudden feeling I'd had, waking up, that someone had been inside our place and looked at us. I'd jumped out of bed and run to Jade's room, where she was asleep, safe, her eyes lightly closed.

'We're still present,' I said.

It was lame, but I couldn't think of anything else to say.

Jade sighed. Going to the beach always made her really tired. I closed my eyes too. Sometimes I fell asleep there, lying on the floor, listening to her breathe.

12.

I knew, I think, when we were kids that something had happened to Miri. But I never said it aloud, or completely acknowledged it. Like I'm not even really acknowledging it here, as I write.

I just wrote 'something had happened to Miri', but what does that really mean? A man assaulted her. I don't know who.

She almost told me, once, when we were kids. We were in one of the fields round the back of her house, hanging out under a line of old pine trees. We liked it there, it was dry and there was a thick layer of prickly pine needles. We'd dragged over some old pallets and propped them up on their sides to make a crappy fort, with an old piece of tarp for the roof.

Miri would sneak into her big sister, Jasmine's, room and steal her Discman and CDs. Then we'd take off for the fort and listen to Destiny's Child, sharing the headphones. Jasmine would be pissed off with us because we'd use up all her batteries.

I was scared of Jasmine but Miri wasn't. She'd scrunch up her nose, throw Jasmine's headphones back at her, and say, 'Mum and Dad should get me my own Discman then.'

Miri would want to listen to every CD over and over, in that way she had of wanting to hear everything, see everything, to know the whole of something. No wonder we used up all of Jasmine's batteries.

I got bored, and I said to Miri, 'Let's go inside and watch TV.'

'Nah,' she said, 'just a few more.' She clicked the skip button to move back to the first track, and I lay on my back next to her, waiting for my turn. But it was getting late and I was cold and the pine needles were spiky.

I heard a car come up the drive and I noticed that Miri had heard it too, because her eyes flicked to a gap between the boards of the pallet.

'Who's that?' I asked.

'Dunno,' Miri said, looking back at the roof of the fort.

We lay there for a while longer as it got darker and darker. Tinny drums and synths leaked out from Miri's headphones as she listened to the songs over again, mouthing the lyrics.

I wanted to go, so I said, 'I think your mum's calling us.'

At that moment, the Discman died and Miri looked at me and I saw, even in the dull evening light, that she was scared, and this scared me, because Miri was never scared. She chased after the boys at school if they threw things at us. She jumped off the highest diving board at the pools.

'Let's go to your house,' she said.

I took the headphones off Miri and said, 'Jasmine will go mental.' And I turned to walk back to the house to take the Discman back, but Miri grabbed my wrist.

'Don't, he's—' she said, snatching it back. 'Promise I'll do it later. She's probably gone out anyway. Let's go.'

She turned and ran across the field towards my place. I followed her. It was night now, but she ran fast, scrambling easily over the wire fences.

We arrived at my back door, kicked off our shoes, and went into the kitchen, panting. Miri's cheeks were pink.

Dad was in the kitchen, moving his hands along the bench until he felt the kettle. He heard us and turned. 'What're you two doing here?' he asked. 'I thought you were staying at Miri's for tea.'

'Mum told us to come over here, cos she had to pop out for a bit,' said Miri.

We went into the lounge, where Mum was sitting on the couch watching a gameshow.

She looked up and said, 'Look at you two. You're freezing. What're you doing running around in the cold? Come and tuck yourselves up, you silly ducks.'

We climbed onto the couch and Mum pulled over a blanket from where it was bunched in the corner and tucked it around our legs. She was wearing her dressing gown and I slid my feet underneath her legs to warm them up.

'I thought you two were having fish and chips at Miri's for tea,' said Mum.

We said nothing and after the ad break the programme came back on. Dad came in slowly with two cups of Milo that he put down on the coffee table, slopping a bit over the side.

'Well, we haven't got anything sorted here,' said Mum, not looking away from the TV, 'but we can get McDonald's. I'll pop out and get it in a bit. Might as well have a bit of a treat, since you two have turned up.'

I felt Miri's body tucked against my side, warming up, our heartbeats slowing after our run across the dark fields.

I didn't know how to talk to Miri about who she was scared of, because I was scared too, and I wanted to snuggle into the blanket and eat McDonald's and pretend that nothing had happened. And Miri didn't bring it up again, not once, and she wasn't the sort of person that you could force to talk about stuff. But I saw how it shaped her, how whatever had happened made her tough and defensive and angry, even when we were kids.

'She's a hard nut, that Miri,' Dad used to say.

And she was, but she was a good friend. We caught the bus together, to and from intermediate and then high school, waited together on the side of the road in the mornings, freezing in winter in our tartan skirts, and always sat next to each other for the short ride to school. I let her boss me around a bit, and I didn't really let other people do that. But with Miri, I didn't mind, because I knew that even when she was being a pain, she was always looking out for me.

She was round at our house all the time. She liked hanging out with Mum and Dad and she tolerated Guy. Even after Dad had his accident, she'd come across the field and let herself in the back door. Some of my other friends were freaked out and they didn't know where to look or what to say when they were in the same room as Dad. When he fumbled with his mug, or suddenly looked in a strange direction, as if he'd heard something that we couldn't hear, it made people feel uncomfortable and they didn't know whether to help him, or ignore him, or pretend everything was the same as it had always been.

Miri figured out the new patterns of our house, though, and when was best for her to come round and how she could be helpful. She has always been quick to pick things up, Miri, and intuitive about people. She'd read Dad the racing results aloud from the paper and knew to tell him if anything had been moved in the lounge, because if things weren't where they usually were, his pathways through the house could get all mucked up and he'd bump into stuff. I guess she knew our place and our lives in a lot of detail then, to know where all the side tables and pens and mugs needed to be. I hadn't really thought about that before. Yeah, she knew us, the Pascoes, better than we probably knew her.

Miri knew about how I coloured for Dad, because, in the beginning, I had started doing it only in short moments, in tiny bits of normal conversation, so that I didn't realise what I was doing. Miri was always at our place, listening to us, so she must have noticed it was happening and how the colouring got stronger and stronger.

Like, Dad didn't ask me, when we got back from school, 'How was the bus ride today?' He'd ask me, 'What'd the bus look like today?'

And I'd reply, 'Fogged up. Drippy condensation. The third formers drew noughts and crosses on the window. There was a Mars bar wrapper scrunched in the seam of the back seat, between its seat and its back.'

I mean, what was that? Who says that kind of thing to their dad?

Dad would be eager, leaning in, hands on the kitchen bench. He'd been waiting all day for this. I think the colouring began with these kinds of after-school questions. Miri and I would've been nine or ten. They weren't questions about what had happened during the day, what we'd learnt at school or what games we'd played, but about what the day *looked* like.

'What colour is the grass on the back field at the moment?' Dad would ask. 'What about your classroom, what's hanging up on the walls? What's on the shelves by the counter at the dairy this afternoon? How's the sea? What's it doing? How's it moving around?'

The questions started out like this, general, and sort of like the usual questions someone would ask another person about their day.

They started a couple of years after his accident, when we were all still figuring everything out. It was hard. I was just a kid but I knew that Dad had been very up and down since the accident. I heard Mum in the morning, coaxing him out of bed, getting him going, helping him through the morning routine. Most days it was a huge effort just to get him to the lounge, into his chair with his radio next to him.

Mum would bring him a mug of coffee and he'd drink it in slow sips. Guy and I would be in and out of the lounge, packing our bags and getting ready for school. Things could feel normal for a bit, and then I'd see Dad in his chair, listening to the sounds of the house and his hands moving about, restless, as if looking for something to do.

He'd been so practical before his accident. He fixed stuff. He fixed our cars. He fixed Miri's mum's car. He fixed Guy's BMX bike. He built me a doll's house for my Barbies with little beds and a stove and a fridge in the kitchen. He knew how things worked. I'd ask him 'Dad, how does the TV work?', and he'd know exactly how it was all put together.

After the accident, I'd go up to him in the morning before I went to school and put my hand on his arm and I'd say, 'Dad, we're going now.'

His face would turn to where he thought I was. 'All right, have a good day then, love.'

'I'll tell you about it when I get back.'

That became our code for the colouring, 'I'll tell you all about it.' Or, 'I'm just going out for a bit but I'll tell you all about it when I get back.'

It made me feel better about leaving him there and it meant I had an extra purpose in my days. I had to remember things for him, specifically remember how things looked, because that's what he really wanted to know, the shape and colour and texture and sheen of things, the *lookiness* of things, I guess.

'What colour are the handles of your tools in woodwork? What pens did you use for your assignment? What about the curtains in the auditorium, what are those like? What posters are up in the halls at school? What happens in that ad on telly? The one with the washing powder? It makes things 'super special bright', but what do the clothes look like when they come out of the washing machine? What colour are they? Sunshine yellow?

'What does it look like? What colour is it? What's there? How many? What's it made of? What colour is it when the sun shines on it? What does it look like in the dark?'

In the beginning, I liked to build up a bunch of interesting things I'd seen during the day, things that I knew Dad would be interested in, and that he might ask about. A strange dog. A new sign at the intersection going into town. A burst of spring flowers. A dead possum on the side of the road. 'It was so flat, Dad, I could tell that it'd been there for ages, because it was squished into the concrete. If you drove over it I bet it wouldn't even make the car bump, it was that flat! And the road all around it was really shiny, small patches of smooth concrete with a lip at the edge, not like the rest of the road around it, which was bumpy and normal. Like, you know, like road is. It was like the dead possum had smoothed out the road, ironed it out with its flat body and its guts.'

I'd go on for ages like this, describing the dead possum I'd seen, for Dad. He'd be in his big chair, nodding, asking questions, happy to have this little piece of the world coloured in for him so that he could see it in his mind's eye.

For a while I found new things, things that Dad might not have seen before. But I quickly ran out of things or people or places that were special. My world was small. I was only nine. I went to school. I came home. I went to Miri's house. When he could see, Dad had seen all these places, and things hadn't changed very much.

'I dunno, Dad,' I said. 'There was nothing new today. Just school. Just the bus. Came home.' I felt bad because I knew how much he looked forward to my colouring. I felt proud that he waited for me to get home and give him this little gift.

'Just tell me about your lunch box then,' he said.

'My lunch box?'

'Yeah, tell me about it.'

'It's pink, but you can see through it. If you put your hand on the other side you can see it.'

'Pink but see-through.'

'Cleary-pink.'

'Cleary-pink.'

'And it's crumby. You know, it's got lots of crumbs in the bottom, from sandwiches, and an old chip packet and my apple, cos I didn't eat it.'

'I won't tell Mum,' he said.

'Okay.' I grinned at him, even though he couldn't see me. Then I said, 'It's got three stickers on the top. Three butterflies. One is orange and yellow, one is purple and blue, and one is lots of different types of green. They're old and fading, but you can still see the colours. Miri put them on.'

Dad nodded. 'Tell me more.'

I paused.

'There's more, isn't there?' Dad asked.

'The orange one has one wing ripped off and you can see the white paper underneath that's attached to the sticky part. It's rough. The different sections of the wings are outlined in black with the coloured part inside. But there's a thicker black line around the whole wing.'

And that's how I went on, describing my lunch box, Dad listening closely, turning the words around in his mind so that he could see the cleary-pink and the faded, ripped stickers.

After that, I knew that I didn't have to find new or special things to describe for Dad. He was happy with anything. He was happy with the driveway, or the kettle, or the ground underneath the macrocarpa hedge. He would sit for ages while I described his toenails, or a milk bottle, or the ceiling, or the sky.

Sometimes, in summer, we would sit outside on the grass at the front of our house. There were two ancient wooden chairs that had been there so long that they were half-sunken into the ground and grass had grown up all around them. I'd lead Dad out to a chair and help him to get settled, and then I'd climb into the one next to him and tuck my legs underneath me and tell him about the sky, its colours and shapes and tones. We'd sit there so long that the evening would fade into night and the stars would start to come out and I would describe them as they appeared.

I thought about the word 'twinkle' a lot. It's such a weird word when you say it over and over again. And I described the way the stars pulsed with light, how they moved very slightly, like light was pouring out of them, coming towards us, how far away they were, how huge, but how small and delicate they were in the night sky above Whakatāne, how they weren't there and then when evening came they appeared, some were the keen ones that appeared first, some clustered together and others stayed on their own, sitting on a backdrop of black. I couldn't name them for Dad, but I could tell him what they looked like. I told him how they 'twinkled', how they 'sparkled', how they 'glimmered'. I used all those words. I told him all about the sky on those summer nights, until Mum came out and said that time was up, and I had to go to bed.

I coloured so much for Dad when I was young that it became second nature. Dad would ask me about something, and I'd quickly slip into its description, looking and describing and saying it aloud for him. I didn't have to think about it. There were certain words I used all the time, words like 'twinkle' and 'rough' and 'peeling'. I had a vocabulary that I built up. And it wasn't clever or fancy, the main thing was to be specific. To get into the detail, that was what Dad liked the best. The back lawn, or the newspaper, or the DVD player's flashing lights, I'd go into a kind of trance telling him about the tiny elements of these things.

Mum helped me. Sometimes she'd be passing through the kitchen, and I'd be describing the Rice Bubbles box to Dad, and she'd chip in with a word or a phrase that'd help describe the right shade of blue.

But it was really our thing. Me and Dad. It was our special thing.

One afternoon I came home from school, opened the back door, and, before I went into the kitchen, I heard Dad and Guy talking, and I paused because Guy was describing a piece of junk mail to Dad.

'It's red and it says 'The Warehouse' at the top,' he said.

'What else?' asked Dad.

'I dunno. Just lots of stuff on the front cover.' I heard Guy turning over the pages. 'Some numbers, you know, stuff is twenty bucks and twenty-nine cents.'

I knew that Dad wanted to know about all the small images of toys and plants and duvet covers that were in the pamphlet. He wanted to know the shape of the font and the thickness of the borders around the outside. Junk mail was particularly interesting for him because there were more images inside it. Images inside of images. Layers of things to dig into. The thickness of the paper too, was it mat or glossy? Did it stayed crinkled when you scrunched it up?

Guy said, 'There are Transformers on sale. Twenty-five bucks each.'

Dad said nothing. I heard his seat creak as he leaned back in it.

I went in and they were sitting across the table from each other, Dad with his hands lightly around a cup of coffee.

'Hi, Jodes,' said Dad. 'I heard you come in. Do you think you could do the pamphlet for me then, love?'

Guy grunted and pushed the mailer across the table at me. It flew off the side and I had to reach down to pick it up off the floor.

'Do your stupid thing then,' said Guy, pushing his chair back and getting up. 'I've got better things to do.'

He stomped into the lounge, and we listened to him plug in his Xbox and turn the volume up.

'It's not that easy you know,' I said.

'I know,' Dad sighed.

'It's not that easy to look right at things, I mean.'

'Things hide, even when you're looking right at them,' he said.

'Yeah. I'm still learning.'

He reached across the table and I put my hand out so that he could find it and hold it. Before his accident Dad hadn't been big on hugs, it wasn't the way he showed his love. But after he went blind, he hugged and held my hand, even when he didn't need to, and put his arm around me. Holding on to the world. Keeping me close.

13.

I remember when social media went crazy. I noticed that everyone on Facebook and Instagram were posting all of the time, pictures of them at the beach, down at the pub, when they got back from their run, #nailingit. It was constant. It was like there was some competition for who could post the most pictures. I mean, of course there are those people who are obsessed with selfies and constantly telling everybody exactly what they're up to, but this was next level, the over-sharers ramped it up and everybody else did too. My feeds were always updating with new posts and I was flooded with notifications. I couldn't keep up.

I liked Facebook and I wanted to know what everyone was up to, wanted to see everyone's kids and stuff, but it was too much. It was out of control. I didn't need to see what everyone was doing every second of the day.

I ran into Bex at the supermarket. Cara and Jade saw each other and giggled and started playing a hand-clapping game and chanting, 'A sailor went to sea sea sea...'

Bex smiled at me. 'How're you guys going?' she asked.

I shrugged. 'Yeah, good, I guess.'

'It's all pretty out there,' said Bex, running her hand through her hair.

The girls had moved down the aisle a bit and weren't listening to us, so I said, 'Yeah, it doesn't seem like anyone's got any control over this anymore, do they?'

Bex shook her head. 'It's everywhere, people are going all the time.'

'Cara told me about her uncle, is that your brother? Is he okay?'

Bex's face stiffened and she looked away. 'He's in Napier, I don't have much contact with him, so...'

We were silent for a moment, watching the girls.

I said, 'Facebook's gone a bit crazy.'

'Yeah, well, you've got to keep up,' Bex said. 'Gotta get out there.'

'Do you?'

'Some of my friends were wondering, you know, since my brother's gone, if I had gone too, and I wanted to show them that I hadn't, that I was still here, and Cara too.' The girls wandered back to us. Bex reached out for Cara's hand and pulled her over so that she was tucked against Bex's legs, and she held her there, close. I reached out for Jade too, and we stood there for a moment, our girls pressed against us, both of them confused about what was going on.

After we went through the checkout, I looked back and saw Bex taking a photo of Cara, standing, hand on her hip, with a shelf of cereal boxes behind her. Would we all go out, I wondered, eventually?

I saw the image of Cara at the supermarket later, on Facebook, and Bex also posted seven more pictures of Cara in the car on their way back home. Everyone kept at it, the overflow of images continued. There were reports of servers failing, storage overloading, and tech companies struggling to keep up. Facebook went down and then came back up, only to be smashed by people posting again. They issued a call for people to stop, to calm down.

'Everyone needs to chill out!' Renee said to me on the phone one night.

But no one was chilling out. Everyone was freaking out. And even after we talked, I saw that Tracey was posting heaps of family photos, pictures of Ari, of Hugo, of Renee, of everyone, way more than she usually did. I saw them on Instagram, they were on the beach at Piha, Hugo and Ari with their backpacks on, ready to go to daycare and school, asleep in their beds, eating breakfast, everything, all the time. Tracey wasn't chilling out.

It was funny, because the more images there were online, the emptier they looked, with empty spaces where people should've been. It was hard to know if more people were going, or if the fact that people were taking so many more pictures meant that we could just see it more, see the spaces, see the nothings. Gaps might have gone under the radar before but now they couldn't escape *not* being in all the photos that poured out of people's phones and spread all over the internet.

There were stories of families who didn't know that their dad, or their nana, had gone, and they only found out after they started posting images, and saw that one of their family members didn't show up. People claimed that they didn't know that it had happened to them. 'I didn't feel any different,' one woman said on the radio. 'I wasn't keeping it a secret. I just didn't know. I'm okay though. I feel fine.'

Did she? We didn't know. She said so, but there was something worrying about them, the gaps, the way they talked, like they were trying to convince us. We didn't believe them, but most of us didn't say anything aloud, we just nodded and were sympathetic.

Jade and I were walking up to the dairy one day when we saw a line of new posters pasted on its outside wall. They were all the same, they showed pictures of the dairy owner, Vikram, and his family, sitting on a couch and smiling.

Jade took my hand and asked, 'What're those up there for?'

I shrugged and frowned. 'I don't know.'

The other posters stuck on the dairy's glass doors and inside the shop didn't make much sense. But it was often like this, you'd walk into a shop and there'd be old posters or advertising campaigns where the model had gone out, so there'd be Coke bottles hovering in midair, or flowers being handed from someone to an empty space. Products were losing the people who were supposed to advertise them, but they still hung around, sadly, often tipped or tilted and pouring hopefully into a mouth that wasn't there.

We went in and I got some milk from the fridge and Jade picked a packet of chips. We went up to pay and Vikram smiled at us.

Jade hopped from foot to foot and said, 'We saw your new posters.'

Vikram looked down at the Eftpos machine and coughed. 'Yes, well,' he said, 'we had some requests, you know?'

'What kind of requests?' I asked. Jade listened closely.

'Some customers, they say, they won't buy, if the owner has gone.'

'If the owner has gone out?'

'Yes, so, you know, I have to let people know, I have to advertise, somehow that my family, we are all still here, and it's okay for people to come in. I saw some of the other dairies had made these posters, to show their status, so I thought I'd do it too. And we've had the community protection group too. They come through and check on us.'

Vikram tried to pass me the receipt, but I shook my head slightly, so he scrunched it up.

'We don't know what this is going to do to business. I have to look after my family.'

'Of course,' I said, 'of course you do.'

He lowered his voice and narrowed his eyes. Jade stood on her tiptoes so she could hear him say, 'I've heard that some of the gaps, they don't need to eat any more, they don't need to consume anything.'

Vikram looked at me as if I should say this was true, but I didn't know what to say. We stood for a moment, listening to the radio playing in the room behind the counter. Then Jade asked, 'Mum, can we get this KitKat?'

I got Jade the KitKat and we left, walking back past the posters of Vikram sitting with his wife and son and daughter, their faces beaming out from the side of their shop.

I'd like to write that I didn't get caught up in the online craziness, but that'd be a lie. I started posting lots of pictures of me and Jade. I couldn't help myself. I felt like I needed to keep up. I told myself that Jade and I were still here and that we were lucky because no one close to us had gone, so we needed to show everyone how whole we were.

We used these words, words like 'whole' and 'empty' and 'halved'. People who had gone out were only partial people, lesser, and the rest of us were more real. I see how stupid this was now, now that we've gone. But we were scared and trying to figure out a situation that was changing every day.

I went on, taking photos of Jade eating her cereal in the morning, or lounging on the couch, watching TV with her feet on the coffee table. 'Stop, Mum!' she'd say, holding up her hand. 'Leave me alone!' And she'd run away.

What did Jade look like then? Small. She'd always been a small kid and, at six, she was easily the littlest in her class. She's a bit bigger now, but then, she had skinny little legs and wrists. I could hold her against me, sitting on the couch, and she'd tuck her head under my chin. Clothes never fit her properly. Her clothes. I wish I could remember more of them. A pair of faded leggings, purple and covered in little gold stars, probably from The Warehouse. A T-shirt with two pink birds on the front. Cotton things, hand-me-downs, worn until they were soft and losing their shape.

When someone goes out, it's not just their body that disappears from images, but their clothes too, and it seems like a stupid little thing, but I lie awake at night now trying to remember Jade's clothes from when she was small, those tops and socks that are all now lost and fallen apart. With no pictures of her, I replay my memories, re-membering moments and writing them down. And as I write, sitting at this computer, a top or a jacket will suddenly appear in my mind, this was the thing that she was wearing at that specific moment, and I smile, to have that thought and get it down here in words. It's the whole point of this, really. Because I might not have any pictures of Jade when she was little, but I can describe her here, and we'll have this, the both of us, this record of the time before we went out.

Though words can be so stupid, can't they? It's so hard to pick the right one. I spent so long picking words for Dad, and now I'm doing it again, by writing this. A word can mean too many things, a 'star' is a starfish, a light in the sky, and a necklace, and everyone sees some-thing different in their mind.

14.

I put Miri out before I knew what was happening. As I write this down, it looks like a lie. But it's the truth, I promise, I didn't know what I was doing or how it would change her. I just responded, right in that moment, to what she wanted, because I wanted to help her, she was my best friend, and she was so scared. And, I think she tricked me. Miri always had a way of getting what she wanted.

When I was with Johnny I was so obsessed with keeping him happy that I lost touch with lots of my friends. It's crazy because Whakatāne is such a small place that you're always running into people, but I realised, when Johnny and I had been together for about six months, that I hadn't seen Miri for ages. The days had just disappeared. It was already May when I checked my phone and saw that the last message I had got from her had been in March.

I texted her: *What's up? Haven't seen you in the ages.* And it was days before I heard back: *Not much. working. chillin. you should cruise round sometime. how's Johnny?*

I knew Miri had a new boyfriend, but I couldn't remember his name, that was how much we'd lost touch. I texted back, saying that I'd come round on Saturday afternoon.

On Saturday, I left Johnny on his PlayStation in the lounge and drove round to Miri's flat. Back then, she was living with her cousin.

I went round to the back door, knocked a couple of times, and then let myself in. Miri was sitting at the little table in the kitchen, on her phone, and she looked up.

'Hi, stranger,' I said, sitting down across from her. 'Why've you been avoiding me?'

'Do you want a beer?' she asked.

I nodded and Miri got us a couple of bottles from the fridge.

'Whatcha been up to?' Miri asked.

I shrugged. 'You know…'

'How's the mill?'

'Okay.'

'How's Nicola? Still being a bitch?'

'She's okay. What've you been up to?'

Miri took a swig of her beer.

'Hey,' I said, 'do you want to get out of here for a bit?' I pushed my beer to the side. 'I can drive. Let's go down to the beach.'

'I can't,' said Miri.

'Why not?'

'Gotta wait till Matt gets back.'

Matt, that was his name, Matt. I was glad that she'd said it before I had to ask. Matt and Miri. It was cute. But I knew, from her voice, from the way she glanced out the kitchen window, that it wasn't that cute.

'How're things going with him? I haven't hung out with him much,' I said.

'Good. He works on Saturdays. He's a mechanic.'

I nodded. That didn't explain why we couldn't go for a drive, why she had to sit around in the kitchen and wait for him. But who was I to lecture Miri? I'd do anything to keep Johnny happy. Even after he lashed out, I'd still glow when he did the smallest thing for me, when he told me the time. It was pathetic.

I wanted to tell Miri about this, sitting across that table from her. I wanted to tell her how I was trapped too. But I didn't know how to start. Any question I asked, Miri would know what I was suggesting, or what I was really trying to find out. We knew each other. We saw each other. And I knew that Miri would never give too much away, and especially never acknowledge any weakness or a mistake. Miri's way was to jut out her chin and tell the world to go fuck itself, which included me if I asked about something that she didn't want to talk about.

So, Miri and I fell back into old habits and watched some stuff on her phone, finished our beers, and then Miri checked the time and asked if I could drive her into town, to the garage where Matt worked.

'He's nearly finished. I'll go and meet him after work, sometimes he likes that,' she said.

We drove through town and I asked her about work. Miri had always been into computers and had taught herself to code in high school. After school she'd gone to Auckland to do an IT diploma and I used to hang out with her when I was there too. She didn't seem to go to many classes, but she smashed her tests, said she figured out what the courses had been about from the questions she'd aced in her exams. I didn't really know what she did now, something IT, something about online security.

She mumbled something about how it was going okay, then she turned to look right at me, and said, 'I saw what you did the other day, at the beach.'

'What?' I didn't turn to look at her but concentrated on the road ahead. I didn't want to meet her eyes.

'With Johnny.'

'What about it?'

'How do you do that?'

'I don't know.'

'Yes, you do.'

'No, I really don't.'

'But you've done it before,' Miri said. 'When we were kids, you did it for your dad. Do you still do that for him?'

'Maybe.'

Miri was silent for a moment. Then, 'He couldn't see you, Johnny couldn't, when we were next to the fire. He looked right past.'

I drummed the top of the steering wheel. I had been shading myself more and more from Johnny but I didn't want to talk about it. Miri was the only person who had seen both sides, Johnny and Dad, and she'd put two and two together. I knew it was a mistake to have shaded in front of her, that night at the beach.

I pulled up across the road from the garage. It was 4:30 and Matt was standing with a group of men out the front, leaning on the bonnet of a beat-up black car. One guy leaned across and they all watched something on his phone, laughing.

Miri and I watched them for a moment, the motor still running.

I said, 'I can take you home, if you want, you can wait for Matt there.' I didn't want her to leave me and shut the door and cross the road and stand with those men.

Miri opened her door. 'Nah,' she said. 'See ya.'

She shoved her hands in her jacket pockets and waited for a gap in the traffic before crossing the road. Matt looked up for a second as she walked towards the group, acknowledging her with a tiny raise of his chin, before he turned back to his mate's phone.

Fuck him, I thought, pulling out onto the road. Fuck Matt. Fuck Johnny.

I wanted to defend Miri because she had always defended me. In 2009, Miri and I were both living in Auckland and one afternoon when I was pissing around in the computer lab at the uni library, wasting time, I checked my Facebook page and saw that a guy from high school had posted on my wall: *Still looking fine Jodie. miss youre ass around in the big W*. Gross. The guy was a total loser at high school, the type who spent his time hassling younger kids, hiding their bags, because he thought that it made him cooler.

I was new to Facebook then, it was still pretty early days for social media, but I knew how to delete posts, and I did. But he didn't let up. He kept posting and commenting on my page and chiming into comment threads that I had going with friends. I didn't want to post any images because I felt him lurking around online and watching me. I didn't want him to know where I was living or what I was up to.

I figured out Facebook's privacy settings and logged on one day so I could unfriend him and shut him out of my page, when I noticed that he had unfriended me already. I clicked around for a bit, to double check, but he was gone. I shrugged. It was weird, but I was happy that he had pissed off.

A couple of days later, Miri texted me, saying that she was at a party in Ōtara, and I went to meet her after my shift finished. I pushed my way through the packed flat and found her on a deck out the back.

She smiled and hugged me when I arrived, handing me a beer. 'You came!' she said, her words slipping and slurring.

Sometimes Miri would leave me at parties, even when we had gone together, she'd wander off and find other people to talk to. But that night, she stayed close, chatting and laughing and getting me drinks. I was tired though, my shift had been full on, and I didn't really feel up to it.

'Miri,' I said, around one o'clock, 'I think I'm gonna go.'

Miri nodded and hugged me and I turned to make my way back through the crowd, but before I could, Miri grabbed my arm and said in my ear, 'Don't stress about Paul anymore.'

That was the Facebook guy's name, Paul.

The party was loud, and I could barely hear her. 'What did you do?' I asked, my voice rose to compete with the Bob Marley thudding out of the stereo.

'We got him,' she shouted, grinning.

'Who?'

'It doesn't matter, he can't get at you anymore.'

It was my first glimpse of Miri's other life, her online life that was mostly hidden from me. She could do things like get Paul to unfriend me and leave me alone. The internet was changing quickly and Miri kept up, kept ahead, learning how it worked, teaching herself new code, new languages, living in chat rooms and comment threads, figuring stuff out. She had always wanted to know how things worked in the background. It was part of her obsessiveness. She wanted to see beyond the top layer of things and under the bonnet, into their inner workings.

I wrote that Miri had always defended me, and it's true, she did, but I suspect that she got rid of Paul to show off to me, as much as to help me out. There was always a touch of that, with Miri, wanting to show me what she could do, and how she was smarter than me.

In Whakatāne, I tried to see Miri again soon after I had dropped her off at Matt's work, but she was hard to lock down. She took ages to reply to my texts and when she did, she said she was busy and couldn't hang out. Maybe I didn't try hard enough. Johnny didn't really like me hanging out with other people.

I did see Miri and Matt, once, in the distance, on the other side of the New World car park. I raised my arm when I thought Miri was looking my way, but she didn't see me, and she turned back to talk to Matt before he got into the driver's side and slammed his door.

It was a grey day. Grey sky. Grey concrete. There was the thud of bass coming from somewhere in the car park, but I couldn't tell if it was Matt's, or another car.

'What kind of grey?' Dad would've asked. 'Grey' is not that specific and it's not that helpful, but all I can write is that I felt that greyness inside of me and in the world around me. Watching Miri put the bags into the boot and climb into the passenger seat, I saw her greyness, and the weight on her shoulders.

I was at Mum and Dad's house when I saw her next. It'd been a couple of months, at least. We had texted a bit, but we hadn't seen each other. We were both moving between work and our boyfriends' flats, hardly going anywhere else, keeping a low profile.

On the weekend, I'd often use Dad as an excuse to get away from Johnny. Johnny didn't like me doing anything without him, but he couldn't object to me going round to take care of Dad while Mum was out for the afternoon. Dad was family and I was needed. He was the reason I was back in Whakatāne, after all.

I liked to go round and tidy the house and cook dinner and read Dad the paper. It was routine and familiar and nice to have some space. Sometimes I tried to do the gardening, but my attempts were half-hearted, and I mostly ended up wandering around the garden describing the old fruit trees and the pond and the clouds to Dad, who would be eagerly asking me what everything looked like. I described the shape of the petals, the colour of the leaves, the texture of the algae in the pond.

Dad and I were in the lounge when Miri came round one afternoon. She had messaged me a couple of hours earlier, *Where you at?*

And I'd replied, *At mum and dads. Do you want to come round? Dad would love it.*

She messaged right back, *be there in 15.*

'Miri's gonna pop in,' I said to Dad.

'She's not been round here in ages,' Dad said. 'There's some lolly cake in the pantry, if you want to get it out for you two.'

'We're not eight anymore, Dad,' I said.

'I know. But I still like lolly cake.'

Soon after, we heard the back door open, and Miri's voice say, 'It's me.'

She came into the lounge and smiled. 'Hi, Ray, long time no see.'

Dad turned towards her voice and laughed. He held out both his hands and Miri took them. 'It's not very nice to go around badgering an old blind man that he can't see, Miss Miri.'

'Yeah, well,' she said, sitting down on the couch, 'I thought you could take a joke. Used to be able to anyway.'

Running under Miri's eye, along the bone of her eye socket, was a deep bruise, slightly yellowed at the edges. She looked across at me, her right eyelid hooded and puffy, and slightly shook her head. She didn't want to talk about it.

I went into the kitchen and made us coffee and put the lolly cake on a plate, before taking everything back into the lounge, where Dad and Miri were still hassling each other. I put Dad's coffee on his little table and guided his hands to where it sat. He was so happy that Miri was there, he forgot all about the drink and it sat there, getting cold, until I emptied it later on.

I sat and drank my coffee, watching Miri and Dad chat. They talked about Miri's work and the All Blacks' last game and Miri's mum and dad. They chatted like old mates because they were old mates.

Miri caught my eye every now and again. She was nervous. She gulped her coffee and sat on the edge of the couch. She had come here because Dad couldn't see her and, with that bruise under her eye, she wanted to be invisible.

Dad tapped his talking clock and its annoying American voice told him that it was ten past four. 'Trish will be home soon and she'd love to see you, Miri,' Dad said.

Miri jumped up. 'Sorry, Ray, I've gotta go. I've got a work thing.'

'Oh, okay.'

'I'll come back and see Trish another time.'

'Come soon.'

'Yeah, I will. Definitely.'

I followed Miri out into the kitchen. 'What's going on, then?' I asked.

'What do you mean?'

I looked at her. I couldn't force her to tell me.

'Look, Jodie, I'm…' she trailed off. 'I'm…' she tried again but didn't finish.

She stared out the kitchen window, her hands stuffed in her jacket pockets.

'Nice to see your dad again,' she said. 'He seems good.'

'He's better now. I'm trying to help out. Things got pretty bad for a while. Mum was really stressed, and Guy is still looking out for number one.'

Miri gave a short laugh.

'It was always good, being able to come round here anytime. That we lived so close. It was easy to get away,' she said.

'Yeah.'

I wanted to ask her what she was running away from, why she had needed an escape route.

I started, trying to find the right way to ask, thinking, after all this time, that we should really talk, 'Listen, Miri—'

But she interrupted, sighing, 'Nah, J, I know what you're going to say, and I don't want to talk about it.' She turned to me, and I saw that her jaw was set. 'I'm actually just totally fucking over it. I'm done.'

'Done? With Matt?'

'How're things with Johnny?'

We stared at each other.

Miri sighed again. 'It's just… I'm gonna need your help.'

'My help?'

The crunch of gravel out the front meant that Mum was home. Miri reached up and ran her fingertips lightly along the line of her bruise. I remember this movement, she did it without thinking, as if she was trying to brush the bruise away, rub it off. I wanted to hug her.

'What do you want me to do?' I asked.

'I've got to go,' she said. 'I'll text you.' And she disappeared out the back door.

Where was she going? Back across the fields, like when we were kids?

I went back into the lounge and looked through the bay window at Mum unloading shopping bags from the boot of the car.

From his chair, Dad asked me, 'What did Miri look like?'

I paused, and then I described Miri's bruise to him, its sickly yellow edges, and the blood at the surface of the skin, how it was like a shadow on her face. My descriptions were tired. I felt tired.

I didn't see her again for three weeks, but I thought about her all that time. Dad was worried too. He messaged me a lot, checking in, seeing if I'd been in touch with her, or if I'd seen her anywhere.

I think you should go and see her, he messaged.

I drove past her flat a couple of times, and I thought about going in, but I didn't see anyone, and Miri's car wasn't out the front, so I didn't stop. I was worried about Miri, but I was also nervous about what she wanted from me. She'd seen me shading, trying to slip away from Johnny. No one else knew that I could hide myself in this way, by bringing up the words of the things around me, colouring them in, and colouring them out. I'd done it unconsciously, in the car that evening with Johnny, and later, at the beach, when he was so angry, when I really needed to disappear, to become unfocussed. I remember the way he flicked his gaze away from the road and towards me, uncertain if I was still there or if he was alone in his car.

I *was* there, but I made myself secondary, lesser than the things around me. I heightened them, strengthened them, so that I became... less defined, shaky, loose.

These are all the wrong words. I've thought about this a lot. I've had time to think, searching for the right word for what it felt like to be shaded. The best word I can think of is *bloodless*. It was like I had been emptied of blood for a few moments, drained, so that I was hollow and pale and fragile, kind of colourless.

It wasn't that Johnny looked *through me* when I shaded, it was more that words couldn't stick to me. I couldn't be described, so I couldn't be seen. There was too much world around me, crowding in. Or, being spoken up, being described by me, I was doing that, I could do that. I could make those things, the sea, the beach, the fire, more real, more *there*, so that I was less there, less visible.

Miri messaged me late in the afternoon when I was at work, *what are you up to after work? meet me at the west end?*

I texted that I'd be there, and she replied, *i know that Johnny will be pissed. sorry.*

I paused, and then I replied, *it's so fucked.*

I waited, biting my lip, hiding my phone from Nicola, who sat across from me in the office. Did Miri understand? Did she see how we were both trapped, twinned, in these messed up relationships? Why were we both in the same situation and we couldn't talk about it?

She replied, *i know. its fucked.*

I stared at those words.

The phone next to me rang, and when I answered it, 'Kia ora, Whakatāne Mill, Jodie speaking,' my voice wavered.

After work, I messaged Johnny that I would be a bit late because I had to go round to Mum and Dad's, then I switched off my phone and got in my car and drove down to the beach.

I was happy that Miri had made the first move. I wanted to help her, but I knew that it would be on her own terms.

Hers was the only car in the car park when I pulled up. She was sitting on the bonnet, legs crossed, hands shoved deep into her jacket pockets, looking out to sea.

I got out and climbed up next to her. I saw that her eye had healed and there was now only a faint purple tinge below her eye.

After I sat down and leant back against the windscreen, Miri said, as if there was no break between our text messages and our conversation, 'It's fucked that we're both with these useless guys.'

'You don't know Johnny.'

'I know Johnny.'

I said nothing. Why did I immediately jump to defend him? It was a reflex. While I was driving to the beach I'd imagined the conversation that I would have with Miri, how I would be upfront with her and tell her how angry Johnny was and how he scared me. And then there were all the other things, piling up, how I felt sorry for him, how he needed me, and loved me, and craved my attention and my focus and my approval, how I was a little bit addicted to feeling afraid, on the edge. I didn't know how to tell her these things.

Miri said, 'You've got to dump him and get out of here.'

'I have to help Mum. You didn't see them before I came back. She was a mess.'

'As long as you're in Whakatāne he won't let you go.'

'Miri, it's not that simple,' I said.

'Yes it is!' she shouted. 'It is that simple, because you're so much better than him, and he will keep you and hold you and stop you from...' She scrunched up her face, running out of words.

'What about you?' I asked. 'What about your eye?'

'Matt did this.'

I was shocked into silence. I hadn't expected Miri to come out with it.

'Miri, I—'

'No,' she interrupted, 'it's my fault.'

'Miri! It's not your fault.'

'It is. I hooked up with him in the first place, even when I knew he was a drunk fuckwit. Like the rest of them. But, you know...' she shrugged.

We sat in silence for a moment and watched the waves crash onto the beach. But, no, I can't get ahead of myself, those words, the sea, the waves, are so much more important later. I need to get the order of this right, so that I can understand what happened. So that Jade can understand what happened.

We sat in silence and looked at the sea, and then Miri said, 'Jodie, I need your help.'

I turned to her. I already knew what she was going to say. 'You saw the shading with Johnny,' I said.

She nodded. 'You call it shading?'

'I don't know… maybe. It's just what it feels like, bringing some things up, sharpening them, so that something else can fade away.'

'Yeah, that night, you got kind of hard to focus on, like, I tried to look at you but then I had to look away.'

'It wasn't meant for you,' I said.

'It was to get away from Johnny.'

'Yeah.'

'Do you do it a lot? With him?'

'It doesn't work so good if it's just the two of us. But yeah, I do it a bit.'

'Does it hurt?' she asked.

'Nah. But it takes it out of me. Sometimes it takes me a while to come right again.'

'But you always do?' Miri asked. 'You always come right again?'

'Yeah, seem to.'

'It's because of your dad, isn't it? What you do for him? Telling him about stuff. You're just real good at it.'

I shrugged. 'Maybe.'

'Does it feel the same?'

'Fuck! I don't know, Miri. Maybe. Maybe it feels the same. Okay?'

Miri was silent for a moment. Then, 'I think you just got real good at describing stuff, because you've been doing it for Ray all this time, and somehow you're good at the other way now, you're good at unde-scribing stuff, making things disappear.'

'Well, you've got it all figured out,' I said.

'So, I need you to make me disappear,' Miri said.

I stared at her. 'What?'

'I need you to do it to me,' she said. 'Shade me out, or whatever it is you said.'

'I can't. I can't do that.'

'Why the fuck not? You do it for you. Why can't you do it for me?'

'But, Miri, I don't know what… I don't know what would happen. I've never—'

'You can do it. Just give it a go. Look,' she waved her arm around, 'I made it really easy for you.'

I looked around at the white sand, the setting sun, the glow of the evening on the ocean. I even started thinking those words, I started thinking about 'the glow of the evening', and 'the rising waves'. No, no, no. I stopped, I put my hands over my ears. I saw the trap that Miri had laid for me. This was a place that was easy to describe, cliched words hovered around it, eager to latch onto things, to sharpen them, to make them fuller and more meaningful, more *more*.

I jumped off the bonnet and started walking towards my car. I heard Miri follow me and then she grabbed my arm.

'Jodes,' she said, 'please.'

I turned and her eyes were full of tears. Miri never cried. 'She's a hard nut,' Dad would say. 'That Miri, she's as tough as old boots.'

'Please,' she said. 'I need you to try. I can't... I can't get out of this by myself. I've tried and I just kept getting into the same shit. There's something wrong with me, like a bit of me is broken. It got broken when I was a kid, and I can't fix it on my own. I've tried and tried. There's a pattern that I can't get out of. When I think I've got out, I'm actually just circling back again.'

'I don't want to hurt you.'

'You said it doesn't hurt. It won't.'

'We don't know that.'

'Okay, maybe, but I'll tell you to stop if it does.'

'You might not be able to.'

'Jodie!' Miri yelled and grabbed my arm. 'Just do it! Come on! I know you can, I've seen you do it, it's the easiest thing, it's just words, just some little words. You were always so clever with them, your little words. Let's see what you've got then, okay? Let's see if you can really do it when it matters, when you're not just looking out for yourself.' She pointed to the sea. 'Start there.'

It was easy really, so easy to describe, the navy-blue water, the swelling waves, the horizon's thin line, all the right words ready and waiting to be used. A container ship appeared in the distance. It was a slow-moving rectangle, heavy but hovering on the smooth surface of the ocean. The beach was empty of people, but thick hunks of seaweed lay on the wet sand, curled and slumped in heavy green piles.

I glanced at Miri. She was standing still, staring out at the ocean, her arms crossed over her chest.

I think I repeated 'thick hunks of seaweed' for a while because I liked the sound of it. Sometimes I would get stuck like this, when I was colouring in for Dad, I'd get caught on a particular phrase or set of words because it sounded so good, and I'd have to keep saying them for a while until I found something else to leap to.

Miri nudged me with her elbow, and I kept going, the words pouring out of me. It was darker now. I heard Miri's feet shuffle on the gravel. The gravel. I described the gravel, the uneven sections of concrete, the speckling of loose stones on top, the tiny indentations they made in the concrete underneath, the thin spread of moss, patchy and pale.

I liked focussing on the smallest things, the moss, the gravel, the texture of stones. I had crouched down to pick up a few rocks so I had something to rub between my thumb and index finger and I gave some words to that feeling.

I stood up again and shook my head, clearing my thoughts, finding another place to work on, the sand on the beach, the pōhutukawa growing in between the rocks behind us, the sky above, the gathering dark. I looked up at the sky and described Venus, glimmering, shimmering, glinting, sparkling, on the horizon, and I knew it was Venus because I had described the sky so much for Dad, and he loved it, and I'd learnt so much by talking about the sky, and there were tears on my cheeks and I was crying because someone had hurt Miri when she was little and she kept getting hurt by men and I wanted to help her and I wanted to help myself but now I was making her disappear, I was forcing her out, and I didn't want to do that, I wanted to keep her there, beside me.

But when I looked down and across to where Miri had been standing, she had gone. No, wait, here I need to slow down and be careful, specific. The words need to be precise. Miri was there, in the dusky car park, and I saw her. And I see her now, as I write this, though the image is hazy with static, like when you are in a darkened room, and the edges of things are hard to make out. She stood completely still, but the hairs escaping from her ponytail were waving in the ocean breeze, and she looked straight at me, her chin slightly raised in that way she had of trying to make herself look tougher, as if challenging me to see her, to find her in the evening light.

And I did, I saw her standing there, but I couldn't tell if I saw her in front of me, or if she stood in my mind's eye. Those two places were the same and I couldn't separate them from each other. I closed my eyes and opened them. She was still there, but I couldn't see her. I felt, I thought, I remember thinking, I'm *thinking* her.

Miri was there, but gone, so my mind projected her image, what I knew she looked like, standing there in the car park.

Miri smiled and pushed her hair back from her face.

I smiled back, shakily. I was tired. 'I'm sorry,' I said.

Miri shook her head and shivered, as if she was brushing something off, breaking free. Then she opened her car door, jumped in, and drove away.

Later, after she had gone, people asked me, 'Where's Miri at? Have you seen her?'

But I'd shrug and say, 'Nah. She moved to Auckland. We haven't really kept in touch.'

Dad was more persistent, asking every couple of weeks, 'Have you heard from Miri? What's she doing with herself?'

'She's in Auckland, Dad, and I think things are better for her there. You know, she has friends from when she did that course. And I think it's good for her to be out of Whakatāne.'

Dad would hum agreement under his breath but would shift and shuffle in his seat in a way that told me he knew something was up.

I didn't know if other people saw Miri in the way that I had, after she had gone. But I knew parts of her were there, for other people, when she wanted them to be. I had a feeling that she had some control over when and how she appeared.

I ran into Miri's mum, Chantal, at New World and I asked her how Miri was going in Auckland.

'Oh yeah, she's good. You know Miri, working, doing her thing. I talked to her on Saturday, and she was going to some dance party thing up north, or something. Techno music. She's always on the move, that girl.'

'Did you... How were things with her and Matt?'

'Did she not talk to you about it? You know, Jodes, I was a bit worried about how he was going to take it, but he wasn't bothered. Helped her pack up her stuff and everything. Wishing her well, like a real gentleman.'

'I don't think he is a real gentleman,' I said.

'No.' Chantal looked over my shoulder, down the dairy aisle, and said, 'I think you're right there.'

I left Chantal and sat in my car in the car park, drumming the steering wheel and watching people come and go through the glass doors.

What had I done to Miri? Shaded her, like I had done to myself, with Johnny. Brought up the world around her so that she was lost amongst the other things that were named and given words. It was about balance. When I shaded, I shuffled around the order of things, things that were normally secondary to people. Things like gravel and windscreen wipers and seaweed and door handles, these got bigger, more *looked at*, and that meant the person could be... not invisible, just crowded out, camouflaged in the wordiness of the world around them.

Miri could talk to her mum and drive her car and wander around Auckland. But, since I had shaded her, she could fade when she wanted to. I didn't know this at the time, but this is what I guessed, what I felt had happened.

A couple of months later, I ran into Matt at a bar. I was drinking with Johnny and some of his mates one night. We were standing around a high table in the beer garden out the back. Johnny smoked and scrolled through his phone. I had had too many beers and things were a little hazy, not messy, just hazy. This is important, because it means I can't remember the exact details of what happened next, and I'm normally very good at that, who was there and what was said. That's how I'm writing this now.

I remember Johnny rested his arm lazily across my shoulders. He often did this. It was a sluggish way of showing his ownership. His arm felt heavy, and I thought about brushing him off, but I didn't move until I saw that everyone had finished their beers and I said I would go and get a round. This was an acceptable way of escaping, acceptable to Johnny.

Inside, it was packed with people and really loud. I had to weave through groups of sweaty backs, ducking under waving arms that were connected to shouty drunk faces. A band sound checked at the other end of the room. The bass drum thudded a dull beat.

I nabbed a spot in the crowd of people waiting at the bar, squished in between two men.

The man on my right looked across at me and I saw that it was Matt.

He raised his chin in greeting. 'Hey,' he said, almost shouting to be heard over the noise, 'aren't you Miri's mate?'

He looked ahead, conversation over. We all shuffled forward, closer to the bar.

Then he turned to me again and said loudly, 'I saw a picture of you on her phone. That's how I know.'

I nodded, showing him that I had heard.

'Have you heard from her?' I shouted.

A man, having bought his beers and clutching three full glasses, pushed between us. Matt was nudged forward from behind by a pushy person, and we were separated for a moment. But I forced myself forward, pissing off the person in front of me, so that I could be next to him again, in the second row before the bar.

I said again, fully shouting now, 'Have you heard from her?'

The band started playing and Matt said something that I couldn't hear.

I held my hand up to my ear to show that I hadn't heard, and he shouted again but I still couldn't figure it out. The crowd moved forward and the woman working behind the bar shouted, leaning on the tap handle, 'Whadda ya want?'

Matt leant across and showed me a picture on his phone, shouting and pointing at it.

'Come on!' the woman shouted again, waving her hand at the crowd of people who wanted drinks.

I shouted my order at the woman, and she filled up two pints of beer and pushed them across the sticky counter. I paid with my card and when I looked up Matt had been shunted further down the bar. He pointed to different beers and shouted his order.

I pushed my way out of the crowd, clutching the beers carefully against my chest. I waited for a second, when I had got out of the main crush of people, but I couldn't see Matt and I needed to put the beers down, and I knew that Johnny would be wondering where I was.

Lying in bed that night, Johnny asleep beside me, I thought about that photo and what Matt had tried to tell me. Should I go and see him and find out? I didn't have his number, but I'd for sure know someone who did. Maybe Miri would get in touch and tell me what was going on. Should I text her? Would she reply?

I turned over, onto my side and buried my face in the pillow. Johnny snored and sighed.

I did nothing. I didn't track down Matt. I didn't message Miri and I didn't ask around Miri's other mates or get more information from her folks. And it would have been easy, I could have done those things, but I was freaking out. I didn't know what I had done to Miri, and I didn't want to think about it. So I buried my head in the pillow and tried to pretend it hadn't happened. I got pissed off with Dad when he asked me about Miri, so he stopped asking. I tried not to think about the photo Matt had shown me in the bar, but I had seen it, and I couldn't not see it. It was a photo of Ōhope, looking across the beach, the sun setting in the distance. A nice picture. A picture lots of people who lived in Whakatāne had taken, we saw those kinds of sunsets all the time.

But I know now, and maybe I also knew then, though I hadn't admitted it to myself, that Matt showed me that photo because Miri used to be in it, running, or laughing, or scowling, or sitting on the beach with her legs bunched up, or putting her hands up in the front of her face, like she used to do sometimes when I tried to take a photo of her. Miri had been in that photo before and then she had gone.

15.

If Dad is listening to this, by now he's probably thinking, Where's Jade? Show me more of Jade.

Well, I hadn't realised I was pregnant until I was already ten weeks. I didn't feel sick, didn't feel tired, and my period had always been all over the place, never that regular, but I can see now that I wasn't listening to myself. I wasn't listening to my body. I couldn't hear anything except Johnny, loud in my ear with all of his bullshit.

I finally figured out that I hadn't had my period in a while, so I took a pregnancy test and there were the two lines. I'd gone down to the pharmacy on my lunch break and I was in the toilet at work. I sat staring at the test while someone came in and peed in the cubicle next to me.

I went back to my desk. What was I going to do? It seemed impossible, that I could look after a whole new person. I didn't know anything about babies.

I went around for a week feeling numb. I looked at my body in the mirror. Did I look different? I felt my boobs. I knew I should go to the doctor, but I couldn't sort myself out, couldn't shake this idea that it wasn't real, that it was happening to someone else.

And I was scared to tell Johnny, scared about what he would do and how he'd react. By then, I was shading myself almost every day, disappearing from his angry focus. It'd become much easier, colouring in the objects around me so that I became faint by comparison. Maybe that was why it took me so long to figure out I was pregnant? I was used to being invisible, to not having a real body that people looked at and cared about.

I'd moved out of Mum and Dad's place by then and was living with Johnny, sharing his small room and his messy bed.

I remember, we were supposed to go to the movies, and I was waiting for him to get home from work on a Saturday so we could go. He was late, so I sent him a message, but he didn't reply. Neither of our flatmates were home and the house was quiet. I sat on our bed, scrolling through my phone. I googled, *eleven weeks pregnant*, and read about the size of the foetus, what it was doing, how it was growing, and how I was supposed to feel.

Then I called Johnny and when he answered I heard loud voices in the background.

'Oh, shit!' he said, when I asked him if he was coming home, 'I'm at Steve's, we're having some beers.'

I heard thumps, as if he had dropped his phone, and then Johnny's voice, 'Nah, nah… it's cool. It's just my missus, yeah, she's always on me about something.'

I hung up. It wasn't that he hadn't talked about me like that before, he had, all the time. It was the image of the foetus that I'd just seen on my phone, its strange bobble head, and its twiggy arms, its tummy tethered to me by the umbilical cord.

(Jade! Here she is! This must be my earliest description of her. Or, at least, a description of an image that looked a lot like Jade.)

I felt that this foetus was listening to our conversation and judging me. Who are you? The foetus thought. Why are you sitting around on this smelly unmade bed waiting around for Johnny to come home? He isn't going to help you. He'll only make things harder. And I need you. We have each other now.

I waited until the next morning to tell Johnny I was pregnant. He was hungover, and I was scared, but I knew I had to do it. I had to sort that shit out.

He wasn't angry, actually. At first, he was charming and attentive. He made me cups of tea and went and got me McDonald's when I craved salty things. I think he saw the baby as something that tied us even closer together and made me more dependent on him.

Those last couple of months of Johnny and I together were, in some ways, our best. Johnny was chill, so I was calmer, and I hardly shaded at all. But there was a feeling, growing inside of me, along with the baby, that I'd needed to do this on my own, that I was meant to do this on my own.

Because I saw Johnny waver, as I grew bigger, and the situation became more real.

We were supposed to meet at the clinic for the twenty-week scan, but he never showed up. In that dark room, lying on the bed-chair thing, I found out that Jade was a girl. The sonographer and I grinned at each other. 'She's looking just perfect,' the sonographer said, 'a perfect little girl.'

I asked Johnny where we should be living when the baby was born, but he just shrugged. Our flatmates hadn't talked about how the house would change when the baby arrived, except to say, 'Fuck, man, that's heavy,' when Johnny had told them.

I was worried about money. I knew I'd be able to move back in with Mum and Dad, but I didn't want to be a burden. I saved every tiny bit that I could from the mill, so I had a little bit extra, and I trawled the op shops for baby things, clothes, blankets, toys. A friend from work gave me her old bassinet and a pregnancy pillow.

So, I had a few things, and a few dollars, when Johnny told me that he was going to his mate's place in Papamoa to 'sort his head out for a bit', as he put it.

'It's too much,' he said, 'it's pretty fucking full on. I didn't ask for this, Jodie.'

I nodded. 'Let's talk about it when you get back,' I said.

I felt calm. I wasn't surprised.

While he was away, I packed up my stuff and moved back in with Mum and Dad. I needed to get out quickly, while Johnny wasn't there. Guy was at home when I arrived and he helped shift things out of the car, a big annoying grin on his face. He put my suitcases down in my old room and said, 'It's gonna be pretty weird being back in here again, eh? Knocked up, back at home. Not how you probably would have planned it, huh?'

Guy was loving this.

I don't know what happened in Papamoa, but Johnny texted me

when he got back, and I met him down at the beach. It was lunch-time, and there were other people around, so I felt safe.

He told me that he'd hooked up with some other girl. 'I dunno, Jodie,' he said, 'it's like I can't really see you anymore. You're never around when I need you to be. And fuck, a baby! Fuck!'

I nodded, but I didn't care. I put my hand on my stomach and thought about the baby, its feet and brain getting bigger and bigger, its tiny hands opening and closing. Johnny needed someone to con-trol, and he couldn't control me anymore because I had more import-ant things to worry about, bigger fish to fry. And I wouldn't let him near me. I didn't want him to hurt the baby. So, I didn't wait for him outside the pub, or pick him up from parties. Johnny was on the edge of my vision, just as I had, so many times before, made myself on the edge of his.

Johnny hung around for a while in Whakatāne, went to work, lurked every now and then at Mum and Dad's place, but he went over to Papamoa more and more and then he said he was moving there, he'd got a job, and he'd come back when the baby was born. But he didn't. He'd checked out. He needed to be the centre of attention, and he'd found some other girl to listen to his bullshit.

Mum's friend Viv was my midwife and she was already at our place having a cup of tea when the contractions started, so Mum and Viv set up a bed on the couch and tried to distract me, put on the TV, played some music, until I was totally losing the plot with the pain, and then Mum drove me to the hospital, and Jade was born an hour later.

The second night in hospital, Jade screamed nonstop, and the ward was full, so the midwives didn't have much time to help. I sat up in my bed and held Jade against my chest, trying to calm her. I didn't know what to do. My boobs hurt and I didn't even know how to hold a newborn right. A scene kept replaying in my head that I would break her or drop her and there were moments when I didn't know if I was asleep or awake.

The clock slowly ticked through the night and when the sun rose Jade finally stopped crying and fell asleep on my chest. She was pressed so close against me that I could feel her little heart beating and the light pressure of her breaths on my chest. She snuffled like a pig. She made a lot of noise for something so small.

My room had a view out to the car park, and, after the midwife had come in and pulled back the curtains, I saw Mum and Dad's car drive past. A huge wave of relief swept over me, they'd be here soon, and I wouldn't be alone with this baby. Someone was here to help me.

A few minutes later, Mum led Dad into my room and helped him into a seat. Then she helped me transfer the baby into her little plastic cot on my other side, managing to keep her asleep.

Mum rummaged through her bag and found her wallet. 'I'll go and find us a cup of coffee.'

I nodded. I was so tired. Was this what it was like, having babies?

Mum patted my hand, as if she could read my thoughts. 'I'll be back in a tick.'

Dad and I sat in silence, the sounds of the busy ward coming through the half-open door.

Then Dad asked, 'Who does she look like?'

I closed my eyes and leant back on my half-upright bed. I took a breath and settled into our familiar routine. 'She's pinky-cream coloured. She has a little bit of dark hair, squashed flat against her head. It's slightly thicker round the back of her head, above her neck.'

'Mmmmm,' Dad said and shifted in his plastic hospital chair. 'That'll be Johnny then.'

I ignored him, and said, 'Her face looks soft, not quite formed. Her nose is flat. Her eyes, when they open, are black. She looks around but she doesn't see anything.'

'She can't see much yet, I don't think.'

'Some of her pores are white and a bit bumpy. The skin around her nose is made up of all these little white raised bits. And there are flakes too, around her eyes. She looks dry, like she's been dried out.' I turned my head to look at her, in her cot, the stripy swaddle wrapped tightly around her. I don't know if I coloured these details for Dad too, these ones that I write down now, maybe I did.

'She's all tucked up. She has green knitted booties. She's very still, but I can see her chest rising and falling. The breath is coming out her nose.'

Dad said, 'Yes. I can hear her breathing.'

'She used to be inside of me. And now she's out here.'

'Yes.'

The baby breathed and I described and Dad listened. We made a pattern, the three of us, passing these things to each other in a sequence around the room. Each of the baby's breaths, a beat, turned into a word, that came out of my mouth, and carried through the air into Dad's ear.

'There's blood, on her head. Blood. Her fingers are like twigs. Her fingernails are so small, they're barely there and they're soft if you touch them, they'd break easily.'

The baby breathed and I described and Dad listened. I had my eyes closed. Like Dad, I couldn't see her, but I knew her already. I had seen her in the night and I had looked at every part of her.

I felt so tired, propped upright in the hospital bed. I couldn't move my arms or legs. I had lost my body. I didn't want to move my mouth, it was tired too, but I knew that if I kept on, and said the words in my mind, if I saw them, then Dad would see them too and he would know.

The baby breathed. She breathed the words out and she breathed them in. The words hovered in the room. Head. Face. Hands. Feet. Tiny. Flaky. Smooth. The raw stump of the umbilical cord. The barely-there hair running up the outside of her ears, a short, curved line. A breath. A word. The baby was taking shape. I was bringing her up, turning her round, colouring her in. I could feel it, and Dad could feel it. The baby could feel it. The skin at her throat. Its two small folds. Her toes tucked up against the soles of her new feet, curled in. All of her curled in, folded in, a body waiting to take on its brand-new form. The line of dark hairs, sparse and irregular, her eyebrows. Her eyelids, puffy, forming the line of her closed eyes.

'I've got her now, J,' said Dad.

The baby cried.

I opened my eyes. They felt heavy. The sight of the hospital room was a shock.

I was still there.

'Can you see her?' I asked.

'Yes.'

The baby opened her eyes and stared at the side of her cot, searching for something.

'I've got her clearly now,' said Dad.

I nodded.

Mum came in with three takeaway coffees in a carry tray and set them down on the table. 'We'll wait a bit, Ray,' she said to Dad, 'they're very hot. I had a lovely chat with one of the doctors, a paediatrician she was, a lovely lady.'

She went and stood, looking down at the baby. 'Hello there, pet,' she said, and the baby scrunched up its nose.

'She'll need a name then, J,' Dad said. 'A colour, I think, so that I can see her better, as she gets bigger.'

'A colour?' I said tiredly.

'What about Rose?' Dad said.

'Don't you remember that gross Rose from primary school?' I said.

'Something else then.'

Mum tucked the swaddle more firmly around the baby's shoulders. 'Jade?' she said.

'Jade Pascoe,' I said, trying it out.

'That's good,' said Dad. 'Jade Pascoe. Jade and Jodie Pascoe.'

'That'll do,' said Mum.

'Jade Pascoe,' I said again.

We all looked at the baby and she squirmed.

I texted Johnny, in the beginning, pictures of Jade, things she'd done. But he told me to stop. *stop trying to guilt trip me,* he texted.

I wish I had those pictures now, those pictures of Jade. I took so many, when she was a baby, and now, of course, they are all gone. Pictures of Jade in her onesie, rolling about on a blanket on the grass out the back of Mum and Dad's place. Sometimes I'd take photos of her at night, sleeping in the bed next to me, lying on a towel so she wouldn't spew milk all through the bed. Those newborn nights with

Jade, in my old bedroom, feeding her and trying to get her back to sleep, I can't really remember them, they are just something we got through together. I remember the photos though, of Jade in the dark, 4:30 in the morning. In the years after, I looked at them again and again. I took the photos because my exhausted brain was generating these repetitive, freaky thoughts that Jade was slipping away from me in the night, and the photos would draw her back, keep her safe next to me and recorded inside my phone.

Now, I think about those early-morning photos all the time, and all the lost photos of Jade. I try to picture them in my mind. The photos were a way that I took care of her, protected her, kept her close to me.

Did I do the right thing, to put us out? All of Jade's short history is lost. How will we be, Jade and I, in the future, now that we can't look back?

16.

It made other parents go crazy, losing the images of their kids, and I understand why.

One night, a couple of weeks after we had talked to Vikram about his posters, Mum called me. It was after eleven, and I was surprised to see her name and photo on my phone's screen. I was always happy to see her, though, and to see that she was present.

'You should turn on the TV,' she said. 'It's the babies, they're gone.'

I put Mum on speaker and turned on the TV.

There was a special report. It was a mess. Babies were born gone. This had never happened before. Kids went. Heaps of them, and it was horrible. But not babies, not newborns. There had been no gone babies, until then.

The camera zoomed in on a mum lying on her bed in hospital. I don't know where she was. I don't know what language she was speaking. There were subtitles that said, *My mother tried to take a photo of us and my baby just wasn't there, she wasn't there! She didn't even have a chance.* The woman leaned closer to the camera and the subtitles said, *We just want to see her, to share her!*

The woman broke off and collapsed onto her bed, tears pouring down her cheeks.

Another shot showed the inside of a different hospital, a woman on a bed in the corridor, sobbing. The empty space of her tiny, gone baby was in her arms. She cradled that space, stared down at it, tightened her arms around it. She looked as if she wanted to pull that space inside of her, make it part of her, make it her own emptiness.

'Are you on channel one?' Mum asked.

'Yeah,' I said.

'That baby is gone. It came out gone.'

'Yeah.' I didn't know what else to say.

The woman looked up and saw the camera. Her face crumpled. 'No! No!' she shouted, hunching her body around the gap in her arms.

'Leave us alone!' she sobbed.

Then there was the sound of a baby crying, a thin, sad wail. The woman looked down at the gap. She rocked her arms and made shushing noises.

The camera lingered and the baby kept crying. It took a deep breath and then screamed again and again, despite all the woman's attempts to calm it.

'If only we could see it,' said Mum, from my phone. 'Do you think it knows? Do you think it can feel that something is wrong?'

'I don't know,' I said. 'It's so small.'

'It sounds like it's in pain,' said Mum.

The person behind the camera asked the woman how she felt.

The gone baby had settled down a little, its wails softening, and the woman seemed to have calmed herself too, in her efforts to comfort it.

She looked up, her eyes wide and suddenly clear of tears, and said, 'I'll never know her, never. She'll always be a stranger to me.'

Her words were so specific, and her voice was clipped and suddenly emotionless. She had no hesitation, none.

The gap started screaming again and the news report shifted to scenes of chaos at a hospital in Malaysia. People ran through the corridors. Concerned doctors hurried out of rooms. There was a shot of a line-up of empty plastic cots. A nurse standing over them reached down to adjust a blanket that was tucked snugly around a gap, and then looked away. Was she scared? What did she see?

Like all footage at that time, there were so many gaps that it was hard to understand what was happening. People twisted at strange angles to move around the gaps, their bodies twitching and flinching, as if they had been bitten or pushed by something. The voices of gaps came and went, confusing the reporting, and interrupting presents.

I put the TV on mute and picked up my phone, turned it off speaker, and held it to my ear.

I thought Mum was just quiet but then I heard a sob and realised that she was crying.

'It's so awful,' she said. 'They'll never see them. They'll forget so quickly. Imagine it, imagine if it was Jade. We wouldn't know her. We'd never be close to her. She'd be so far away.'

I said nothing. I watched the silent TV. A mother walked down a hospital corridor, her damp hair clung to her forehead, blood on the cuff of her gown. Her hand cradled the head of her newborn gap. I imagined it, so delicate, so tiny, so new to the world. She held that head against her shoulder, her eyes were fierce, wild. 'Don't fuck with me,' her eyes said. She rushed past the camera and out of the hospital's sliding door, out into the car park.

I jumped when Mum's voice came whispering out of my phone. I'd forgotten that she was there.

'Did you do this, Jodie? Did you start this?' Mum asked.

I hung up, almost throwing my phone across the room.

I turned off the TV and sank down onto the couch. Mum's question was in my head. She blamed me. How could she think that? We didn't know. There was no way we could know. The question burrowed its way inside of me, into my chest. I wanted to rip it out. I wanted to stop this, to bring these babies back. Did Mum think I was a monster?

Because it was monstrous, horrible. When babies were born gone, their parents' sense of time became all messed up. Without photos of their child, they couldn't hold themselves in a time and place. They couldn't look ahead or look back. They got caught in a kind of intense hyperactive present of trying to remember every moment, and they were riddled with anxiety about their undocumented children. What would it be like if the baby had never seen itself in an image? Would the baby understand itself? Would it feel whole or real or normal? Nobody knew.

Present parents appeared on TV saying that since their newborn had been born gone, they themselves felt like they were gaps. One dad said he felt 'unanchored'. He said, 'I wake up and I don't know if it is morning or afternoon. It's like I'm jetlagged, and my body clock is totally out of sync.'

After the babies started going out, people really wanted to advertise the fact that they hadn't gone, not just online, but in the real world. Like Vikram, business owners put up posters showing themselves and their families outside their shops. Families covered their letterboxes with printed photos of themselves to show that the family inside the house was still present. These always flaked off in the rain. When Jade and I went out for a walk around the neighbourhood, there were little photos of faces scattered on the grass and the footpath. Jade would pick them up and pile them back around what she guessed was the right letterbox.

One day I was at the pharmacy getting a few things when I saw a stack of small, printed cards next to the till, each about the size of a credit card. I picked one up. It showed a photo of a white man with his name and qualifications printed underneath. The pharmacist looked up from behind the high counter where he was working, and I realised it was his face on the card. 'Please,' he said, waving his hand at the cards, 'feel free to take one.'

'Okay, thanks,' I said, and tucked it into my wallet. It was weird, I didn't know what it was for.

Soon these cards were everywhere. I had one printed for myself, and Jade demanded some as well. 'Everyone at school has one!' she said.

Our cards were simple. We both had the same one. I found a nice photo of us together at the beach and had our names printed underneath, the same on both sides. *Jade and Jodie Pascoe.* That was it.

We gave them out to our friends. It quickly became a thing that we did, a short transaction, say hi, swap cards. At the vege market, I'd pass over my cash with one of my cards, and the store owner behind the table would throw one of their cards into my bag, along with my tomatoes and bananas. At the mill, every visitor left one of their cards in a tray at the front desk and, at the end of the day, we collected them up and filed them away in an alphabetised system that I had created.

Jade swapped our card for the cards of other kids and teachers at school. She started a collection and bought a special book to stick them in. She had categories for friends, family, sports players. Celebrities had their cards printed in editions and they became collectors' items. Jade carefully looked after her cards of her favourite singers and vloggers.

We did it because, if we were present, we wanted everyone else to know.

There were the cards and letterboxes and posters, but bigger, louder images also started popping up, billboards and TV ads and flyers placed in every letterbox. In a small town like Whakatāne there weren't that many billboards around, but that changed as more people began to go out. People had hoardings printed with their smiling faces alongside their names. It wasn't a political thing, they weren't running for council or trying to get our vote or anything like that. They wanted to let everyone know that they were present, and that they could still be imaged, still be seen.

There was one roundabout that we drove through on our way to Mum and Dad's place, I remember it started with only a few small hoardings, but within a week it was crowded with hundreds of them, each stuck into the grass with two wooden pegs. When I drove round, smiling face after smiling face stared in through my passenger window.

The council tried to organise specific areas for people to put the hoardings and posters up. There were articles in the paper, encouraging people to put them on the berm by the beach, or on certain traffic islands. And people did obey the rules for a while, but then Graham Patterson, the captain of the All Blacks, went out and everyone freaked.

Patterson was the first famous person in New Zealand to go out. At the time, he was the captain of the All Blacks, and he was hot, funny, and in the media a lot. Where is he now? I don't know.

They said it started on YouTube, someone was watching a clip of Patterson scoring a try and he disappeared from the video. The viewer posted a comment underneath the video and shared it around. In minutes, seconds even, the news was everywhere that Patterson had gone. All the matches, all the ads, all the interviews, all the social media. This very *seen* person had gone and nobody knew what to do.

Patterson released a statement on Instagram that said he and his family were well and appreciated the support of his fans and fellow players.

Did his fans support him? Not really. I went round to see Mum and Dad soon after it happened, and I found Dad in the kitchen listening to talkback radio. I made him a cup of coffee and started making dinner. The tone on the radio was mean. The host was trying to keep things civil but mean-sounding men kept calling and accusing Patterson of lacking leadership, letting himself go, of not playing in the 'spirit of the game'.

'What was he supposed to do? He can't stop it,' I said.

'He's a goner,' Dad said, shaking his head.

'He can still play rugby,' I said.

'Yes, but nobody can watch him play rugby,' said Dad.

Patterson was a goner, just as Dad said. The All Blacks dropped him, with New Zealand Rugby citing their broadcasting contracts and other obligations. He didn't fight back, like other sportspeople did, who went out later. Tennis players and gymnasts tried to figure out ways that they could still play their sport and make money from it, like invitation only matches, exclusive in-person events, that kind of thing. But nothing worked. If you couldn't be filmed and broadcast around hundreds of countries, then you couldn't be a professional sportsperson. So, if you went out, that was the end of that.

Patterson was famous and he had gone. It could happen to anyone. It *was* happening to anyone. The hoardings and billboards and cards multiplied. People in Whakatāne totally ignored the council's requests and put them up everywhere, the streets were lined with grinning faces.

Some rich dude in Auckland got hundreds of thousands, maybe millions, of his cards printed and had them delivered to houses all around the country. Jade and I got one in our letterbox. A photo of this guy, with a Photoshopped wooden frame, his name underneath with a message that sounded like he was in the army, *Justin Clayton: Present and Accounted For.*

I saw pictures of Times Square, where the same thing happened, except on an American scale. Some billionaire tech entrepreneur paid for his image to be shown on those giant billboards around the square. It was creepy and lots of people objected, but he had heaps of money, so he could do whatever he wanted. Then it became this pissing contest, especially among those Silicon Valley types, those types who lived online, constantly sharing everything about their lives. They needed to be present, they needed to be seen, because they saw that the whole world they had created, the world of social media, was falling apart around them, as more and more people went out and left their online lives behind them and retreated into the place that those of us who were present didn't want to follow, or know about, or think about.

I read about a town in Kenya where everyone went out all at once. The whole town, all gone, just like that. There were reports that the gaps then got together and decided to seal themselves off from the rest of the country. They didn't want to be interfered with, they felt that they'd been chosen to be separate and they wanted to keep it that way. I don't know what they did for food. The town was at the foot of a mountain range, next to a river, and I guess the people knew how to farm for all they needed.

They rejected the internet. They couldn't be seen there anymore, so they said they didn't need it. They said they wanted to return to a simpler way of living, one that was more grounded in the present.

Other gaps started migrating to this Kenyan town. They said they were drawn there, that they wanted to be somewhere where they belonged. International travel was still working, but things went up and down, routes would be cancelled because of some security collapse and then be reinstated again. So the gaps who were able to get the right visas and permits flew around the world to Kenya, where they were welcomed. There were reports of initiation rituals, of spoken-word systems being set up so that the gaps could record events and communicate with each other online.

'We're building a new society,' said the woman who called herself their 'communications representative'. She came out of the town every now and then to talk to the waiting media. She said, 'Our society is free from the tyranny of the image. Free from the constant desire to be seen. Our citizens are alive with connection but without vanity. We are no longer alienated from our true selves.'

She spoke in clearly pronounced English, her voice rich and warm. I wanted to know what she looked like because she sounded beautiful.

It pissed people off, this idea that the gaps were in some way better than the rest of us, and that they were living better lives. Up until then we'd enjoyed feeling sorry for them, shaking our heads and saying how terrible it was and wasn't it a shame and that everything would be okay and work out in the end. But then they started getting together in groups, like in this town in Kenya, and it freaked everyone. We didn't want them to have power, we wanted them to be weaker and smaller and simpler than us.

I wish I could write that I didn't think like this. But I did. I was worried about me and Jade. I thought about the person who had come into our house a few months before. What were they looking for?

Once, and only once, this Kenyan town let a camera crew in to film. I saw bits of it on my Instagram feed, the empty streets, cars moving down the roads, the voice of the communications woman talking about the collective model of governance they had set up, how they were producing and distributing their food.

'No one goes without,' the communications woman said. 'Everyone's needs are met and everyone is equal. And, above all, everyone is *seen*.'

But they couldn't be, they just couldn't be seen. They couldn't be captured in an image. They easily slid under the radar and slipped between systems. They couldn't be as easily traced and tracked and accounted for, and everyone was worried about these shadows, these untraceable elements in their countries. We knew that gaps didn't appear in photos, but rumours began that they were also harder to see in real life when they stood in front of you. People said that they looked shaky, unstable, blurry around the edges, and that you could tell, just by the look of them, that they'd gone. That's what people said.

17.

One evening, in the middle of the social media frenzy, I sat on Mum and Dad's couch and watched the six o'clock news and listened to the gaps saying they felt fine, that they were happier this way, that they felt that one day they might appear in their photos again. 'I think it'll just come back, at some point,' said an old man. Then, in a sadder tone, 'But I miss those photos, I do. My wife and I, we've been married fifty years, and those wedding photos... I'm gone now. That's a bit sad, isn't it?'

'Oh, that's sad,' Mum said, sitting next to me on the couch. 'I'd miss that too, if I went.' She looked across at the photo of her and Dad on their wedding day that always stood on the sideboard in the lounge. Mum held a bunch of purple roses and Dad grinned at the camera, in a brown suit and thin tie. Mum's hair was pulled back into a French twist and her high-necked dress was pale yellow.

'It won't happen to you, Mum,' I said.

She pursed her lips.

I looked at the photo again. I'd never thought to ask, until then, but I suddenly said, 'Was your wedding dress really yellow, Mum? Why not white?'

She frowned a little. 'Do you know what? I can't remember. The most important day of my life, and I can't remember. I remember Shirley helped me make it. But... was it yellow? Maybe. Maybe a pastel yellow. How silly! I'll have to ask Dad later. He'll remember.'

We watched TV for a bit longer. I remember Jade lying on the carpet in front of us with her felts, drawing on the back of Mum's old genealogy papers.

Dad came into the lounge and as he crossed the room to his chair, Jade made a chirping noise, which she sometimes did so he'd know where she was and wouldn't bump into her.

Dad walked around her and felt for the arms of his chair before slumping into it.

I untucked my legs. 'I suppose we should go home,' I said to Jade, who rolled onto her back.

'Jodes, be a love and put the kettle on before you go,' said Mum, who had picked up the TV Guide and started the sudoku.

I pushed myself up and off the couch and went into the kitchen. As I was filling the jug, I heard the phone ring. Mum and Dad still had a landline that sat on the shelf in the hall. Guy and I always complained about the loud ring, but it was so Dad could always hear it wherever he was in the house.

I heard Mum get up and go into the hall to answer it. The jug boiled, and I filled two mugs, sharing a teabag between them. It was gross, watery, but it was the way Mum and Dad liked it.

'Jodie?' Mum said. 'Yes, she's here. Can I say who's calling?'

Silence. Then Mum appeared at the kitchen door and said, 'There's a man on the phone for you.'

'Who is it?'

'They wouldn't say.'

'Wouldn't say?'

'Said they just needed to talk to you.'

I went into the hall and picked up the phone. 'Hello?'

Silence on the other end. I heard Mum shuffling in the kitchen and opening the fridge door.

'Hello? Who's there?'

Someone breathed at the other end. Breathing so that I could hear them breathing.

Mum paused in the hall on her way through to the kitchen, watching, a mug in each hand.

'Hello?' I said again. 'Can you hear me?'

Jade came into the hall as well, her toys packed up, her backpack on. She stood still, watching me.

Muffled noises and a thump on the end of the line.

'I think you've got the wrong number,' I said, and hung up.

'Who was that, Mum?' asked Jade.

I shrugged. 'I think they had the wrong number.'

'But they asked for you,' said Mum.

'Who was on the phone?' Dad yelled from the lounge.

'Someone for Jodie!' Mum shouted back.

'What did they want?' Dad yelled.

I went and stood next to Jade and Mum in the doorway to the lounge so that Dad could hear me. 'It was a bad connection. I couldn't hear them,' I said.

I grabbed my bag and coat from the hallway. 'Come on, Jade, let's go.'

'Will they call back?' Dad asked. 'Who was it?'

Mum frowned. 'They asked for you, for Jodie. How did they know you were here?'

'It was probably just Vodafone or something, they'll have me on record as living here from an old contract. Come on, Jade, have you got all your stuff?'

Jade touched Dad's hand so that he knew she was next to him, and then she gave him a hug.

'See ya soon, pet,' he said.

Mum saw us to the door.

I said, shepherding Jade in front of me, 'If they call again, just give them my cell number. Sometimes they don't give up. They can be a real pain when they want to be.'

I drove home, replaying the noises at the end of the line. The breathing. The soft muttering and the thud. Not a broken line, someone at the other end, making noises, and wanting me to know that they were there.

The streets were crowded with people's faces, smiling out from posters and billboards and hoardings. The council hadn't been able to stop people from putting them up wherever they wanted. Occasionally, there'd be a blitz and the council would get rid of a truck load, but the signs sprouted up again, more than before, alongside the beach road, on fences, the side of shops, in the windows of office buildings.

I'm writing about these signs, as part of that time, because when I think back to that drive home from my parents' house, the signs were already an established part of our landscape. Those faces, those images. The continuous line of smiles, like a barricade against going, the void that we were all terrified of. 'I am here!' the posters shouted. 'I am here! I am here! I am here! See me!'

They demanded to be seen, but I had already stopped looking at them. It had only been a couple of months since Jade and I had spoken to Vikram and the signs and cards and billboards had started to appear. But, already, there were so many that it was impossible to look at them. The faces blurred into a stream of teeth and eyes and necks.

Jade and I had made a poster of ourselves, the same as our card that we gave out at the vege market and to Jade's friends. We'd stuck the poster to our fence. But I didn't see it as I turned off the road and into the drive. My mind was on other things. I was thinking about the phone call.

'Guy!' Jade banged on the inside window of the car when she saw Guy sitting on our front steps.

'Jade, stop it!' I said, grumpy because I was annoyed to see Guy.

Guy stood up and came over to the car as we pulled up. He opened Jade's door and she leapt out, grabbing his hands so that he could spin her round and round while she shrieked and laughed.

When he dumped her down on the grass, she said, panting, 'We've been at Nan's place. Come on, I've got new Lego.'

I grabbed my bag, followed them round the back, and unlocked the door while Jade chatted and clung to Guy's hand.

In the kitchen, Guy put a bag down on the bench and took out a packet of biscuits and a bag of chips. 'I got you guys some stuff at the super,' he said.

'Can we have some chippies now, Mum. Can we?' Jade begged.

I opened the packet and put some in a little plastic bowl for her.

'Chippies before bed,' I said. 'Just the thing.'

Guy took a box of beer out of the bag. 'And something for me and J,' he said. 'Do you want one?'

I shrugged and Guy opened two beers, handed one to me, and jammed the rest of the box into the fridge.

'Where's this Lego, then?' he asked.

Jade grabbed his hand and led him down the hall to her room to show him the Lego that I had got second hand from a mum that we knew from kindy.

I called down the hall, 'Time for bed in fifteen minutes, okay? It's already way past your bedtime, Jade.'

I went back out the door to collect the load of washing that I had left on the line. It was dark, and the clothes were cold and slightly damp.

I took the basket back inside and hung them out on the little clotheshorse. It was always such a mission to get the washing dry, I could never get the timing right. Guy came back and opened the fridge to get another beer. He took a swig and looked at me, leaning on the bench.

'What do you want, Guy?' I asked.

'Can't I come and see my niece?' he said, spreading his hands.

'It's bedtime,' I replied. 'She's tired.'

'I'll go in a bit.'

I kept hanging up the clothes.

'How're you guys going?' Guy asked.

'Jade is freaked out, I can tell. She's worried, anxious.'

'She's smart. She's always up with the play.'

'That's the thing, sometimes too much. But, it's not as if I can keep it from her now, with all the posters and signs.'

'I saw your poster on your fence. Nice photo,' said Guy.

'Yeah well,' I sighed and sat down at the kitchen table. 'What can I do, though? Jade wanted one. All the kids at school have one now.'

'Fuck yeah,' said Guy, 'gotta have one. Gotta let people know you're still present.' He took his wallet out of his back pocket and handed me his card. He was facing the camera, arms crossed, set against a sepia background. 'Pretty sweet, huh?'

I nodded and he put it away.

'This shit is not going away any time soon. We've got to get ready.'

'How am I supposed to get ready, Guy? After the rent goes out tomorrow, I have fifty-three dollars in my bank account until Monday.'

I glanced down the hall to check that Jade was still in her room.

Guy gulped his beer and said nothing for a moment. Then, 'People are going to learn how to control this and they're going to force people out, you know what I mean? Certain people will go, others will stay, that's just the way it's going to be.'

'I don't know what you're talking about. It's just random, no one can control it, it just happens.'

'Yeah, they say that now because that's what they want you to think.' He waved his beer bottle at me. 'But I saw on this website, on this map, and you can see patterns. There are more gaps in the Southern Hemisphere, there are areas of the world that they want gone.'

'Mmmm, maybe,' I said.

I heard Jade in the hall and then she appeared at the doorway. 'Are you going to play with me, Guy?'

'Course, yeah, I will,' said Guy.

'It's bedtime, Jade, it's late,' I said.

'Awwww.' Jade scrunched up her face.

'I'll come back tomorrow,' said Guy. 'We can go to the movies.'

Jade skipped on the spot. 'Yeah! Can we, Mum?'

'Course. Can you get your PJs on?'

Jade went back down the hall.

Guy finished his beer and put the bottle on the bench.

'You should take the other ones,' I said, gesturing towards the fridge.

He started shoving the bottles into his backpack. 'I'll leave you a couple, you know, to get you through to Monday.' He zipped up his bag. 'You know, J, you're doing a good job, with Jade and everything. Jade is cool.'

He smiled his familiar, charming Guy smile. Charming Guy. He could really turn it on when he wanted to.

I should've told him to piss off, but I wanted to hear how cool Jade was, how I was doing a good job, holding everything together. I never stopped wanting to hear those things.

I followed him out the back door and walked him to his car. What was that night like? There are moments that are harder to remember, harder to describe. It was winter. I hadn't been able to dry the washing. Did we hear a car door slam? Did we hear the thuds of Jade walking inside the house? I suppose I could just make some stuff up.

The time between leaving the house and arriving at the car was important, though, because when we left, Guy stumbled on the steps and I wondered if he was okay to drive. Did I say, 'Are you okay to drive?' I think so. I'm sure I would've said that.

He threw his bag over to the passenger side and went to climb in, but then paused and turned to me, leaning on the top of the door. His movements were suddenly precise, measured. He didn't seem drunk, though I'd thought he'd been slurry only seconds before.

He asked, in a clear voice, 'Do you still do that thing for Dad?'

I paused, worried. I could only see the outline of his face in the dark.

'What thing?' I asked.

'You know, telling him about stuff.'

'Nah, I haven't done that for years.'

'I was just thinking about it the other day, the describing, all that boring stuff.'

'Okay.'

'You did it for people too, right? Described people to him? What they looked like?'

I nodded and crossed my arms. I didn't know if he could see me properly, in the dark. 'Who was that man you were with?' I shot back. 'We saw you in town, talking to someone.'

If he was watching me, I wanted him to think that I was watching him too.

Guy paused, then rapped the top of the car door with his knuckles. 'Okay then, see ya later, J.'

I watched him back the car out and drive away. I knew he'd already forgotten about his promise to take Jade to the movies, and that he wouldn't text me the next day to organise it. Guy didn't remember things that he had promised other people, and he made a lot of promises.

I told Jade the next morning that Guy had messaged to say he had to go to work unexpectedly, so he couldn't take her to the movies. She threw her spoon into her bowl of Rice Bubbles.

'Can we go anyway, Mum?' she asked.

I had no money. I was worried about what we would even have for dinner. 'Next weekend,' I said. 'I promise. And I keep my promises. Do you want to see if Cara wants to come round later?' I tried to distract her.

'Why does Guy always say he can take me to things and then he doesn't. He never does. He's dumb,' Jade said.

I started clearing the breakfast table and Jade stormed into the lounge and flopped down on the couch.

18.

Even when Guy and I were kids, I couldn't tell where his loyalties lay. I mean, they should've been with me, or with Mum and Dad, but they weren't. It was as if he was missing a part of his brain, the part that made him want to be a member of our pack.

At school, he wanted to be popular, to be liked. And he was, he was really good at rugby and had heaps of friends at school. Heaps of friends, but no group, and no close friends like Miri, who was always at our house, and who Mum and Dad chatted to and knew stuff about, and were just normal with.

Guy hung out with random dudes who'd wait in their cars in our driveway, their engines running, hidden behind tinted windows, while Guy grunted, 'Later,' and left by the back door.

Mum and Dad worried. They'd ask me, when he hadn't been around for ages, 'Who's Guy hanging out with? Do you see his mates at school?'

I wasn't much help. 'Nah,' I'd say, 'don't see him much.'

And just when they'd be about to intervene, to say something, or check he really was where he said he was going to be, he'd appear in the lounge, and help Dad with his screen reader, or offer to unpack the groceries for Mum, or make everyone a coffee, all charm and chat and jokes. Mum would grin at him and pat his hand, and Dad would lean on his arm going down the hall.

Guy could switch it on and switch it off. You never knew which Guy you were going to get, the Guy who unpacked the groceries, or the Guy who snarled and turned his back on you.

Once, in high school, when I was sixteen and Guy was seventeen, I remember a party we went to in a small hall just out of town. Miri and I got ready at my place, and I remember us, how we looked, how it felt to be there, and I like to write about us then, at sixteen, this memory, this description comes easily.

We were in my room, listening to Rihanna, Miri lying on my bed and watching me try to outline my eyes with dark eyeliner.

'You need to do it like this,' she said. She reached over with a tissue and wiped the eyeliner off my right eye. 'Close your eyes.' I felt her hands on my face, one pushing up my eyebrow, and the other resting on my cheek bone as she drew a dark line across the top of my eyelid, her warm breath on my cheek.

'Open,' she said.

I opened my eyes, blinked, there was Miri right in front of me, sixteen, her eyebrows scrunched in concentration, examining her work. Miri. Who, later, would plead with me in a car park to help her fade away, escape from the men who followed her and hurt her, who I would push out from the world of images, who I would make indescribable. Miri. Gone. Vanished.

I'll try and fix things and bring her back here, on the screen. Miri at sixteen, dark hair pulled back into a ponytail, grey eyeshadow, a patch of bad skin on her chin, thickly covered with foundation, red top from Glassons, nose ring in her right nostril. Is that right? Yes. This face, Miri's face, I see it, as I write this. I bring her back. I can bring us both back, for a moment, but only in words.

'Fucking A, you look great,' she said. 'Now can you do a bit more on mine?'

She closed her eyes and I leaned in to run the pencil over her eyelids. Our postures switched, our faces doubled, drawing each other into being, outlining each other so that we were clear and defined. Visible.

Mum came and stood in the doorway. 'You two look nice,' she said. 'Do you want to go now?'

'Yup,' I said, pulling on my jacket and tucking my phone into the pocket.

Miri turned off the stereo and checked herself again in the mirror.

In the hall, Mum called out to Dad in the lounge, 'You all right?'

'Yeah, beaut.' Dad was listening to the rugby on the radio.

In the car, Mum sang along to ABBA and Miri and I cringed at each other, though Mum is actually a good singer.

The party was in a small hall just out of town. I peered in the dark for the street sign, and made Mum stop on the corner when we found it.

'It's just down there.' I pointed through the dark to where we could see the outline of the hall. When I opened my car door we heard thudding bass.

'Why don't I just drive you down?' said Mum.

'No! Just here's good, and then you can turn around easier.'

Miri and I had talked about how we didn't want people to see Mum drop us off.

'Yeah, this is good, Trish,' Miri said. 'We can just walk down.' She already had her door half open.

'Well, okay. But I want you to text me when you get there. And Guy is bringing you back, okay? At twelve.'

Miri and I walked through the thick grass on the side of the road. A couple of cars drove past us and turned into the car park outside the hall. Mum waited a moment, but when I turned around she was driving away.

The hall was already crowded and the music loud. Miri unzipped her backpack and took out a couple of beers. Her dad had given her a six pack for us to share. She twisted open a bottle and looked around.

A boy standing next to us stepped back slightly to let us into his circle, and we stood and sipped our beers, trying to be cool. Miri started talking to the boy next to her. I looked around the hall. There were lots of people I didn't know. I saw Guy in a dark corner, surrounded by a huddle of his mates.

The boy said something and Miri laughed, but I couldn't hear what they were saying above the music. I took out my phone and sent Mum a text, *All good. saw Guy here. will come home with him.*

The hall had a small stage at one end, and I saw a group of mates from school sitting along its edge, legs dangling. I touched Miri's elbow to let her know I was going, and she nodded at me, so I went to join them.

We soon moved from the edge to sit as a clump in the middle of the stage, listening as two boys fought over what music to play. 'Just leave it the fuck alone!' someone shouted into the moment of quiet when a track was cut short for the third time in a row. Two boys smiled and shrugged sheepishly from the corner next to the stereo.

The music played on, uninterrupted, and people flowed in and out of the doors opposite the stage. Behind me, two girls lay down and spread-eagled themselves on the floor.

Miri found me and handed me another beer. I smiled at her, and we clinked the bottle necks together.

'What was that guy's name?' I asked. I thought he was hot.

'Luke.' Miri looked across the hall.

'Is he at Trident?'

'Yeah.'

I was jealous of how Miri talked to boys. She did it like she didn't care, like she could just say anything and didn't care what anyone thought.

The boys ruling the stereo allowed Kanye to play and everyone on the stage jumped up. Miri and I tucked our beers behind the curtain at the back and started dancing. Beyoncé came on next and everyone went wild, more people swarmed the stage, lifting their arms.

Sometime in the next couple of songs, I lost Miri, but I didn't care. I was a bit drunk and with friends on the small stage, dancing and shouting and stamping. A girl passed me a pre-mixed drink and I took a swig, so sweet. Someone stumbled backwards and stepped on the bottom of the curtain that hung at the back of the stage so that it was pulled off half of its rungs and sagged. People crawled underneath, forming a small fort.

Later, I jumped down off the stage, hot and breathless, my jacket bunched up under my arm, and joined some members of my soccer team who were leaning against the side wall.

I'd lost track of time and I was surprised when I saw Miri weaving through the crowd towards me.

'It's twelve,' she said.

'You okay? I'm a bit wasted.'

'Yeah, I—'

I couldn't hear her, and I put my hand up to my ear.

'I was looking for Guy!' she said loudly.

We walked through the hall together, looking around for him. All the boys in their dark hoodies looked the same.

Out the front of the hall, the air was thick with weed and the concrete was wet, it must have rained while we were inside. Cars were coming and going from the car park, engines growling and stereos thudding. A car horn barked near me and I jumped. People stood around in groups, smoking, murmuring, clouds of smoke rising off them, lit by the one stark light shining down from the eave of the hall.

It was hard to make out faces in the dark, but I couldn't see Guy, and I didn't recognise anyone else either, they looked older, not at school anymore.

It was cold and I put on my jacket. I checked my phone, no messages. I sent one to Guy, *where are you?* It was 12:15.

'Where the fuck is he?' said Miri.

'He's probably just gone,' I said. 'He doesn't give a shit.'

The sound of an engine came from the corner of the car park, then tyres grating across loose gravel.

'You ladies looking for someone?' A boy standing near had overheard and turned to us.

Miri and I stared at him. His face was in shadow, backlit by the light from the hall.

'My brother,' I said.

'Giving you a ride?'

I nodded. 'Yeah, but he's pissed off, the fuckwit.' I wanted to sound cool, like I didn't care, but I did, I did care.

The group of boys around him shuffled and moved closer to us, interested.

'Ride with us,' said the boy.

One of them finished a ciggy and dropped it on the ground.

'Nah, we're okay,' I said.

'We were just going now, eh boys? Phil's got his car.'

I looked to Miri, but the light was right behind her and I couldn't see her face either.

'What's your name anyway, gorgeous?' I heard his drunk voice slip around the edges of his consonants.

I was drunk too. Struggling to make sense of things. Should we go with these guys? 'Jodie,' I said.

One of them swigged a can of bourbon and Coke. He grunted, 'The other one's all right.'

People were leaving, there were only a couple of cars left in the car park. Taillights disappeared down the road and it started to drizzle again.

Miri turned so half her face was in the light and I saw her scowl. I reached out and held her forearm and, I remember the shock of it, she was trembling.

'Call your mum,' she said quietly.

The boys laughed. 'Call your mummy to come pick you up!' said the one drinking the bourbon.

I moved away from them and called Mum and she answered after one ring.

'I can't find Guy,' I said.

I heard Dad in bed next to her, asking what was going on. She said she'd come straight away.

Miri and I stood in the rain by the side of the road and waited. When the carload of boys drove past us, one of them shouted out his window, 'Frigid fuckin' bitches!' And they gunned it away down the narrow road.

Mum turned up not long after and took us home, angry at Guy, worried about where he was.

The next morning, after Guy had been dropped home by his mates, she shouted at him in the kitchen, 'You promised me you'd bring Jodie home!'

He shrugged and leant back against the kitchen bench. 'She's okay. I went to Phil's place.'

'What is wrong with you, Guy? You can't leave your sister in the middle of nowhere.'

'She's okay.'

I was in the lounge, watching music videos on TV. Guy came in and slumped down in an armchair.

'You could have just got a ride home with someone,' he said. 'You didn't have to call Mum.'

As if I had called Mum deliberately so he'd get in the shit.

'You could've just waited for us and given us a ride,' I said.

'Went to Phil's place for a smoke.'

'Real nice, thanks Guy. What a winner.'

Dad came in and felt his way through the lounge to sit next to me on the couch. He put his hand on my shoulder briefly, marking out where I was.

'You need to look after your sister, Guy,' he said calmly. 'I've told you before, you have to do some of the things I can't do.'

Dad didn't get angry. Guy crossed his arms. He was only eighteen months older than me. He didn't want to be responsible for me.

'Now, show me these ones then,' said Dad, gesturing at the TV and settling into his spot on the couch.

Describing music videos was a regular Sunday morning routine for Dad and me. I was honing my skills, because the images were so quick, I had to be selective and precise. 'A boat. Clear seas. The singer is white. He's hauling up the sail. Steering the boat. A storm is coming. Dark sky.'

I liked it, and I'd got better at this type of colouring as the years went on. I'd been terrible at it to start with. I'd get tongue tied and muck it up. By that time, though, when I was sixteen, I'd done it so much that I could go into a kind of trance, throwing out words like cards from a pack, so that I didn't have to think, I only spoke. I was a funnel that turned images into words. 'The singer is in front. Two dancers behind. In a club. Bright lights. Inside a car. Glasses with whisky. Pink light. Red lips. Plaits. A mirror ball. Squares of colour, bright colours, all on top, on the dancers, on the floor. Lips again. Ears. The dancers fanning out, backs arched.'

I rambled on. I could keep going for hours. Dad told me once that I was like a ticker tape machine, and I had to look up what that was, but when I did, I saw what he meant, and when I described the music videos I imagined the long paper strip of words pouring out of my mouth, launching off my tongue, and out into the room, like a white snake, a live thing.

Dad and I settled into our comfortable Sunday morning pattern, together on the couch, me colouring, my legs stretched out on the footstool, and I forgot that Guy was in the room with us until he moved suddenly, and I looked across at him and he was staring at us, unblinking.

19.

I was worried about my job at the mill. A production assistant went out and they gathered us into the staff room to make an official announcement, even though we already knew, and it was all anyone could talk about.

They said that the person who'd gone out was on leave for a couple of weeks while the mill's parent company figured out what to do.

Someone put up their hand and asked, 'But it doesn't make any difference, eh? I mean, she can still do her job, right?' We all nodded, because that's what we'd all been thinking.

The manager nodded and looked nervously at his colleague standing next to him. 'Yes, ah, well, we're not sure. Maybe. That's what we're working to ascertain. There're health and safety implications we have to work through, for those people who have gone. We want to ensure the safety of our employees.'

As we filed out of the staff room, a woman stood at the door and handed everyone small cards. By this time, we were used to receiving these. I looked at the card. It showed the board of directors of the parent company, a row of men sitting around a long table and grinning at the camera.

It was bullshit. She could still do her job, but going out made people harder to track, harder to trace, impossible to record on the company's CCTV. The mill was owned by a parent company in Singapore and we'd heard stories of employees in the company's other businesses losing their jobs after they had gone. Contracts were dismantled. Severance pay was offered. People disappeared from the workforce. What these people were doing now, I didn't know. Were there still jobs for gaps? They could do the same things the rest of us could do. I remember the administrator at Jade's school. She was still working, though she was gone.

I went home after that staff meeting and looked at my bank account. I had about three hundred bucks and $1700 owing on my credit card. The electricity bill would come in the next couple of days, and Jade needed new sneakers and a winter coat. She was getting taller. Suddenly, her tights didn't reach her ankles and her pale wrists poked out of the ends of her sleeves. Six-year-old Jade. Jade looking out at me from under her fringe, understanding all that was going on in the world.

I stared at my bank balance and I felt my heart start to thud. I couldn't lose my job. Mum and Dad had my old bedroom at their place, but I didn't want to move in with them again, I was supposed to be supporting them, not the other way round. And they didn't have much cash. Mum still worked as a relief teacher and pieced that income together with Dad's welfare. I couldn't put more stress on them.

I googled the Singaporean parent company and read on their website about their response to the de-imaging of people and how they respected the rights and entitlements of those who had gone. *This is new territory*, they wrote, *and we are working with our lawyers to ensure employment practices are in place that establish stability and best practice in a period of change.*

What did that mean?

I tapped through to a page about the board of directors. The page was dominated by the same photo that had been given to us on the cards at the meeting and I stared at it for a moment before reaching into my pocket to take out the card again, and I held it up, next to my phone. Comparing the two images, I could see that one of the men in the back row had gone out. On my phone, I pinched the image to zoom in and saw that they had Photoshopped another man into his place. He had a glitchy outline and his jacket didn't match up with the space he had been given.

Huh. One of these guys had gone and they had said nothing to us and just Photoshopped some random man into his spot.

I looked up from the screen and took deep breaths to slow my rising panic. People in charge would protect themselves and the rest of us would be left scrambling, on the outside. People who were present would be given precedence for jobs. Gaps were already a lesser, undesirable part of a different community.

I shook my head. It didn't make sense. People still needed boxes, cartons, paper, all the things that the mill produced. People still needed their hair cut and buses to be driven and kids taught. Gaps could still do all these things. It made no difference that they couldn't be photographed.

And yet, by then it was happening everywhere, gaps losing their jobs, having their contracts cut short. Job adverts had started to say 'Candidates must be present'.

I stared at the image of the board of directors on my screen. These people were so far away, and yet their decisions could make or break things for me. And for Jade. I looked at the image for so long that my focus shifted, and I saw myself reflected in the glass of the screen. It was comforting to see my face, to see it replicated. I was still here, doubled, seen.

I was jolted out of my trance by my phone ringing. Tracey's name came up on the screen, but it was Renee.

'I messaged you!' she said. 'Are you ignoring me? You didn't reply.'

'Sorry, sorry. We had this meeting at work about redundancies, what they're going to do with employees who've gone. I'm freaking out a bit.'

I got up and poked my head through the doorway to check that Jade was still watching TV.

'Yeah, I know. It's pretty messed up,' said Renee.

'They can't fire someone as soon as they've gone, though. Can they? I mean, I could still do my job.'

'It's happening already.'

I felt dizzy and sat down again at the table.

'Oh my god, Renee. What's going on? What's happening?'

'Breathe, Jodie, breathe. It's okay. They're going to figure out a way to stop it. Did you see that announcement? From those trials in Switzerland? They said it looked really promising.'

'Yeah, I saw that.'

Renee requested to switch to a video call and her face came up on my screen, and I looked at her and at myself, the small square of my face down in the right-hand corner of the phone. It was calming, seeing our faces, holding us together there, snug inside the phone's frame. Seeing those images of us made me feel a little more in control of the situation.

Renee told me a story about Hugo and Ari and what they'd been getting up to. 'I love to hear them talking to each other when they think no one's listening. Ari told Hugo he was going to get a real dinosaur for Christmas,' she said.

I laughed. 'Yeah, Jade's already started asking me when it will be Christmas, pointing stuff out that she wants.'

Renee paused, then she said, suddenly serious, 'Listen, Jodie, someone came to the door asking about you, the other day.'

I'd been slumped at the table, but I sat up and pulled the phone closer to my ear. 'What do you mean? Who?'

'A man. I was at home, by myself. He knocked at the door and asked if I knew you, or where you might be.'

'Did he give his name?'

'I asked him. I asked him why he was looking for you. He said that he was trying to return something to you. He wouldn't say what.'

I was silent, biting my lip. Renee frowned at me through the screen.

'Jodes, what did he want? Is this about Miri?'

I shook my head. 'I don't know.'

'What happened to Miri? I used to see her around sometimes, after she moved back. But... has she gone? Did Miri go out? It's okay, you know, if she did. But she's your best friend, maybe they think, you know, that there's a connection, maybe they're trying to track down people who knew her. I've heard that they do that.'

'Maybe,' I said.

'I think you should tell me, Jodes. Because I don't want strange men coming to my front door. How did this guy know that I knew you?'

I saw my small face on the screen. My voice was small. 'Did you tell him? Did you tell him where I was? Did he make you tell him?'

'No. It wasn't like that. He wasn't angry. I told him that I thought you were in Whakatāne, but I only told him that because I think he already knew. That's the only reason I said anything. I'm sorry.'

'It's okay. You're right, he probably already knew. I don't want dodgy men coming to your door, either.'

'Is it to do with gaps? Where was he from? Do you know something about it?'

'I don't think so. At least... no, I don't know anything. I don't know why they want to talk to me.'

'Who wants to talk to you?' I turned towards Jade's voice and she'd appeared in the doorway. She came over to stand next to me and waved at Renee.

'Hi, Jade!' said Renee. 'Cool T-shirt! Hey, sorry guys but I've gotta go, I can hear Ari outside, someone's fallen over or something. I'll call you later in the week, okay?'

Jade reached over and pressed the red button to hang up and our faces disappeared off the screen.

'Who wants to talk to you?' Jade asked again. I didn't know how long she had been standing in the doorway.

'Someone from work. It's a work thing,' I said, and I stood up and went to put the kettle on.

Jade. Whenever she walks into this writing I want to slow down and look at her on the page. I want to walk around her and see her from all angles, drink her up, think about all her tiny details, the soft hair at the nape of her neck, the sudden energy that made her hop up and down on one foot. I don't really want to describe all those other things, what happened with the gaps, with me, with Guy, and with Miri. I just want to describe Jade.

In the kitchen, after talking to Renee, I felt Jade watching me as I made a cup of tea. She knew Renee and I had been talking about something important and she wanted to know what it was.

'Do you remember when someone came into our house at night?' she asked.

I looked up. 'No, when?'

'You know, just before. It was in the morning. You said no one had been here, but they had. Were you talking to Renee about that?'

'No one had been here. I wouldn't let anyone come in.'

Jade was sitting at the kitchen table and she shifted onto her knees and then onto her bum again. There was something about sitting at the table that made her fidgety. She was always moving around in her seat, bumping her knees against the underside of the table and making the plates and cutlery jump around.

'Cara said that gaps can make themselves invisible in real life too. Like, you can't see them walking around and stuff.'

'Well, you know that's not true. It's just their pictures where they can't be seen, they can't be in photos anymore.'

'Do you think a gap came into our house? Do you think it came in and looked at our stuff? Do you think it was there but we just couldn't see it, like a ghost?'

I sighed. 'You know Donna? Donna at the school office? She's gone and you see her every morning, right?'

'Yeah, but just some of them, Mum. Some of them can do it, that's what Cara said.'

I grabbed my keys off the bench. 'Come on, let's go get an ice cream.'

My distraction worked and Jade jumped up and started hopping up and down on one foot.

We drove the couple of blocks to the dairy, Jade wondering aloud about what ice cream she was going to get.

As we pulled up, I saw that something was wrong. There were no signs on the footpath and the front doors were shut.

'What's happened, Mum?' Jade asked. 'Why aren't the lights on?'

We got out of the car and went up to the shop. Among the signs for Coke and chips there was a small bit of paper taped up to the inside of the door.

Jade tugged my hand. 'What does it say, Mum?'

I scanned it quickly, then read aloud, 'Dear Valued Customers, we regret to inform you that a member of our family has gone. We are closing the shop until further notice while we look after them.

We thank you for your continued custom and hope we will return to business soon.'

'Vikram has gone?' Jade asked.

'Maybe Vikram, maybe just someone in his family.'

Jade tugged on my hand. 'Do you think he has disappeared too? Do you think he's one of the ones that you can't see, in real life?'

'Jade!' I raised my voice. 'That isn't what happens! It's just photos! They are still here!'

Jade looked up at me, her face crumpling. When she spoke, her voice came out in a whine. 'I don't like it when you shout at me.'

I looked at Vikram's sign and then down the empty street.

'I'm sorry,' I said, crouching down, 'shall we try somewhere else?'

She nodded and reached out for my hand.

Vikram's dairy was the first shop we saw that closed. In the months after, more and more shops shut, the hairdresser, the baby supplies store, the beauty therapy place. People said they needed to care for family members who had gone, and that their businesses were facing discrimination, threats, and harassment. The community patrol was out all the time.

A voice played on TV. 'This is not something we can control,' he said. 'People need to protect themselves. Gaps have rights too.'

We were advised against holding events. They said it was to protect those who were still present from the 'potential threat' of going out.

The A&P show was cancelled, and the school's winter fair. The library closed while the city council assessed how to 'most effectively manage its services, in light of recent events', or something like that.

I read reports about gaps massing at hospitals in Auckland, seeking medical treatment, demanding to see doctors. There were violent scenes in emergency departments. One gap attacked a nurse and smashed a window before security brought them down.

The director of the hospital appeared on the news. 'There are serious mental health considerations about going out that need to be addressed. People can become unstable and violent. In many cases, their sense of self has completely collapsed, and they're looking for answers. We're doing the best that we can, but with limited resources.'

I didn't buy Jade a new winter coat. I got the small block of cheese. I stocked up on tins of baked beans and pumpkin soup at the back of the cupboard. At night, after Jade was asleep, I kept checking that the doors were locked and the windows were shut. After I'd looked for the fourth time, I'd go into Jade's room and watch the rise and fall of her breathing.

And I took photos of her. I took photos of her face, up close, her closed eyes, her tangled hair, how it curled a little bit around her ears. I took photos of her hands, floppy with sleep, her fingernails.

Then I went to bed and scrolled through these photos, and all the photos I'd taken of Jade during the day. Jade outside school, Jade at the supermarket, Jade on the front doorstep, Jade at the kitchen table, Jade on the couch. Sometimes I'd fall asleep while I was looking at these photos, and I'd wake up with my phone on the bed next to me, battery dead, screen blank, and the real Jade crawling into bed next to me.

20.

It's only now, as I write this down and piece things together, that I can bring back the moments that I've tried not to think about. I'd forced myself to forget things, certain events, because I knew they put me in danger, but I can see now that they are part of this picture, of what happened to me and Jade.

Even before people started going out and the world changed, I'd blocked things out. I was scared. I felt the shaky energy of what I could do and it freaked me out.

Here's one moment that I've tried not to think about.

One afternoon, when I was about sixteen, I wandered into the lounge to find Dad sitting in his chair. It was quiet, no one else was around, and he didn't have anything with him, not his braille, or his radio, or his computer, any of the things that he used to keep busy and connected. He looked so alone, so still, so trapped inside his dark world. My heart ached.

'Hey, Dad,' I said loudly, breaking the silence, though he would have heard me coming down the hall and into the room.

'Hi,' he said, his blank eyes turning towards me.

I flopped down on the couch. 'Do you want me to do the paper for you?' I asked, picking up the newspaper.

'Go on then,' he said.

I liked describing the newspaper for Dad. I liked doing the images, but I also really got into the words, I'd read what they said, and also describe different fonts and styles of lettering, and the way they looked. The words could sometimes be just as good as the images, to colour, to make an image out of.

I flicked the paper open and, leaning back into the couch, started with the image on page three, it was a white middle-aged man with his arms crossed, standing with a rickety wharf behind him that stretched out into the ocean. He was worried about something going on at the port in Tauranga. Next page. An ad for Countdown, stacks of oranges, clipped out against a bright white background, Tararua butter, on special for $5.50, yellow, a solid blocky rectangle, the packaging with red lines, the emerald-green frame of the ad around the edge of the page.

I don't know why it happened on that day and not on others. I remember that I was talking quickly, colouring at speed, like I had learnt to do when working on the music videos. An ad for a funeral home, four women half turned towards the camera, all wearing black blazers, arms firmly at their sides, straight hair. The printing was slightly off, so the red of their lips was smudged, bleeding across the page onto their cheeks. *Bay Funeral Directors, Here to support you and your whānau in their time of grief.*

On the next page there was a photo of a woman in a supermarket, pushing a trolley, her arm raised to take an item off the shelf. It was a stock photo, the woman's expression was calm, her gaze unfocussed. The cans on the shelves were bold in primary-colour labels of red and green, but there was no writing on them, no brand names, nothing to identify them. The supermarket could be anywhere, with its gleaming white floor and tidy shelves.

I coloured in the shelves, and the walls, and the words of the article all around the image, its caption, and I was colouring in the items in the trolley when I noticed the woman's face start to disappear. It was only the smallest change, and I wouldn't have noticed unless I was so involved in the image, pressed right up against it. As the words were coming out of my mouth, the woman's face became slightly transparent, and behind I could see another row of shelves, with their blank packages and cans, become visible. The woman was still there, but she had faded, become see-through.

I threw the newspaper down and stood up, my heart thudding and my palms suddenly sweaty.

'What is it?' asked Dad, worried. 'Was it in the paper?'

'I… I just realised that I have a thing with Miri. Now, actually. Sorry, I've got to go. I'll come back and do some more later.'

I left, went to my bedroom, and sat on my bed, head in my hands. I knew that I had done something new and caused that woman to fade. I had felt the power of the words on the tip of my tongue. If I had kept going, colouring all the things around her, she would've gone out. I'd felt the rhythm of it, felt it building up.

This was way before anyone had gone out. I was sixteen, maybe seventeen, and I tried to pretend it hadn't happened.

I didn't colour for Dad for ages. He kept asking me and I made up excuses. I said I had to meet someone, or I was too tired. I stayed in my room on Sunday mornings so I wouldn't have to colour the music videos for him.

But I felt like shit. It was our thing, me and Dad. Dad needed it to stay in touch with the world, to feel like he was among things and people and colours and life. So I started again, but I was a lot more careful. I went very slowly, to begin with. I kept an eye on the people in the images, made sure they stayed clear and present and seen. I didn't go too deeply, or too closely. I needed to be able to stop at any moment.

I knew Dad could sense things were different, that I was leaving things out, giving him an edited version, but he didn't say anything, and neither did I.

21.

Paul Irons. I hadn't heard of him before, but as soon as he went out, his voice was everywhere, on TV, on the radio, playing out of Facebook and Instagram. Hearing his voice takes me immediately back to that time, when we were on the precipice, waiting, watching, unprepared for how out of control everything got.

Paul Irons was a preacher from Auckland. I think he'd had a bit of a following before he went out, was in charge of a big church somewhere, but now he was all over social media.

After he went out he became a force of nature. He thought that being a gap was what 'God intended'. He was always saying that. 'This is what God intended for us, this is God's true design for humanity.' He was pure, he said, and 'uncorrupted by the shadow of images that surround every person in the modern world'.

Jade asked me, one day, in the car, 'Mum, what's 'manifest error'?'

I looked at her in the rear-view mirror, strapped in her booster seat. 'What? Manifest error? Where'd you hear that?'

'I heard that man on the radio. He said that worshipping images was in manifest error. That man that we always hear, you know, with that crazy voice.'

It was a crazy voice. Deep and rumbly and persistent. I didn't know what 'manifest error' meant but it was exactly the kind of thing Paul Irons was always saying. He said that images had corrupted us and that it was only after he had gone that he was able to truly understand the word of God, and that he could be a mouthpiece for that word.

Gaps flocked to him. They loved him. He told them that they were pure and true and real. Someone rich gave him a plot of land in Central Otago to build a bigger church and a centre for gaps who wanted to be near him. It was called Purity. Irons was always on the radio, saying, 'We call all those who seek the truth to come to Purity and learn about the future that God has planned for the world.' Gaps would learn about the truth of their new state, he said. They would learn what it meant and how they could 'harness their new power to make change in the world'.

Irons was always saying 'power' and 'purity' and 'energy'. What could gaps do that we didn't know about?

On the news there were interviews with people who lived in the small town near Purity. 'It's not right,' one man said, 'them coming in here and building that big place. Shouldn't let them get all together like that. Nothing good will come of it.'

Another woman said, 'Well, we can't see what they're up to, can we? Can't go in unless you're one of those… gaps. Can't see them and can't control them.'

Irons ignored any criticism. He kept on calling gaps to Purity, saying that it was a place that had been 'freed from the tyranny of the image', a place where 'people lived in the full glory of the present'. And it grew and grew, thousands of gaps moved there, and there were buildings quickly built to accommodate them. They took lots of the kids who had gone out too. Parents dropped their kids off there, or moved in, scared and freaking out about their gone kid and what they should do.

Irons clearly had money behind him, rich gaps supporting him. I saw images of the centre taken from above. It had rows and rows of buildings, all arranged around a central meeting area, where the community apparently met every morning.

Other countries began to build their own versions of Purity, places where gaps gathered and lived, where they felt safe and with their own kind.

It was during this time, when gaps were starting to flock to these places that I asked Mum if she'd heard anything more about Terri McKenzie. 'Have you talked to Pam recently?' I asked. 'Do you think Terri will go to one of these new centres that they're setting up for gaps?'

Mum had all her genealogy papers out on the kitchen table. She was a regular at the Whakatāne Library, going through old newspapers and stuff. She loved telling us stories about what she'd found and new people she'd added to our family tree.

She looked up, over the top of her reading glasses, to where I was standing in the kitchen. 'I don't see Pam now. She doesn't come to Weight Watchers. I texted her but she didn't reply. I thought maybe she'd, you know, gone too. They say it can run in the family.' Mum frowned and looked back down at her papers. 'It's so awful, you know,' she said quietly, as if she was speaking to herself, 'these women, going, because they're already so hard to find.'

I put a cup of tea down on the table next to her and sat down. 'What do you mean?'

'Women didn't get to sign documents, or get loans from the bank, or really *be*, in the written record. So, they're that much harder to track, to find out about. It's a real pain. Men are in reports, in the news, in property deals.'

'Easier to find, in the past,' I said.

'That's right. All the men in my research have that much more information about them, but the women, I often know hardly anything about them. It's a different history.' She sighed. 'And it's got me thinking, with the going, that, in the future, all these women who have only just become part of the picture, will disappear again, be lost.'

I laughed. 'Part of the picture.'

'Sorry, wrong choice of words. But I'm always thinking like that, how people in the future will find out about us, what they will think about what's happening.'

'They may have found a cure. People might reappear. It might only be this tiny blip, we don't know.'

'Maybe,' said Mum. 'I can't help but think that if this gets into the wrong hands, whole histories will be deleted, stories that are dangerous or just not in the mainstream. Us genies know that history can be changed, things can be lost. We see them all the time, these spaces.'

I stood up. 'I've gotta go and pick up Jade.'

Mum walked me to my car. I chucked my bag into the passenger seat and turned to see her taking photos of me. I took my phone out of my back pocket and took a few of her, photos of her, taking photos of me. We had started doing this by then, when we met up with someone, we reeled off a bunch of photos and they did the same in response. We still handed over the cards too, with our pictures, and often we did both. The more of our images that we could get out into the world, the better.

I knew how Mum felt. I wanted to take photos of Jade all day long.

Mum put her phone away and gave me a hug. She held me a moment longer than was necessary and when I stepped back, she kept hold of my shoulders. She looked tired, Mum did, old. Behind her, the garden was growing wild, long grass, bits of corrugated iron were propped up against the side of the shed.

'People are going to be lost, in all of this,' Mum said.

She pulled me close again, into a hug, and she whispered in my ear, 'Someone called again, last night, asking for you.'

I tensed.

Mum said, 'You have to be careful.'

'I know.'

'You can't colour anymore, for Dad.'

'I know.'

'He'll understand. Maybe just for a while, we'll see.'

I wanted to stay like that for a while, inside Mum's hug, protected by her. But Mum had a lot on her plate, and I didn't want to be another thing for her to worry about, so I stepped back. I took another couple of pictures of her, to show I wasn't worried, and that I had everything under control.

'I'll tell Dad,' she said, crossing her arms.

I drove away. Irons's voice was gravelly on the radio, telling me that only gaps could 'truly see the world, be in the world, understand the world. It is only gaps who can build real, meaningful connections with each other'.

What a useless daughter I am. Stop! Mum told me to stop describing things, stop giving words to things! And here I am, writing it all down. Writing about the long grass in her garden, her tired eyes, her papers strewn across the kitchen table. Stop! Stop!

It was dangerous then, but not so dangerous now, maybe. I don't know.

Can I write about myself driving to pick up Jade, that night? It feels so good to describe, to write, and to remember. I lean into the words and see myself, taking a left turn in my crappy car. Hair in a ponytail. The tiny nodding rabbit stuck to the dashboard. Blue hoodie. The back seat covered in Jade's clothes, books, and toys from McDonald's. I'm frowning and my mind is turning over, thinking about what Mum said. Stop colouring, stop bringing things up and putting them out, stop finding words for things. Switch it off. Stop it. Stop.

22.

I didn't talk to Dad about the colouring, but Mum must have, because he stopped asking me to do it.

At first, I couldn't handle it. I had to frown, bite my tongue, and physically stop myself from saying the words. I'd be looking at the newspaper, or a cereal box, or the inside of the fridge, with Dad nearby, and I'd open my mouth to begin, to start showing the world to him, then I'd remember, stop, and push all the words out of my head. Sometimes I had to leave the room, tears in my eyes. It felt so wrong. This line of words that had connected us for so long had been cut. I didn't know what to say to him, at those moments. Everything else seemed so stupid. 'Hello. How are you? What have you been up to today, Dad?' Blah blah blah.

Dad felt these moments too, but he pretended that he didn't miss the colouring, and that he didn't need it. He'd say something to fill the silence, or he'd turn on the radio, turning up the noise and static of horse racing, or Dire Straits.

I was tense. Trying not to say the wrong thing, feeling the words build up inside me. Someone was looking for me, and I didn't know who, but I sort of knew why. I tried to avoid Dad. We stayed away, didn't go round very often. But I felt bad about not helping Mum, and Jade was always pestering me to go and see her Nana and Pop. She loved it there.

I followed the news obsessively, though the internet was breaking apart and it was more and more difficult to piece together information. For every website that was working, there were three that had collapsed because of gaps in their pages. News websites, with their pages and pages of information were hard to navigate because people who had been in the background of images came forward into the main space, and interviewers in videos spoke to people who weren't there.

There were more stories about groups of gaps getting together in the Philippines, South Africa, Argentina. Some of them were rounded up and kept together in compounds, but there were breakouts, resistance. There were reports of cures, of people coming back, of pills you could take, of spells you could say to stop yourself from going.

We had to get away for a bit, get out of town. It was school holidays, so I took a week off work, bought a tank of petrol on my credit card, and Jade and I drove to Auckland, to Renee's place.

Tracey wasn't keen for us to come, at first. I could tell when I talked to Renee. It was because of the man who had come to their door and asked about me. 'It's all good,' I lied. 'I talked to them. They came here, to my place, and it was a misunderstanding, they thought that I had been at this event where lots of gaps had been. But I hadn't. They were following up on some leads, so I set them straight. I didn't have anything to do with it.'

I felt shit about lying. But I told myself that they already knew Renee was connected to us, to Jade and me. Whoever was interested in us knew where we were and knew who our friends were, so it wouldn't make any difference if we went to Renee's place. We weren't putting them in danger. That's what I told myself anyway.

We had to stop at two roadblocks on the way. Police looked through the car and took photos of us to make sure we were present. I handed over our card and let out the breath I was holding when they waved us through.

We had to sit in long queues before each checkpoint, so the drive took ages. It was late by the time we arrived, and Jade was asleep in her car seat. Renee and Tracey came out when I pulled into their driveway and helped me carry Jade to the bed that they had prepared for us, tucked in their small office.

In the morning, Jade and I heard Ari and Hugo giggling outside our door and Tracey telling them off. Jade was shy at first, but she soon warmed up, and sat down with Ari to play with a set of Duplo in the lounge.

I hugged Renee. We took photos of each other and gave each other our cards. She looked tired, her dark hair pulled back into a ponytail.

Tracey came into the kitchen and took her hand and we all stood together for a moment, before Hugo started screeching that Ari had stolen his toy and Tracey had to go and sort it out.

Later, Renee and I drove the kids down to the park. Every fence carried a sign with smiling faces looking out. There were billboards even, with the faces of whole families looking down at us, advertising their presence. People had put their signs up along the fence around the park too, anywhere there was space there were faces. Nobody seemed to be controlling it anymore. But lots of them had half come away, or had fallen off completely, so the playground was cluttered with these bits of cardboard and plastic, the grinning faces staring down into the bark around the swings and slide.

Renee and I gathered them up and made a stack in the corner of the field and I found a rock to weigh them down.

The kids invented a game about crocodiles on the swing bridge. Hugo, the littlest, ran to catch up with the older two.

Renee and I sat down on the nearby bench, took out our phones, and took photos and videos of the kids playing. Ari smiled and waved and Renee took a burst of photos. Her phone made the rapid-fire noises of a gun.

'It's not even me I'm worried about,' said Renee, 'it's them. What will happen if they go out? I read this story about a kid in Aussie who went. He was seven, maybe eight, I think. He went and then his parents forgot his name, forgot who he was. Like, they couldn't see him anymore, even in real life, they couldn't remember him. I saw this interview with them, they were just shaking their heads and they wouldn't believe it, they wouldn't believe that he was their son.'

'They have homes now, special places, I think, in Aussie, for kids like that. I think it's happened a lot,' I said.

'But how can they not know? How can they forget their kids?'

I shook my head. 'I don't know.' It's fucked. Like their brains are too connected to their phones, and if their kids aren't in their phones, they can't really see them anymore.'

Renee looked at me, and her eyes were glassy. 'I won't forget, I won't, there's no way I can.'

'I know. Me neither,' I said.

The kids ran and played and screamed. Jade was a crocodile. Hugo fell and bashed his knee. When we were bored, and they were getting tired, we herded them into the car, bribing them with ice creams.

'We'll have to go over to Newmarket, it's the closest place,' said Renee. 'Everything else is shut up.'

We drove past closed shops, their doors and walls plastered with posters of presents. I looked in the rear-view mirror at the kids. Ari and Hugo, and Jade in her car seat in the row behind, tracing something with her finger on the window. I liked seeing an image of them, even if it was just in the mirror.

We found an open dairy, while the kids took forever to decide which ice creams they wanted, the woman behind the counter handed us a stack of her cards, and we gave her ours. The owners hadn't taken down any old posters and ads, and the shop was filled with images that made no sense. Food floated about, disconnected. Ice blocks, licked by invisible tongues.

I wanted to get out of there, so I rushed the kids, made them choose quickly, and got them back onto the street. Renee and I wanted to keep the ice cream drips out of the car, so we found a bench a little way down the road and sat everyone down.

'Come on, Jade,' I said, 'don't let it melt.' Her ice cream had already started to drip down her hand.

'But what's wrong with them?' Jade asked, pointing her ice-creamy hand at a group coming towards us, but walking on the other side of the road.

'What do you mean?' I asked.

'They're weird. Look.'

A group of about four adults were walking down the road.

'They're gone,' said Jade.

I looked down at her. She ran her tongue around the edge of her ice cream, smoothing the edges.

'How do you know?' I asked.

'You can just tell,' she said, 'it's all in their bodies, they're all fuzzed up.'

Hugo was crying. He had ice cream smeared across his face and his cheeks were red with tiredness.

One of the women glanced across the road at us, and Jade raised her hand in a small wave. The group stopped and they all took their phones out and held them up, sweeping them, in one movement, across us. They were sussing us out, checking if we were present.

'Do it back to them, Mum,' said Ari. 'Check them! Get your phone!'

Renee and I looked at each other.

'I think we should head home,' said Renee. 'Mum will be back from work soon, and we've got to get dinner on.'

The kids were still halfway through their ice creams, but we hurried them into the car, where they wiped their sticky hands on the seats and dripped on their T-shirts.

Renee drove down the street, past the group. I didn't look at them.

'What do you think?' I asked quietly, after we had passed.

'Gone,' she said. 'Gone, gone, gone.'

That night, after the kids had gone to bed, we sat down in the lounge with glasses of wine.

I was tired. Stressed after the long drive and the weird day and the feeling that Tracey didn't want us to be there. I'd hoped that Auckland would be good for us, give us some space and a change of scene. But it felt like everything was closing in. Jade had been clingy all evening. She sat close to me and refused to eat her dinner and was rude to Tracey. She kept asking about the people we'd seen on the street and Renee and I gave vague answers and tried to change the subject, so she frowned at us, annoyed that we weren't giving her more information.

In the lounge that night, I let Renee describe to Tracey the people we had seen on the street.

'They seemed, kind of, confused,' Renee said, 'like they didn't know which way was up or down. Like they didn't have any purpose, they could have just kept walking forever, and never arriving anywhere, and not caring. I don't know, they just didn't look... normal.'

'It messes with your head, going,' said Tracey. She got up, halfway through her thought, left the room, and came back a moment later.

Renee looked at her, confused.

'Checked the doors' said Tracey. She finished her wine with a gulp before pouring herself another.

We sat in silence for a moment. I felt the unsaid words hovering around the room. I was putting their family in danger. A man had come to their door and asked about me. But he already knew where I was. He knew where he could find me. Why did he come to Renee and Tracey's door? Why was he circling me? He was telling me that he knew about me, that he knew what I could do. That he could find me if he wanted to. That he was waiting, watching.

I shivered and pulled my legs up to my chest, sinking into Renee and Tracey's fancy grey couch. Everything in their house was expensive. Big square pillows and those wine glasses that were huge bulbs.

'Going out makes you lose your sense of time. I think those people had kind of become disconnected. It builds up, after you've been gone for a while, which is why we're only seeing it happen now,' said Tracey. 'I read about it yesterday, in the UK, but I didn't think it had happened here yet.'

'What happened?' Renee asked.

'Groups of gaps, massing, like you said, walking together. Walking but not going anywhere, just moving around. They said they didn't know how to stop anymore, stop and be somewhere, that they couldn't connect to places anymore.'

I picked up my phone and found the article Tracey was talking about. I wanted to see these gaps, but, of course, I couldn't. I found a sound bite and turned up the volume so an English-accented voice filled the room.

'I'm just looking around, you know?' he said. 'Looking around for things. It's hard, when you're gone, to stop, and be with people, because you don't know if you're really there. You know what I mean? There's no way to really get into it, the being there, no way really to make sure you're in it. So, we're just moving around, keeping our options open, keeping it loose.'

The interviewer said something we couldn't hear because the gap paused, then continued, 'What? Oh yeah, it's better with other gaps, because they understand, they know what it's like, to go somewhere and not be able to really see, to really get into it… I can't really explain it. Like, say, if you go to a football game, you can see it all happening, right? All the goals and what not. But, if you're gone, you can see it, yeah, but you feel like you aren't really there, and you don't know if you'll be able to remember anything, once you've left the stadium, or whatever. I'm always thinking, did I really go to that place? Was I really sat there? Did I really see that thing? Parties and the like, they just seem to slip away.'

The clip finished and I put my phone down on the coffee table.

'It's happening to gaps who've been out for a while,' said Tracey. She rubbed her eyes. 'We'll see it more here now. We'll see them around, these groups.'

'What're we going to do about the kids?' asked Renee. 'They'll want to know what's going on. Hugo was freaked out.'

'They won't hurt anyone,' I said. 'They're just, like that guy said, looking for something to help them.'

'They're not hurting anyone now, but who knows what will happen in two weeks. There's going to be a fight about how to control this.' Tracey leant forward in her armchair. 'Think about it, whoever can put people out can control what people remember. They could just erase a whole event if they can find the right people and make them gaps. You can just see it, can't you? It would be so handy for people to make certain things disappear. All the people gone, gapped, easy. Nothing to see here.' Tracey swiped her hands together, as if she was wiping them clean.

'But they don't know, Trace, no one knows how to put people out, it just happens, it's random,' said Renee.

Tracey shrugged and had another sip of wine. 'We don't really know that. Things from fifty years ago, eighty, it'd be easy as to just wipe the slate clean. That photo at Tiananmen Square? Put that one man out and it's not a problem. Protests? Land claims? It could all be changed, if you knew how to make gaps. That's why they're all scrambling to figure it out.'

Tracey sat back and arched her neck.

'You're stressing me out, Trace,' said Renee.

'I'm sorry, but it's true.'

Tracey took her phone out and took a few photos of Renee and me on the couch, as a way of saying sorry.

'Look at you two lovelies,' she said. 'Old mates.'

I crawled into bed that night and watched Jade sleeping. I thought about the people we had seen on the street. They hadn't looked sad or hurt or angry. They had just looked lost, and in between, like something had been taken away from them.

Renee had taken the week off too, and we made plans for fun stuff to do with the kids. I suggested things that were cheap, or free, but Renee wanted to take them all to the zoo.

She checked her phone in the morning and said, 'It's closed!'

'How come?' I asked, relieved, thinking about my credit card.

'It just says, 'Due to the current situation we are closed until further notice.''

We looked at each other as the kids ran around the kitchen.

'Maybe some of the staff went out and they're just trying to sort out what to do,' I said.

We decided to take the kids to the mall for milkshakes instead and, I remember, when we got all the kids out of the car, through the car park, and in through the glass doors, I thought, straight away, Something's not right here.

It was the noise. It was too loud, echoing. I thought that maybe it was because of the school holidays, and there were too many excited kids, high on sugar. But then I saw that the escalator had stopped and people were running down, trying to get to the ground floor, pushing other people out of the way, and running to a shop, where a crowd had gathered outside.

We got caught up in the flow of people. I grabbed Jade's hand. Renee had Hugo and Ari on either side of her, holding them close.

It was a tech store. It was packed with people, pulling things off the shelves, pulling down posters, passing things between each other.

A man ran out of the shop, his arms filled with DVDs. Other people stuffed Bluetooth speakers into their backpacks. There was a loud crash as a TV fell off a shelf and splintered across the floor. Luckily, no one seemed to be hurt, they just moved around the mess of plastic and glass, and kept grabbing, shoving, and taking photos.

We hustled the kids away.

'What's happening, Mum?' Ari asked.

'We should go,' I said to Renee.

She nodded. 'We're going to go somewhere else for milkshakes, okay?' she said to the kids.

They all nodded silently, scared.

There was a group of security guards standing by the doors, huddled in conversation, their radios crackling. I tapped one on the shoulder as we hurried past, and he looked up.

'What's going on?' I asked.

He was pissed off. 'Kim Kardashian's gone.'

In the car park, a group of about twenty gaps walked towards us in between the cars, heading in the direction of the mall. A car tried to back out of its spot and all the gaps turned, as a group, to look at it, but they didn't move any faster to let it out, they just stared and stared and kept walking, as if they knew the car was there, but didn't matter to them and they could go wherever they wanted, they didn't have to wait for things, or worry about things, or follow the rules.

We bundled the kids into the car and quickly drove home. Renee frowned at the road, her hands gripping the steering wheel.

'Where are we going?' Jade asked. 'What were those people doing? Are we still getting milkshakes?'

Hugo started singing 'Jingle Bells' at the top of his voice.

We made it home, got out a bag of chips for the kids, and turned the TV on.

In the kitchen, we checked our phones. The news was everywhere. A video popped up of a scene from *Keeping Up with the Kardashians*. Kourtney argued with an empty space. I tried to open Instagram but it didn't work.

On another app, I read about looting in Spain, and in the UK. People had stormed department stores and run off with TVs and computers and clothes. The reports said that the Kim had gone a few hours ago and major websites and social media had collapsed because of high traffic. People searching. Bots crawled the web, looking for images of her.

We stayed at home for the rest of the day, taking turns with the kids, and keeping an eye on the news when we could. The apps on our phones stopped and started. Websites came and went. Renee turned the radio on but kept the volume low so the kids wouldn't hear. There was too much traffic, too many people on the internet and everyone had gone crazy taking pictures. Everyone everywhere was taking as many photos as they could. It was a flood, too much, a tidal wave. Servers couldn't keep up and they crashed. People lost all their backed-up files and started taking more photos to make up for this sudden loss.

I read about large groups of gaps, now wandering around in lots of different countries. They wanted to be closer together. They said that they needed to be with other gaps who understood what it was like to have gone. 'Only other gaps can know what I'm searching for,' a gap on the radio said. 'We are in this together.'

It was a long day. In the late afternoon, Renee signalled to me that she'd managed to get through to her mum on the phone, and she went into her bedroom to talk. I took the kids into Hugo and Ari's room to give Renee some space, and we built a fort out of pillows and blankets.

We squished inside, the four of us, and lay down on our bed of pillows. The blanket above us was bright blue and all our faces and arms looked blue.

'We're in the sea,' said Ari, looking at his hands.

'I'm a giant squid,' said Hugo.

I could hear Renee's voice, urgent in the bedroom next door.

What were the gaps searching for? I wondered, as I lay on my back. Why did they look so lost?

I turned onto my side and let the kids climb over me. I liked being in that small blue cave with them, the four walls around us, the saggy blanket on top, keeping us safe. Our world was muffled and soft.

Jade whispered in my ear, 'We're down in the Mariana Trench.'

'Jade,' I said, 'your face is so jade!'

She giggled, pressed her face into the pillows, and said something that I couldn't hear.

I heard the front door slam. Tracey, home from work. Then, Renee's and Tracey's raised voices in their bedroom, arguing. Another door slammed.

When the kids got bored, we climbed out through the gaps in the blankets. Tracey was in the kitchen. She bent down and pulled Ari and Hugo close.

'Mum, we saw so much smashing today,' said Hugo.

'Yeah, TV smashing,' said Ari.

Tracey made eye contact with Renee, who was standing by the sink. 'Those weren't very nice people, were they?' she said. 'It's not good to break things, especially other people's things.'

She pulled them close again. 'Do you guys want to watch a bit of TV while we get dinner ready?'

'Yay!' they said, running into the lounge.

After the kids were asleep, we sat down in the lounge to watch the news and talk about what had happened. There were more scenes of looting, fires, and police trying to restore order.

'There were police on my train,' said Tracey, 'checking IDs.'

We put the TV on mute and sat in silence. We watched the silent images of people pulling clothes off shelves and breaking windows. Gaps made the footage glitchy and warped. Some duvets and microwaves and speakers moved by themselves, as if by magic, because the person holding them had gone. They floated around, gripped by invisible hands. Cricket bats hovered and swung by themselves at windows and broken glass fell to the ground.

The growing number of gaps put pressure on video footage. We were seeing it more and more, on the news, on social media. In those early riots, objects moved around by themselves, but the presents were also pushed and jostled by gaps so that they had this strange way of moving. Their legs fidgeted, and they dodged invisible obstacles, so it looked like they were dancing, or struggling against a strong wind.

Tracey paced the lounge, scrolling through her phone.

'We should go home,' I said. 'This is crazy.'

Renee looked up from her phone and said, 'You don't have to go.'

Tracey cleared her throat. 'I think she should.'

'I need to check on Mum and Dad. They'll be scared. And Guy won't be any help,' I said.

'Yeah, my mum's going to come up from Kāwhia,' said Renee. 'She's going to stay here for a while until things settle down.'

Tracey nodded. 'They'll stop people moving around soon,' she said. 'They'll try to keep everyone in their place so that the gaps can't organise. Things won't settle down, this is going to get a lot worse before it gets any better.' She paused, then said, 'Fuck! I can't believe the kids saw that today. They're not going to forget. Ari asked me, just before, in bed, 'Will gaps come and smash our windows, Mum?' What can I say? We don't know what they're doing, wandering around in packs. Where are they going?'

'Presents are smashing stuff too,' Renee said.

'But it'll be the gaps that get away with it,' said Tracey. 'The presents are all on CCTV and they'll be tracked down and charged. The gaps can just run off with their new TVs and do whatever the hell they want! It's not right! Something needs to be done.'

I hardly slept that night. Jade lay next to me, and I watched her for hours, worrying that she was getting a cold. I must have dropped off at some point because I woke up and checked my phone at 5 am. The house was silent. Birds chirped in the garden and the light beneath the curtains slowly grew stronger.

I thought about the people grabbing stuff in the tech store. The bright yellow signage falling to the floor. The broken glass crunching underfoot. People pushing, elbowing through the door. The force of the gaps and their invisible pressure on the presents.

I heard myself telling Dad about it. He was in his chair, in the lounge at home, listening close. I could give everything its right word, dig into the scene, draw it for him. I could be so specific. And he relished it, the detail. Colours, clothes, the materials of the things in the world, their roughness, their shininess, their yellowness. I could describe for him particular faces. One woman with dyed red hair, pulled high on her head in a ponytail, leaving the shop with a stack of records clutched against her chest. Another woman, in a black puffer jacket, looking at her phone at the same time as she pushed a pair of grey speakers into her backpack. She was still staring at her phone as she left the shop, oblivious to the people bumping and pushing her.

As I lay in that bed, in Tracey's office, I went over the scene and its words. I wanted to tell Dad but I knew that I couldn't. I felt the clot of these words inside me, trying to get out. And I feel the release now, typing them out. They needed somewhere to go, and it's good to get them down on this page, all of the things I remember and their words, all of the things that I had to stop colouring for Dad.

In the bed, Jade rolled over and I watched her wake up. She yawned and scrunched up her nose as if she had smelt something bad, then her eyelids opened, and her pupils shrank as they adjusted to the light. She blinked. Grey eyes.

We looked at each other across the blue pillowcase.

'Hi, Mum,' she said.

We left Auckland in the afternoon. Renee hugged me and Tracey stood on the doorstep behind her, arms folded.

I told Jade that we had to get back to Whakatāne because Nana needed some help with Pop. She didn't believe me, but she nodded and sat quietly in her car seat.

I half-filled the car with petrol in Papakura. I was sure that my credit card would be rejected and I watched the terminal processing, my heart thudding until it went through. I bought Jade a packet of chips and a Chupa Chup and took them back to the car.

My tiredness caught up with me on the drive home. My eyes felt rough, sandpapery. I put Hauraki on the radio and sang along to crappy songs to wake myself up. We played I Spy, and then Jade told me a long story about a mermaid who lived in a fountain and grew legs at nighttime so that she could walk around.

'Where did she go?' I asked.

'Just to the supermarket to get some fish,' said Jade. 'She likes fish so much because she is a fish.'

I glanced at her in the rear-view mirror. Jade. Here she is. Her window is open a couple of centimetres so that her brown hair flies up around her face. Her grin. Her two bottom teeth, in the middle, overlapping slightly.

We had to stop at three checkpoints and wait for ages in the queues. I wound down my window and a policewoman leaned in to look at my driver's licence, check my licence plate, and take two photos of me and two photos of Jade.

'New policy,' said the policewoman at the first checkpoint. 'Need to keep track of where everyone is going. You saw the looting?' She shook her head. 'Terrible stuff, awful. It's the gaps, they think they can get away with it, but we'll soon put a stop to that.'

She waved us through.

Jade was asleep by the time we reached the last checkpoint. Her head lolled sideways onto her car seat. Her pink T-shirt was rumpled and there were chip crumbs on the seat all around her.

The officer took two quick photos, click, click. Jade asleep. Jade when she was six. I think about the lost images of her on other people's phones. Even the moments when she was caught in the background of another photo, because there must have been lots of images of her like that, running on the beach, or at the pools. What holes did she make in the internet when she went? Do other people notice the spaces where Jade was, in their photos? Do they think, I'm sure there used to be a little kid in this. She must've gone. Stink. How sad.

The petrol light was flashing when we finally arrived back home. I pulled into the driveway, thinking, I'll deal with that tomorrow.

I pulled Jade, half-asleep and floppy, out of the car, through the front door, and tumbled her into bed. She was asleep again quickly, so I walked through the small house, looking to see if anything had been moved, if anyone had been here, if anyone was still here. But the house was silent and everything was in its right place.

I wanted to feel like we had made it, through the checkpoints, and were now in our safe place. But I didn't feel that way. Our house felt small and shaky. I turned on all the lights except Jade's, and stood by her doorway, watching her sleep.

23.

Maybe there were some people who knew how humans would react to going out, how it would mess with their heads and make them crazy. Maybe there were warnings. Alarm bells. There must've been. But I can't remember now if I heard any anxious predictions about how it would change people, how it would change the world.

Maybe I heard but I didn't really take it in? Maybe I thought it wouldn't make that much difference? That someone would figure out a cure and everything would go back to normal. Gaps would go back to their families, their jobs, and they would return to all their precious images. They would reappear on their phones and computers and tablets, as if they had never gone, as if it had just been a horrible dream, where they had lost, for a moment, who they really were.

There was more talk about a cure. Scientists in South Africa had apparently discovered one. Then scientists in Sweden. Then a big research project in London was 'on the brink of a major discovery'.

Meanwhile, people kept going out and the world kept falling apart.

After we got back from Auckland there was still another week of school holidays and I had to go back to work. I had no idea who could look after Jade.

Mum and Dad could do a couple of days, but Mum was working three days a week, and Dad couldn't take care of Jade on his own, it was too much for him.

I sent Ange Reweti a text but she didn't reply, so Jade and I went down the road to see if they were in. All the curtains were closed. We knocked on the door, but no one answered.

Jade ran round the back to jump on the trampoline, and I stood on the doorstep stressing about what I was going to do.

The guy from the house next door poked his head over the fence and said, 'They've gone to Wairoa.'

'For the holidays?' I asked, taking a photo of him as I walked over.

He took a picture of me too, and then said, 'Longer, I think. Went to their marae. Ben's folks are out there.' Brian paused, and then he said, 'I think Ben went.'

'Gone?'

'Yeah, I mean, I don't know for sure, they were keeping it real quiet. But did you notice things were a bit weird last week?'

I hadn't noticed. I'd been picking up Jade after I finished work and not noticing anything was up. I felt bad. I was too wrapped up in my own worries.

'We've just been in Auckland,' I said, hoping this might explain why I hadn't kept an eye on the people who looked after my kid every weekday.

'Yeah, well, I kept seeing him, Ben, wandering around at night, leaving the house at weird times. He'd walk down the street and back, not really going anywhere, just kind of... walking. The lights were on in the house at weird times.'

'Did you come over and talk to them?' I asked,

'Nah. It's their business really, isn't it? I didn't want to be a sticky beak. I saw him at the supermarket, and he was chatty enough. But there was nothing in his trolley, even though he'd been walking up and down for ages. I'd seen him. You know? It was strange. He didn't picture me, at the supermarket, and, you know, if someone doesn't, to you, sometimes you don't want to back, because you don't want them to feel bad. You know?'

'Yeah, I know what you mean. Did you look in your phone?'

'Yeah, I did, after a bit. Even though it felt sort of wrong, like I was spying. I knew I had some photos of the street Christmas barbie and I can't see Ben in there. But I don't know if it was because he wasn't in the photo in the first place, or if he had gone.'

'Mum! Come see this!' Jade shouted from the backyard.

The neighbour looked down the driveway, then said, 'Someone said they're being rounded up now.'

'Gaps?'

'Yeah, cos of the looting, they've gone too far.'

'But presents were doing it too,' I said.

'But the gaps started it, cos they aren't on CCTV they think they can just do whatever they want. They're being rounded up until someone figures out how to bring people back. Maybe that's why Ben got out of town. Wairoa is pretty far away from anywhere. Easy to stay under the radar.'

'Mum! Come! I'm doing it!' Jade again.

I went and watched Jade do flips on the tramp. At the time, I didn't see her. I just made supportive noises and stared in her general direction. The Rewetis had left, Ben had gone, and I was fucked. I was sorting through all the possibilities of who could take care of Jade after school.

Now, as I write this, I stop and picture Jade in my mind, and how she looked on the tramp. I see the moment I didn't see at the time. Her face, so serious and focussed before she flips. Her arms at her sides, steadying her bounces. Her orange T-shirt flips up as she spins round and lands on her back, legs in the air. Here she is.

'Look, Mum!' she says, springing onto her feet. 'I'll do it again, take a video!'

I sent another text to Ange that evening, *I heard you're at the east coast. Hope everything is okay. Let me know if you need anything done at the house while you're away.*

I was surprised when she replied quickly, *needed to get back to whānau. Ben has gone. am worried. doesn't know where things begin anymore.*

Then, another text, a couple of minutes later, *Sorry bout Jade. sorry didn't tell you. I hope you find someone to look after her. not sure when we'll be back.*

Doesn't know where things begin anymore, Ange had texted, and I began to see much more of this on the news. Gaps said that they had lost their sense of time, of where they were up to in the day, or what they were supposed to be doing.

A gap on the radio said, 'I can't look back, you know, at pictures of myself, so it makes it hard to look forward. Or to think what the next day will look like, or the next hour, or the next minute even. And there are no reminders from my phone, of stuff from before, stuff that kept me on track. Like, oh yeah, remember that thing that happened. I'm just, a bit, lost…'

'It wasn't always like this,' another gap said. 'It didn't start out like this when I first went. But it's got worse. I keep thinking it's Saturday, but then it's actually Wednesday and I've forgotten to pick my kid up from school again. It messes with you. It messes with your head.'

Things got out of hand at this massive Justin Bieber concert in Auckland. I watched clips online. The footage was taken from a camera above the stadium, maybe it was a drone. I want to write that the crowd was 'filled' with gaps, but that's not the right word. The crowd was empty because of how many gaps were there. Pockmarked by them. And I saw again the pressure of their invisible bodies, pushing and jostling, they were there and not there. The presents moved sharply, their bodies making awkward angles and sudden flinches when they were pushed by the gaps, or when they had to dodge around them. Sometimes the presents looked like they were in pain, as if something had bitten them.

On stage, Bieber sang and danced but he seemed confused. On either side of the stage there were two big screens that showed Bieber and his band. They looked normal enough, but when the cameras zoomed back out to show the crowd, the gaps showed. And there were so many of them, maybe half of the audience had gone. So, on screen, the stadium looked empty and sad.

Bieber's eyes kept flicking over to the screens, and to the row of monitors along the stage in front of him, which must have shown the same footage. The two things were so different, the scene in front of him of the packed stadium, and the half-filled space on the screens, with the presents moving in their weird way, as if there were gusts of wind pushing them from every angle.

Bieber got through the first couple of songs but he looked more and more stressed and he kept looking back at his band for reassurance. He forgot the words and didn't come in at the right times.

Of course, lots of the presents had their phones out and were filming the gig. They must have realised too, from their phones and from the big screens, how many of the audience were gaps. They were everywhere, all around, surrounding them.

After the third song, Bieber left the stage. The band looked around at each other and kept playing what was filler music. Strobe lights flashed. The screens flanking the stage changed from showing the crowd to images of huge, animated words, swirls, and fireworks.

For several minutes, Bieber didn't reappear, and the energy of the crowd started to shift. The presents started moving so that they were gathered in the middle of the stadium. They wanted to get away from the gaps, but they couldn't tell, in the arena, who was present and who had gone. Lots of them had their phones out, but they'd stopped filming the stage and had started filming the people around them, trying to suss out who was present.

The backing band played on. The music looped around and around. Fights broke out between presents and gaps. On my Facebook feed, I watched the presents wrestle with their invisible enemies under the lights of the arena, filmed by other people at the gig.

No one made an announcement, nobody said that Bieber wasn't coming back to the stage, but the crowd started breaking up and drifting away. Footage on the news showed lines of presents leaving from the exits, moving down the concourse and out into Auckland.

Later, in an interview, Bieber said, 'I've got nothing against them, gaps, but I didn't know there was going to be so many and it just kind of got to me, that I couldn't see them on the screens. People think they're just for the audience, but I use those screens to keep, you know, myself in the right place.'

The interviewer pressed him a bit and asked again why he didn't come back.

Bieber replied, 'It was just wrong, all those people, not there. I could see them looking at me, but I couldn't feel them there. And then, on the screens, they weren't there. I wasn't getting anything from those pictures of the crowd, no energy, and I need that, as a performer, that's how I get going, how I get the gig going, keep it going.'

Other events were canned. Concerts, rugby games, conferences, parties. Organisers announced that events were 'untenable in the current environment' and that they couldn't 'ensure the safety of audiences'.

As more and more people went, it became harder to understand what was happening overseas. There were other big events that became chaotic. Political rallies and an election in Brazil where gaps were stopped from voting and where there were violent protests. Gaps were hard to control, but they could also be suppressed. They couldn't be imaged, and their anger couldn't be shared. There were no images for them to rally around around, and it made it difficult for them to organise themselves.

In Brazil, there were reports of police violence against gaps and that they were being barred from shops, schools, and other basic services.

But we couldn't see them in the news. We couldn't see the protests or the gaps gathering to demand the return of their rights.

I watched a clip of the Brazilian police at a gap rally. The police stood with their batons and visors against an invisible crowd. I tried to imagine the gaps facing them. I tried to imagine how angry they were, how desperate. But I couldn't. It was impossible, beyond what I could see, in my mind's eye. I watched the police join their shields together and push against the mass of gaps. The police jostled and leant back and shook under the pressure of the gaps shoving against them. I watched a policeman raise his baton and lay into an invisible person, his face focussed and frowning.

It was horrible, but I couldn't register it, take it in. I read about the situation in Brazil, listened to the news, but I didn't feel any real empathy with the Brazilian gaps because I couldn't see them. Their cause felt lost. It slipped away from me, there wasn't anything that I could hold on to, to understand. I needed to see it.

I remember, it was late at night, and I was on the couch watching a reality show where people battled against each other in a huge gym. There were pools of plastic balls and conveyor belts and massive walls to climb over. A crowd of people sat around the arena and, behind them, flame throwers shot bursts of fire high into the air.

It was a battle, the finale of the whole series, but all the participants had gone, except for one woman. She bashed invisible people with her huge, padded paddle. She pushed them out of the way in the pool pit and clawed at them as they tried to pull her down from the wall. Her face was grim, set in a frown, and she sweated and fought with all the gaps around her.

A sound behind the couch made me jump. I turned and Jade was standing in the doorway, looking at the TV. Her eyes were half open. I wasn't sure if she was properly awake or sleep walking.

She stepped forward. 'What is she doing?' she asked, pointing at the TV.

'It's a competition,' I said.

She came around the couch and snuggled into me.

Here she is. I see her now. Look. Jade in her PJs, hair messy around her face. She is holding her toy lion. She rests her head against me and tucks her free hand into the folds of my jersey. I stroke her dark hair. I want to keep her like this forever.

'Who is she fighting against?' Jade asked.

'Everyone else is gone,' I said.

'Gaps all around?'

'Yeah, just her.'

Jade's voice was sleepy. Was she even awake?

'Then why is she still fighting?' she asked.

'It's in the past. This has already happened, before the other people went.'

The woman was on a red path in the middle of the arena and she kept running into something, or someone, who was pushing her back. She bounced off this force, landing on her butt and scrambling back up again.

'But why does she keep going?'

'They are still there, to her, the other people, she can see them.'

'In the past?'

'Yes, she could see them, when she was there. It's only now, that we can't.' Saying it aloud was always so stupid, so weird.

Jade said nothing and when I looked down, she was asleep, the light from the TV flickering on her face.

On the programme, the woman ran up onto the final podium and jumped up and down, grinning. Red lights flashed. A gap must have joined her because she put her arms around someone, wrapping herself around a space, an emptiness that pushed her slightly off balance, almost tilting her off the small winner's platform.

24.

Bex said she'd look after Jade for the last two days of the school holidays. Thank Christ. Jade and I made lolly cake to take round and Jade packed some of her favourite toys to share with Cara.

When I picked Jade up after work on Friday, Bex said, 'I heard they're going to close the school.'

'What? Why?' I asked.

'The ministry are worried about the kids being in groups. They are going to put everything online until the gaps are sorted out.'

We were watching the two girls jump on the trampoline.

'What about the gaps, online, I mean, they won't be there,' I said.

Bex shrugged.

Two weeks later, Jade's school said it was closing. All the schools were closing. They said it was a temporary measure, for 'the safety of learners across the country, and for the safety of teaching staff'.

By then, lots of kids had gone and schools had been trying to figure out how to manage gap students. Some had set up special classes or recruited new teachers. Others just kept going as if everything was the same and let the gaps and presents sort it out among themselves in the playground.

'Mum, I need a computer,' Jade said, the evening that we'd heard the news. 'I have to have a computer for school now. Mrs Davidson said so.'

I was cooking dinner. We didn't have a computer. I just used my phone and my desktop at work. I stared into the fridge. I was expecting the bill for the internet in a couple of days and I had only just enough to pay it.

I called Mum that night after Jade was asleep. 'It's totally crazy,' I said. 'Why would they put all the kids online when it's harder for them to see the gaps there? Surely they want everyone to be together so that they can at least see the gaps and make sure they're doing okay.'

'I don't think they're really thinking about gap welfare,' said Mum. 'I think they just want to get them out of the classrooms.'

'But we know that that's not how it happens now, don't we? I don't know what I'm going to do.'

'I can take Jade tomorrow,' said Mum. 'And there'll be other people in your situation too, people who have to work, so they'll have to sort something out.'

Mum and Dad had a computer that Dad had been given by the Blind Foundation. He used his screen reader and spent a lot of time on the internet, listening to sports results and reading the paper. I couldn't ask to borrow Dad's computer. He needed it and Jade would mess with it, or change some setting that was important.

Mum must've said something to Guy because he turned up the next weekend with a laptop in his backpack. He took it out and showed it to Jade and she clapped her hands and danced on her tiptoes. 'Thanks Guy!' she said.

'No worries, Jadey,' he said. 'You need one of these for school now, right?'

We took the laptop into the lounge and Guy helped set it up.

'The battery doesn't work,' said Guy, 'but she runs sweet if you keep her plugged in.'

After Guy had sorted out the Wi-Fi connection Jade begged me to watch Peppa Pig, so I found it on YouTube for her.

Guy followed me into the kitchen. 'Where'd you get that from then?' I asked. 'Or maybe I shouldn't ask.'

'Thanks, Guy, thanks for getting a laptop for my kid when I really needed one,' Guy said, pretending he was hurt.

'Yeah, well. I'm just not used to stuff turning up magically when I need it.'

'Magic Guy, that's what they call me.' Guy wiggled his fingers in the air and smirked.

I hated asking him, but I said, 'Can you stay here for a bit? I really have to go to the supermarket. We have nothing to eat.'

'Sure, sure, of course, sis. I can stay.'

'Thanks. Just keep an eye on her, make sure YouTube doesn't take her to watch something weird.'

Guy saluted. I hated it when he did that.

I drove to the supermarket and rushed through the aisles grabbing stuff. I tried to be as quick as I could, but shopping took longer because prices were so up and down and lots of things weren't there. I stopped to check the price of bananas. Too expensive. I couldn't get tomatoes. There were no two-minute noodles. Supply chains were broken and international trade was falling apart because the situation with gaps was different in each country. Some borders were closed, and some were open. Thousands of gaps had lost their jobs.

The woman at the checkout smiled at me briefly and we pictured each other. I glanced at the photo I had taken. The woman looked tired, her hair was pulled back in a ponytail and the fluorescent lights made the skin on her nose shine.

In the car park, a policewoman was taking photos of everyone who came out and a voice repeated, over the loudspeakers, 'Gaps must identify themselves to security on arrival. Special protocols are required in-store.'

Looting and more targeted thefts kept happening across the country, especially in places where lots of people had gone. Technology shops were on high alert. Some gaps were convinced they could find themselves again, find an image of themselves, if they just got hold of the right phone or the right computer. Others were sure that it was a conspiracy, and that the government still held their images on a server somewhere, and if they could just find it, they'd come back.

Gaps stole laptops and iPads. They got together in gangs and busted into computer shops, into archives, and into government departments. They were looking for themselves. Looking for an answer. Where did they go? Could they come back? They felt as if they didn't have to follow normal rules, that they were outside of things, and they could do what they liked.

I drove back to our place, pulled into our driveway, and lugged two shopping bags into the kitchen. I found Jade still in front of You-Tube and Guy on the couch next to her, scrolling through his phone. He looked up, startled.

On the laptop, a skateboarder attempted a trick and arsed over. 'Fuck this shit!' he yelled at the camera, and the frame filled up with poo emojis.

'Guy!' I said, 'What the hell?'

I leant over and snapped the laptop closed.

'She wanted to watch some skater fails. This channel is awesome,' Guy said.

'For Christ's sake, I can't leave you with her for two minutes,' I said.

'I know that word already, Mum,' Jade said.

'See,' said Guy, 'Jade knows, eh, Jadey? That channel is sick.'

Jade looked at him and frowned.

'Oh my god, you're like a kid yourself,' I said.

Guy stood up. 'Okay, well, then I won't come round with a new computer for you two, and I won't stay here and look after Jade while you go out and do whatever it is you need to do. I'm helping you out here, Jodie. I'm the brother who comes round and gives you a hand.'

'Yeah, I'm so fucking lucky that you come round here and sit on the couch while my kid watches inappropriate videos. What an awesome babysitter you are, Guy. What a life saver.'

I stormed out of the living room and went out to the car to grab the other shopping bags. I took a moment, my head leaning against the top of the boot, to take a breath. I shouldn't swear in front of Jade. I closed my eyes, my hands gripping the handles of the last two bags. I did need Guy. That was what annoyed me so much. I needed all the help I could get.

I went through the back door into the kitchen. I was going to say sorry. But Guy was there, and he was scrolling through my phone.

I dropped the bags and lunged at him. 'What are you doing?' I hissed.

He leant back, holding my phone above his head and out of reach.

'Give it to me!'

He grinned, holding me off with his free hand. 'Now, now, Jodes. Don't get all feisty. I was just looking for a photo of Miri. She hasn't been around, and I want to remember what she looks like.'

'Miri? What? Guy, give me my phone. I'm serious!'

He had my photos open and was still scrolling through with his thumb. Did he know my passcode?

'The thing is, Jodes, that Miri's gone, hasn't she? She's a gap.'

I stepped back and crossed my arms. I wasn't going to let him bait me. I heard Jade in the lounge, watching more crap on YouTube.

'So what if she has? So what if Miri's gone? Have you seen the news recently? You may have noticed that she's not the only one? It's not like she's special.'

Guy moved to stand by the back door, still holding my phone tight against his chest. He wasn't looking at it now but was staring at me from across the small room.

'Guy,' I said, taking a deep breath, trying to keep my voice calm, 'no one cares about Miri, just give me my phone back.'

I held out my hand.

'But here's the thing…' he trailed off.

'What's the thing? Tell me, what's the thing?'

'Miri has gone, but she went ages ago. When you guys were, like, twenty-two.'

'What are you talking about? There's no way Miri could have gone then.'

'No, she did.' He pointed a finger at me. 'And you did it, Jodie, didn't you? You made her go.'

'I made her go?' My heart was thudding. I was trying to keep it together. 'What're you talking about? How would I do that? Why would I do that?' My hand was still held out, palm upward. 'Can you give me my phone back?'

'Don't try and act all innocent. I know what you can do.'

I laughed. 'What I can do? I'd like to know too, what can I do? Just what exactly is this secret?'

'You can put people out. You put Miri out and you've probably put other people out too. It's cos of your colouring for Dad. You learnt how to do something… something when you were doing all that for Dad when we were kids. Or maybe Dad taught you, I don't know, maybe you figured it out together.'

'You sound crazy. I have no idea what you're going on about.'

'Don't give me that, Jodie. Don't fucking patronise me.' His voice was tight, vicious. 'You were always doing that, with Dad, talking to me like I didn't know shit, keeping your secrets, the two of you.'

'There's no secret, Guy. You're paranoid.'

'Who knows about it then? No one fucking knows! Of course it was a secret. But I know, and it's different now, with all this shit going down. There are people who want to know what I know.' He pointed at his chest.

We stared at each other. I heard Katy Perry singing through the crappy speakers of the laptop in the lounge. I thought, How has Jade managed to find Katy Perry by herself? Does she know how to type words into Google?

I said quietly, 'Who wants to know what you know? Who have you been talking to?'

He shook his head and put my phone down on the bench. I didn't move. We both stared at it. A photo was open on the screen. It was Jade at the beach. Guy looked like he was about to say something and then he turned and went out the back door.

I grabbed my phone and shoved it in my pocket. What did Guy know? Who was that man I had seen him with? I needed to talk to Dad, but I couldn't think what I'd say. We had talked to each other so much, but there was so much more that we hadn't said, so much that we couldn't say aloud.

Here's the truth. I'm writing it down here. I didn't know what I had done to Miri. Had I made her go? I remembered that evening in the car park by the beach. All the words rushed back from that colouring, 'thick hunks of seaweed', 'the navy-blue water', 'the horizon's thin line'. Those words were so easy, so ready to be used, rising up around Miri, blocking her out, pushing her back. I didn't have to think about it.

I remembered the way she had smiled at me afterwards, a strange smile, as if she had shaken something off, broken away. Did she go? Did she get a new freedom, away from the eyes of men?

'Mum!'

I jumped. Jade was calling me from the lounge and I went through to her.

'Mum,' she said, 'look, I think Katy's gone. Do you think she looks weird?'

I watched the music video for a moment. Jade was right. Katy Perry had gone, but someone had replaced her with a new Katy. Someone almost like Katy Perry sung and danced in the music videos. She was in a forest wonderland, gnomes and fairies flying around her. She wore a cupcake costume and spun around.

It was almost Katy Perry, but it wasn't her. Her face was too smooth, too serene. When she sung the corners of her mouth didn't move in the right way. They tightened, shifting upwards, but not in the right way, not in the way that would release a real voice.

'It's wrong,' said Jade. 'I don't like it.' She slumped back on the couch. 'Has she gone?'

I clicked through to another music video. It was the same thing, the fake Katy Perry with sparkles and glittery flowers pouring out of her mouth, the angles of her face not quite right, her jawline not quite distinct enough from the mass of glittery pixels behind her, her hair flicking up into a mess of distorted animation. Not quite Katy Perry. Too perfect. Not perfect enough. Too cleanly outlined. Edges fuzzy from the pixels sitting behind.

I closed the laptop.

'Will she come back, Mum?' Jade asked.

I slumped on the couch too. 'I don't know.'

'What were you shouting with Guy about?'

'You know us, sometimes we just argue. It's dumb. We get upset.'

'It was nice of him to bring the laptop.'

'Yeah, you're right, it was nice.'

I put my arm around her shoulders.

Jade asked, 'Can gaps come back? Did Katy go and then come back?'

'I don't think so, no, I think someone just made a new version of her. But because she was a gap, it doesn't look exactly like her. It didn't look right. Something about going out means there can't be real fakes, fakes that look too much like the gap, like the person.'

It was hard to explain this to Jade because I didn't know how it worked, no one did. Gaps could have their portraits painted. They could be animated, sketched, and CGI'd into existence, created by Photoshop. They could be drawn, but they couldn't be duplicated by a camera, by a phone, or anything with a lens. Any technology that showed them exactly as they were, this didn't work.

So, of course, there was suddenly massive demand for painters, for artists who could capture people and in their tiny, specific details. They could charge whatever they wanted, these artists, and the prices for portraits that I heard thrown around were insane.

Animators and developers were also recreating gaps and making them real again on the screen. I don't really know how they did it, but I think they could wire up a gap's face to see how they moved, and then use this information to create a specific animated version of them. I don't know. Back then, it didn't really work. I could always tell when it was a gap. Like this new Katy Perry and her too-smooth face and her eyes that didn't seem to focus on anything.

That night, after fighting with Guy and watching the gone Katy Perry, I got Jade into bed and paced around the house for a while, checking the locks and scrolling through scrambled news on my phone. Protests in Vietnam. Special rehabilitation centres had been set up for gaps in Russia. Further measures were being put in place to prevent people from moving around the country. Stricter monitoring was required, the news said, to ensure gaps were held accountable for their actions.

I called Dad. I pictured his phone ringing on his side table in the lounge, and him telling Siri to answer.

We chatted about the news and other small things until there was a pause. Dad was waiting to see why I had called, but I didn't know what to say. I didn't know what I really wanted to ask him. So many words had passed between us, but now I was stuck.

I told Dad about Guy and the laptop.

'Oh, that's good,' he said, 'that'll work, won't it? While they get everything sorted out.'

Dad never questioned Guy, never gave him a hard time, always thought he was doing his best.

'Yeah, well, I'm not sure where he got it from, but it seems to work.'

Another silence.

I cleared my throat. 'Listen, Dad, Guy thinks that…' I started again, 'Guy thinks that, you know, he thinks my colouring for you means that I can do things, other things. He said, just before, when he was round here, that the colouring meant something different.'

Dad said nothing.

'Dad?'

'Yes, I'm here.'

'Did you hear me?'

'Yes, I just think… I'm not sure…' he trailed off.

'I didn't stop and think that much about it, Dad, the colouring, I didn't think about it. It just became this thing we did, part of the day.'

'You could do it with your eyes closed,' said Dad.

I frowned. I didn't want to joke. I wanted someone else to help me understand what I did when I coloured. Because it was so natural to me, gathering words, naming things, listing, circling around an object to find its colours and textures and corners. It was more of a feeling than a planned activity, as if all the right and good words already existed inside their objects and I just reached out and took them, said them. I didn't invent them, they were already there, waiting for me to find them. When I coloured, I didn't have to try.

I needed Dad to tell me what he saw when I described for him, and when it had changed, when it had become something else, something bigger and more powerful. I had tried to ignore what I had done to Miri, tried to ignore the hungry look in her eyes as I coloured in the beach and the ocean and the car park around her. Even though I had tried so hard not to think about it, I could remember everything about that evening, every second, every wave on the shore.

I shook my head and said, 'I'm trying to remember, when the colouring changed. I think it was with Johnny.'

In the background, I heard Mum say something to Dad.

Dad said, 'Jodie, I don't think we should really talk about this.'

'But, Guy is threatening me, Dad, he's been around here talking shit and I need to figure this stuff out. It's doing my head in.'

'J, I don't really know what you're talking about.'

'Dad! What? What do you mean? I need your help, because—'

'Jodie,' he cut me off, 'look, it's late, I think you need some rest, let's talk about this later.' And he hung up.

I stared at my phone, tears in my eyes. So much for fucking family.

In the morning, I saw a message from Mum appear on my phone, *let's take Jade to the beach we'll pick you up in ten.*

I wanted to tell her to piss off, but Jade was bouncing off the walls and we needed to get out of the house for a bit.

Mum and Dad picked us up and we drove through town to the beach at Ōhope with Jade chatting all the way about the different types of clouds and the phases of the moon and other random information that she had picked up recently, all the adults nodding patiently and not looking at each other.

At the beach, Mum led Jade down to the shore with a bucket and spade and I sat on the bank next to Dad.

Dad said, 'It's funny when things feel normal, like today, this morning, just normal stuff.'

I grunted. I sat with my arms crossed. I didn't look at him. I felt so betrayed.

Dad shuffled his walking stick from one side to the other. He said, in a quiet voice, 'J, we can't talk about it on the phone.'

I looked straight out to sea.

He continued, 'We can't talk about it on the phone because Mum and I are worried that they're listening, these blokes. You remember that call? When that bloke asked for you? We think they're listening in too.'

I felt something inside me drop away. Of course. What an idiot I'd been. And Jade, I had put Jade in danger.

'This isn't a joke,' said Dad. 'We have to be careful.'

When I spoke, my voice croaked, 'What do they want, Dad?'

'They'll be looking for how this all started, looking for the beginning, where the first person went.'

'They know where we are, they went to Renee's house, to ask about me.' My mind was racing. 'And the phone call, at your place, that was just so we'd know they were watching.'

Down on the beach, Jade yelled, 'Mum! Look!' and held up a shell. I gave her a thumbs up.

'What is it?' Dad asked.

'Just a shell,' I said. Then, 'Dad, what are we going to do?'

'We don't know how much they know. We just lie low, keep quiet, no colouring, no shading, zippo.'

'I wish I had never shaded Miri. She made me. She kind of tricked me, I didn't want to.'

'J, what did you do?' Dad asked.

I pulled my knees up and rested my forehead on them. I wanted to hide.

'Did you meet her boyfriend? Matt? He was a real dickhead. Kind of like Johnny. She needed to get rid of him. She was afraid. But, it's like, sometimes, women need help, it's hard, when someone has this power over you, even for Miri, and you know Miri, she wouldn't take any crap from anyone.'

'She's a hard nut, Miri,' said Dad.

Did Dad know about what had happened to Miri when she was a kid? Could he hear that pain inside her?

'She knew I could shade myself. She'd seen me do it with Johnny, only once, at the beach one night. I forgot she was there, Dad, and I was scared of Johnny, and I just forgot and I started bringing up all the beach things, you know that's some of the easiest stuff, all the words are so easy, and Johnny didn't see me, but Miri saw, she saw what I could do. I wish I'd just kept quiet.'

'Miri never missed a trick,' said Dad.

'And she remembered, and she asked me, she made me shade her, to get away from Matt, but this time it was more, something bigger.' I raised my head. 'We were at the beach. I think she knew. She took me there on purpose, Dad, where it would be easiest. I wish, I wish I hadn't done it.'

I looked behind us. The car park was empty except for one car at the end of the lot. I lowered my voice and said, 'I didn't know what would happen, but I felt like Miri knew. It's always been like that with her, she's one step ahead.'

'She wouldn't have asked if she didn't really need your help, J. Miri never asked for help.'

'And I wanted to, Dad, you know I wanted to help her.'

'I know. We all did.'

I wanted to stop talking then, but Dad kept going.

'J, what happened to Miri? Did she go out?'

Thinking about it, my chest felt empty, like I couldn't properly fill my lungs. 'Yes. Maybe. I don't know. She seemed different, when I had finished. Dad, she seemed happy, I think. It didn't hurt her.'

'Did you check your photos?'

'Later, when I did, she was still present. I didn't think about it. I didn't think to check again for ages.'

'And now?'

My voice felt very small. I'd put my whole family in danger. I was a dick who didn't know when to keep her mouth shut. I said, 'She's gone. I don't know when it happened, but she's gone.' I rambled on, not making much sense. 'But it could've happened any time, right? It definitely didn't happen right away, I looked, and she was still there. But I didn't even think, back then, to keep checking, I knew I'd changed her, but I didn't know what it meant. I knew she needed my help.'

'J, you did the right thing,' Dad said.

'Did I, though? Did I?'

'We don't know if she was the first. And neither do they.'

I couldn't wrap my head around what we were talking about, the size of it. Was Miri the first gap? Had it started with her? The weight of it pressed down on me for a moment, the pressure of this thought was too much to take. It didn't seem possible that everything, all around the world, could come circling back to me, and to that desperate evening on the beach with Miri. It wasn't real, it seemed like a joke, a fucked up joke.

I lashed out. 'It's all cos of Johnny. I'd never have started shading if it wasn't for him.'

Dad said, 'They obviously know something, and they know where we are, but they can't prove anything, else they would've done something already. They're just keeping an eye on us.'

'Guy knows. He said he's been talking to someone. Maybe he's said too much already.'

'I will talk to Guy. He knows how to keep a secret.'

I thought about the feeling of someone having been in our house, nearly a year ago. Jade had been so grumpy when I'd pretended that nothing was wrong. Someone had been watching us for a long time. Watching and waiting.

I shivered and stood up. Mum and Jade were walking up the beach towards us. 'They're coming,' I told Dad.

Here she is. Jade is running ahead. Her feet are covered in brown sand. She grins and holds a yellow bucket. She runs up to me and waves half a crab shell in my face. 'Look! Mum! I found the claw piece too!'

I took a bunch of photos of her, standing with her crab shell.

When Mum arrived, she asked, 'You two all right?' She looked meaningfully from Dad to me.

'We've had a good chinwag,' said Dad.

I felt embarrassed about the night before, calling Mum and Dad, ready to reveal everything to whoever was listening on the line. Mum and Dad must've been talking about this for ages, trying to figure out what to do, but they'd said nothing until now.

I helped Dad get up and handed him his walking stick.

As he took my arm, he said, 'I think maybe you should find our old mate Miri.'

'Miri?'

'Yes, but we can't use phones.'

'How can I do that? She's in Auckland, or up north, or something. I haven't been in touch with her for years, definitely not since the gaps started.'

Mum and Jade walked ahead of us across the car park, Mum carrying Jade's bucket, which was stuffed with the bits of driftwood and shells that Jade always collected.

Dad said, 'She'll be able to tell us what happened. When she started going, what it felt like. Maybe it was nothing to do with your shading. Maybe something else happened and she went much later.'

'Her ex, Matt, showed me a photo and she'd gone. It was maybe a month after, I'm not sure. And then I checked my photos, and she wasn't there.'

'So, there's a month, maybe, when we don't know what happened. It's unaccounted for. She could have gone then.'

'I don't know, it seems risky, Dad. I don't know how—'

Dad stopped me, his hand on my arm, halfway across the car park. 'If we try, we can get ahead of them,' he said. 'They know you did something, but they don't know exactly what. Maybe you put Miri out, but maybe you didn't. And if we get to Miri before they do, we can warn her not to lead them back to you.'

I shook my head. 'I don't think she'd do that.'

'Mum! Mum!' Jade was shouting from the car. 'Mum! Hurry up!'

'We owe it to Miri,' Dad said quietly. 'To try and warn her.'

'Mum! Mum!' Jade again.

'I'll think about it,' I said.

25.

On my lunch break, I went to the garage where Matt worked and sat in my car across the road for half an hour. I didn't know if he still worked there or even if he still lived in Whakatāne. I hadn't seen him around, didn't know anyone who hung out with him.

The outside of the workshop was covered with the billboards of presents, their grinning faces looking out at the road. The owner of the workshop was right in the middle, a huge image of his smug face in front of a setting sun and a blue ocean. There were so many signs that the name of the workshop and its prices for WOFs and new tyres were completely covered up. Lots of businesses were like this, their advertising had been consumed by signs for presents showing that they hadn't gone out. Being present and making sure everyone knew was more important now.

I had started the engine, and was just about to leave, when Matt walked out, talking with a customer and wiping his greasy fingers on a cloth. Six years on, he looked the same, relaxed, confident. He laughed with the other man and clapped him on the back.

I watched him for a moment and then drove back to work, thinking about what I would say to him.

The next day, again on my lunch break, I sat in my car across from the garage and checked my rear-view mirror. No cars parked behind me. Everything normal.

I opened my door, crossed the road, and went into the empty reception. I rang the bell and waited, my heart thudding.

Matt came in through a side door. He reached into his pocket, took out his phone and, without saying anything, we took photos of each other.

He slapped his photo down on the counter and leant against it, arms crossed. 'Jodie, right? Can't seem to get rid of your family at the moment.'

'What do you mean?'

'Your bro was in here the other day. Guy. You looking for Miri too?'

'Yeah, I am.'

'Thought you two were great mates.' He tapped the counter with his index finger. 'She's not been in touch?'

I shrugged. 'It's been a while.'

'Yeah, well, she's gone, you know that, right?'

'Yeah, I saw. She was... she must have been early.'

'Thought she'd fucked with my phone. She deleted all her social media.'

'So, you tried? Did you try and track her down?'

Had I hidden her enough?

He shook his head. 'Nah, didn't need to, got a new lady.'

'Is she still in Auckland?'

'Dunno.'

The phone rang and we both stared at it. Matt made no move to pick it up. It stopped.

I said, 'That time at the bar, when you tried to show me your phone. You were trying to show me that she'd disappeared? That she'd gone?'

'Yeah, I didn't know though, what it was. Hadn't seen it before, back then.'

'Didn't you think something was wrong? Weren't you worried about her?' I asked.

'I, sort of, forgot. Don't look back at old photos much.' He paused. 'If you give me your number I'll text you, if she texts me.'

I looked at him. He grinned and tilted his head to the side. Fuck-wit.

'You've got a kid, though, don't you?' he asked.

'And why would she text you, Matt? Why would she text you after all this time when you treated her like shit when you were together?' I spat out the words.

Matt held up his hands. 'Hey hey! No need to get pissy with me. I don't know what sort of fucked up shit is happening here, but I do know that your brother came in here a couple of days ago and now you're here and now I'm wondering what's up and why everyone is looking for Miri all of a sudden, like, why's she so special?'

He picked up his phone, tapped on something, and smirked before tapping out a reply. What a dick. He didn't know anything about Miri or where she was. He cared so little about her that when she'd gone he didn't even wonder what had happened, why she'd disappeared, what had happened to the photos on his phone. He just forgot about her, as if she'd never been there, as if she was nothing.

I should've kept quiet and walked out the door, but I was so pissed off. He was the reason that I'd put Miri out. He was the reason she'd begged me to shade her, tears in her eyes, because she was so scared and needed to get away from him, and she knew that I'd understand because I was trapped too. I looked at him and I saw Johnny and all the stupid decisions Miri and I had made to end up with these wasters who messed with our heads and hurt us. I'd made her disappear, made her less than she was. I'd lost my best friend because of him.

I tightened my hands into fists. My voice broke when I said, 'You don't know where Miri is and there's no way she's going to waste her time on a dickhead like you anymore.'

Matt looked up, his eyes narrowing. 'I wouldn't talk to me like that if I were you. I know some stuff.' He tapped the side of his head.

'You know shit.'

He started coming out from behind the counter and I moved to the door.

'I'll tell your brother then, shall I? Where Miri is. We're old mates now, me and Guy. Just like this.' He held up his hand with two fingers folded around each other.

'Fuck you, Matt.'

I opened the door and walked quickly across the road to my car. My hands were shaking and I held the steering wheel to steady them. I sat there watching the cars drive past, half an eye on the garage in case Matt came out.

I took out my phone. The last time I had texted Miri was in 2015. I had written, *hey what's up? haven't heard from you in a while. hope all is good.*

Then, after there had been no reply, *hey, hope you're ok. just hadn't heard from you in a bit and was wondering what you are up to. let me know. xx*

Then, just, *???*

No reply. Nothing. I'd sent them to the number that I had always had for her.

Matt didn't come out of the workshop. I checked my rear-view mirror again. The street was empty. There were no cars with darkened windows or men watching me from across the road.

I turned on the engine and pulled out onto the road. I didn't know who was after me. I didn't know what they wanted. I didn't know what I was looking for.

Later that evening, after Jade was asleep, I fired up the crappy laptop Guy had given us, which he had obviously nicked, or bought for nothing from some dodgy dude, and logged into my Google Drive.

I scrolled through, looking for photos where Miri should've been, but my folder only went back to 2015 when I had set it up. Miri had gone in 2012. I would have only just got a smartphone. It was probably my first one.

And I didn't see Miri much around that time anyway. She was caught up with Matt. I was always with Johnny. Both of us too ashamed to talk to each other and acknowledge that we were weak and desperate and damaged.

On my drive, I paused on a photo of Dad and I sitting on deck chairs out the back of Mum and Dad's place. Mum must have taken them. Dad is laughing, his face turned upwards. I'm drinking a can of beer. I'm in the middle of saying something, my mouth in a strange position.

What were we doing? What were we talking about? I couldn't remember. But it was comforting, like it always was, to have that photo, and to have Dad and I locked in the past together. My mouth looking weird. His unseeing eyes looking up to the sky. He must've heard a noise, a plane maybe. Mum there, but not there, behind the camera, looking at us.

I scrolled through some more photos, looking for gaps, spaces where people should have been. Some photos looked a little strange, bodies in awkward positions because of where gaps used to be. I couldn't remember who used to be there, or what faces had been lost.

I sat up, straightened my back, and thought for a moment in the quiet house. Then I went to the cupboard in the hall and found an old box where Mum had stashed my old school reports, letters, bits of paper from the past.

I knew what I was looking for. Tucked in the bottom, where I'd hidden it after I had taken it out years ago, when I was trying to find out what had happened to Miri, there was a printed photo that I half-remembered being taken.

I held the photo up. Look. Here she is. I'm down at the beach, the sea behind me. I'm ten, maybe. I'm young. My hair is all over the show and I'm wearing a black puffer jacket. My left arm is raised in the air and the other is wrapped around an empty space where Miri would've been. My face is big and happy and smiling. I look so happy to be with Miri, to have her there close beside me.

I tried to remember her face, her expression, whether her hair was also whipped up by the wind coming in from the sea. But I couldn't remember. I couldn't remember if she was sad or happy or just nothing. I couldn't remember if she was looking at the camera, or looking away.

I'm good at remembering. I'm writing this all down. It's a bit of a mess, but I can remember what people said and how I felt at different times. I can remember Jade, that's the most important bit. I can remember Jade and I can write her down. There are words I can give to her and words I can put around her to put her in place on the screen. I can colour her in, even now that we are gone.

Sitting in the hallway, I closed my eyes and tried to see Miri, tried to remember her when she was ten, when we were ten together, on the beach.

I found the words for her and I said them quietly. They had to be plain and precise.

'She scowls, looking across her left shoulder, away from me. She doesn't want to be in the photo. She has a thin top lip. Her hair is long, past her shoulders, but thin. It's wispy and there's baby hair around her face. Her eyebrows are dark and straight. She doesn't want to be in the photo, but her body is warm next to me. She wears a grey hoodie. Her feet are bare, and her toes are buried in the sand.'

I opened my eyes and stared at the photo. I was still there, my protective arm around an empty space. My face was still big and happy and smiling. I was gripping that space, gripping Miri, making her stay in the photo even though she didn't want to stay, even though she was pissed off and saying something mean, or kind, or meaningless.

I had held her then, on the beach, but she was still gone, and I couldn't bring her back.

I had put her out and then I had tried to forget about her, tried to pretend that I hadn't done anything, and that she was okay.

I slumped on the floor of the hallway, my back against the wall, and felt the loss of her in my arms and legs. I wanted to tell her things. I wanted her to meet Jade. I wanted Jade and Miri to talk to each other and I wanted Miri to be grumpy with me and boss me around and tell me to piss off because I was annoying her. I wanted to see her face.

I sat on the floor in the hall. When I shook myself and looked up, the house was dark. I didn't know what the time was. My legs ached when I stood up. I felt old and useless. I wanted a smoke. In the bathroom, I splashed my face with water.

I went round the house, pulling the curtains tight. To break the silence, I turned on the radio and switched on the jug. On the radio, a woman was screaming, 'It burns! Arg! It burns! Please! Please! Make it stop! Please!'

I turned it down, worried about Jade waking up.

The audio cut to a reporter who said there were new reports coming in of gaps in severe pain. When they went out, gaps were complaining of needle-like pains in their wrists and legs that lasted for several hours. Specialists were investigating, the reporter said, and tests were being undertaken. Gaps were being taken to hospitals and treated.

Paul Irons's gravelly voice came on. The reporter asked him what he thought about these reports? Had he seen any cases of this in Purity?

He said it was all part of the trial, of the path that some gaps had to take. It was necessary, he said, to cut away the error of their images. For some, he said, the bond was deep, much deeper than others, so the split was more damaging, more painful.

'But they will come through,' he said, his voice calm and warm and so familiar by then. 'They will come through into the light and they will be free. And they will know what it is to return to their true selves, to their true bodies, to those bodies that are unblemished and uncopied and fully in the present, and more fully realised in the present.'

'Will Purity be treating these gaps?' the reporter asked.

'Purity has all the facilities to accommodate those solos who need our help. Our centre is state of the art.'

'Solos?' the reporter asked.

Irons chuckled. 'We do not subscribe to this term you use, 'gaps'. We are not gaps. We are not absences. We are unique. We are not copied and diluted and replicable. We are singular and precious. So, I am a solo, a person solely in the here and now. I am no longer one of the many.' He laughed again. 'Nor do I wish to be. In fact, I cannot imagine anything worse.'

I turned the radio off and went to bed, poking my head in to check on Jade as I went past her door.

Tossing and turning in the dark, I couldn't stop thinking about the gap's pain, her cries, and her pleading. I thought about Miri, where she was, what she was doing. Had I hurt her, when she'd gone? Or did she feel unique too? Like Irons had said.

26.

The online version of school started again. It was temporary, the school insisted. What they were hoping for, what they were protecting the kids from, I don't know, but lots of things were closing down.

It was being in groups that people found hard. At gatherings, it was difficult to tell who was a gap and who was present, so people took photos constantly. Sorting through the crowd, they saw a different version of the event. Some gaps took photos too. They didn't take part in the event, but they liked to record from the outside of it. They said that it gave them a purpose, a sense that they were really there, and standing in the world.

Schools fell apart. Teachers didn't know how to treat gone kids, or how to talk to their parents. School is so much about recording, being counted, and marking the time that passes, and gaps messed with all of that. They just seemed less *there*, less accountable, like they slipped through the systems of documentation that schools were so dependent on.

There were a few gaps at Jade's school and she said that they sat together at lunchtime.

'No one knew what to do, Mum,' she said, 'at the whole school photo. You could just tell, the teachers felt weird. One gap just walked away. She walked out of the hall and didn't come back. She's one of the big kids.'

The school sent Jade a bunch of activities to do, and she had to log on to the school's web portal every morning for a chat and short activity with her teacher. She was only six. Kids that age don't have much of an attention span.

Jade was excited because she got to go into work with me. I didn't have any other options or any other favours I could call in. I couldn't ask Mum. She was still working and supporting the other teachers at her school. Lots of gaps just stopped turning up for work and there were staff shortages.

I would never have asked Guy. And he supposedly had a job at the time, helping a mate with his haulage business, apparently. Guy's jobs came and went.

I asked Alan, my boss, and he said it was okay, for a trial period, but he looked pissed off when I arrived on the first Monday with Jade holding my hand. He was standing at the back of the office and talking on his phone, and he frowned at me, as if he'd forgotten our conversation and that Jade would be coming in.

He reached into his pocket, as we passed, and took a photo of us with his phone.

I set Jade up at an empty desk in a tiny alcove off the reception area. 'Do you know what you need to do?' I asked. She gestured at two pages of numbers and letters.

'I have to follow the arrows,' she said. 'I'll be okay, Mum.'

Her little face was serious.

I wanted to stay and help her write the letters. I didn't want her to have to teach herself.

I sighed and went to my desk. The phone rang. Lots of our international clients were cancelling or downsizing their orders, ones that had been the same for years were being adjusted or deferred. The mill made specialist paperboard for packaging, and not the kind that you could get just anywhere. But many countries were looking inward, preferring the semi-stability of local suppliers, rather than the uncertainty of international trade, where rules were changing rapidly as gaps left, or were forced from, the workforce.

My phone rang all the time. My inbox was stacked with messages.

Jade lasted about half an hour before she came over and pulled on my elbow. We went back to her little desk, and I opened the laptop and waited for it to come to life. It was a miracle when the Wi-Fi connected and we managed to log on to the school's portal.

When I got back to my desk there were two red message lights flashing on my phone. Nicola, who sat across from me, said, 'Your phone rang.'

Yeah, no shit.

After lunch, Jade crawled under my desk, curled into a ball, and fell asleep for an hour. When she woke up I gave her my phone and she watched music videos of the glossy gone Katy Perry with the volume turned down low.

My boss walked through reception in the afternoon. He didn't ask me how I was doing or if I needed any help. He took a photo of me. I kept my head down, not catching his eye.

When we were driving home, I glanced up to the corner of my windscreen and saw that the WOF was due.

Fuck! Fuck! Fuck!

Ever since we drove back from Auckland the car had been making weird grating noises when I turned it on, and I knew that something was up, but I'd been ignoring it. I couldn't deal with it. I knew I would take it into the garage and they would say it needed some super expensive thing that I couldn't afford.

I hammered the steering wheel with the heel of my hand.

'Are you okay, Mum?' asked Jade.

'Yeah,' I said, 'I'm just a bit worried about the car, it's been making funny noises.'

'Maybe Guy could fix it?'

'Yeah, maybe, maybe he could. Or maybe Pop.'

'He can't see.'

'No, but he still knows a lot about cars. He used to fix stuff all the time.'

'What was he like when he could see?' Jade asked.

'Pop? He was... he was the same as now, but he could just do more stuff. You know, get about a bit more. He worked at the mill, like me.'

Jade was right, if Dad could still see I would've taken the car round and he would've sorted it out.

'Why don't you see for him anymore?' Jade asked.

I glanced at her in the rear-view mirror. She was looking out her window.

'You used to see for him all the time but you don't do it now,' she said, turning to look at me in the mirror. 'I liked listening to it. I liked it when you did the TV, it was so fast. Like, blah blah blah blah!' She waved her hands in the air.

'Pop doesn't really need me to do it anymore,' I said.

'Why? He liked it.'

Tears welled in my eyes. 'Um, we're just taking a break for a bit.'

'It's okay, Mum.'

'Yeah, I know.'

I turned into our driveway and switched off the ignition. Would the car start again when I next turned it on?

I opened the back door and undid Jade's seatbelt. She leapt out and put her arms around my waist, resting her head against my stomach. I stroked her hair, held her close.

Here she is, warm, trying to comfort me. She wears pink leggings and a white T-shirt with a unicorn on the front. She has lost one of her big front teeth and she is always pushing another wiggly one with her tongue. It makes a clicking noise that she likes.

'It's okay, Mum,' she said again.

We separated and walked around the house to the back door, Jade holding my hand.

'But where do they go now, Mum?' Jade asked. 'What do you do with all your words that you don't use?'

I said, 'I'm just storing them up, I guess.' I unlocked the back door. 'I'll use them later.'

And here they are, Jade! Here they are. I'm writing them down now, for you, for me, for us.

We had baked beans on toast for dinner and jelly for dessert that Jade had made with Mum a few days before.

I got Jade into bed and called Bex and asked if she could look after Jade a couple of afternoons a week. I hated asking but I had to, there was no way Jade could come into work with me every day for the whole week. I had to figure something else out.

Bex said, 'Yeah, sure, Cara would love that.'

'Thank you. Thank you so much. I'll pack some of Jade's toys, and make some biscuits.'

'Yeah, fine, all good,' said Bex. She paused, and then she said, 'I heard that you went round to see Matt the other day.'

'Matt? What? Oh yeah, maybe.'

My mind was racing. Why was Bex asking me about Matt? How did she know him?

'He just said something the other day, that you'd been into the shop, and Guy too. Bit weird, you two going in on the same day.'

'I don't know what Guy gets up to most of the time, to be honest. We don't really get along. How do you know Matt?'

'He's mates with my brother. He said you were looking for Miri.'

'Just, you know, asking if he'd heard from her.'

'She was your best mate, wasn't she? And you don't know where she is?'

'We sort of lost touch a while ago.'

'Yeah, I remember you said.' Bex paused, and then she said, in a rush, 'Because, some of us noticed, Matt showed us, that Miri had gone, but ages ago. We didn't even know what it was then. We didn't know what to think. It was just... really weird.'

I said nothing. Who else was listening to this call?

'Did you know, Jodie? Did you know that she had gone?'

'She didn't talk to me about it.'

'But, if she did, then how? How could she, when it was so long ago?'

'I don't know.'

'She was always a bit weird, Miri, you know? A bit different.'

I gritted my teeth. Bex, you don't know the first thing about Miri. You don't know what happened to her, how brave she was to even walk around in the world, to be seen. No wonder, when she saw the opportunity, that she wanted to take a step out of it, that she wanted to disappear for a while.

Bex lowered her voice and said, 'Do you think... do you think it could have started here? With Miri?'

'Look, like I said, we lost touch. I don't really know.'

'It was ages ago. I checked, I don't think I had a phone then. I mean, one that could take photos. I wanted to see if she was still there, but I didn't have any photos of her.'

I desperately wanted to get off the line and to stop talking, but I couldn't offend Bex, I needed her to look after Jade. I needed her to be on my side.

I said, 'I'd just been thinking about her, you know? I thought Matt might know, but he didn't. I'm sure she's all good, though.'

'It would be so crazy, if it had started here in Shitsville Whakatāne.'

I laughed. 'I don't really think—'

Bex interrupted, 'You could ask her mum, Miri's mum. She's still out on Pembroke Road, I think. She'll know.'

I had to get out of this conversation. I said, 'So I'll drop Jade round at lunchtime on Thursday? Is that okay? Thank you so much.'

'Oh, yep, all good.' Bex seemed a bit pissed that I'd dropped the subject. She fancied herself some kind of detective, solving a big mystery. And she was, I guess. We both were.

On Thursday I gunned it out to Bex's house on my lunch break and dropped Jade off. They lived ten minutes out of town, so I didn't have time to settle her in, or to stay and chat with Bex. I just had to drop her off and be rude and not make any small talk.

I kissed Jade and said, 'Don't forget to read your book from school.'

Cara and Jade were excited to see each other. 'Come on,' Cara said as they rushed off, 'Mum's got a 360-degree camera, she's going to take lots of photos of us.'

Bex laughed as we watched them go. 'I thought it'd be something nice to do, while we can, you know.'

I quickly drove back to work. My boss had been keeping a close eye on me and Jade. I'd told him I was figuring out some other child-care, but I just needed a little more time to finalise things. I planned to make it obvious that Jade wasn't around that afternoon. I'd work really hard. Sort out a bunch of tricky supplier contracts and email them all through to him just before I left.

Bex had asked that I pick Jade up at five, so I'd have to leave a tiny bit early. Just a tiny bit. Hopefully he wouldn't notice. Hopefully Nicola wouldn't take lots of photos of me leaving. She was photographing me all the time, smiling in this annoyingly sweet way when she did. It was completely normal, by then, to picture friends and family, when you met up with them or said goodbye. It was how we confirmed everyone was present. But Nicola was constantly up in my grill. In the staff room, when we were at our desks. The day before, I had been coming out of the toilet and she was there, in the hallway, with her phone at the ready, smiling sweetly before she took a series of pictures.

I couldn't tell her to stop. It would have made people suspicious. Only gaps would protest someone taking photos of them. Presents were supposed to love it. I just stared back down the camera on her phone, keeping my face emotionless, letting it make copies of me, showing Nicola that I had nothing to hide.

I got back to the mill, parked, and jumped out of the car, checking my phone as I did, because I knew I was running late. As I went to put my phone back in my bag it slipped and fell onto the concrete. I watched it falling. I saw the screen smash and the case pop off.

I stood in the car park out the back of the mill and stared at the broken phone. Fucking phone. Fucking WOF. Fucking closed schools. Fucking screwed up world with disappearing people. I looked up at the sky, holding back tears. Seagulls circled overhead.

I bent down and picked up my phone. The screen was blank. What if something happened to Jade and Bex needed to get in contact with me? What if Mum and Dad needed something? What if someone new imaged me when we met and I couldn't picture them in return? It would be rude. They would worry and think something was up.

I tried the power button, but the screen stayed blank.

I had to get back to work, so I stuffed the phone in my bag and went back to my desk. Nicola looked up at the clock as I came in, but I ignored her and stared at my screen.

I focussed on getting the contracts sorted and sent to Alan. I pushed all the other worries out of my mind. I would figure something out. I had before, and I'd do it again.

I rushed through the contracts as well as a bunch of Nicola's invoices. Later in the afternoon I reached down to grab my phone and tried to turn it on again. Behind the splintered lines of broken screen, the phone flashed into life. I nearly cried.

I quickly tapped in my passcode and it all seemed to be working okay. No messages from Bex. Nothing gone wrong.

The screen was smashed, but I could still mostly see my apps and I could still take photos and sort of see them. I could still keep in touch with people. A new screen would be too expensive. This would do for now.

I clutched the phone against my chest and said a small prayer for it to keep working. Don't die, little phone. I need you. Then I grabbed my bag and snuck out of the office, while my boss wasn't around, to go and get Jade and get us home and keep us safe and together.

27.

I thought about going round to see Miri's mum, Chantal, but I was nervous about driving around too much without my WOF.

Though, the police had bigger issues than a single mum with a smashed-up phone in Whakatāne not having her WOF. There was more and more looting across the country. Gaps were moving around and doing whatever they wanted and something needed to be done to stop them.

News came through thick and fast, but it was messed up and confusing. I couldn't hold on to it. I couldn't make sense of it. It was harder and harder for reporters to tell us what was happening, with more people going, and the constant but random flare ups of violence and arrests and empty shops and checkpoints.

I remember a confused security guard on the news. He said, 'I must have seen them come in. Yeah, I must of. I don't see how they could have got in otherwise, there's no other way through. But sometimes, with gaps, it's like you can't really focus on them, eh? You can see 'em but, yeah, nah, they just sort of aren't there. It's pretty wild.'

There were different groups of gaps all around the country setting up spaces where they could gather together. The media kept calling them 'gangs', but they weren't really. Mostly they were just gaps who wanted to be on their own. A group of gaps in Whanganui had taken over an old warehouse, set it up as some kind of headquarters, and were refusing to come out. I don't know what they wanted or what they were trying to achieve.

One of them said on the radio, 'If we can't be seen, then we don't want to see either. We just want to keep to ourselves. We don't want to let other people in. Anyway, no one was using this old building.'

The police couldn't seem to keep a lid on things. There was the sense that gaps lived outside the law and that they could do what they wanted, move around wherever they wanted, grabbing stuff, not caring about presents or what they thought. Like they weren't in the real world.

A new police force had been set up to take care of gap crime. 'They're a special group in our society,' said the Prime Minister, 'so they must be treated as such. They have special requirements, there are particular measures that the police must take in order to ensure the safety of all citizens.'

Irons's smooth voice was always on the radio. 'We won't be treated as second-class citizens. The government needs to consider its priorities. We don't know how many of us will pass through into the light. There may well be a large voting block of solos in the near future and I'm sure this will change the way the government is handling the situation.'

When asked if he condoned the looting, he said, 'Of course not. But you must understand, these are solos who have not yet realised the plenitude of their new existence. It's about education, acceptance. You can understand that seeking your image is a natural response, that some solos will stop at nothing to see a photographic representation of themselves again. It is how they understand themselves and their place in the world. I welcome those lost and confused solos to come to Purity, and be amongst our community, and they will come to understand the new depth they have in their lives, in their truly real and unrepeatable bodies. What a gift! What a blessing! To be finally whole.'

I spent several weeks worrying about my WOF and Jade and my broken phone and Miri and the people who were watching us, sitting at the kitchen table, trying to decide what to do, and then Chantal came round.

Jade and I heard someone knocking quietly on the front door and we went to answer it, Jade standing close behind my legs as I opened the door a crack.

'Chantal!' I said, opening the door wider when I saw her.

'Jodie. Long time, no see. Look—'

I held up my hand. 'Jade, honey, shall we go round the back to the school? I think we should go for a walk, don't you? Jade wants to have a hoon on the playground while no one else is there.'

Jade looked at me suspiciously, but I took her hand and put my other arm around Chantal's shoulders, guiding her down the driveway.

There was a small gate cut into our back fence that led through to the school field. We crawled through. Jade hung close while Chantal and I made small talk. She knew something was up, but she couldn't resist running to the playground when she saw some other kids from down the road hanging from the monkey bars.

'How'd you find where we were?' I asked Chantal, as Jade ran away across the field.

'Jodie, it's Whakatāne! Don't you want to talk at your place?' She nodded her head back to our fence.

'Nah, I'm just...' I was trying to figure out what to tell her, how to make sense of it all. I didn't really know what exactly I was worried about. 'I'm just a bit stressed, because of the gaps, because of that new police force.'

Chantal nodded, as if she understood. 'They onto you cos of Miri?'

I shrugged. 'I'm not sure, maybe.' I paused. 'Chantal, did you know, did you see that she had gone?'

Chantal glared at me. 'Course I knew! I'm her mum! How could you think I didn't notice a thing like that?'

'When? When did you notice?'

'It only happened in bits at first, cos, you know, it was before I had one of these fancy phones, so I didn't have lots of old pictures of her on my phone back then. So I didn't see straight away, like I would now. But I was looking through an album, from when you guys were kids and I thought that Miri used to be in that photo. I stared at it for ages. But I wasn't sure. And then next time I looked, she was there again, so I forgot about it, just thought I was going a bit funny in the head.'

She tapped the side of her head and was quiet for a while. The playground had a big, wooden frame with thick knotted pieces of rope that the kids could swing on, and Jade was pushing one of her mates and then dodging the rope as it swung back. I didn't want her to come over and listen to us.

'Then there was something that I couldn't forget,' Chantal continued. 'That photo of Miri with her nan, in Rotorua. That one that we had on the wall in the hall, you remember the one, eh, Jodie? It was the last time Miri saw her nan, when that photo was taken. She went, from that one.' Chantal's voice broke then, and she looked away from me. 'I didn't look at it much, because when something's on the wall you don't look at it anymore, it's just part of the furniture. But one day, I don't know, I looked at it and Miri wasn't there. Just Nan. Just Nan smiling at this empty space. Miri was gone.'

Chantal looked down at her hands. 'I called her, straight away, I called her and I told her what I had seen. I was standing in front of the photo when I was talking to her. She said she was fine, all good. She said she was in Auckland, that she was working, that she was busy. I asked what was happening with the old photo and she said that she had asked you to do it. You, Jodes. She said something like, she wanted to be 'less seen', and maybe what was happening with the photo was because of what you'd done. She said she'd probably come back, in the photo, that she was okay.'

'Did you know about Matt? That's why I shaded her. She begged me to. She wanted to get away from him,' I said.

'I knew about him. I knew he was bad news, but you know Miri, there's no telling her. There's no telling her what to do. She stopped listening to me a long time ago.' Chantal shook her head. 'I kept walking past that photo in the hall. It wasn't right! And I kept calling her, checking up on her, checking that she was okay. I told her to come home, but she just laughed at me. What did you do? What did you do to her?'

I stared out at the field. 'It's because of Dad,' I said, 'because I told him how things looked. I can colour things in, by describing, so that other things disappear, other people can disappear. She begged me to. She took me to the beach and forced me to do it.' As I said this, I felt how pathetic it sounded. I didn't want Chantal to think I had hurt Miri. I would never hurt her.

I rushed on, 'I didn't know what would happen, but she seemed fine afterwards. She seemed really happy actually. And she got away from Matt. I saw it, he just wasn't interested in her anymore, couldn't control her. And he hit her, Chantal. He hit her. I had to do something.'

Chantal said nothing and when I turned to her I saw that her eyes were full of tears.

'I know,' she said quietly. 'I know he hit her. I couldn't... I couldn't protect her. Even before.'

I asked, 'Did you tell anyone? Did you tell anyone that she had gone?'

Chantal shook her head. 'No, no. I didn't know what was happening. I took the photos down. I hid them. I put them all in a box, but I'd take them out and keep checking, looking for her. For years, sometimes she was there, and sometimes she wasn't. She came and went. I missed her, I missed seeing her, I was always so happy when I'd open the box and see that she had come back. And then, maybe two years ago, I checked and she had gone, all of her, everywhere, and she didn't come back.'

'She stopped replying to my messages. Do you know where she is?' I asked.

'We talked all the time, on the phone. She said she wouldn't come back, to Whakatāne, because of Matt, because of... But then, after she'd gone, for real, she stopped answering and I didn't know where she was. I tried to find her. Then, she left a message for me, online, on this forum I'm in.' Chantal laughed, wiping her eyes. 'It's about that planting we're doing, down at the beach, the dune regeneration. We have this group, and she started messaging me, so the others couldn't see. Now she finds other places online, other forums, to let me know she's doing okay.'

'Where is she?' I asked.

'Up north, I think. She won't tell me exactly where.'

I could see that Jade would run back to us soon. She was arguing with one of the kids about the rules of their game.

'Listen, Chantal, you can't tell anyone. If they know that I can do that...'

Chantal shot back, 'I haven't told anyone all these years. Why would I say something now?'

'I know, I know, of course,' I said. I didn't want her to get angry. I needed her to listen to me. 'It's just… people are following me. I think they know. They may have got to Miri. She has to be careful.'

'I'm taking care of Miri now,' said Chantal. 'I'm keeping her safe.'

'Yes, of course you are.'

Jade started running across the field towards us, her hair flying.

'I actually came here because Miri had a message for you.'

'A message?'

'She said something big is going to happen and things are going to get more messed up. She said you should come up north. She said it was important. She made me promise to tell you.'

Jade tackled me around the legs. 'Stella wouldn't be the tiger!' she yelled, grabbing my hand so that I almost fell over. 'Mum! Mum! Stella was being a shark!'

'Okay, okay,' I said, trying to get her off me.

We walked back across the field.

'Do you want a drink?' I asked Chantal as we climbed back through the fence.

'Nah,' she said, 'I've gotta go.'

Jade skipped up the back steps and I walked Chantal to her car.

She opened her door and then she appeared to make up her mind about something and she turned and said, looking me straight in the eye, 'You shouldn't have done that to Miri. I was going to help her, with Matt, with everything. I was going to sort it.'

'She forced me to, Chantal, she made me do it. She had to get away from here, there was too much bringing her down.'

I wouldn't be blamed. Miri had forced me. She had tricked me, taking me down to the beach. Miri with the sea behind her, the words rising up, yelling at me.

Chantal said, 'Last I checked, nobody could force you to do any-thing, Jodie. You and Miri, both the same, always were.'

She got in her car and drove away.

I know now how much Chantal missed Miri, and how helpless

she felt. Now I know what it's like to have a daughter who has gone. I know that loss, that feeling of something having been taken away. And Chantal was still present, there was that huge barrier between her and Miri, they were in different worlds, and Chantal missed her. She mourned that box of empty photographs, all those memories of Miri that had disappeared.

I remember when Miri's nan died. We were ten. Miri came round to our place early in the morning. It was still dark, and I was in bed. The back door must've been left open, or she crept in a window because she came into my room and took her shoes off and crawled into my bed, facing away from me. She felt cold. How long had she been outside?

'What happened?' I asked, still groggy with sleep.

'Nan died.'

'Oh! Are you okay?'

I leant over to look at Miri's face. Her eyes were closed, her face pressed into the pillow.

'She was in the hospital. She was, like, old,' she said.

'She was cool, your nan,' I said.

'Yeah, she was way better than most of the losers round here. She taught me how to gut a fish.'

I lay down and put my arm around her. She didn't push me off. We must have fallen asleep for a while because I remember waking up, confused, and Miri wasn't there.

She never asked for help, Miri, until that night on the beach, but she got close to me. She always found me when she needed to.

After Chantal left, I went back into the house and found Jade and gave her a hug. She put her arms around my waist and asked, 'But why is Chantal so sad?'

I wanted to say so many things, but I said, 'She just doesn't feel too good. She'll get better.'

Would Chantal go after Miri? I wondered. Had Miri told Chantal to go up north too? And what was Miri trying to warn us about? What could be bigger than what was happening now? I thought, when I was scrolling on my phone later that night. In India, Rahul Jakhar had gone out. I recognised his name, but I didn't know that he was the prime minister. Theories had been all over the place that he had gone ages ago. He hadn't been seen in public for months, and this always made everyone suspicious. I read posts that said there was a huge team of people patching up his gap in the internet, building deepfakes, cutting and splicing, doing anything to keep him present and in the public eye.

There was desperation to it, especially with politicians, because no politician had survived going. In New Zealand, some MPs had gone and they had been quickly demoted, or quietly shuffled out of parliament in some reorganisation, the PM giving some stupid reason for their disappearance. Politicians needed to be present, seen, plastered all over social media and all over billboards.

In India, someone broke into Jakhar's official home and caught him and his security off guard. It looked massive, the Prime Minister's residence, and covered in guards, so I've no idea how they did it. The intruder caught Jakhar coming out of a side building and filmed him. Jakhar was gone. The man was quickly caught, but he had already uploaded the footage and it was suddenly everywhere and being pulled apart by the internet.

Scrolling on my phone, it looked like things in India were being pulled apart too, and factions were doubling down. Supporters of Jakhar discounted the footage, but the Prime Minister didn't appear in public to disprove it. People wanted him out. They said he was a liar and a cheat. Why should they trust him when he had spent however long and however much money filling the internet with fakes and doubles and phonies? The Prime Minister had to be present, they shouted, pouring out into the streets and motorways and public squares.

It didn't take long for Jakhar to remove the protesters. Police moved in and there were violent struggles. It was clear that Jakhar wasn't going anywhere anytime soon. He had support and he was convinced that he could stay in power, even as a gap. He'd be the first big politician to set up a new kind of authority, outside of his image. He organised a press conference, but there were no phones or lens-based devices of any kind allowed, and he installed loudspeaker systems throughout Delhi so his pronouncements could be broadcast. Instead of continuing with the deepfakes on the internet, he let his image disappear, let it fall away, and stopped trying to patch it up.

Presents didn't like it. They didn't trust him. They couldn't see him. They couldn't even see deepfakes of him. They didn't know what he was up to.

Later, he began a campaign to erase phones, cameras, and computers from India, anything with a lens. Jakhar thought that if he couldn't be imaged, then no one could. He wouldn't let presents, especially political rivals, exercise that kind of authority. A country as big as India! It was insane. Jakhar spoke about it with an intense sense of purpose.

I remember all the words he used about sickness and plague and infection and how he flipped things around so that he was a martyr. 'India must be purged,' he said, 'of the images. It is a sickness, this obsession with the image of ourselves. I am doing this for the good of the people, for the good of India, our beloved nation.'

Sitting at the kitchen table, I put down my phone and laid my cheek against the cool table. I felt overwhelmed, exhausted, my mind buzzing. Miri, I thought, did we start this? This thought seemed so big, so impossible. I thought about the crowds in India, demanding to know the truth, to see the truth. The riots in Brazil. The gathering community in Purity around Irons. The faces of looters in the mall, hauling out TVs and computers. Why hadn't Miri told me what I needed to prepare for? Why did she feed this message through Chantal?

I got up and went and checked on Jade. She was fast asleep, her arms flopped up above her head. I went into my room and got out the old suitcase that Mum had lent me when we went to Auckland. I packed clothes and toiletries. In the kitchen, I looked in the cupboards. There wasn't much, but I took out a stack of two-minute noodles, a couple of cans of baked beans, a box of muesli bars, and some small packs of chips.

I wandered about the house finding other useful things. What would we need? I packed an old torch, a box of matches, towels, bottles of water.

I stared down at the suitcase of random stuff. It wouldn't get us far. It looked a little pathetic. But I felt like we needed to be ready, in some way at least, for this big thing that Miri had especially warned us about. She hadn't been in touch with me for so long, so it must be important.

I checked all the locks again, and then got into bed. Could we go up north? I wondered. How would we get there? Where up north, exactly? What would we do and where was Miri?

I took out my phone and checked my bank balance. I had $437 in my account. I'd get paid next week. I didn't know how my credit card was looking. I needed my job. We couldn't just leave everything, leave Mum and Dad behind, leave Jade's friends. Who were we running from? What were we running towards?

I lay awake for ages, these thoughts running through my head, but I must have fallen asleep at some point because I woke up and found Jade standing next to me.

As I write this, I see this moment so clearly. Here she is in the dim light, in her purple nightie, her hair messed up and sticking out everywhere. She holds her toy lion in one hand. She moves slowly. I don't think she's actually awake. She looks at me but she doesn't see me.

'It's too late,' she says.

I move over. 'Too late for what?'

She crawls in next to me. 'Nothing's coming back,' she says.

I lie next to her. Here is the back of her head, covered in its single strands of brown hair. Here are the lumps of her spine leading up to her skull. Here she is. Look.

I didn't go back to sleep after Jade crept into bed with me. She wriggled and shifted next to me, sighing and snuffling in her sleep.

After she woke up, we had Rice Bubbles for breakfast and I made myself a coffee with lots of sugar.

'I don't want to go to the mill,' said Jade. 'I want to go back to school with my friends.'

I rubbed my eyes. I felt so tired. 'I know it sucks,' I said. 'It won't be for much longer.'

Jade watched me from across the kitchen. 'Until they figure out how to bring people back,' she said.

'Nana is going to come and pick you up at lunchtime,' I said. 'So it's just for the morning.'

We grabbed our stuff and got in the car. We were already running late, but I stopped at the dairy on the way to get some snacks for Jade's lunch. Mum and Dad shouldn't have to feed her, on top of everything else.

As I was leaving, I noticed a group of people across the road stop and take photos of me. My hands were full and I couldn't return the imaging, so I just nodded and stared at them. They frowned and moved on.

I always felt a flicker of fear when this happened. Had I gone and I hadn't realised? Were these strangers the first to find out?

In the car, I dumped the groceries on the passenger seat and quickly took out my phone, switching the camera round to look at me. Christ, I looked awful. But I was still present, still there, still hanging on. I needed to be.

At the office, there was a strange mood. Nicola was flitting about, running out through the side doors, into the factory, and back to her desk, then hammering away at her keyboard. I saw Alan in the boardroom, yelling into his phone.

I tried to set Jade up in her alcove as quietly and quickly as I could. The school had sent a couple of activities for her to do on her laptop and I gave her a little pack of chips. I said she could watch some gone Katy Perry clips later. She was sick of working in the office though and munched her chips grumpily, spraying crumbs everywhere.

I sat down and tried to work but my eyes felt scratchy and tired and I couldn't stop thinking about Miri and Chantal.

Nicola hurried past me and went into the boardroom, slamming the door behind her. I watched a bunch of other managers come down from the offices on the floor above us and go into the boardroom. Something was up.

An email went round at 10:30, calling an urgent staff meeting at eleven. We filed into the shipping area at the back of the factory where there was a large forecourt.

'What do you reckon?' the woman next to me asked.

I shrugged. I didn't want to say what I thought aloud. It'd make it too real.

Dean, the big boss, the one from Auckland, appeared on the small podium and told us that the mill was closing down.

Orders had dried up. Our international customers were turning to local suppliers as trade across borders became more difficult.

'We've been exploring all the options,' Dean said, 'but unfortunately our parent company wasn't able to prop us up any longer. International trade is just not what it was. Governments are looking locally. They don't want the risk of dealing with international partners with the global situation the way it is.'

I tried to focus in on what he was saying but my heart thudded in my chest.

The mill was closing. I didn't have a job.

One of the union reps got up and explained that we'd get a payout. It wasn't huge, but it was something.

People put their hands up and asked questions but I couldn't hear them, I was too far away.

The woman next to me gave me a nudge and pointed to the door that went back into the offices. Jade was standing there, the empty chip packet in her hand, watching us.

I crossed the factory floor and took her hand.

'My computer ran out of batteries,' she said, 'even though it was plugged in. It just stopped.'

'That's okay,' I said, 'we're going home anyway.'

'But what about work?' she asked.

'It's finished for the day.'

We went back to the office and I packed up Jade's things and grabbed some stuff off my desk. My inbox was open on my screen and I stared at it for a moment. There were cancelled orders coming in from Indonesia, from Vietnam. People had lost how to communicate across borders. We couldn't see each other anymore. We couldn't understand each other, couldn't understand what other people were experiencing. Everyone was turning inwards. Countries were turning inwards.

I closed my inbox and shut down my computer.

Nicola appeared beside me. 'You can't just go,' she said.

I wish I'd said something cool like, 'Watch me', or 'Yes I fucking can'. But I didn't say anything. I just looked at her and then picked up a sad old banana from my desk and put it in my backpack.

I took Jade's hand and we walked out the doors and into the car park.

People stood around in groups, smoking and scrolling on their phones.

Jade looked up at me. 'We aren't coming back for ages,' she said.

'Yeah, not for a while,' I said, squeezing her hand. 'The mill is closing for a bit.'

Dean had come out of the factory and was talking to Alan by the big roller doors. There was a small mirror hanging from a lanyard on his belt. As he was talking to Alan, he pulled the mirror and the cord extended so he could look into it. He glanced at his reflection for a moment, and then let the mirror hang back to his hip.

Jade looked at them. 'What're they doing, Mum?'

'They've gone,' I said. 'Him too. It's a thing now, with the mirrors, so they can see themselves. They like it.'

Dean and Alan reached down at the same time to grab their mirrors. They kept talking as they pulled them up to their faces, took a quick look, and then dropped them again.

I said, 'I think it makes them feel better.'

I piled our stuff into the car and we drove round to see Dad.

'I heard on the radio,' he said as Jade and I walked into the lounge. 'Damn stupid.'

'There were no overseas orders,' I said. 'Too risky. Too many gaps. Supply lines are a total mess. People don't know how to talk to each other.'

'It's been through rough times before,' Dad said. 'After the '87 crash, you should've seen it, we had this huge shipment that nobody would buy, nobody wanted anything to do with us, but we bounced back.'

Dad had started at the mill when he was fifteen. He still knew heaps of people who worked there. Even after his accident, he'd ask me all the time about new clients and new products and new equipment. And he kept in touch with his old mates who still worked there, old dudes who knew every little detail about the boilers, the rollers, and the lifts. These guys could fix anything.

'I don't know what we're going to do,' I said.

'Let's go for a walk,' said Dad.

Jade took Dad's hand. 'I'll take you, Pop,' she said.

We walked out through the messy back garden and then Jade passed Dad's hand to me, and ran ahead, yelling, 'I'm just running to the gate!' so that Dad would know what was happening. She opened the back gate and held it open for Dad and me, hopping from foot to foot as I guided Dad through. We walked through the neighbour's paddocks and down to the track that ran next to the creek.

Miri and I used to play there all the time when we were kids. Chantal cut up her stockings for us, and stuffed cat food down the end, in the bit where toes go, and we'd take them down to the river and try to catch eels. Once, one bit at Miri's stocking, and she half-pulled it out of the river. We both tried to grab it, but it was so slick we couldn't get a hand on it.

'Mother fucker!' said Miri.

'Mother fucker!' I said too because it seemed a cool thing to say.

I remember how we grinned at each other. We'd nearly caught an eel.

Down at the river with Dad, he said, 'I remember my first day at the mill.'

'What'd you do?' asked Jade.

'Dog's body.'

'A dog's body! That's not a job!' Jade cracked up and ran ahead of us again, trailing a big stick behind her through the dirt.

I said to Dad, 'Chantal came to see me. Miri sent a message, she's up north, she said that I should come. She said something big was going to happen.'

'And did Chantal know, that Miri had gone?' Dad asked.

'Yeah, she knew, of course. It was like we thought, Miri came and went for a while. She said she hasn't told anyone. I think I believe her.'

'Okay, okay.'

'She misses her,' I said. 'She hasn't seen her for a long time. Maybe she will go too, up north.'

'I think you should go,' said Dad. 'It must be important. I think you should get out of town.'

'I won't leave you and Mum,' I said.

'Guy is here,' said Dad.

I snorted.

'He helps his old man,' said Dad.

Jade yelled, from up ahead, 'Look! Pop! A spider web!'

'What does she look like?' Dad said to me quietly, so quietly that I almost couldn't hear him.

I had my hand on his arm and I gave him a squeeze.

'I can't, Dad, I can't,' I said. I shook my head.

We felt the space between us again. Dad wanted to see, wanted me to colour for him, wanted to be back in the world of colours and shapes and forms. And I wanted to get the words out, the words that had piled up and pressed against the inside of my head. I wanted to be the line of sight that connected him to the world.

Sometimes, at night, I'd lie in bed and whisper them to myself, just to get them out. No harm done. No one around. No one could get hurt. I described the things I'd seen in the day. I liked doing the most boring things. I liked the cereal packets, and the rubbish trucks, and the men's shirts, and the fence posts. I liked the boring words. 'Flat', 'green', 'puffy', 'shiny'. I said them, and let them out into the night. Words for things. All the boring things that Dad couldn't see.

So, Dad, here she is. Look. Jade, six years old, on the track down by the river, round the back of our house. She hops on one leg and points at a spider's web in the knot of a tree. Her eyes are wide. She waits for me to nod and say, 'Yeah, cool,' and then she runs down the path. The spiky energy inside her that means she won't stay still, can't stay still. She has a pink hair tie on her wrist that has a unicorn stuck on it with a bit of hard glue. Dad, here she is. I want to hold her here, in these words, but she's gone, she's gone, she runs down the track and disappears round the corner.

28.

Jade and I stayed at home for a few days. It was quiet. I helped Jade with her schoolwork. We drew pictures. I found *Monsters, Inc.* on some dodgy site and we watched it twice on the laptop. I looked at job ads online, but listings appeared and disappeared, sites flickered in and out, and the internet was unstable.

I went into work to get the forms so that I could get my payout.

'They're boarding it up,' the woman at reception said. 'They're worried about looters. Lots of businesses that have shut up shop have been hit. Gaps looking for opportunities.'

'What would they want to steal?' I asked.

'There's lots of equipment in there that'd be worth a mint. Gaps, they don't give a shit. They just do whatever they want. They'd make a mess of the mill, given half a chance.'

At night, I checked our suitcase, the packets of two-minute noodles. Should we go up north? How far would we get with the road-blocks and the closed businesses and the stacks of posters that cluttered every playground and every roadside, taking over every public space? And what if we went before we got to Miri? We'd be stopped, rounded up, sent back, or sent somewhere else.

I checked the windows were closed. I had two smokes left in my pack, and after Jade had gone to sleep at night, I sat on the backdoor step and before I knew it, I'd smoked both of them.

By Saturday, we really needed to get out of the house, so we went round to Mum and Dad's.

When we arrived, the kitchen smelt good. Mum had dug up some of the wild potatoes that grew down the back of their garden, roasted them, and fried some sausages.

We sat on the old deck chairs in the long grass by the fishpond.

Jade had her sausage in a piece of bread with lots of sauce. Mum and Dad and I each had a beer.

It was calm, sunny. We didn't talk about Miri. We didn't talk about the gaps. Mum got up and took a photo of us and I smiled. Jade had sauce on her cheek.

Dad was always the first to hear when someone turned into the driveway. He turned his head and tilted it slightly, as if that helped him hear better. That's when we knew that someone was coming.

A car pulled up on the other side of the house and a door slammed.

'That's Guy,' Mum said. 'I told him that we were having sausages. I'll go and make him a plate.'

She went into the kitchen and Guy came round the side of the house.

'Guy!' Jade jumped up and gave him a hug. 'I watched gone Katy Perry all afternoon.'

'Cool cool,' Guy said, sitting down and putting his feet up on an upside-down crate. 'Looks like you need to get the lawnmower out, old man. Bit of jungle back here.'

'I'd end up mowing down the washing line,' said Dad.

'And the fishpond,' said Jade, 'and all the fish.'

Mum brought out a plate of food and Guy cracked open a beer. 'I'll come and do it for you, Dad. I'll come on the weekend, got nothing on.'

Guy had been offering to do the lawn and not doing it for ten years.

We ate our dinner. Jade told Guy all about gone Katy Perry, how she was the same and not the same. The sun set behind us and cast our shadows onto the grass. Guy crushed his beer can and chucked it in front of him and Mum brought us all another one. A truck rumbled along the road, behind the macrocarpa hedge. Guy told Dad some joke that he had seen online, but Dad didn't get it. I tucked my legs up underneath my bum and sipped my beer. My worries felt far away. The mill closing, the looting, Miri and her message.

Jade ran down to the back of the garden where she was building fairy houses out of bits of plant pots and wildflowers.

Dad tilted his head, 'Jade's not here?'

'Yeah,' I said.

'Can we listen to a bit of the news?'

I didn't want to interrupt the still evening but I put the news on my phone and balanced it on the arm of my deck chair. Radio was so much easier than TV. We could follow the flow of information on radio, but video was broken. Gaps pushed the image around from their invisible places. They had too much power to control what we saw.

More gone babies. More riots. Hospitals being overrun by panicking parents who demanded answers. A detention centre in Greece where gaps had started a hunger strike, protesting against their conditions.

'Christ almighty,' said Dad.

'Maybe we should turn it off for a bit, eh?' said Guy and he stood up to grab my phone, but he never made it. As he reached over, his arm seized up and he shuddered and fell onto the grass.

'Arg!' he yelled, clutching his arm at the wrist. 'Arg!'

Mum leapt up. 'Guy! Guy! What's wrong?'

Guy writhed around on the ground, grabbing his wrist and then his stomach.

'What's going on?' yelled Dad, standing up and knocking over his chair.

Guy tried to speak but he choked and spluttered, spit gathering around his lips. 'I'm—' he tried to get words out but couldn't.

Jade ran across the garden to us, her eyes wide. 'What's wrong? What's wrong with Guy?' She grabbed Dad's hand to stop him from bumping into the fishpond.

Guy grabbed at my leg, one hand closing on my ankle. 'J—', he started to say.

'He needs you, Jodie, he needs your help!' yelled Mum. 'What is it, Guy?' She knelt down next to him, cradling his head.

My phone had fallen onto the grass but the news presenter's voice droned on. All the terrible news. All of the world, falling apart.

'He's going out,' Mum yelled. 'He just said, he's going! He's going!'

And here's where I start to remember every single tiny detail, as if, above us, a bright light had been switched on and it revealed every blade of grass, every wrinkle on Mum's hands, every sequin on Jade's T-shirt.

Guy's voice. 'I'm going,' he said. 'Fuck.'

'Do something!' Mum turned to me, shouting. 'Do it!'

Guy groaned and shook.

'He's in pain, Jodie!' said Mum. 'Oh god, look at him! Make it stop!'

Jade yelled, 'Do it, Mum! Don't let him go!'

'Hurry, Jodie, hurry! Oh god!' shouted Mum. Her trembling hands held Guy's head.

Then, from behind me, Dad's voice, calm, steady, 'J, do it. Do it. Please.'

Guy's face was turned away from me, but it didn't matter, I knew him. I knew everything about him. I knew his black jeans and his faded blue T-shirt. I knew his little red lighter in his front pocket. I knew his three-day-old stubble, his hands, a little shaky, a little unsure. His beat-up sneakers, the laces tied up differently on each shoe.

I said these things. The words came easily, especially with Dad behind me, listening, his hand on my shoulder. It was the way I'd always coloured for Dad. Take something, hold it up, look at it closely, and find the right words. Not fancy words. Just the right words. The right words had the right power in them.

I knelt on the grass and said Guy's words. Grey eyes. Freckled arms. His dark hair, a little too long at the back, scruffy.

Mum cried. Jade knelt down next to me and put her hand on my leg.

Guy, when he was a kid, ran with his head down, talking to himself, and looking at the ground, as if that might make him go faster. And he was fast, when he played rugby, running on the wing. Guy in his red and white rugby strip, muddy, holding a trophy above his head and grinning. Guy with his black headphones on, slouched on the couch. Guy in his car, gunning the engine. Guy taking Dad's hands and showing him where his cup of tea was. Guy scrolling on his phone. Guy on his skateboard. The arm he broke when he was sixteen, trying to be cool and do an ollie. A white cast. A sling. The scar just below his elbow where the bone had come through. The skin there was so smooth, almost shiny, as if it had been ironed or flattened or melted and reformed. That bit of Guy's skin. Only three centimetres across.

I sank back and sat down fully on the grass, tired. Dad took his hand off my shoulder.

I picked up my phone from the grass and trained it on Guy's back. He was present. 'He's here,' I said.

Mum sobbed.

'You did it, Mum,' said Jade. 'You did it!'

Guy turned towards me and as soon as I saw his face, I knew what he had done. His little smile. His look of satisfaction. He got up, brushed off his jeans, and tapped something on his phone.

'Yeah,' he said, 'funny that.'

Mum looked up at him, wiping the tears from her face. 'Are you okay?'

'Yeah. Thanks, sis,' he said.

I stared at him. 'What've you done?' I asked.

He laughed. 'Nothing, nothing, I'm here, aren't I?' He dismissed me with a wave of his hand. 'Your little thing must have worked. Colouring, that's what you two call it, eh?'

'Guy—' Dad's voice held a warning.

'Calm down, calm down,' Guy said, laughing again. He glanced at Dad though, a little worried, and looked away again. 'I just wanted to know, you know, if Jodie could do it. We all thought so, didn't we? We all thought that her thing might have something to do with it? I mean, come on, it's obvious.'

I said again, standing up, 'What've you done? Were you even going?'

Mum had her phone out and was checking Guy was present. 'He's here! He's still here,' she said.

'I know that, Mum! But was he even going? How do we know he was going?' I asked.

'He said! He said he was. Guy, were you? Were you going?' Mum looked at him, frowning.

Guy shrugged. 'I dunno. I think so? I gotta say, Jodie, it was pretty interesting, what you said, how you said it. It's, like, sorta boring, right? But that's the point, eh? Boring?'

Guy's phone pinged and he took it out of his pocket. 'I gotta go. Thanks for the feed.'

Thanks for the feed? I was so pissed. I was burning up. I walked towards him. 'Where are you going, Guy? Who messaged you?' I asked. Guy was working for someone. Guy was feeding someone information about me. 'Who was that man?' I asked. 'That man with saw you with in town?'

Guy smirked. 'Just Matt. You know Matt, right? At the garage?'

'Give me your phone,' I said.

'I'm not giving you my fucking phone.'

'Did you just record me colouring? Is it on your phone?'

'What? No!'

He was such a liar. Someone had asked him to gather information about me and he was doing it. He didn't care. He didn't give a shit about his own sister.

'You know that they're watching me, right? You know that they—'

'Jodie,' Dad interrupted me. 'Let's just calm down. Guy didn't record you.'

This was fucking typical. Dad had always trusted Guy, always believed that he was better than he really was.

Guy gestured to Dad. 'See? See? It's not always about you, you know? You're not always the centre of the universe.'

I was about to yell at him again when Jade stepped forward and put her small hand inside mine. I looked down at her. I had forgotten that she was there. Here she is. Her eyes large with worry. Grass stuck to her knees. Sauce on her T-shirt.

She asked, 'Were you really going, Guy?'

He looked at her and the asshole lied again. 'Yeah, I was. But lucky we've got your mum around though, eh? She's got some sweet skills. Special skills. She's pretty onto it, your mum.'

I watched Guy leave, heard his car growl down the driveway. Was he going to report back to the people he was working for?

I thought about following him but I felt so tired, and scared, and I wanted to stay with Jade and make sure she was okay.

Mum picked up the plates from where they had been left on the grass. As I led Dad into the lounge, he said, 'You did the right thing. He was going. He needed you. Family have got to look out for each other.'

I led Dad to his chair.

'Jodie,' he said as he sat down, 'I'm sorry.'

'What? What for?'

'For the colouring. I shouldn't have asked you to do it. I... it's just very dark for me in here. I was scared. But I shouldn't have done that, it was too much.'

I took his hands. 'Dad, I wanted to. I loved it. It was our thing.'

'Yes, but... I didn't know. I didn't know that it would get as big as this.'

'We shouldn't, you know, talk... we don't know...'

He nodded.

That night, Mum made up the beds in my old room for me and Jade.

I lay in bed and watched Jade sleeping. I kept thinking about Guy. He hadn't been going, I knew it. He had just tricked me into colouring so he could give information about me to someone.

When would these people make a move? I thought about emptying my mind of words, disconnecting all the things from their right names, from the words that let them be in the world, be an image, and letting them melt away. Could I switch it off, if I needed to? They couldn't force me to do it. I wouldn't. Fuck 'em.

I woke at five in the morning and checked my phone in the dark, Jade's even breathing in the bed next to me. Overnight, Paul Irons and a crowd of Purity gaps had taken over a neighbouring farm. As usual, the news was pockmarked, split apart and hard to understand, but there were some reports of violent resistance, of guns, of shots fired.

At breakfast, Mum put on the radio in the lounge. Irons was being interviewed. 'If the government are going to try and introduce their draconian new measures, then we will fight back,' he said. 'It's as simple as that. We will not be reintegrated into wider society, which is what they claim to want to do. But we are not fooled by these spurious claims. We are set apart and that is the way we wish to stay. As we see it, it is a simple request.'

'What's he talking about?' I asked Dad.

'They're going to tag the gaps,' Dad said, 'announced it late last night. Can't see them on CCTV, so gotta keep tabs on them some other way.'

On my phone, I watched aerial footage of the farm next to Purity. A barricade had been set up, made out of old pallets and tyres and other stuff dragged from off the farm they had taken over. Bits of wood shifted and moved, bumped around by the gaps that I couldn't see. The drone moved over the nearby fields, searching the area. The fields were possibly full of gaps, but in the footage they were empty, there was no sign of violence or the attack that the media was reporting.

'They're going to start locking things down, shutting up shop,' said Dad. 'They're going to stop people from moving around the country because of this joker down south. There were more protests in Auckland, they took over the harbour bridge.'

Dad was right, the government moved quickly to stop anybody coming and going from Purity. On TV, we watched the Prime Minister announce the new tagging system for gaps. The recent violence near Purity was 'further proof that this action was warranted', he said. Gaps would be tagged with a microchip under the skin so that they could be found at any time. 'It is the simple requirement of citizens of New Zealand that they are able to be seen by their government,' said the Prime Minister. 'This measure is for the safety of both gaps and the communities of presents that they live among. We need to understand their needs better, so we need to see them, in any way that we can. We need to look closely.'

On my phone, Mum and I watched police put up roadblocks across the country. In Central Otago, around Purity, people were advised not to travel unnecessarily. 'The area is unsafe,' a policeman said in a clip, 'and we can't guarantee the safety of people when there are gaps at large.'

I remember the news building up throughout the day. Things escalated quickly. Gaps around the country moved towards Purity to support their movement. Dad and I heard an angry voice on the radio, 'You can't tag us like rats for some experiment! This is an outrageous breach of privacy!'

Footage showed a convoy of cars, empty of drivers or passengers, moving through Christchurch, and more shots taken from above Purity, searching for some sign of what they were doing in there, what they were planning.

We hated it, the fact that we couldn't see them. We felt like it was our right to see, to know what they were doing. I read some of the angry comments spreading online. These comments had mostly been buried in underground forums until then, but now pissed-off presents were everywhere.

I wish I hadn't felt that way too. But I did. I watched the footage of the empty paths and playgrounds that they'd built at Purity and I felt excluded, angry. What were they doing in there? It felt like a contract had been broken, something fundamental was being ignored by the gaps in Purity. They weren't giving us their images and that felt like an insult. They were giving us the finger. And they didn't care.

I remember that day. It was fast and slow at the same time. Riots erupted all over the country and police spread out to stop them. The gaps at Purity extended their barricade and Irons's voice was all over the radio, issuing his demands.

But it was all so hard to keep hold of. It came from all angles and was broken up, confused, empty images of Purity, scenes of people arguing with empty spaces, policemen defending a line against invisible attackers.

Dad used his screen reader to read news websites on his phone but it didn't make any sense, the words didn't link up into sentences, and the voice leapt from place to place. 'It's from the code,' said Dad. 'It reads from the code. It must be broken.' He turned the robotic voice off.

In the late afternoon, I stood at the kitchen window, peeling more potatoes, and watched Jade follow Mum around the garden with the hose. I could see Jade chattering away, her mouth opening and closing, and Mum nodding, half listening. Mum looked over and saw me at the window. She pushed her hair out of her eyes. She looked worried.

Dad was at the kitchen table. The radio was on and the announcer was talking about how 'unnecessary travel was not advised' and how it was likely that 'further measures would be implemented to curb the threat of rogue gaps'.

I watched Jade. Here she is. I thought about Guy falling down onto the grass, his body shaking, his back towards me. Mum in tears beside him. What had it felt like, for him, when I had coloured? Could he feel himself coming back in, just as I had felt myself fading when I shaded from Johnny? Or did it make him hate me more? Me trying to do this thing for him, the thing he'd always hated. The radio droned on. Things falling apart. Gaps moving about in their secret, hidden world. They could do whatever they wanted. They'd bring everything down. They didn't give a fuck. Guy turning back to me, that small smile on his face. He knew! He knew! He knew exactly what he was doing. He had laid a trap for me. Maybe it was the final piece in the puzzle that they needed before they came after me, this proof that Guy had recorded for them.

Dad turned off the radio. He said, 'You should go up north.'

I put down the potato peeler. I wiped my hands on a tea towel. 'Yeah, we should go.'

'Soon,' Dad said.

'Now,' I said. 'Right now, before we can't get out. Miri will be able to help. Guy is talking to someone.'

'I'm sorry,' said Dad.

'It's not your fault, Dad.'

'I should've done more for Guy. I should've included him. I should never have asked you to colour.'

'Dad—'

'No!' Dad raised his voice. He had forgotten who could be listening, the danger we were in. 'It wasn't right. I was a selfish prat. It pushed Guy away. I should've—'

'He wanted to be pushed away,' I said. 'That's just the way he is.'
Dad said nothing.

'I'm going to go and get our stuff,' I said. 'Can you tell Jade that I've just gone to pick something up?'

I drove back to our house through the quiet streets. No one was out. Everyone was at home, listening to the news, watching the images that made no sense. But as I drove past the fire station the roller doors were up and it was filled with a big group of people. Some kind of meeting, the community patrol, maybe. People turned and looked as I drove past. I checked my rear-view mirror and their eyes followed me down the road.

I unlocked the door and went into the dim lounge. I flicked on the light and saw open drawers and cushions thrown across the floor. Jade's schoolbooks had been pushed off the coffee table. Someone had been in our house.

I stood still, listening, my heart thumping. The house was silent.

I left the door behind me open and went into the kitchen, turning on lights as I went. It was a mess. The backdoor was closed and I couldn't see any broken windows. I glanced out at the backyard. Nothing.

I quickly went down the hall and checked all the rooms. No one. I went into my bedroom and the bag I'd packed was still there, under my bed. Clothes had been pulled out of my cupboard and lay on the floor. The drawer in my bedside table hung open, Panadol and hair ties and other crap had been rifled through and scattered around.

I tried to focus. I had prepared for this, sort of. We had to get out of there. Fast.

I went around our house grabbing the things that I could find in the chaos. Toothbrushes and shampoo, Jade's favourite toys, togs, sunscreen, plasters.

Outside, I chucked the bag in the boot along with sleeping bags and blankets. I went back into the kitchen and grabbed all the last tins and packets and put them in a box. I checked the fridge. There wasn't much in there. I poured the milk down the sink. I don't know why, it was all such a mess anyway.

I stood and looked around and then I heard a car on the street outside. Was it idling right next to our place? I went through the house and closed all the curtains, and the car moved on, growling down the road.

I paused, thinking, then went to the cupboard in the hall. The sheets and towels had been pulled out, but, in the box at the back, I found the photo of Miri and me when we were ten, my arm around the space where Miri should've been, and I put the photo in my pocket.

I took a last look around, then turned off the lights, locked the door behind me, and jumped in the car.

Empty streets on the way back to Mum and Dad's, now much darker, streetlights on. I took a different route to avoid the fire station and the gathered group.

When I got back, Dad was on the couch with Jade, playing a book for her with his screen reader. He tilted his head when I came in, listening for me. 'All okay?' he asked.

'Yeah.'

Mum was in the kitchen, packing food into a bag. She turned towards me, but didn't look up, and I saw that she had been crying. She reached over and turned the radio on and its blaring music drowned out our conversation.

'I'm just putting in some things,' she whispered, panicked. 'Crackers, some Vegemite.'

'Mum—'

'I just got a text,' she said. 'There's some kind of group in town, a protest. Gaps, maybe. They're smashing windows.'

'Mum—'

'Guy was going! He was! I saw. He wouldn't hurt you, Jodie. He won't tell anyone.' She brushed tears off her cheek.

'It doesn't matter,' I said. 'It's not safe here for us, we should've gone weeks ago, but I was freaked out. I didn't know what to do.'

She nodded. 'Where will you go?'

'Up north. We'll stop at Renee's. We'll see if we can get in touch with Miri. Chantal might be able to help.'

I told her this plan, but I was making it up. I didn't know what I was doing, where we were going. We should go to Renee's first, yes. She would know what to do. She might've even been in touch with Miri. She'd let Miri know that we were on our way, that we were coming to find her.

I said, 'I'll drive to Auckland tonight and we'll stop there for a bit.'

'The roadblocks,' Mum said.

'We're present. We'll be sweet. It's okay.' I didn't mention the WOF.

She put the bag down on the bench and pulled me towards her, putting her arm around me. She whispered in my ear, 'It wasn't you. You didn't start it, you didn't. It was just between you and Dad. It made him so happy. You helped him see all the things in the world.'

I pulled away, tears rising. We looked at each other for a moment, and then Mum turned away and put more things in the bag.

While Jade sat with Dad, I grabbed some more things and put them in the car. Pillows, Jade's gumboots. Mum came out with me and tucked the bag of food into the last corner of the boot. The car was stuffed.

'Take this,' Mum said, and held out some money.

'No, Mum, no.'

'Take it. Don't be stupid. It's only two hundred bucks.'

She tucked it into the pocket of my jacket.

I didn't protest. I needed that money.

We went back inside and found Jade asleep on the couch, curled up next to Dad. The screen reader was still loudly telling the story and the radio was playing music in the kitchen, drowning out any noise we made.

We didn't say much, though, so there wasn't a lot to hide.

I gently lifted Jade up. I could still carry her. Look. Floppy arms and legs, that sleepy heaviness. Her pink polar fleece. Her eyes flickering, not really awake, not seeing anything as we walk down the hall. Mum and Dad are behind us. Jade's head is warm against my shoulder. My hip holds her up. Here she is.

Outside, Mum opened the car door and helped get Jade into her booster seat, where she was quickly asleep again.

I closed the door and turned to Mum. She held her finger to her lips, showing that she didn't want to talk, even out in the still silence of the night. She pulled me close. The security light above the front door went out and we were suddenly in darkness.

I reached out for Dad. He came closer and put his arms around me and Mum, locking us together. None of us said anything. I remember how we stood in the dark. I thought about what it was like for Dad, always in darkness. I didn't want to leave that space, to drive away into the falling-apart world, but I had to, I didn't know what Guy was up to, who he was talking to right now, and I had to answer these questions about myself, it was messing me up, not knowing. I had to find Miri and find out if I had put her out, if she had been the first, if it had all started with her.

I shrugged them off and got into the car. I flicked on the lights and reversed down the drive, watching Mum and Dad fade into the darkness.

A little way down the road I pulled over and put the car in park. I rested my forehead on the steering wheel and took deep breaths. I looked up and out at the dark road. I didn't know what was ahead of us. I wanted to text Renee but I couldn't. We'd just have to turn up.

I heard a car in the distance and I saw the headlights coming up behind us. I looked at Jade, slumped in her seat. I had to get going. I had to harden up. It was eight o'clock. We could get to Auckland by midnight.

I let the car pass us and then I pulled out onto the road.

29.

I drove for three hours and Jade slept. I blasted the heater. I left my phone face up on the passenger seat so I could see if anyone messaged me. I glanced down at it now and again. I thought about throwing it away. Someone was using it to track me. But what would I do without it?

Focus, I told myself. Get to Renee's first and then figure out what to do with your phone. I could get a new SIM card. Would that help? Was Renee going to freak out when we arrived in the middle of the night? Tracey definitely would. She never really liked me, Tracey. I was a piece of Renee's past that she didn't want around.

Well, she'd just have to suck it up. We wouldn't be there for long.

On the outskirts of Auckland I slowed and turned off into a petrol station. I was worried that if the car stopped for too long Jade would wake up, so I jumped out, quickly put the nozzle in the tank, and pressed 'fill'. It was self-service, so I swiped my credit card.

The forecourt was empty. It was late, 11:30 at least, maybe later. The fluorescent light above me buzzed and flickered. Jade wriggled in her seat and I watched the numbers on the pump spin past, willing it to go faster. Tick, tick, tick.

I glanced across the forecourt at the night window to see if anyone was there, watching me. The main window of the shop was smashed. The glass hadn't fallen out onto the concrete but it was broken and splintered into a web of thin lines.

The front door hung open on a weird angle and I could just make out that the shop had been looted. Packets of chips were scattered across the floor. Lollies and toilet rolls and tissue boxes were everywhere. The lights in the fridges at the back flashed on and off, illuminating bottles of Coke and then letting them fall into darkness again.

I was standing there, staring, when another car drove into the station.

I tugged out the nozzle, slung it back into the machine, and jumped into the car. I started the engine and pulled out and onto the motorway.

I glanced in my rear-view mirror. For a moment, nothing. And then I saw it, the car coming out onto the motorway too, following us.

I gripped the steering wheel to stop my hands from shaking and sped up. The streetlights flicking past. My heart thudding.

Jade stirred and opened her eyes, confused. 'Mum?'

'It's okay, we're nearly there.'

Her head drooped and she went back to sleep. I hadn't even told her where we were going or what we were doing. She might freak out when she woke up at Renee's place.

I sped down the southern motorway, heading into Auckland. The car following us kept a little way behind, not too close, not too far. But there, keeping up.

A couple of trucks appeared on the road ahead of us, and I overtook them. I was going too fast. The car disappeared from view, caught behind the trucks, and then the flashing lights of a roadblock appeared ahead and we all slowed down and were guided into different lanes.

I'd been waiting for a roadblock since we left Whakatāne, expecting one to appear at every turn in the road, and I knew what I had to do.

A police officer waved us into the area in front of the barrier arm and I wound down my window so she could take my photo.

I had to be quick. I didn't think. I whispered the words for the edge of the window frame, the car door, the windscreen. Just the simple things. The boring things. Quietly, a murmur. Just enough, so I was shaded the tiniest bit, to confuse them, to cover myself from the camera. Someone was looking for me, and I wouldn't let them know that I was here. The camera would see me, yes, but it wouldn't know who I was. I had to shade myself, but just a little bit.

I whispered the words as I gave my face calmly to the photo, but I had taken my hands off the steering wheel and pressed my fingers into my thighs until it hurt. I wanted to feel something, my body hurting, my being, being *there*, like it would protect me, make sure I hadn't gone, and stop them from seeing inside me, into my mind, into my thoughts, and the cloud of words that sat inside my head.

The police officer took the photo and frowned at her phone. She walked away and showed it to her team.

I waited on the dark motorway. The flashing lights of the road-block threw an orange glare into the car. I checked Jade. Still sleeping.

I wasn't worried that it wouldn't work. I felt more and more sure about what I could do and how to do it. As soon as I started whispering the words, I knew what to say and how much. It felt normal, like reaching for something that was always next to me, always ready.

The police officer came back, and without saying a word she motioned at me to lower Jade's window. Looking in the rear-view mirror, I shaded Jade, whispering. The band of her seatbelt. The texture of her car seat and the scruffy carpet at her feet. Everything was grey or black or dark. The material of the car seat had tiny red diamonds on it.

The police officer took a photo of Jade, then she tapped and scrolled, her head tilted to the side. I watched her. I felt the urge to take a photo of her too. I wanted to keep looking at her forever.

'Where are you going?' the police officer asked, not looking up.

'Visiting a friend in Sandringham.'

'Might not want to stay long,' she said. 'It's gonna get harder getting in and out, real soon. People are gonna have to stay put. Auckland specially.'

She looked up and we made eye contact for the first time. What did I look like to her? I still felt slightly shaded, hidden, powerful. Maybe that was why I asked, 'What're you going to do with the gaps that try and get through?'

'Gonna stop them and ship them out,' she said. 'Out to the new centres.'

She looked bored. Her gaze slipped past me to a van in the queue behind me. I looked too, in my wing mirror, but I couldn't see the car that had followed us.

The barrier arm swung up and the policewoman waved us through.

I drove out of the roadblock, fast, but not too fast, checking all the time in my mirror for the other car, but it must have got caught up further back in the queue.

I turned off the motorway and into the suburbs, a lot of shops were boarded up, and the streets were dark and empty. I stopped at a red light and saw a group of gaps standing on a nearby corner under a streetlight. There were about eight of them, and I knew they were gaps because they had mirrors hanging on cords. Some of them took out their phones and started taking photos, desperate to record something, desperate to be part of the world of images that they had been rejected from.

As soon as the light changed to green I gunned it down the road, the gaps snapping photos of us as we disappeared into the night. They could take my photo, but that meant nothing really, I couldn't save them, no one could.

I parked outside Renee's house just before twelve. All was quiet and dark. Jade was slumped in her seat. Her head rolled forward like a doll's. I undid her seatbelt and picked her up.

Next door, a dog started barking. Shut the fuck up! I screamed in my head as I struggled round the side of the house with Jade heavy in my arms.

I tapped on the back door with my free hand. No movement from inside. The dog kept barking. Maybe it'd help to wake them up. I tapped again. Jade opened her eyes and lifted her head.

I was thinking about going round to tap on Renee and Tracey's window when the light came on in the kitchen and I saw Tracey's face peer out at us from the window, frowning.

She opened the back door, her hair messed up and her face furious. She was pissed.

'Jodie! What the hell? What're you doing here? It's the middle of the night,' Tracey said.

'I'm sorry, I can explain. I couldn't text.'

Tracey didn't move from her spot in the doorframe, her hand on the door.

'Can we—' I said.

I moved to step inside. There was a moment when I thought Tracey wasn't going to let us in, and that she was going to shut the door

231

and send us away. I wanted to get into the light of her kitchen and close the door behind us. I wanted to forget about the drive through the night and the roadblock and the shading and the group of gaps staring at us from the side of the road.

And then Renee was there behind Tracey, her worried face, and she was pulling us into the house and closing the door behind us and hugging us, and Jade was waking up and saying, 'Renee!', all confused and sleepy, and I felt this wave of relief break over me, that we had got this far, and that we were safe here for the night.

Renee got sleeping bags out, and I settled Jade down on the couch in the office. I sat next to her for a while before she dropped off. I could hear Renee and Tracey speaking quietly in the kitchen.

'Why are we here?' Jade asked.

'We're going to go up north, on a little holiday,' I said.

'Did we drive here? In the night?'

'Yeah.'

'This is Ari's sleeping bag,' she said, and then, out of nowhere, 'We're going to see Miri.'

She closed her eyes and fell asleep.

When had I talked to Jade about Miri? I couldn't remember. Jade never stopped surprising me with what she remembered and the tiny things she noticed.

I went to the kitchen and stood in the doorway. Renee and Tracey turned to look at me, hair all over the place, dressing gowns on.

'I'm sorry,' I said. 'We won't stay. We're going up north. We're going to find Miri.'

Renee and Tracey began to talk at the same time, but Tracey's voice rose over Renee's.

'You don't get to turn up here in the middle of the night and scare the shit out of us, Jodie,' Tracey said. 'That's not a thing that you get to do.'

'We're not staying. It's just for one night,' I said.

I knew Tracey would be pissed off. She had a right to be. Here I was, knocking on her door in the middle of the night, with my kid sleeping on my shoulder. I just had to ride it for one night and then get the hell out of there.

'Why didn't you text me?' Renee asked.

'I can't text,' I said. 'It's... it's just not safe, for us, at the moment...' I trailed off.

'For fuck's sake,' said Tracey. 'It's not safe for anyone, anywhere at the moment! Did you come through a roadblock? They're screening everyone, they're rounding gaps up and sending them away.' Her voice broke and Renee put her hand on her shoulder.

'We should go to bed,' Renee said. 'Let's sort it out in the morning.'

I got a couple of hours of sleep. When Jade woke up she rolled off the couch onto the floor next to me. 'You slept on the floor!' she said, like it was the funniest thing she'd ever seen.

'Do you remember getting here last night?' I asked. 'You were pretty sleepy.'

'Yeah,' she said. 'We're going to see Miri.'

'How do you know about Miri?'

'You told me about her, she's a gap, but she's your friend. Is she your best friend? Cara is my best friend.'

'Yeah, she's my best friend. I've known her since I was little, like you. She used to live next door to me.'

'Cool. I wish Cara lived next door to me. Maybe Miri can be my new best friend.'

I thought about Miri on the couch with Dad and me on Sunday afternoons, watching music videos, me colouring for Dad, and Miri just sitting there, not even really listening to us, like it wasn't a big deal, it was just a normal thing. Miri was the only person outside of our family who knew about it, that's how close she was. She was part of it. Sometimes I felt as if Miri could colour too, like if I'd got up and walked away, into the kitchen to put the kettle on, she'd just be able to pick up where I stopped, in the middle of a sentence, like I wasn't sure where I ended and Miri began, our words could just blur into each other.

I struggled out of my sleeping bag. 'Yeah, I reckon Miri would want to be your best friend too,' I said.

'I'm gonna see Hugo and Ari,' said Jade.

'Okay, but, Jade, remember, we're not staying here for long. We're gonna get going this morning. We've got to get up north, to meet Miri.'

Jade ran down the hall into Hugo and Ari's room and I packed up the sleeping bags and tidied the little office, trying to make it look like we'd never been there at all.

Renee was in the kitchen, leaning against the bench and scrolling on her phone, when I went in. She looked up at me, biting her lip, her eyes wide.

'We'll just have some breakfast and then we'll go,' I said. I didn't like the way she was looking at me. 'You okay? Look, I'm sorry that we came—'

'You shouldn't have come here, Jodie,' she said.

'I know, I know, we're—'

'Why didn't you text me?'

'There's someone, I think, who's keeping an eye on me, on my phone.'

'What? Why?' Renee shook her head. 'Oh my god, I don't know what the fuck is going on.'

I walked over to her. I hated seeing her like this. She was normally so together. 'Hey, it's going to be okay,' I said. 'No one followed me, no one knows I'm here, we'll be gone in an hour.'

I could hear the kids screaming and laughing down the hall, excited to see each other. A loud thump as one of them jumped off a bed.

'Are you guys okay?' Renee yelled.

No reply, more laughter.

Renee rubbed her eyes. She looked so tired. 'Jodie,' she said. 'It's Ari, he's—'

Tracey was in the doorway. 'No, Renee, don't!' she said.

'She should know!' Renee said.

'No, it's just for us, for whānau,' Tracey said. Her eyes were red and glassy. She had been crying. I couldn't imagine Tracey crying. I had stepped into the middle of something messy. 'Who's after you, Jodie? And why?' Tracey demanded.

'I'm not sure,' I said, and Tracey snorted. 'It's true! I really don't know, but I think it has to do with something I did a long time ago, with Miri. That's why I'm going to find her, to sort it all out. I haven't seen her in so long, I need to talk to her, face to face.'

Renee said, 'Don't go through the CBD, they've taken over some buildings there, I just heard it on the radio. Gaps.'

'Taken over buildings?'

'Yeah, they're kind of burrowing in, throwing stuff out, taking over. There are fires on Queen Street.'

'I can go another way,' I said. 'The bridge should be okay.'

'There are roadblocks now, they're checking everyone,' said Tracey.

'It's the tagging,' I said. 'They're going to tag all the gaps.'

Renee made a strange sound, sort of half whimper, half gulp, as if she was trying desperately to hold everything in, but some small pain escaped. 'Jodie, it's Ari,' she said, her voice choked, 'he's gone.'

Tracey stormed out of the kitchen.

'She can't handle it,' said Renee, pointing towards Tracey. 'She can't talk about it.'

'When? When did it happen?' I asked.

'A couple of days ago,' said Renee. 'Hugo noticed first, because of—' She pointed down the hall at the photos hanging on the wall. 'I was putting him into bed and he said 'Ari has gone from the wall'.' Renee's eyes filled with tears. 'I hadn't even noticed. I hadn't even looked, and then I went into the hall, and he was... gone. He's gone. How could I not have seen?'

I walked over and hugged her. 'See,' I said, talking into her dark hair, 'you didn't notice because he's fine, right? It didn't hurt him. He's the same old Ari, it doesn't change him.'

I was shocked. I said some other stupid things to calm her, because I didn't know what to say. Down the hall, I heard Tracey telling the boys to get their clothes on, her voice loud and angry.

Renee pulled away, wiping her cheeks with the back of her hand.

'Did you talk to him about it?' I asked.

'Yeah, a bit. He seems... confused. But, I guess, we don't know how to talk about it really. Tracey's a mess and Ari can tell. Jodie,' her voice broke again, 'I don't want him to be tagged, it's not right, he's just a kid.'

'They won't, Renee, they can't do that to kids.'

'Yeah, but, on the radio—'

'Don't listen to the fucking radio! Listen to me, it's going to be okay, you just have to look after him, look after Tracey.'

Renee crossed the kitchen and flicked the kettle on. 'I think it would be good for us to get out of here for a while, but I kind of don't want to leave the house. I've heard some crazy shit about what's going on in town.'

The kids thundered into the kitchen, eyes bright, demanding breakfast. Renee and I put out Weet-Bix and milk, and peaches. I realised I was starving. I couldn't remember the last time I'd eaten.

I watched Ari. He seemed happy. Renee sat close to him, giving him extra peach juice from the tin. Tracey came into the kitchen, her hair damp from the shower. She wanted to know how many bowls Ari had eaten, and whether he wanted some more. 'Do you want a glass of juice?' she asked.

I watched them watching him, trying to see if anything had changed. Was he in pain? Did he feel things the same way? They wanted to hold him close, stitch him into their sides and never let him go, but he'd gone, and a part of him had slipped away. He felt less real to them now, and it scared them, this feeling that he wasn't quite there, that he couldn't be reached.

I understand this feeling now. Now that Jade has gone. I understand the women I'd seen in the maternity wards on TV, clutching their babies to their chests. Gone, gone, gone. Babies that only half appeared in the world. Babies that slipped away, unseen, unimaged, a person that would never be controlled, because they couldn't be photographed, a person that'd never be connected, linked, or understood.

Tracey reached over and filled my cup with more coffee. I smiled at her, but she didn't make eye contact with me. 'Thanks, Trace,' I said.

Ari leapt up and, standing on his chair, Weet-Bix on his chin, he shouted, 'The moon is made of cheese!'

Hugo took up the chant too, and then Jade. 'The moon is made of cheese!' They marched into the lounge, kicking their legs out in front of them.

'Jade, I'm going to have a quick shower, then we'll brush our teeth and go. Okay?' Jade wasn't listening. 'Is that okay, if I jump in the shower real quick?' I asked Renee, and she nodded, distracted.

I cranked the shower on really hot, scalding myself red. I nicked some fancy shampoo and washed my hair.

Getting out, I swiped the steam off the bathroom mirror and stared at myself, frowning. I wanted to feel clean, ready, on top of things. I didn't know where we were going, or what we were really doing. I just knew that we had to go and find Miri, and she was up north.

I loaded our stuff into the boot of the car, repacking things and tidying up. When Renee came out to help me, I asked her, 'Can we borrow your tent?'

'Jesus, Jodes, where are you guys going? You're going into the bush? Are you going completely off the grid?'

'It's just in case, you know, we need it.' I shrugged.

'Do you even know where Miri is, exactly?'

'She's going to get a message to me, somehow, she'll let me know.'

'Why can't she just call you? She's gone, right? But she could still call you.'

'It's not that easy now, you've seen what they're doing—' I stopped myself when I saw Renee's face begin to crumple. I didn't want to freak her out. 'You know Miri, eh? You remember what she's like. Nothing's ever easy with Miri. Nothing's ever straight down the line, there's always some drama.'

I went inside to get Jade into some clean clothes and convince her to brush her teeth. Ari and Hugo came into the bathroom to do their teeth too, and they all stood up on stools in a row of three in front of the mirror.

Hugo pointed at Ari's reflection and said, 'There you are!'

Ari grinned, toothpaste smeared all over his chin. 'Yeah, but I'm gone actually, out of the photos.' He said it proudly, like it was something special, and spat into the basin.

Hugo started making monkey noises and contorting his face, but Jade turned to Ari, worried. I was trying to brush her teeth but she pushed me away. 'Mum!' she said. 'Ari's gone!'

'It's okay, lots of people have gone now, you're okay, aren't you, Ari?' I said. It was a bit lame, but I didn't know what to say. I just wanted to get out of there, get on the road again.

'But, Mum, you could bring him back. My mum can do this thing, Ari, where she brings people back, she can do it with words, a big cloud of them.' Jade was talking and spitting toothpaste everywhere.

Ari looked a little interested. I kept going on Jade's teeth so she couldn't speak. I didn't want to try to bring Ari back. I didn't know if I could and I was scared. I knew what to do. I found the words. With Guy, the words had been right there, so easy to pick from the air and give to him, to put around him, comfort him. But it had been freaky, that feeling of drawing him back down, drawing him back in, putting his body into space. I didn't know what would happen to Ari, who'd been gone for so long, and I didn't want to attract the people who were following us, the person who had been in our house, who had gone through our stuff. I had this feeling that they could sense it, when I coloured, and that it brought them closer to us. I didn't know if this was true, but I didn't want to risk it.

'We're going up north for a bit, and we'll stop and see Ari and Hugo on the way back, maybe we can try then,' I said.

Jade scrunched up her face. 'But, Mum—'

'Jade!' I raised my voice. 'I said, not now! Later, we'll try it later.'

Three little faces stared at me.

'But that'll be nice, won't it? We'll come back and see these guys again soon. Maybe we can go to McDonald's, all of us.'

Jade frowned at me. She couldn't understand why I wouldn't help Ari. She jumped down off her stool and said to me, under her breath, 'Why don't you just do it, Mum?'

I ignored her, took her hand, and we went out into the driveway, Ari and Hugo trailing behind us.

I checked the boot of the car one more time and buckled Jade into her car seat. Renee handed me an ice cream container. 'Some snacks for the road,' she said.

'Thanks,' I said, taking them. 'Hey, I'm sorry this is all so messed up. I'm sorry we stopped here.'

'Take care, on the road. I heard some crazy stuff on the radio this morning.'

I nodded. I'd thought about what I was going to say next, and whether I should say it. 'If someone comes, asking for me—'

'We know,' Renee interrupted. 'We don't know where you're going anyway.'

We hugged.

I waved to Tracey, who was standing on the deck, looking down at us, and she waved back, before going back into the house and pulling the sliding door closed behind her.

'She's stressed,' said Renee quietly. 'It's Ari, you know?'

I nodded.

Hugo and Ari were running around the car. 'Hey, you dinos!' Renee said. 'Come here, get out of the way.'

She pulled them close to her and kissed them on the tops of their heads. Hugo squirmed. I gave Ari a high five.

'It'll be okay,' I said to Renee as I climbed into the car.

She nodded, tears in her eyes. Ari put his arms around her middle, squeezing her. She held him close. It was the only thing that she could do. She wouldn't let him go.

As I drove down the driveway, Jade turned in her seat and waved to Ari and Hugo and Renee. I looked in my rear-view mirror and saw them all. Ari and Hugo waving and jumping and pulling on Renee's arms. Renee, her dark hair, curly around her face, her orange top. The lawn behind them with the tramp and the big lemon tree by the fence.

And Jade. Here she is. She's twisting around, pressing against her seat belt, and it cuts into her neck. She's waving at Ari and Hugo. She laughs at them. She loves it when they're being crazy. She loves that there are two of them, that they look the same. She still has her pyjama pants on, purple with white stars. 'Mum! Look! They're crazy!' she says, pointing through the dirty glass.

I want to hold them all there, in that space, and in these words, in the neat frame of the rear-view mirror. All these things kept them safe and contained, seeable, visible. Even Ari, a gap, he was there, an image of him in the little mirror, a copy of him, another version. People were lost without the images of themselves, and Renee, in that moment, had a lost look in her eye. Taking photos of Ari was a kind of care, a way of protecting him, of making him mean something.

I switched back to the road ahead of us. I had to focus. It was sunny, but the streets around Renee's house were empty. Schools were closed. Shops were closed. People were staying at home, waiting to see what would happen at Purity. What would the gaps do?

I didn't know what was happening in town. Were gaps taking over the office buildings? What had Renee said? 'Burrowing in'? We had to head west. We drove through New Lynn, Henderson. We drove past long fences covered in sign after sign of people's faces looking out, bright smile after bright smile, people desperately holding on to their presence, claiming it.

At a set of traffic lights, the car next to us gunned its engine. Its windows were tinted and I couldn't see inside. I looked straight ahead, ignoring them.

'What do those guys want?' Jade asked.

'Just looking for trouble, I guess,' I said as the light changed and the car hooned away from us, disappearing down the empty street.

'We're not looking for trouble,' said Jade. 'We're looking for Miri.'

I laughed. 'That's right. Tell me if you see her.'

'Where is everyone?' Jade asked, pressing her nose against the window. 'This is boring.'

'I think everyone's staying at home because of the trouble with the gaps. Schools are closed up here too.'

'Everyone's forgotten how to do the normal stuff,' said Jade.

'Yeah, they have.'

'People have forgotten how to do normal stuff without being able to take photos. It's all gone wrong,' she said.

I nodded, biting my lip. She was right.

'It's going to be okay, though. We'll find Miri and she'll help us,' I said.

'And then we'll go back to Nana and Pop and Guy?'

'Yep. We'll go back.'

I reached over to the passenger seat and found the magnetic drawing pad that Mum had got Jade for Christmas. 'Do you want this?' I asked.

Jade nodded and I handed it back to her, along with a biscuit from the container that Renee had given us.

We kept going, headed west after Massey and were soon out in the country, green fields on either side. I thought about driving on country roads with Johnny, shading myself from him, plucking the words out of the air to give myself cover, give myself space. And giving that space to Miri, that was a gift. Would I do it again? Had I saved her? Or caused a domino effect? People going out, all over the world, like streetlights switching off, one by one, a kind of darkness falling. Had it started on a beach in Whakatāne, when Miri had gone? When I had picked out the words of the beach and the evening and the sea and pulled them up around her?

A roadblock appeared up ahead and I slowed down, falling in line behind a short queue of other cars.

'Jade,' I said. 'I'm going to shade us, okay? When the cop talks to us.'

'I know, Mum. Will you do me too?'

'Yep, just don't say anything, okay?'

I watched the car ahead of us. Something was going on. The police officer waved another cop over and they both spoke to the driver. They pointed to another lane that had been marked out by cones, where a police van was parked at the end. The car ahead didn't move, and another officer came over and stood by the boot, talking on his phone.

A couple more cars lined up behind us.

I glanced down and checked my phone. A message from Mum, *dad picking up beer at the supermarket.*

She was worried about us, wanted to make contact but couldn't say anything specific. I didn't reply. I had turned off the location info on my phone. I didn't want to give any information to the people who were following us. It seemed useless though. They probably knew exactly where we were and were watching, waiting.

Jade was busy with her drawing pad, so I turned on the radio, keeping it down low.

Dead people had started going out. In Mexico, first, and then more reports in Puerto Rico. The announcer sounded slightly breathless, as if the information was coming at them quickly.

There was a translated interview from a woman in Puerto Rico, her voice desperate, raised, behind the robotic voice of the translator. 'My mother, my mother! She's gone. I saw yesterday, the photo on my wall, she's gone. She's been dead fifteen years. My mother, rest her soul. Let her rest in peace. Oh my dear god.'

The car ahead of us finally moved into the left lane and the police officer waved us through.

I turned off the radio and wound down the window to let the police officer lean in and take our photos. I was more efficient than last time, quickly and quietly bringing the words together, serving up the most boring, the most normal things. The black textured plastic of the dashboard. The bottom of the windscreen, where the glass turned to a faint blue. And for Jade, the crumbs in the seams of the back seat, and the red button of her seat belt, chipped at the sides.

The police officer took our photos and frowned at her phone, tapping and scrolling.

She looked over the top of the car, out across the fields, and then back to me, meeting my eyes but not saying anything, as if she was trying to think of something to say.

'You going through?' she asked.

'Yes, to Whangārei,' I said.

The woman sighed, then said, 'Okay, on you go then,' and waved us through.

I sped up to 100 on the open road and the roadblock disappeared behind us.

Jade leant forward and tickled the bit of my neck that was exposed under the headrest. She said, 'That lady couldn't see us.'

'No, I shaded us, just a tiny bit,' I said.

'But we were okay in her phone,' said Jade.

'Yeah, I just do it a little bit. It's not strong, and we stay in the photos. Just so that we can get through the roadblocks without them really noticing us.'

Jade nodded and went back to drawing. 'I'm not gone,' she said to herself.

I turned the radio on again, changing the balance so the sound was only coming from the front speakers. More news from Mexico. People in the streets, empty photo frames clutched to their chests, sobbing. A translated interview with someone from a museum. 'I'm going through the collections,' he said, 'they are falling apart. There are gaps everywhere, more and more every time that I look. Important events where there used to be crowds, now they're empty. Will they all go out? All the people who have passed away? What will happen to our history, to our memory?'

A curfew was in place in Mexico City and other parts of the country. Airports closed. Any unnecessary movement restricted. The government said they were going to find whoever was responsible for this catastrophe, and they were going to put a stop to it.

The news changed to the Auckland CBD. Renee had been right, gaps had taken over several buildings and were hollowing them out, setting them up as centres for some special activity, or a base, it wasn't clear. Police were moving in, surrounding them, a special new division that had been set up to deal with gaps. And Purity was spreading its boundaries, taking over new properties, a steady march that was forcing the armed forces to fall back and regroup.

The Prime Minister's voice came on, saying, 'Our duty is to protect the livelihood of all right-thinking New Zealanders. Those that are present, those that are whole, those that are committed to sharing themselves with their communities, and our sense of shared history as a nation. We will not be bullied by those individuals who operate in the shadows and seek to bring us down.'

I glanced in my side mirror. Nobody behind us, just the long road stretching out. Jade had put her drawing pad down and was staring out the window, looking sleepy. I turned the radio off.

People wanted someone to blame. Governments wanted to find a cause so that they could be seen to be doing something and taking

243

action. The panic was rising. I could almost feel it, coming up the road behind us.

I sped up. I wanted to drive away from it all, leave the mess behind. I thought of Miri. Go north, go north.

30.

Whangārei was quiet. Only a few people on the main street. A few parked cars. A corner dairy covered in the signs of its smiling owner, all piled on top of each other, overlapping, so that I couldn't see the door or any windows, it looked like a building made out of faces. I couldn't tell if it was open or closed.

We drove past the rugby fields and saw a crowd of people gathered near the stands. I slowed down and saw a man with a megaphone, shouting something above the heads of the group. Others drifted in groups of twos and threes across the field. One man, near the road, pointed at us as we drove past at a crawl. He shouted something and held up his phone, aiming at us and taking a photo. I kept one hand on the wheel, opened the window, and held out my phone with my other hand. I fumbled, nearly dropping it, but managed to hold down the button to take a series of photos, the images quickly stacking on top of each other underneath my splintered screen.

The man yelled something at us and waved his arm.

Jade said, 'Go, quick, Mum!'

I wound up the window and sped past the field, past a school, and out of town on State Highway 1.

I handed my phone back to Jade, and she said, 'I knew it, they were gaps, Mum. Can't see them.'

'Nobody there at all?' I asked.

'Gone,' she said. 'All gapped.' She paused, and then she asked, 'Do you feel sorry for them?'

'Yes, maybe. They're just people, right? It's not their fault.'

'Yes, but not really, eh? They're not really there. Cara's mum said it was selfish to go out, not letting other people see you. It's like hide and seek when you don't come out when someone is looking for you and they've been looking for ages and ages and they get all pissed off.'

'Don't say 'pissed off', Jade.'

'You do.'

I smiled. 'Yeah, okay, I guess you can say it.'

'I'm pissed off about these cracks in your phone,' she said.

'Me too,' I said.

I didn't want to drive at night. I'd checked on my phone and there was a motel north of Whangārei where we could stay for $90. There were no more roadblocks, no more police, just quiet roads and fields and cows. Jade watched cartoons on my phone until it ran out of battery and then she fell asleep for a bit, my phone falling out of her hands and onto the seat.

I drove on, and the motel didn't appear, and I started to freak out, but then it was there, and I was pulling in, onto the gravel driveway, and Jade was waking up and looking around.

The units were all connected by a long deck, with a reception building out on its own. A broken fountain sat in between the buildings, the water around it a gross brown. Jade went up and peered in, hoping to see a fish.

'I miss Nana and Pop,' she said.

We went into the reception and waited for a moment before a small old woman came through a door behind the counter. She reached into the pocket of her skirt and took out her phone and took a photo of us, Jade and me, there in the doorway, the light behind us.

I wonder what that photo looked like. I wish I could see it now. I wish I could see us together, held in the frame of the picture, tired, scared, not so long ago. Was Jade holding my hand? I think so. What was I wearing? My grey hoodie, probably.

Now, writing this, I close my eyes and I try and see us, but I remember other annoying details about that motel and they get in the way. A fish tank on the sideboard, with one fish swimming round and round. Brochures fanned out on a coffee table. A row of black and white images of Whangārei's main street that are framed on the wall.

I wish I could turn my memory around and see me and Jade in the doorway, as that woman had seen us, as that camera had seen us, and held us, and stored us away in its memory. I keep writing, because it helps, it helps me to see the moments that we've lost and bring them back.

'My phone died,' I said, to explain why I wasn't taking a photo of the woman in return.

She smiled, shrugged, and said, 'What can I do for you?'

'Just a room for the night, thanks,' I said.

She looked at her computer. 'Oh, so you must be Jodie and Jade,' she said. 'Yes, that's right, isn't it?' She looked up.

I froze. Jade tugged on my hand. I stepped back, about to run away, throw Jade in the back of the car, and speed down the road.

'It's okay, my dear,' said the woman. 'Miri called, she said you would be stopping in. She left you a message.'

'Mum!' Jade whispered.

My mouth was dry. 'Miri called?'

'Yes, yes, lovely girl, isn't she? She said to tell you…' She paused. 'Now, I've written it down somewhere.' She picked up a bit of paper and put her reading glasses on. 'She said to tell you that you should keep going, up to Karikari, and she'll meet you there.'

She put down the paper and smiled at us, bending her head so she could look over the top of her glasses. 'There. That's nice, isn't it? She'll meet you there. Not long to go now, you two.'

'She said that? A message for me?' I said, stepping forward.

'Mum!' Jade said again. 'Miri!'

I gave her hand a little shake and said, 'Ssshhh.'

The woman said, 'She just called this morning! And she's paid for your room too! She gave me her credit card. All sorted.'

She took us down to our unit and after she left I plugged in my phone. No messages. Jade and I sat on the bed and looked at each other.

'Mum!' Jade said. 'Miri knows we're coming! She's waiting for us.'

I nodded. If Miri knew where we were, who else knew?

Later, Jade had a shower and washed her hair with one of the small packets of shampoo.

'Mum,' she said, after she had hopped out and wrapped herself in a towel, 'it's pretty awesome staying in a hotel, eh? Like, all those little packets of things, they're pretty cool.'

I helped her into her PJs. 'Look!' I said, holding up the little hair dryer. 'Let's do your hair.'

I dried her hair and brushed it out. Here she is. Look. Jade. So soapy and clean. Pink cheeks, flushed from the shower. Humming to herself. Faded pink pyjama top. She sits on the floor and I'm on the bed, drying her hair, and she leans back against my legs. The fine straight line where I part her hair and brush it down on both sides, each tiny dark hair, each little boring nothing part of her that I want to remember. Here she is. Look.

She got into bed and I played some of her favourite lullabies on my phone, ones that I used to put on when she was a baby. She sighed and turned over and was quickly asleep.

I stretched out on the bed beside her and thought about switching on the TV. It was tempting to just lie beside Jade, in the warm motel room, and not look at my phone, and not look at the TV, and just keep away from everything and try to get to Miri, because she'd know what to do.

But it was still early and I felt wired, kind of hyper, so I found the remote and turned on the TV. Sucker for punishment, I guess. For a couple of minutes I watched some Australian soap where half of the cast must have gone. I don't know why it was still being broadcast, because it was completely messed up. A woman had a huge argument with an empty space, sobbing, throwing things, tears pouring down her face, but there was no one there, just some poor gap, their voice without a body, so her big melt down was for nothing, for no one.

I changed to a news channel. More people in the streets, clutching the empty photos of their dead relatives. Gunshots outside Purity. The Prime Minister appeared, standing with the Chief of Police by his side. 'We are calling for calm,' he said. 'People can rest assured that the government of New Zealand is in charge of the situation and force will be used as necessary to ensure that both gaps and presents, and their families, are kept safe.' He continued, 'We will not be held ransom by unlawful gaps, but nor will we mistreat them. We are also committed to uncovering the cause of this threat and determining new strategies with our allies and partners.'

I switched the TV off and lay in the silent room for a while, then I got up and had a hot shower.

Eventually, it must have been around two, I fell asleep. I dreamt about the crowd of gaps we had seen in the field in Whangārei, their angry faces turning to look at Jade and I as we drove slowly past. Guy was there in the crowd, looking at me, his mouth opened and he said something, waved at us as if he wanted us to stop. And then I saw Johnny, leaning over a fence, grinning. We didn't stop. We just drove on and on and left them both behind.

In the morning, Jade had another bath, because she wanted to use another one of the small shampoos, and I packed up our stuff. I checked my phone was fully charged. No messages.

'We'll get McDonald's for breakfast,' I said. 'We'll see if we can find one.'

I figured that we'd saved some money with Miri paying for the motel, so I could splash out a little.

I put our bags in the boot and then we went into the reception to return the key. The woman was there, sitting at the desk, and she looked up as I came in. 'Did you have a good night, my dear?'

I nodded.

'Off to find Miri then, are we?'

I didn't want to talk to this woman about Miri. 'Got to find breakfast first,' I said.

'We're having McDonald's!' said Jade, then she pointed at the old photos that sat on the wall and asked, 'What're those?'

The woman came out from behind the counter and stood beside us. 'That's Whangārei, back in the day. See, this is Bank Street.' She pointed at one of the photos. 'See that horse and cart, that's how people used to get around. And it's so sad, it is, there are lots of gaps in these now. I don't know what to do about it, can't get them fixed, can't put the people back in, dear me.'

She pointed at another street scene with old wooden buildings. 'See here, there used to be a lovely little girl down the bottom here, but she's gone out. And there was a lady crossing the street, wearing one of them long skirts that they used to wear, and this big hat, but she's gone too. She's always been in there, crossing the street, and then I noticed the other day that she had gone. And it's funny, I miss them, I do. I wonder where they went? Where do they go, the old gaps, when they disappear?'

Jade looked up at the woman and patted her arm. 'It's okay,' she said, 'maybe they'll come back.'

'Can they do that? Maybe you're right, love,' she said, 'maybe they will. I'll keep an eye out for them. Because it's so sad, isn't it? All the old photos not making any sense, all these people we've lost. We won't be able to remember them, won't be able to remember things right. How things looked. I miss that little girl from this photo. She was lovely.'

She walked out with us and stood on the small deck while I got Jade into her seat. 'Drive safely, it can be a bit of a dodgy road up to Karikari, specially in the wet.'

I didn't like that she knew where we were going, but Miri had told her, so there was nothing I could do about it.

'Maybe you can stop back in on your way back through,' she said.

'Maybe,' I said. 'Thanks.'

She watched us turn and go down the drive and I saw her wave as I turned out onto the road.

31.

I didn't know when we drove away that morning that a state of emergency had been declared. Jade sensed something though. She looked out the car window and said, 'There are hardly any cars on the road.' And I saw that she was right. 'There's something,' she said, so quietly that I could barely hear her, 'something has happened.'

There was no McDonald's for ages, so Jade ate biscuits and I played songs for her on my phone.

After we'd been going for about an hour, I turned on the radio and the reporter said that there was a state of emergency and everyone had to stay where they were. There'd been explosions near Purity and the army was moving in. Everyone had to stay put until the 'situation had been resolved', the reporter said, because there was 'significant risk of danger to the public'.

I didn't know what to do. I checked the petrol. Half full. We'd probably be able to get back to Auckland. Or, maybe we could stay at the motel another night. Wait it out a bit and see what happened. If we kept going, how far would this tank take us?

But I didn't want to stop now. I remembered the smashed-up petrol station and the car following us. We couldn't stop, someone would notice us and wonder what we were doing. I just wanted to get to Miri and for her to sort everything out. If we stayed in the car and kept going, we could make it, I knew we could. If we got to a roadblock I'd shade us, I'd pull up the words and help us slip through.

I gripped the steering wheel. Miri had said Karikari, and we could do it, we could get there, I just had to focus.

As soon as I'd decided this, Jade had to pee. I slowed down and pulled the car over onto the side of the road. Jade got out and I helped her take off her leggings and undies and she crouched down in the tallest patch of grass.

'Can anyone see?' she asked.

'No, I can only just see the top of your head. Try not to pee on your leg.'

I looked down the road. Empty. Cicadas making a racket. Not even the sound of traffic in the distance. I checked my phone. Nothing. I checked that the location tracking was still off, and then I turned the phone off completely and chucked it into the glove box.

'Come on,' I said to Jade. 'We're not really supposed to stop.'

She stood up. 'How come?'

'Just because.'

A car appeared in the distance. I moved next to Jade and pulled her down so that we were both crouching together in the grass. 'What are we doing?' Jade whispered.

'I don't know,' I said.

The car didn't stop, it didn't even slow down. It just gunned it straight past us. We heard a few seconds of music from its radio, as it went past, and then the road was empty again.

I helped Jade put her undies and leggings back on and we got back in the car.

'Is someone following us?' Jade asked.

I pulled out onto the road. 'No, no one. It's okay.'

'It's so lonely,' said Jade. 'We haven't seen anyone for ages. We'll see Miri soon though, that'll be cool.'

'We should try and not stop again. Can you try and hold on?' I asked.

'Okay, Mum, I'll try.'

'If you're desperate, we can stop though.'

I turned on the radio again, to get a better sense of what was going on at Purity, but the information was confusing. A barn had exploded. The gaps there were refusing to be tagged. They wouldn't be rounded up and put in a centre, like they were doing with other gaps. They wanted to be free. Free of their images, free from everything.

They should have never been allowed to get together in the first place, I thought. They could move as a pack, they didn't leave any information behind them, they had rich supporters, and they were armed.

Irons was on the radio, calling from a phone somewhere, his familiar voice broken up by static. I remember he said, 'We didn't want it to come to this, but this is the position the government has put us in because of their antagonistic activities. The government may think we are not organised, but we are. The government may think we are not powerful, but we are. You do not know the immense power that comes with disassociation from one's image. It is in this split that true power is released, like a bomb, like the splitting of the atom.' The phone line cut out and when his voice returned it was in mid-sentence, '—because the subject is no longer beholden to their image, to the weight of it, to the weight of having to generate it all the time, to that immense burden and alienation. Solos can travel light, move quickly, and you will soon find out what my subjects are truly capable of, now that they are untethered.'

I remember that weird word he used, 'untethered'.

I turned the radio off, shook my head, tried to clear my mind, and kept driving. I kept us on State Highway 1 because I didn't want to get lost. My phone was off and I couldn't quickly check where I was, but I knew that if I kept on this highway we'd have to turn off to the right somewhere after Kaitaia.

We ate lunch in the car. Jade passed me Burger Rings from her packet, and I searched through radio stations until I found one that was playing Bob Marley, and we sung along.

I took the turn off after Kaitaia and followed the signs all the way up to Karikari. It was mid-afternoon. Jade was grumpy and tired. She hadn't fallen asleep, even though it looked like several times that she'd been about to. She'd done so well. We'd come so far and she'd come up with all sorts of games to pass the time.

There was no roadblock as we drove into Karikari. Strange. I'd been preparing to shade. Hopefully everyone was looking the other way. Purity, with its explosions and gangs of armed gaps, was down south.

I stopped the car on the road next to the beach and we got out. I stretched my arms up above my head. I was exhausted. My legs ached. My mouth was dry.

'Where's Miri?' Jade asked. 'She's meeting us here, right?'

I looked around, and then pointed to a dairy down the road. 'Do you want a drink?'

'A chocolate milk,' said Jade.

'We'll see what they have.'

'I want a chocolate milk!'

'Well, I said we'll see what they have.'

Jade kicked a stone along the footpath.

She was just about done. I had to keep her going a little bit longer. I looked out at the beach. There were a couple of people in the distance. Where was Miri? How would she find us?

I opened the glove box and took out my phone, thought about turning it on, but decided against it and put it in my pocket. 'Come on,' I said, taking Jade's hand.

We walked down the empty footpath that ran along the beach. A cold wind blew off the sea and I wished that I'd brought Jade's jacket.

'Mum, something's wrong,' said Jade.

We were close to the dairy and I could see that she was right, in the way that Jade was often right before I'd clocked something, like she could see a tiny bit into the future. The side of the shop was covered in signs for the owner, but they must have gone out, because the signs were empty blue backgrounds, piled on top of one another. There must've been hundreds of them that had been stuck to the exterior wall in a frenzy. They were on the front windows too, but now they were unsticking and falling off. I remember there were piles of them around the door and they'd even been stuck on the roof, the corners of the posters flapping in the wind.

We stood at the front doors and Jade tightened her grip on my hand. It was dark inside because of the thick layer of posters on the windows, and no one had turned on a light. There was a TV high in the corner of the room that was playing some show, but all the actors must have gone, because it was all just empty rooms, a kitchen, a living room, the camera moving backwards and forwards, as if searching for the gaps, searching for the people that used to live inside the frame. There was a shot of a table where a gap must have sat, and a cup moved up and down, to their invisible mouth and back to the table again.

'Hi?' I called. 'Hello?'

The counter was at the far end of the shop. There was a shuffling noise from the room behind it and a woman appeared.

'It's okay,' she said. She held up her phone and took a photo of us, before waving us in.

'We're just getting a few things,' I said, and she nodded. I couldn't be arsed explaining about my phone, or turning it on, and she didn't seem to care.

Jade was quiet at my side as I took a couple of cartons of chocolate milk from the fridge. The woman watched us as I grabbed a pack of chips too, and took everything up to the counter.

'Thank you, thank you,' she said softly, as she tapped the buttons on the register.

'Are you okay?' I asked. 'The posters...'

'Yes, yes,' she said. 'it's just with the state of emergency going on and on. We've been trying to stay open a little bit each day. But no one's around. It's tough for business.'

What did she mean about the state of emergency going on? Hadn't it just started that morning?

The woman smiled at Jade and said, 'Would you like a lollipop?'

Jade stared up at her, nose just above the counter, and nodded, then asked, 'Have you gone?'

'Jade!' I said. I didn't think we should ask. The woman seemed so sad and alone. My phone was still switched off and in the car, so I hadn't tried to take a picture of her.

She handed Jade the lollipop with a little smile. 'Yes, a little while ago, my husband too. But you can see, can't you? Because of the posters... We need to take them down, but there's no one around anyway.' She pushed our chips and drinks over to us and I put them in my backpack. 'And, it's funny, I can't remember exactly when it happened now. When you're gone…' She looked away into the distance, out the door, before continuing, 'when you're gone, the days don't stop, like there's no beginning and end, just this… nowness. You can't remember what's happened, or where you've been, or who you've talked to.'

She frowned and blinked and looked at me again, as if she had forgotten that we were there.

'Are you okay? Do you need anything? A doctor?' I asked.

She didn't need a doctor but I couldn't think of anything else to say.

'No, no. I'm fine. My husband, he's around too.' She looked back over her shoulder, into the little room behind the counter. 'But I lose track of him sometimes, during the day. And I have the TV.' She pointed up at the TV in the top corner of the shop, where the empty sitcom continued, the camera moving across a little kitchen, searching for something, for a body to focus on.

Jade turned when we reached the door and raised her hand in a wave and the woman waved back before shuffling away into the back room again.

It was bright outside, after the darkness of the dairy. I looked down the empty road. There were a few cars parked about 100 metres down from us, but otherwise nothing, no one.

We went back to the car to get our coats and I grabbed my phone. Jade spotted a playground, so we crossed the road and she ran around for a bit, but the emptiness made us both feel weird. No traffic. No one else around. No other kids making noise. I was on the lookout for anybody coming towards us, or watching us, because we were so exposed. I kept looking down the road, but there was nothing.

Jade jumped off the swing. 'Let's go down to the beach,' she said.

We found a bench tucked against the bank, facing out to sea. Jade sat down and bunched her legs up inside of her jacket. 'When's Miri going to come?' she asked. 'I'm cold.'

'She'll be here soon,' I said.

I stabbed a straw into a chocolate milk and gave it to Jade, hoping it would distract her. I didn't know where Miri was, or when she would come, or even *if* she would come. I took my phone out of my pocket and looked at its blank screen. Did Miri need me to turn it on so that she could find us? Had she sent me a message? She'd said Karikari, and here we were, in the middle of nowhere. We made it, Miri, I thought, we did it, come and get us now.

Jade munched the chips and then ran down to the tideline and threw shells into the sea. The sun came and went, clouds moving quickly across the sky. With my phone switched off, I didn't know what time it was. I guessed, maybe, late afternoon, but it was hard to tell. Was this what the woman in the dairy felt like all the time? No anchor, no sense of time passing?

Jade chased after a seagull and it ran about for a bit and then swooped up into the sky, flying away low over the sea.

I'm writing these words now, this description of the beach, but I was also thinking them at the time, watching Jade run around, in the lazy way that I always did, picking up words, testing them, and putting them down again. If I stopped for a moment, sat still, the habit of colouring came back. I'd imagine what I'd say for Dad, if he was there, listening quietly. Jade at the beach. He'd want to see her. He missed her. From the moment she was born he missed her, missed seeing her every day. He'd want me to pick the right words for him, to show him Jade at the beach, and the light, and the waves, all the things around her, all those everyday things, those normal words that meant so much to him, that gave him a path back into the world.

So, I'll keep going, here you go, this is for you, Dad.

Jade dragged a long stick behind her through the wet sand, look-ing at the pattern that it made, the small canyon, the crumbling wavy line. I'm writing this sentence, I was thinking this sentence, thinking about how I'd say it for Dad, and Jade looked up and saw someone down the end of the beach, someone blurry and dark, too far away to really make out, but they were walking towards Jade, coming straight along the tideline. They got closer and suddenly there were too many words, all rising, and I was probably saying them out loud without realising it, because the person was Miri. Her dark hair was blown all around by the wind and she wore a khaki jacket, with her hands stuffed into the front pockets, and big black boots. Jade dropped her stick and ran towards her, splashes of wet sand and sea flying up as she ran, and when she reached her, Miri crouched down and gave her a hug, and Jade turned and pointed to where I sat on the bench, and I didn't know what to do, so I just waved, I waved at my mate Miri, as if we'd just run into her at that beach, like we'd known she'd be here, which I guess we did, we'd known that she'd come here to Karikari and get us, she'd said so, and here she is. Look.

32.

Miri said, 'It's getting dark. We should get back to camp first, then we can talk.'

I had so many questions for her, but I also wanted to follow her instructions and for someone to tell me what to do. It was a relief, after having spent so long making decisions by myself, to be bossed around by Miri.

Miri said, 'It's about an hour's drive, then a walk, you can follow me.'

We were standing next to my car, Jade waiting in her seat. Miri pointed down the road to a beat-up van.

I opened my door and then stopped and turned. 'Miri, there's a woman in the dairy, she's gone, and I think she should come too. She needs help.'

Miri paused, then said, 'Okay. Go get her, quick.'

I ran down to the dairy and the door was still open, so I went inside. It was much darker, nearly night, and the dairy was still wrapped in its layers of blank posters, keeping out any light. It was like the burrow of a small creature.

The TV glowed from its vantage point in the corner.

'Hi, hello?' I called out, and the woman came out to the counter.

I said, 'My friend Miri is here and she's going to take us to her camp. She's gone too. She knows what it's like. She might be able to help you. She *will* be able to help you. She knows what's going on.'

The woman looked at me. 'But—'

I interrupted her, speaking loudly. 'Your husband isn't really here, is he? He's pissed off, hasn't he?'

She paused. 'Yes, but... he might come back.'

'Trust me,' I said, 'he won't come back. Come with us, you'll see, Miri can help. I'm Jodie.'

'Okay. I'm Rita. Can you wait? Let me get some things.' She disappeared into the back room and I waited nervously in the dark dairy. A car drove down the road outside and my heart thumped in my chest.

Rita came round the counter. She wore a thick raincoat and a backpack. We went outside and Rita locked the front door and then tugged down a metal grate. It got stuck on all the blank posters, so I helped her, and we managed to get it in place so she could trap it with the padlock at the bottom.

'When did you go out?' I asked as we walked back to my car.

She looked straight ahead. 'I can't remember,' she said. 'A while ago, I think, but it's hard to tell. I know it sounds crazy, but I lose track of the days. I'd be sitting out the back, in our house, and I'd think a couple of minutes had passed, but then I'd look up and it was four hours later.'

We got to my car and Miri was sitting in the back, next to Jade. She climbed out and I said, 'This is Rita.'

Miri nodded. 'Let's get out of here. Follow my van.'

We followed the taillights of Miri's van out of Karikari and headed south. Rita sat next to me, in the passenger seat, her backpack on her lap. She didn't ask any questions, just sat looking out the window, into the dark fields.

I watched Jade in the rear-view mirror, thinking that she might fall asleep, but she craned her neck so she could see out the windscreen, at the taillights of Miri's van, just ahead of us in the night.

We took a turnoff onto a gravel road. Miri slowed and we matched her pace. I gripped the steering wheel, focussing. The road turned and there were several tight corners. It was hard to see in the dark, but the fields seemed to have gone and we were driving into thicker bush.

It was about half an hour, I think, before Miri slowed again and stopped the van in a small clearing off the side of the road. Everyone got out. The bush was all around us. In the distance, I thought I could hear a river.

Miri already had her head torch on and she handed three more out to us. I put on Jade's coat and helped her tighten the strap around her head. She twisted around to shine the light on the trees and grass.

'It's not far,' said Miri. 'It's just a bit dark now, so we'll go slow. You don't have to worry about your stuff. Lauren and Taryn will come and get it. They've got to sort the cars anyway. Jade, you stay right between me and your mum.' She looked at me and Rita, then asked, 'Are your phones off?'

Rita reached into her jacket pocket and checked.

We walked into the bush, Miri, then Jade, then Rita and me. There was a track, but it was hard to see. I could only see just ahead, to the reach of the torchlight, to Rita's backpack in front of me, and to the wall of bush on either side. I wasn't scared. I trusted Miri to look after us. I didn't know where we were going, but I knew we were going somewhere safe.

We came to a small stream and Miri helped Jade across. I heard them talking to each other, but I couldn't hear what they were saying.

I remember looking down at the dry ground, covered in leaves, and thinking how it mustn't have rained for ages. I remember the quiet of the bush that night and as I walked, words crowding in about the thick dark and the flash of silver and green when the light from my head torch moved across the trees next to me. When it was quiet, or I was doing something repetitive, the words always came back, they were always there, at the edge of my thoughts.

I looked up and realised that we were in a clearing, and there was a hut, and rows of small tents on a patch of flat lawn next to it.

Jade took my hand, and we followed Miri up some steps and into the hut. Inside, people were sitting around long tables that were dotted with candles and lamps. There was a long metal bench at one end with a sink where two women were washing dishes.

'This is Jade, Jodie, and Rita,' said Miri, taking off her head torch. 'Come on, sit down,' she said, pointing to a spot on the bench.

I sat down and Jade climbed onto my lap. Rita sat next to us, and Miri went to the other end of the room where she spoke quietly to a dark-haired woman.

'How're you doing?' asked a woman across the table from us.

I stroked Jade's hair. 'She's very tired,' I said. 'We've come a long way today.'

'Of course, yes. Jade, isn't it? I'll get you a Milo.'

Jade rested her head against my shoulder, her face up against my neck. Rita was talking quietly to the woman next to her, and I looked around and saw that it was only women in the room, about thirty of them. There were no kids, but I guessed that they might have already been in bed.

The woman came back with the Milo, but I could feel by Jade's breath against me that she was asleep.

Miri crossed the room to be with us. 'You need to get her into bed,' she said, nodding towards Jade. 'Follow me.'

I stood up and Jade hung heavily on my body, her arms around my neck. We left the hut and I followed Miri to a tent, where she unzipped the door and we crawled inside. She unrolled two sleeping bags, and I took off Jade's shoes and socks and pants and got her to crawl inside. She made grumpy, half-awake noises, but quickly turned over and was asleep again in seconds.

'I'll stay with her,' I said to Miri.

I couldn't see Miri's face, only the bright light of her head torch, and I had to look down. 'I'm going to check on Rita,' she said and then left.

I slipped outside and peed in the bush, then returned to the tent, stripped down to my T-shirt and undies, and climbed into the sleeping bag beside Jade.

I lay and listened to the quiet around us, to Jade's breathing, to the creak of the hut door as it opened and closed. Then, I was asleep.

Later, I woke up with a sore neck. It was still night, totally dark, and I had no idea what time it was. When I opened my eyes I couldn't see anything. I reached out to where I thought Jade's head should be and touched her hair, heard her regular breathing.

I felt Miri lying against my back, her arm resting on my waist, and heard her breathing too. I knew it was her. I thought about the three of us, me, Jade, Miri, and how we would look from above, tucked up against each other. I thought about Miri's face, how it was different now, older, changed, a few lines around her eyes, like me. We were thirty-one. I wanted to look at her in the light, to see her up close, find the right words for her, for her hair, for her neck, her lips.

Next to me, Miri stirred and rolled over onto her other side. 'Don't,' she said, as if she was talking in her sleep, and I sighed and went back to sleep.

33.

Jade was excited about waking up in the tent, and the camp, and the hut, and the Milo, and the generator, and everything. 'Mum, this is so cool!' she said, running around.

The sun was out. A couple of women laid out breakfast in the hut and we took our toast and cereal and ate it out on the deck. Rita sat next to us and drank a coffee.

At the edge of the clearing, I watched Miri talking to a tall woman. Miri was giving directions. She was in charge. Women kept coming up to her and asking her questions.

Miri turned and walked over to us. 'Jade, do you have your togs?' she asked.

Jade looked at me. 'Do I, Mum?'

'I think they were in the back of the car,' I said.

'Doesn't matter,' said Miri. 'Come on, get your shoes. Rita, you too. I want to show you guys something.'

Miri led us round the back of the hut and pointed to the outside wall. 'Rita,' she said, 'this is where we keep time. You'll need this.'

Running along the wall was a series of small straight notches, carved into the wood, and arranged in groups of seven. Above each notch was a shape, a crescent, or a full circle, or a semi-circle. Underneath each notch was a name, or a group of names.

'So, here,' said Miri, 'these are the days, and this is the cycle of the moon. Here, I'm going to put your name into this one.'

She took out a Swiss army knife and scraped *Rita* into the wood below the last notch.

'This is the day you arrived. Now you can count, see? You'll know how long you've been here. And we put it in here.' She patted the wall. 'You can touch it, it's there. You can come along here and feel the time and it'll help you remember.'

Rita reached out and ran her fingers along the row of notches.

Miri put her hand on Rita's shoulder. 'I know it's hard,' she said. 'Because when your image goes, you can feel... you can feel empty, and the time, it just goes, you can't hold on to it. I know what that feels like.'

Rita said, 'It's too slippery, too fast, too slow, you can't stop it, to look at it and know what is there, to know that *you* are there.'

Miri nodded. 'I know, I understand. But, it'll get better, and now that you are here, we can help. Start here, each day, with the chart.'

'You've been here six weeks?' I asked.

'Yeah,' said Miri. 'But we've been planning it for ages, getting organised, sussing out good spots. We knew there was going to be tagging, we just didn't know when, and then when we saw what was starting at Purity, we knew we had to get out here fast.'

'Everyone here has gone?' Rita asked.

'Yes, some for ages,' said Miri.

'We're present!' said Jade.

Miri smiled. 'I know, but you guys are a special case.' She looked me in the eye. 'Shall we go for a swim?'

Rita stayed at the camp and Jade and I followed Miri up the hill behind the hut. We walked through the bush, sometimes on a track, and sometimes not, for about ten minutes until we reached a small stream that we followed for a while. Jade took off her shoes and leapt from rock to rock.

'Where are you taking us?' I asked Miri, a bit worried about leaving the track behind.

She laughed. 'You'll see. It's okay, I know how to get back.'

Jade, who was just ahead of me, shouted, 'Look, Mum! So cool!'

Ahead of us was a group of rock pools, cut into the side of a small cliff, and overhung by ferns and moss.

'It's warm,' said Miri, 'oh my god, it's so nice, you would not believe. We call it our private spa, Taryn found it.' She was already stripping down to her undies and bra, and I did the same.

'You can just be a nudie, Jade,' I said, and I helped her take her clothes off.

'This is the deepest,' said Miri, walking carefully along the rocks to the largest pool, and dipping her foot in.

We slipped into the water and Jade shrieked and laughed. It was so good, so warm and relaxing. A faint steam rose off the surface of the pool and into the green canopy overhead. Miri dunked her head under and came up again, slicking back her hair. I bobbed around, keeping an eye on Jade and bouncing on the rocks with my tiptoes. It felt so good to be clean, to be far away from everything, to be in the bush with Miri.

Jade started to build a stack of rocks at one end of the pool, and I anchored myself in a spot next to Miri.

'I can't believe we made it,' I said. I took out my hair tie and dipped my head back to wet my hair.

'Sorry about all the weird messages,' Miri said. 'We're trying to keep under the radar, buying some time. But I knew you'd figure it out. Mum's coming up too, she should be here soon. I'll go and get her at Karikari.'

I let my arms float on the surface of the water. 'Has she gone?'

'No.'

'Is it okay that we're here, me and Jade, and present?'

'They understand.'

'Did you tell them about what happened?' I asked.

'No.'

'Miri, what did happen?'

'You put me out.'

'Did I?'

'Yes, I made you do it.'

I stared at her, her mouth just above the water, and she stared back. Our knees bumped against each other.

'Were you the first one?' I asked.

'I don't know, probably not. Don't you think it's probably happened before? Somewhere else? It didn't happen right away, at the beach, but maybe a month later. The first time I saw it, it was on my driver's licence. I remember, I took it out when I got ID'd somewhere.' Miri laughed. 'I was like 'Oh, sorry!' My picture just wasn't there. Shit! They must've thought I was being real dodgy. But I didn't go everywhere, all at once, it happened in bits, and I'd come and go. And, I wasn't freaked out, J. I think I knew, when I made you do it, what would happen, and I wanted it. I figured out how to hide it from people, not to be in photos, got myself offline, just to be on my own.'

'I'm sorry,' I said, 'I didn't want you to go out.' My voice broke.

She moved next to me. 'Jodie, I wanted to, I wanted you to do it, I didn't want to be seen. And I couldn't have got away, from Matt, from any of those fuckers in Whakatāne, looking at me, if you hadn't helped.' Under the water, she took my hands. 'It's not a darkness, J, it's a light, being gone, it's my right now, to decide who sees me, and all the women here, they have that right too. You gave me the best thing, the best thing! I promise.'

'I missed you,' I said, 'I couldn't see you. I really wanted to.'

'I'm sorry I couldn't come back and explain, but it took me a while to figure out what was happening, and then there were other gaps and I had this feeling, like I didn't want to put you in danger, because you had Jade too, and you can do it, Jodie, you can make people go and come back, and they want to control it because then they can decide what people will remember, and what people see, and they'll fuck it up, J, and we can't let them.'

I nodded, yes. All the photos that could be changed, all the events that could be erased, all the people that could be forgotten. I thought about the woman at the motel, staring at the spot in the photo where the little girl had been.

'If they can control it, they can change history,' said Miri. 'And it's our right! We don't want to be seen! I'm not going to let them take that away from us. I'm not going to let them look at us.'

'They're coming after me,' I said. 'Guy made me bring him back, and recorded it, so that he could show them. I thought he was going, but he wasn't.'

'I don't know that anyone is that interested in you, right now. They want to control what's happening at Purity, and that's good for us, because it gives us a bit of time. They're busy.'

'How do you find out what's going on down there?'

'I've got some connections,' said Miri. 'People who tell me stuff.'

'I think they've been keeping an eye on me for a long time. Someone came into our house once, ages ago, they're watching,' I said, and I felt tears in my eyes, the stress of the last year washing through me, the feeling that something was wrong, that I had made a huge mistake that I could never take back. 'I'm worried they'll follow me here,' I said. I turned, suddenly thinking of Jade and wanting to keep her close. Over a line of rocks I could see the top of her head bobbing around in the pool next to us. 'Are you okay?' I called.

'I'm making a whirlpool!' she shouted back.

Miri smiled at me. 'She's cool,' she said.

'Yeah.'

'How long did Johnny hang around for?' Miri asked.

'Not long.'

'Did he want to see her?'

'No, he left.'

'Does he know that you put me out?' Miri asked.

I shook my head. 'Nah, I mean, I don't think he really knew what was happening, when I shaded. You saw him, remember? He just went quiet, like he couldn't remember what he was doing.'

Miri nodded.

'He didn't know that I was going to meet you on the beach, that time.' I paused, then said, 'I don't think he knew.'

Miri bobbed in the water. 'It was crazy, that night. I was desperate.'

'I know, but I wanted to keep you close, for myself. I wanted to see you, but I knew that you wanted to go, and I was freaked out, by what I could do, the feeling of it, like knowing, but not knowing, not knowing what'd happen. I didn't want to hurt you.'

'It didn't hurt. It just felt... I don't know... like getting my body back. It's better, I promise, J, it's, like, way better. And you can see me now. And it's better, right, in the moment?' She smiled, dunked her head under, and came back up. Her cheeks were pink, her hair dark and wet. I felt all of the words I wanted to use for Miri rising inside of me, new words. She was so beautiful.

'We need to get back,' she said, standing up.

34.

Over the next couple of days we learnt the way the camp worked, where the food was kept, how to help with the meals, where the shower bags had been rigged up in the bush, and how to fill them with warm water.

Jade made friends with a bunch of other kids in the camp and they built huts in the bush and we took them up to the hot pools to float around.

Rita seemed more relaxed. I watched her going back to the notches on the back wall of the hut and running her hand along them, whispering something under her breath.

There were other structures too, that the women had built to mark time passing. I overheard them talking about it, and they all agreed it was the hardest thing, the way time felt different when they had gone. One woman, Zoe, I think, said, 'I've been gone a year, I'm pretty sure, and I still have mornings where I wake up and don't know what time it is, what day it is, how old I am. I mean, I had days like that before too, but not like this.'

In the middle of the camp, in front of the hut, the women were building a stack of rocks. Each day, someone was put in charge of finding a rock the right size, because they all had to be as similar as possible. Someone else added it to the stack the next morning, before breakfast. The women often sat around the pile and talked. I noticed that they liked to be close to it, liked to touch it.

There was another sort of calendar too. At the far end of the camp, past the tents, on the edge of the bush, someone had strung up a tight line of nylon between two trees. Every day someone found something from the bush, a stick, or a large leaf, or a bit of bark, and they put a hole in it, and tied it to the nylon. It was like a mobile, a bit of nature for each day. The women liked this calendar too. They would go into the bush to look for things that could be hung up, and then talk about which one would be best, getting together in a group and holding them up on the line before deciding.

No one seemed to have a phone, but Miri must have had one, because she somehow knew what was going on, out in the world. She let everyone know what was happening with the state of emergency, with Purity, with the dead gaps. She gave little speeches at breakfast time with new information. She was busy in the camp. She was in charge and everyone came to her with questions and problems.

The kids didn't care, but some of the women were a bit weird with me and Jade. We were present, then, and it made us different, made us outsiders.

At night, in the hut, around the tables, I overheard the women talking to each other and caught bits of their stories. It was interesting to hear about when they'd known they had gone out, how they had heard about the hut and Miri and the plan to stay there. Some of them seemed stoked to be gone, proud and confident. They talked about their past lives, their feeling of being watched, consumed, and of wanting to fight back. 'I was so exposed, so open,' said one woman, 'to anyone who wanted to look at me. It seems so crazy to me now, that I would even have let that happen. Now, if I had it, all I'd want to do is keep my image close to me, right next to me, here, not for anyone else.' I remember the way she pressed her chest with her open palm, as if she wanted to push her image inside of herself, or eat it and make it part of her body.

But there were others, like Rita, who seemed lost and a bit messed up. They stayed close to the calendars, touching them all the time. They would try to help prepare the meals, or help out with some other little job, but then they'd wander away and forget to come back. They easily forgot where they were and what they were doing.

One afternoon, I watched Rita playing with the kids on the lawn. She was cross-legged on the ground, making a daisy chain. Then she stood up, the daisies falling to the ground, and wandered away through the tents. The kids watched her, confused. One girl called after her. Rita's mouth moved as if she was whispering something to herself.

Miri was sitting on the deck next to me, drinking a cup of coffee. 'Don't worry,' she said, 'she's going to be okay. It affects everyone differently. I'll help her.'

'But what can you do?'

Miri shuffled a little closer. 'I think it'll help her if she can come and go, if she can control it. Then she'll still have an anchor, but she'll be able to pull back, hide herself, if she wants to. I can do it, I'm still practising, but I'll be able to do it soon and then I'll teach everyone.'

'You can come and go?'

'Sort of, almost.'

'I tried to bring you back once, but it didn't work,' I said quietly.

Miri looked at me. 'I reckon you'd be able to do it too. If you went, you could come back, and maybe just in some photos, the ones that you really wanted to be in. I can't do that yet, but I think that's what we've got to work on. We need to be able to pick and choose where we can be seen, women do, these women do, especially.'

A couple of women came out of the hut behind us, and we were silent until they had moved away.

'What do you do when you're trying to come back?' I asked.

Miri laughed. 'You know!' she said. 'You showed me how to do it. I colour myself in. I hold my phone out, with a picture, and I've seen myself flicker back, as I'm talking, but I can't hold it, I can't keep myself there, it always collapses and I'm gone again. I can't really describe it, it's like I'm trying to hold on to something slippery.'

I said, 'It's about the right words. And also not thinking too hard, just letting them bubble up.'

'I know, but that's what you're good at, because of your dad. You could do it, Jodie, you could come and go, then you could teach me, and everyone else who needed it.'

I finished my cup of tea. 'You're asking me to go out,' I said. 'To put myself out.'

'I'm just saying, think about it,' Miri said.

'I can't, Miri, there's Jade. I just can't do that to her.'

Miri shrugged. Why did she do that? Acted like it was such a small thing? 'You have so much power, Jodie. I wish I had what you have.'

'It doesn't feel like power,' I said, struggling to keep my voice down. 'It feels like a weight, like, if I could just stop the words, none of this would've happened. I wish I could go back to the first time I coloured for Dad, I'd shout at myself, 'Don't! Stop it! It's going to be a fucking mess!' But it grew and grew and I could feel it changing, getting bigger, stronger, and then with Johnny, he changed it too, and I had to, I needed to disappear, because he hurt me.' My voice broke. 'He hurt me, Miri, and I could use the words to step away, to step out of the world, just for a few minutes, because I was so scared. So, I did, and it's totally fucked, and I'm sorry.'

Miri put her arm around me. 'See, you've just said, it *is* a power, and imagine if you could give it to everyone else here, what they could do, what we could do.'

I shook my head. 'I couldn't do that to Jade.'

Miri stood up. 'Take her with you.'

I stared at her. I didn't know what to say. Miri was asking me to put Jade out. Who would do that? Who would ask that? Who would do that to their own kid? I thought about the women I had seen on TV when their babies had been born gone, their absolute terror, their desperation. The woman walking down the hallway of a hospital, holding a tiny gap in her arms, blood on the hem of her hospital gown. Another woman waving a phone over her tiny baby, nothing there, emptiness, nothing to remember, a blank space.

'I can't believe you're asking me to do that,' I said to Miri. 'What parent would do that?'

'It wouldn't be forever. You could bring her back, I know you could. Just think about it, okay?'

Miri went back inside the hut, and I found Jade in our tent, playing with a torch. I lay down on the sleeping bag next to her.

'How long are we going to stay here, Mum?' she asked.

'I don't know, a bit longer, it's safer for us here at the moment,' I said.

'It's okay, but we need to get back to Nana and Pop, and Guy too. Maybe they could come here? They could drive.'

'Maybe.' I lay on my back and stared at the blue roof of the tent, the shadows cast by the trees above, then I turned on my side to look at Jade. I wanted to hold her close and never let her go. I wanted to protect her. I wanted to take a thousand photos of her, write a million words about her. I thought about what I'd write. I thought about writing this book, how I'd hold her in here, all the tiny bits of her that I didn't want to forget.

'What're you staring at?' Jade asked.

'You,' I said.

She shone the torch at my face, blinding me. 'Stop it!' she said, laughing. 'You look so weird.'

I avoided Miri for a while after that, I didn't want to talk to her, and I kept Jade close. We kept ourselves busy, helping round the camp, gathering firewood, washing clothes in the river, cutting the grass around the tents with some old shears and hammering in the tent pegs to make sure everything was safe.

Jade was happy most of the time, but she asked a lot about Nana and Pop and when we would see them again. 'We haven't even got a phone!' she complained. 'We need to check if they're still present. We should send them a message.'

I was a bit restless without my phone too. I went to check it all the time, put my hand in my pocket, before I remembered it wasn't there. Even though the internet was useless and broken and made no sense, all the images and videos emptied out, I still missed it. Jade kept asking me to put on a video of gone Katy Perry and I had to remind her that I couldn't, and she'd scrunch up her face and sulk.

One breakfast, I asked Rita if she missed her phone, and she said, 'No, it's not for me, after I had gone, it was just... confusing. It reminded me too much of what I had lost. But I'd like to take some photos of you and Jade, to see what you're really like. It'd be nice for the two of you, to have a few phones around.'

I helped wash the dishes and then went out to the deck. Miri was there, and she turned to me and asked, 'I know you're pissed off at me, but I'm going to go and get some supplies from Coopers Beach. Wanna come?'

It was tempting to get away from the camp for a bit. 'Can Jade come?' I asked. 'Is it safe?'

'Nobody cares about us at the moment, you should see all the shit that's going down at Purity. Nobody cares about a bunch of gone women camping in the bush. The Four Square is still open, we just run in and run out again. Even with the state of emergency, people can still go to a supermarket. It's better with two, because we can do two separate trolley loads. We'll see how much stuff they have.'

'Okay,' I said, and then, because I was sick of being annoyed at her, I said, 'I'm not pissed off at you. I'm just... thinking.'

Miri smiled. 'Okay, let's go then.'

I went and found Jade and then filled a backpack with our jackets and water bottles.

We met Miri at the start of the track and followed her through the bush, Jade walking in between us. We hadn't been along the track since the night we'd arrived, and it was beautiful in the daytime. Everything was so green and rich. Sunlight came through the canopy and made patterns on the mossy rocks. I wanted to stop and describe it, like I'm doing here, but Miri kept us walking quickly, until we reached a small clearing where the white van was waiting.

Miri had told me that they had a few secret spots where other cars were parked. I'd hoped to see my car there, I was worried about it, but Miri told me it was fine, and it made sense for us to all go in the van.

There was a booster in the back for Jade and I strapped her in, before climbing into the front seat next to Miri. She gunned the engine. 'I'm always stressed this old dunga isn't going to start,' she said as she looked over her shoulder and reversed out onto the road.

We drove on gravel for about twenty minutes, before we turned out onto the sealed road. The van rumbled along and the bush became farmland.

'Do you need some money from me?' I asked, thinking about the two weeks of rent that had gone out of my bank account since we'd left home.

'Nah,' Miri said. 'We'd been saving before we moved to the camp, preparing. Anyone who was part of the network started putting money in. We should have enough for all the food for a while, and then we'll have to make other plans.'

'Hunting for wild boar?'

Miri smiled. 'Something like that.'

'Should I put the radio on?' I asked.

'Give it a go, let's see what's going on out there,' said Miri.

Everywhere in New Zealand, the internet was out, a reporter said. Servers had crashed. Overnight, cyber-attacks had brought down key government digital infrastructure. People couldn't message each other, or send images, or post to their social media accounts. Purity was blamed. 'This is a deliberate and targeted attack on presents,' said someone, 'on our way of life, on our images, on our right to be seen. We know Purity has been recruiting gaps with an anti-present agenda to conduct these malicious attacks. But we will hold tight to our images, we will share them, as is our right as individuals, and we will not be intimidated by this group of gaps.'

'Maybe we should go back, it sounds like a bit of a shit storm,' I said.

'We really need food,' Miri said, speeding up on a straight patch of road. 'Let's do this real quick, it might be our last chance for a while, and then get back to camp and make a plan.'

We drove into Coopers Beach. All was quiet. There was a row of billboards on the side of the road leading into town. A couple of smiling faces were still present but most of them had gone.

We pulled up outside the Four Square, alongside two other cars. I got out and opened Jade's door and took her out of her seat.

'We're going to be real quick,' Miri said, taking Jade's hand. 'No pissing around, we just get in, get some food, and get out again.'

Jade nodded, her eyes wide and scared.

We crossed the car park and went in the front doors. I scanned the shop. The aisles were quiet except for a couple of other people moving at the far end of the space, near the fridges. There was some food on the shelves and things looked mostly normal. A teenage boy stood by the door, looking after the check out.

'You open?' Miri asked.

'Yeah, but we haven't got much stuff,' he said.

He reached into the pocket of his jeans and took out a photo of us. Miri nudged me forward so that I was a little in front of her, and transferred Jade's hand into mine.

The boy took the photo and looked at his phone. 'You're gone?' he asked, looking up at Miri.

She nodded and jutted her chin forward, challenging him.

He shrugged. 'Can't do anything about it now. I'm supposed to report you, but internet's down. Doesn't make any difference anyway, too many of you now.' He watched us grab a couple of trolleys and push them inside. 'You gotta pay cash,' he said.

'Grab what you can,' Miri said to me. 'I'll check out the veges.'

Jade and I went to the first aisle and I took cartons of soy milk down off the shelf, then tinned peaches, then all the pasta that they had. What would we do when we couldn't shop here anymore? I needed to get back home, I thought. I needed to get back to Mum and Dad and check that they were okay, or send them a message, or something. But we couldn't go back, and I also wanted to stay close to Miri. There were riots in Auckland, and police moving in to tag the gaps. I didn't know if my phone was still working, and I didn't have a job.

I stood in front of the shelves of cereal, my mind buzzing through all these thoughts, and I heard someone next to me say, 'Which one are you going to choose?'

I turned. A man was standing next to me. I hadn't seen him come in. I knew him straight away. It was the man I'd seen with Guy on the street in Whakatāne.

He was totally calm and gave a little smile. 'Whichever one you don't want, I'll have it,' he said and looked in my trolley. 'I imagine you'll need a lot of Weet-Bix.'

I stared at him, silent.

'Okay,' he said, 'I'll just take this, shall I?' He reached past me and took a box of cereal and put it in his basket.

'We know what you can do, Jodie, and we need you to help us,' he said. 'You have a huge power, if you learn to use it properly. I think of it like a dimmer. You could turn the lights up and down all over the world, if you wanted to.'

My heart was thudding and I gripped the trolley. 'Who are you?' I whispered.

'We're simply trying to get everyone under control,' he said, 'and you can help, Jodie. Everyone deserves the right to be seen, and you can help people hold on to that right, because it shouldn't be taken away. You've seen yourself what it can do to people, to their minds, and it's only going to get worse.'

'How did you know I was here?' I wasn't really thinking. The questions just fell out of me.

He laughed gently. 'We know a lot, Jodie. And there are others, like you, who we have been watching. You are not the only one. We want to bring you all together, we feel that you could learn a lot from each other.'

I stared at him. Where was Jade? I remember how quiet the supermarket was, the hum of the fridges. His body there, next to mine, was such a shock, but I also had this feeling like he'd been there for ages, watching, waiting, learning about us, and in a weird way it was nice, to have him finally appear there, in that supermarket in Coopers Beach. He didn't seem angry. He just seemed interested.

'We can help you,' he said, 'and you can help us. But it's imperative that we act, and that we stamp out the threat.'

'Did you come into our house?' I asked. 'Did you break into our place?'

He smiled.

I thought about him in our house, picking up our things, and putting them down. That was what Jade and I had felt in our space, his looking, his eyes.

The man's phone chimed and he took it out of his pocket and looked at it. So casual. Like we were just having this totally normal conversation at the supermarket. He had never been afraid. He had never been observed. He had never had to run, in the dark, not sure what was coming, who was there, who had seen him, who was watching him. He did the looking and he looked at whatever the fuck he wanted.

I turned away from the man and looked down the empty aisle. Where was Miri? And where was Jade? I left my trolley and ran down the aisle and into the next one. Empty. Had they taken her? I couldn't hear her voice. 'Jade!' I yelled. 'Jade!'

I ran to the next aisle and there she was, standing with Miri. Miri grabbed her hand and looked at me, confused. 'We have to go,' I said. 'There's a man here and he knows about me.'

I didn't have to say anything else. We ran down to the checkout and Miri reached into her pocket and handed the teenager a stack of cash. 'Keep the change,' she said, 'we don't need the other stuff, sorry.'

Miri pushed the trolley out the door and down the ramp and when we got to the van I opened the side door and strapped Jade into her seat while Miri chucked the groceries in the back.

When Miri started the engine it made a weird grunting noise, as if it wasn't going to start. I shouted, 'Miri!' and looked at her, freaking out, my hands on the dashboard. I turned to the supermarket and there was the man, standing on the ramp that led to the front doors, calmly looking at us. He leant forward, onto the metal railing. He wasn't nice anymore. I wanted to get away from him. I didn't want him near us, near Jade.

Miri was focussed on the van. She let it rest for a second and I remember the silence of that moment, nobody moved, not us, not the man. Then Miri turned the key again and the engine started and she reversed out onto the road and drove away, going too fast.

Nobody spoke for a while. Miri kept looking in the rear-view mirror, and I checked the wing mirror, expecting to see a car behind us, or something, but there wasn't anyone following.

'We left our other trolley,' said Jade, after a while. 'Who was that man?'

I looked over at Miri. She was frowning, focussed on the road. 'We don't know,' I said.

'He wants your mum to bring people back,' said Miri.

'She can do that!' said Jade, excited. 'She did it for Guy!'

'I know, she's got some sweet skills, your mum. But I don't know if she wants to work for that man, I don't think he's a good man, not everyone wants to be present.'

Miri sped the van down the road, but when it came to the turnoff that led back to camp, she kept going and drove straight past. 'Do you guys want to go and see a new beach?' she asked, looking back at Jade. 'It's pretty special.'

'Can we swim there?' Jade asked.

'Yep! It's real nice,' said Miri.

I leant my head back on the headrest. I was still shaking. I thought about what the man had said, that there were others like me. Did they do it the same way? Did they use words like I did? And did it feel the same for them?

Miri turned sharply and drove down a steep gravel road. We passed farmland and a few houses, then we turned right again, onto another road that led down to a small bay that was framed by pōhutukawa trees and scrubby bush.

Miri parked on the grass bank. 'So cool!' said Jade, as we got out of the van. 'And they won't follow us down here, eh? That bad man.'

Miri and I looked at each other. 'We're all good here,' Miri said. 'Hey, why don't we stay the night?' she said. 'It'll be cool. There're some blankets in the van, and we can make a fire. We can put the seats down and sleep in the van.'

If he was following us, I guessed that Miri didn't want to lead the man straight back to the camp. She wanted to buy us a bit of time and space.

'And we've got heaps of food!' said Jade.

'Too true,' said Miri. 'Okay,' she said, clapping her hands together, 'I'll move the van somewhere a bit better, and why don't you guys go and find some firewood?'

I watched her. She kept her voice bright, optimistic.

I took Jade's hand and we wandered along the beach. It was a small bay, rocky at one end where a river fed into the sea. But I won't describe it here, I'll wait, let me get to the right part to start all of that.

I kept scanning the hills behind us, listening for the sound of a car, or a plane, or a boat, but there was nothing, we were alone. I'd spent so long, over the last years, listening, watching, waiting for someone to come out of the shadows and blame me for everything, for the gaps, for the chaos, for all the confused and fucked up people. But the man had said that I wasn't alone, that it wasn't me. That it wasn't *just* me.

All the wood on the beach was wet, so we returned to Miri with nothing. She'd driven the van down closer to the beach and dragged rocks into a circle to make a fire pit.

'We couldn't find any wood,' Jade said.

'It's okay, we've got heaps of time to look for some later,' Miri said. 'I know where to get some, there's a sheltered bit.'

We had a pretty random collection of food. Miri got rice crackers and apples and a packet of salami out of the boot and we sat on the grass to eat our lunch.

Later, Miri took Jade down to the mouth of the river and they built a protective circle out of rocks and put in a few things from the supermarket that were in plastic and needed to be kept cold. Then we went into the bush behind the beach and found firewood, carrying it in armloads back to the campsite.

'That stuff will be okay for one night,' said Miri. 'We'll go back to camp tomorrow. There's just one thing we've got to do and it's better to do it here, just the three of us,' she said.

She didn't look at me, but I watched her moving the groceries around in the back of the van, panic rising in my chest.

'Wanna go for a swim, Jade?' I asked. I wanted to get far away from Miri.

'Okay!' she said.

I took one of the blankets that Miri had found in the van. 'We can dry with this. If we leave it in the sun, or next to the fire, it'll dry by nighttime, for bed. Let's go!'

Jade ran towards the sea and I turned to follow her but Miri grabbed my arm. 'Don't be scared, it's gonna be okay,' she said.

I pulled away. I didn't want her to comfort me.

On the dry sand, Jade and I stripped down to our undies and we walked into the sea. Jade still couldn't really swim, so we stayed in the shallow water, splashing each other, the sun hot on our backs.

Here she is, Jade in the sea. Look. Her pale body and her blue undies, flecks of sand on her cheeks and caught in the stray bits of hair around her face. I see her in these words, in that moment. She pushes her toes into the sand and takes them out to look at the holes she's made filling up with water. She's happy but she knows something is up, something isn't right. She wades out into the deeper water, but she keeps looking back at me and checking that I'm still there, and Miri too, back at the camp. She waves and Miri waves back.

I didn't want to, but Jade came out of the water, shivering, so we headed back to our little campsite and lay on the blanket in the sun to dry off, and then we got our clothes back on and sat in the shade of the van so we didn't get sunburnt. I felt cold inside though, a shaking that had started when I saw the man in the supermarket and hadn't gone away.

Jade helped Miri start the fire. Miri had scraped together some scraps of paper from the van and she nestled these under smaller pieces of dry wood that she had found somewhere. The wood was rough, hollowed out by saltwater, and it caught quickly. Bright, orange flames crackled and rose up into the air.

Here I go, bright flames, rising up. And here are the other things, I'll put them down here, the sunset, the fading light, the blue sky blending into purple at the horizon line, and the sea deepening to a dark blue underneath. These words started rising inside me, I said them, and then I shouted at Miri, 'You can't make me do this!'

Miri sat down beside us and chucked a piece of wood on the growing fire. 'Jade,' she said. 'You and Jodie have to go out.'

Jade turned to look at me, her eyes wide. 'Mum?' she asked.

I shivered and bit my lip. What could I do? I had no choice, we had to go, we had to get away from the people who were following us, we had to join Miri and the others.

I sat beside Jade and put my arms around her. 'It's going to be okay, it'll be sweet, look, Miri has gone, and she's okay, it won't hurt.'

Jade wrestled away from me and went to stand on the other side of the fire, looking at me, tears in her eyes, the evening sky behind her, the dark forest on the hills. I said those things. I said those words.

'Mum! You won't be able to see me!' Jade cried.

'I will always see you,' I said, 'always.'

I had to keep going, because if I stopped, I didn't know if I could start again. The gold sparks from the fire, flying upwards, and its hot, orange centre, where the heat glowed and grew. The ring of stones that Miri had found, the brown sand, and the dry grass around us, one blade of grass with its flat stem and head of seeds, bits of seed flaking away.

'Mum! Mum! Stop! Please!'

Jade was still on the other side of the fire. Miri went to her and put her arms around her but didn't say anything. She didn't want to break the pattern of words. Miri looked at me through the flames and nodded.

I had to keep going. I had tears in my eyes. I turned away, out towards the bay. I had to describe this place around us, draw it in closer, tightly, with the right words. I tried to settle my thoughts. I had to look, to *really* look. I wiped away the tears so I could see properly.

The dark bay. The waves with their white lines stroking the beach. No horizon line, the sky was navy blue, inky. I looked up at the stars, tiny and perfect and random in the sky, and I thought about describing them to you, Dad, and how much you loved it and how we sat in the backyard and walked around the sky together, looking. And then I saw it, the full moon, appearing over the hill at the end of the bay, and I stuttered, repeating myself, because all the words rushed off it in a flood, almost a physical thing, a taste in my mouth, and it was so easy, describing the moon, white and grey and slow and relentless, and I could feel myself relaxing and going out and it was like someone tugging each of my fingers, one after the other, at the knuckle, like I was being opened up, unlocked, loosened, but also, at the same time, I was closed away, shut up, so that no one could see me anymore, and I could keep my secrets and not let anyone in. It felt like both of those things at the same time.

I was still finding the words and saying them, and then I realised Jade was in my lap, her head tucked against my chest, one half of her warm from the fire, and she was still, and I put my arms around her and held her close.

'I will always see you,' I said, pressing my face into her sea-salt hair. 'I see all of you.'

Miri stood up and I looked at her. She smiled back at us and prodded the fire with a stick, sending a burst of glowing sparks up into the dark sky. Those are the right words for the sparks. I thought about those words, at the time, but I'd stopped speaking. I didn't have anything else to say. The world went on, sparks in the sky, without any words. I'd done what I needed to do. I held Jade and the fire warmed us.

35.

I'm up to where we are now, in the camp, with Miri. I've written everything. I read it back, and I've remembered it right, got all the important bits down. Maybe I should take out the place names. Would that make us safer? Maybe that doesn't matter anymore, I don't know.

I've been writing this on Miri's laptop. At night, I charge it from the solar panel that Miri rigged up, and make sure it's ready to go for the morning. I'm always worried it won't start and there'll be no way of getting back to my writing.

I've been writing in the afternoons, mostly, when Jade plays with the other kids, or helps the women around the camp. It's taken a while. But I have quite a bit of spare time, while we figure out what to do next.

I can see Jade right now. She's working on one of the new time sculptures. It's a pile of dirt that everyone adds to. She's pressing leaves around the base and there's a line of mud on her cheek.

Whenever I write about her, I think how you'd want to see her, Dad, and hear these words read out loud. I wish I could sit on the couch with you and read you this from start to finish. Some parts would be hard for you to hear, but you'd love it, really, because you'd see so much. That's all you wanted, right? Words, words, and more words. Words about anything and everything, but especially words about Jade.

I need to get this writing to you, but I don't know how, with the internet not working. We get our news in tiny pieces when someone goes out to find food, and they come back with strange stories of destruction and decay, of the world breaking down and history coming apart.

We're stuck here but we're safe. We're okay. We haven't seen the man again, but we know that he'll be back. The stakes are too high.

He needs me. The world needs me. That sounds a bit full of myself, but it's true.

Miri reckons he doesn't know where we are. But I know he'll be looking.

Miri doesn't say anything to me, but I know she wants me to start trying to come back. She wants to see if it will stick, if I'll be able to come back and then go out again. She has some kind of plan, I think, though she hasn't told me what it is.

Jade and I are still getting used to being gone. We wake up in the morning in the tent, our faces close together, and stare at each other in the blue light, reminding each other that we're still there. I think we're okay. We use the time sculptures to measure the days.

To be honest, I'm scared I won't be able to do it, to bring myself back, and I can feel Miri waiting for me to start, can feel her getting tired of waiting. She just walked past me, here, in the hut, and looked down at me typing. She thinks I'm wasting my time.

Christ, she's always been like this. She's so impatient, always has to get her way.

I told her I needed to write it all down first, about how Jade and I got to be here, and why I put us out. I said that it'd help me find the right words, that I'm practising.

Writing is not the same as talking, but it helps to get things in the right order.

I told Miri that it's different, bringing someone back, because I have to describe the person, not the things around them. Bodies are different. They need other words to be seen, to bring them into the light. And some bodies don't want to be seen, and I can already feel that resistance too, in some of the women in the camp. They won't let me bring them back. Some of them think I'm a bit suss. That's okay. That's their right.

But Miri thinks it'll help, if people can come and go, and I guess I agree. If they can decide where they're seen, Miri says, people will feel more in control and less lonely, less freaked out. There'll be less difference between presents and gaps, more of a middle ground, and that'd be a good thing.

I still have the photo of the beach, where me and Miri used to be, smiling at the camera with the wind in our hair. I keep it hidden in my backpack. I don't want to show Miri because I don't want to tell her that I've tried before, to bring her back, into this photo, and it didn't work. I couldn't do it.

But maybe it'd be different, to bring myself back? That's what I've been saying to myself, that's what I've been hoping. Maybe that's where I should start, and then it might get easier.

Sometimes I tuck the photo underneath the edge of the laptop as I'm writing, and I think about the words I'd use to put myself back into this image, and be close to Miri on that beach, and be ten years old, and be happy. What should I say? What do I look like, really?

I look at my hands writing with the keyboard, my fingers bringing letters together into words. Maybe I should start here, just with my fingers. That should be easy, right?

I hear Dad's voice in my head. 'What does it look like?' he asks. 'What's it looking like out there?'

Acknowledgements

Thank you to first readers, Flora and Ollie, who gave such helpful feedback on a rough manuscript.

Thank you to my writing group, Holly, Lucy, and Michelle, who read bits of *The Words for Her* and had thoughts that sharpened it, shaped it, and made it a lot better.

Thank you, Brannavan and Murdoch, for all your hard work and friendship; it's been wonderful making books and eating kebabs with you for all these years. Ngā mihi to Tīhema Baker for printing and launching our books together.

Ngā mihi to my friend Judith, who always says yes when I come to her with a new book and creates such thoughtful and beautiful covers.

Thank you, Brydan, for your quick and incisive editing.

Ngā mihi to my mum and dad, Sally and James, who always brought me lots of books to read when I was a kid. Thank you Callum, Pip, Olivia, Will, Scott, Jo, and Holly, my family in Te Awakairangi ki Tai. You support me every day so that I can squeeze in time for writing.

Finally, thank you, Mark, Corin, and Toby. I'm very lucky to wander around this world with you three.

AD LIB

THOMASIN SLEIGH

"The camerawoman zooms in on the photo, the lens of the camera lingering on the image. After a moment, the camerawoman reaches out and touches it and Kyla copies her, tracing the outline of her mother's face and the straight line of her raised arm. 'She will be in our thoughts always,' whispers the camerawoman."

When celebrity singer Carmen Crane passes away, her only daughter inherits a reality TV show. As Kyla Crane adjusts to this new scrutiny, strange things start to happen: the house is rearranged overnight, unknown characters appear, the show's narrative loses its way, and the camera crew begin to echo events. When fragments of her mother's past surface, Kyla is compelled to scroll through the footage and come to her own conclusions about life in the public eye and her ambiguous inheritance.

Ad Lib was Thomasin Sleigh's debut novel and was listed as one of the best books of 2014 by the *New Zealand Listener*.

www.lawrenceandgibson.co.nz

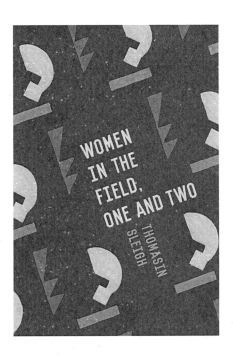

"*I kept going, and I couldn't go back. I had to make it work, because... because that was all I could do. I didn't know that there were special rules, a special game, about whose art gets seen and whose art is remembered.*"

A young British woman in post-war London is tasked with recommending acquisitions for New Zealand's National Art Gallery. When she ventures into the basement of a charismatic Russian painter three decades her senior, she discovers a solution that reconciles her idea of that far-away country and her own modernist sensibilities. *Women in the Field, One and Two* explores two women's creativity and freedom against the backdrop of art history's patriarchal biases.

Thomasin Sleigh's writing about art and culture has been published widely. *Women in the Field, One and Two* was released in 2018 and is her second novel.

www.lawrenceandgibson.co.nz

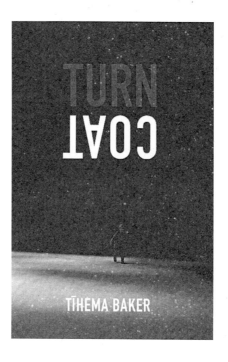

Daniel is a young, idealistic Human determined to make a difference for his people. He lives in a distant future in which Earth has been colonised by aliens. His mission: infiltrate the Alien government called the Hierarch and push for it to honour the infamous Covenant of Wellington, the founding agreement between the Hierarch and Humans.

With compassion and insight, *Turncoat* explores the trauma of Māori public servants and the deeply conflicted role they are expected to fill within the machinery of government. From casual racism to co-governance, Treaty settlements to tino rangatiratanga, *Turncoat* is a timely critique of the Aotearoa zeitgeist, holding a mirror up to Pākehā New Zealanders and asking: "What if it happened to you?"

Tīhema Baker (Raukawa te Au ki te Tonga, Ātiawa ki Whakarongotai, and Ngāti Toa Rangatira) is a writer and Tiriti o Waitangi-based policy advisor from Ōtaki.

www.lawrenceandgibson.co.nz